BEYOND THE CURTAIN
OF DARK

Edited by
Peter Haining

D0889235

PINNACLE BOOKS • NEW YORK CITY

*For my wife, Philippa, who has shared me
with the monsters for a long time.*

CONTENTS

ACKNOWLEDGEMENTS

The Editor is indebted to the following authors and their agents for permission to reproduce copyright material in this anthology: Robert Block for "Lizzie Borden Took An Axe" and "Return to the Sabbath"; Patricia Highsmith and A. M. Heath Ltd. for "The Snail Watcher"; Harry Harrison and E. J. Carnell for "At Last, The True Story Of Frankenstein"; Theodore Sturgeon and E. J. Carnell for "The Other Celia"; Ray Bradbury for "Fever Dream"; Fredric Brown for "Come And Go Mad"; August Derleth and Scott Meredith for "The Survivor" and "The Ancestor" by H. P. Lovecraft and August Derleth; Henry Kuttner for "By These Presents"; Henry Slesar and Theron Raines for "Whosits Disease"; Harold Lawlor for "Mayaya's Little Green Men"; Edogawa Rampo and Kurt Singer Features for "The Human Chair"; Isaac Asimov for "Eyes Do More Than See." I should also like particularly to thank Kurt Singer who has proved an invaluable source of information throughout the compiling of this book.   P.H.

FOREWORD

By Judith Merril

I am not ordinarily partial to the weird or horror story —at least not those which depend, as many do, on nothing but the statement that something Strange and Terrible Did Happen, for their effect. But I think the Editor's selection in this volume is extraordinary, both in the selection of individual stories, and in the complementary character of the combination.

In hindsight I am not sure whether I was more pleasantly surprised at seeing such overlooked items as *The Snail Watcher* by Patricia Highsmith and *The Other Celia* by Theodore Sturgeon included, or at my own first reading of the Harold Lawlor, Francis Marion Crawford and Edogawa Rampo stories—as well as Mary Shelly's *The Mortal Immortal,* which I had heard of but never seen.

But, to be sure, all the stories are pleasing and I have no hesitation in recommending *Beyond The Curtain Of Dark* as a fine collection.

BEYOND THE CURTAIN
OF DARK

all around us—day or night—and in every situation we are likely to encounter.

But before taking up this invitation to be frightened to death, a few notes on the men who have concocted these masterpieces of the macabre may be of interest to the horrorphile. For instance . . . .

Robert Bloch, who opens the collection with a gruesome piece on the hatchet-wielding activities of Lizzie Borden, is a mild-mannered, quietly-spoken American who is far more ready to talk about his hobby, baseball, than his explorations into the haunting regions of the unknown. Mr. Bloch, whose reputation was assured immediately the critics saw the brilliant suspense film, "Psycho," based on his book, also contributes a topical second story featuring horror movies and those who make them, "Return to the Sabbath."

Patricia Highsmith, who follows Robert Bloch, is another writer who came to public attention through a film of her novel, "Strangers On A Train." This was made in 1951 by Alfred Hitchcock and is regularly revived for the benefit of crime aficionados. In "The Snail Watcher," Miss Highsmith has, however, turned to a subject far removed from that crime. But—strangely—a subject which is close to her heart. For she is an avid *collector* of snails and even takes her "pets" with her whenever she travels abroad. Her knowledge of these creatures—so repulsive to most—is quite extraordinary as the reader who explores the world of the snail watcher will discover.

Miss Highsmith was born on the same day (January 19) as another of our most notable contributors: *Edgar Allan Poe.* This extraordinary, tormented American genius, who was without doubt the first great modern horror story writer, has left an indelible mark on the genre. His work has been reprinted endlessly and I count myself lucky to have found two of his lesser known stories for this collection—"The Oval Portrait" and "King Pest," the latter surely one of the finest

10

pieces of Black Humour ever penned. In Poe's homeland his high standard of writing is commemorated each year by the Mystery Writers of America who award the Edgar Allan Poe Prize to the best mystery work of the year. Not surprisingly, this honour is much coveted in the writing world. Appropriately, Poe's modern "pupil" and fellow Capricornian, Patricia Highsmith, has one!)

If the prize had been instituted during the lifetime of *Ambrose Bierce,* one cannot help feeling that this fellow American would have been certain to qualify for one. Bierce, who came to be known as "Bitter Bierce" because of his morbid and acid writings, was a mysterious, restless man who travelled endlessly in search of an illusion and suddenly disappeared at the height of his fame while visiting Mexico in 1913. His stories are often preoccupied with war and death and the particular example included here, "Chickamauga," is a brutal exposé of the effect battle can have on both soldiers and civilians.

Harry Harrison, the next contributor, is first and foremost a Science Fiction writer, but in "At Last, The True Story of Frankenstein" he has taken a new look at the old legend of the mad scientist and produced one of the most original horror stories for many years. Harrison, who occupies his time in between writing novels with working on film scripts, often chooses the most unlikely themes for his short stories and recently published a chilling little piece about a "Pop" group who literally devour their fans!

In *Ray Bradbury* we have a modern writer who also lets his imagination free in the dark corners of human terror—and comes up with small masterpieces like "Fever Dream." Bradbury is unquestionably the most famous horror story writer alive and his work is always eagerly sought after for every new anthology. The story I have selected appeared originally in "Weird Tales," the ill-fated pioneer horror story magazine which was

11

produced in the United States in the 1920's and first published such now-famous names as Robert Bloch, August Derleth, H. P. Lovecraft and Bradbury himself. Copies are now collectors items and change hands for quite large sums of money.

Theodore Sturgeon, the next in line, is another American writer who had early work published in "Weird Tales." His contribution to this anthology, "The Other Celia," is very typical of his outlandish fantasy and illustrates why he is often referred to as "one of the most gifted explorers of the strange byways of other worlds."

W. C. Morrow and *Fredric Brown* who follow Sturgeon are separated by nearly half a century, yet both have strangely similar comments to make about obsessions in their respective stories, "The Monster Maker" and "Come And Go Mad." The settings are in no way alike, yet the indefinable force which drives the crazy old surgeon to destruction is encountered again in a somewhat similar manner by Brown's alert and cynical newspaper reporter on the look-out for a story.

Following these two tales I have thought it most suitable to introduce the "scoops" in the collection—"The Survivor" and "The Ancestor" from the joint pens of *H. P. Lovecraft* and *August Derleth.* Behind them lies a remarkable story which involves two of the most famous names in the genre.

Howard Phillips Lovecraft is still considered today —some forty years after his death—as one of the all-time greats of the horror story. Living quietly in Rhode Island and subsisting almost entirely on sweet, black coffee (which eventually contributed to his early death), Lovecraft produced a brand of lurking evil quite unique in its macabre fascination. His output was at no time phenomenal and after his death his admirers naturally believed they had read the last of Lovecraft.

This was not so, however, and it is thanks mainly to the efforts of August Derleth, horror story writer, publisher and anthologist, that a cache of forgotten tales came to light. Derleth, who was himself a fan of H.P., learned that before his death the master storyteller had deposited a number of notes and outlines with a friend, Mr. R. H. Barlow, who in the meantime had also died. After extensive enquiries these papers were again brought to light—a find of no small magnitude for Lovecraft enthusiasts. Derleth then set himself to work on the notes—some of which were almost complete plots—and the result was a collection of new stories faithful in every way to Lovecraft's style.

The two I have chosen for "Beyond The Curtain Of Dark" have never been anthologized before and I am greatly indebted to August Derleth for his permission to reproduce them here. They are the gems of the collection.

Henry Slesar is one of the most prolific of today's short story writers and is as frequently found in Science Fiction magazines as in crime and mystery publications. "Whosits Disease" which has been taken from this profusion, is one of his shorter works but lacks none of the nuances of black humour and carefully constructed shudders usually associated with the name of Slesar.

The next three stories are all on a favourite theme of mine: immortality. They were all written at entirely different periods and each author has his own very special ideas on the subject. *Mary Shelley*—wife of the poet and creator of the most famous of all monster makers, Frankenstein—discourses on the dangers of living for ever in "The Mortal Immortal"; *Nathaniel Hawthorne,* author of the world-famous "The House of the Seven Gables," is in a skittish frame of mind in "Dr. Heidegger's Experiment" while *Henry Kuttner*

13

describes the unexpected results of signing a pact with the Devil in return for eternal life in "By These Presents." I think you will find them all fascinating.

Harold Lawlor concerns himself with the strange powers of the West Indies in "Mayaya's Little Green Men"—and a maid who can almost charm the kitchen utensils into doing the housework themselves! A quick trip back in time then takes the reader straight into the terror-laden atmosphere inhabited by vampires in *Francis Marion Crawford's* "For The Blood Is The Life." This unearthly tale of a bloodsucking creature of the night is perhaps the best short story Crawford ever wrote, though, strangely, probably the least reprinted. He is most noted for his Italian romances and the national ode he wrote in 1887 to celebrate the centennial of the American Constitution.

After Crawford, I have picked a new story by the leading Japanese author, *Edogawa Rampo*. He appears here to ensure that no reader will ever again sit quite so comfortably after learning the truth of "The Human Chair."

Joseph Sheridan Le Fanu is another of the great masters of the ghost/horror story in the same mould as Poe and Ambrose Bierce. Born in the middle of the nineteenth century in Ireland, he saw a decaying culture all around him and reflected this in his work. "The Fortunes of Sir Robert Ardagh" is a masterly study of a man's disintegration through fear of the supernatural.

So, finally, we come to the last two contributors in the collection—*Clive Pemberton,* a virtually unknown —but nonetheless outstanding—newspaperman who wrote horror stories for his own amusement (some of which appeared in "The Morning Leader" at the beginning of the century) and *Isaac Asimov,* the internationally famous Science Fiction and Science Fact authority. Mr. Asimov's very short piece, "Eyes Do More Than See," may seem at first reading to be strangely out of place in a collection such as this. But a second

14

look will show that in a few precise words the author has brilliantly described the ultimate horror that could overtake humanity. It is a salutary lesson in our world which may no longer seriously fear the shapes of night but has hanging over it the much more dreadful fear of global annihilation.

Peter Haining

LIZZIE BORDEN TOOK AN AXE . . .

By Robert Bloch

*"Lizzie Borden took an axe
And gave her mother forty whacks.
When she saw what she had done
She gave her father forty-one."*

Men say that horror comes at midnight, born of whispers out of dreams. But horror came to me at high noon, heralded only by the prosaic jangling of a telephone.

I had been sitting in the office all morning, staring down the dusty road that led to the hills. It coiled and twisted before my aching eyes as a shimmering sun played tricks upon my vision. Nor were my eyes the only organs that betrayed me; something about the heat and the stillness seemed to invade my brain. I was restless, irritable, disturbed by a vague presentiment.

The sharp clangor of the phone bell crystallized my apprehension in a single, strident note.

My palms dripped perspiration-patterns across the receiver. The phone was warm, leaden weight against my ear. But the voice I heard was cold; icy cold, frozen with fear. The words congealed.

"Jim—come and help me!"

17

That was all. The receiver clicked before I could reply. The phone slid to the desk as I rose and ran to the door.

It was Anita's voice, of course.

It was Anita's voice that sent me speeding towards my car; sent me racing down that desolate, heat-riddled road towards the old house deep in the hills.

Something had happened out there. Something was bound to happen, sooner or later. I'd known it, and now I cursed myself for not insisting on the sensible thing. Anita and I should have eloped weeks ago.

I should have had the courage to snatch her bodily away from this atmosphere of Faulkneresque melodrama, and I might have, if only I had been able to *believe* in it.

At the time it all seemed so improbable. Worse than that, it seemed *unreal.*

There are no legend-haunted houses looming on lonely hillsides. Yet Anita lived in one.

There are no gaunt, fanatical old men who brood over black books; no "hex doctors" whose neighbors shun them in superstitious dread. Yet Anita's uncle, Gideon Godfrey, was such a man.

Young girls cannot be kept virtual prisoners in this day and age; they cannot be forbidden to leave the house, to love, and marry the man of their choice. Yet Anita's uncle had her under lock and key, and our wedding was prohibited.

Yes, it was all sheer melodrama. The whole affair struck me as ridiculous when I thought about it; but when I was with Anita, I did not laugh.

When I heard Anita talk about her uncle, I almost believed; not that he had supernatural powers, but that he was cunningly, persistently attempting to drive her mad.

That's something you can understand, something evil, yet tangible.

There was a trust fund, and Gideon Godfrey was

18

Anita's legal guardian. He had her out there in his rotting hulk of a house—completely at his mercy. It might easily occur to him to work on her imagination with wild stories and subtle confirmations.

Anita told me. Told me of the locked rooms upstairs where the old man sat mumbling over the moldering books he'd hidden away there. She told me of his feuds with farmers, his open boastings of the "hex" he put on cattle, the blights he claimed to visit upon crops.

Anita told me of her dreams. Something black came into her room at night. Something black and inchoate —a trailing mist that was nevertheless a definite and tangible presence. It had features, if not a face; a voice, if not a throat. It whispered.

And as it whispered, it caressed her. She would fight off the inky strands brushing her face and body; she would struggle to summon the scream which dispelled spectre and sleep simultaneously.

Anita had a name for the black thing, too.

She called it an *incubus*.

In ancient tracts on witchcraft, the incubus is mentioned—the dark demon that comes to women in the night. The black emissary of Satan the Tempter; the lustful shadow that rides the nightmare.

I knew of the incubus as a legend. Anita knew of it as a reality.

Anita grew thin and pale. I knew there was no magic concerned in her metamorphosis—confinement in that bleak old house was alchemy enough to work the change. That, plus the sadistically inspired hintings of Gideon Godfrey, and the carefully calculated atmosphere of dread which resulted in the dreams.

But I had been weak, I didn't insist. After all, there was no real proof of Godfrey's machinations, and any attempt to bring issues to a head might easily result in a sanity hearing for Anita, rather than the old man.

I felt that, given time, I would be able to make Anita come away with me voluntarily.

19

And now, there was no time.

Something had happened.

The car churned dust from the road as I turned in towards the tottering gambrels of the house on the hillside. Through the flickering heat of a midsummer afternoon, I peered at the ruined gables above the long porch.

I swung up the drive, shot the car past the barn and side-buildings, and parked hastily.

No figure appeared at the open windows, and no voice called a greeting as I ran up the porch steps and paused before the open door. The hall within was dark. I entered heedless of knocking, and turned towards the parlor.

Anita was standing there, waiting, on the far side of the room. Her red hair was disheveled about her shoulders; her face was pale—but she was obviously unharmed. Her eyes brightened when she saw me.

"Jim—you're here!"

She held out her arms to me, and I moved across the room to embrace her.

As I moved, I stumbled over something.

I looked down.

Lying at my feet was the body of Gideon Godfrey— the head split open and crushed to a bloody pulp.

2.

Then Anita was sobbing in my arms, and I was patting her shoulders and trying not to stare at the red horror on the floor.

"Help me," she whispered, over and over again. "Help me!"

"Of course I'll help you," I murmured. "But—what happened?"

"I don't—know."

"You don't *know?*"

Something in my intonation sobered her. She

20

straightened up, pulled away, and began dabbing at her eyes. Meanwhile she whispered on, hastily.

"It was hot this morning. I was out in the barn. I felt tired and dozed off in the hayloft. Then, all at once, I woke up and came back into the house. I found—him—lying here."

"There was no noise? Nobody around?"

"Not a soul."

"You can see how he was killed," I said. "Only an axe could do such a job. But—where is it?"

She averted her gaze. "The axe? I don't know. It should be beside the body, if someone killed him."

I turned and started out of the room.

"Jim—where are you going?"

"To call the police, naturally," I told her.

"No, you can't. Don't you see? If you call them now, they'll think *I* did it."

I could only nod. "That's right. It's a pretty flimsy story, isn't it Anita? If we only had a weapon; finger-prints, or footsteps, some kind of clue—"

Anita sighed. I took her hand. "Try to remember," I said, softly. "You're sure you were out in the barn when this happened? Can't you remember more than that?"

"No, darling. It's all so confused, somehow. I was sleeping—I had one of my dreams—the black thing came—"

I shuddered. I knew how *that* statement affected me, and I could imagine the reaction of the police. She was quite mad, I was sure of it; and yet another thought struggled for realization. Somehow I had the feeling that I had lived through this moment before. Pseudo-memory. Or had I heard of it, read of it?

Read of it? Yes, that was it!

"Try hard, now," I muttered. "Can't you recall how it all began? Don't you know why you went out to the barn in the first place?"

"Yes. I think I can remember. I went out there for some fishing sinkers."

"Fishing sinkers? In the barn?"

Something clicked, after all. I stared at her with eyes as glassy as those of the corpse on the floor.

"Listen to me," I said. "You're not Anita Loomis. You're—Lizzie Borden!"

She didn't say a word. Obviously the name had no meaning for her. But it was all coming back to me now; the old, old story, the unsolved mystery.

I guided her to the sofa, sat beside her. She didn't look at me. I didn't look at her. Neither of us looked at the thing on the floor. The heat shimmered all around us in the house of death as I whispered the story to her —the story of Lizzie Borden—

3.

It was early August of the year 1892. Fall River, Massachusetts lay gasping in the surge of a heat-wave.

The sun beat down upon the home of Fall River's leading citizen, the venerable Andrew Jackson Borden. Here the old man dwelt with his second wife, Mrs. Abby Borden, stepmother of the two girls, Emma and Lizzie Borden. The maid, Bridget "Maggie" Sullivan, completed the small household. A house guest, John V. Morse, was away at this time, visiting. Emma, the older Borden girl, was also absent.

Only the maid and Lizzie Borden were present on August 2nd, when Mr. and Mrs. Borden became ill. It was Lizzie who spread the news—she told her friend, Marion Russell, that she believed their milk had been poisoned.

But it was too hot to bother, too hot to think. Besides, Lizzie's ideas weren't taken very seriously. At 32, the angular, unprepossessing younger daughter was looked upon with mixed opinion by the members of the community. It was known that she was "cultured" and

22

"refined"—she had travelled in Europe; she was a churchgoer, taught a class in a church mission, and enjoyed a reputation for "good work" as a member of the WCTU and similar organizations. Yet some folks thought her temperamental, even eccentric. She had "notions."

So the illness of the elder Bordens was duly noted and ascribed to natural causes; it was impossible to think about anything more important than the omnipresent heat, and the forthcoming Annual Picnic of the Fall River Police Department, scheduled for August 4th.

On the 4th the heat was unabated, but the picnic was in full swing by 11 o'clock—the time at which Andrew Jackson Borden left his downtown office and came home to relax on the parlor sofa. He slept fitfully in the noonday swelter.

Lizzie Borden came in from the barn a short while later and found her father asleep no longer.

Mr. Borden lay on the sofa, his head bashed in so that his features were unrecognizable.

Lizzie Borden called the maid, "Maggie" Sullivan, who was resting in her room. She told her to run and fetch Dr. Bowen, a near neighbor. He was not at home.

Another neighbor, a Mrs. Churchill, happened by. Lizzie Borden greeted her at the door.

"Someone has killed father," were Lizzie's words.

"And where is your mother?" Mrs. Churchill asked.

Lizzie Borden hesitated. It was hard to think in all this heat. "Why—she's out. She received a note to go and help someone who is sick."

Mrs. Churchill didn't hesitate. She marched to a public livery stable and summoned help. Soon a crowd of neighbors and friends gathered; police and doctors were in attendance. And in the midst of growing confusion, it was Mrs. Churchill who went directly upstairs to the spare room.

Mrs. Borden rested there, her head smashed in.

By the time Dr. Dolan, the coroner, arrived, questioning was already proceeding. The Chief of Police and several of his men were on hand, establishing the fact that there had been no attempt at robbery. They began to interrogate Lizzie.

Lizzie Borden said she was in the barn, eating pears and looking for fishing sinkers—hot as it was. She dozed off, was awakened by a muffled groan, and came into the house to investigate. There she found her father's hacked body. And that was all—

Now her story of a suspected poisoning was recalled, with fresh significance. A druggist said that a woman had indeed come into his shop several days before and attempted to procure some prussic acid—saying she needed it to kill the moths in her fur coat. She had been refused, and informed by the proprietor that she needed a doctor's prescription.

The woman was identified, too—as Lizzie Borden.

Lizzie's story of the note summoning her mother away from the house now came in for scrutiny. No such note was ever discovered.

Meanwhile, the investigators were busy. In the cellar, they discovered a hatchet with a broken handle. It appeared to have been recently washed, then covered with ashes. Water and ashes conceal stains . . . .

Shock, heat, embarrassment all played subtle parts in succeeding events. The police presently withdrew without taking formal action, and the whole matter was held over, pending an inquest. After all, Andrew Jackson Borden was a wealthy citizen, his daughter was a prominent and respectable woman, and no one wished to act hastily.

Days passed in a pall of heat and gossip behind sweaty palms. Lizzie's friend, Marion Russell, dropped in at the house three days after the crime and discovered Lizzie burning a dress.

"It was all covered with paint," Lizzie Borden explained.

Marion Russell remembered that dress—it was the one Lizzie Borden had worn on the day of the murders.

The inevitable inquest was held, with the inevitable verdict. Lizzie Borden was arrested and formally charged with the slayings.

The press took over. The church members defended Lizzie Borden. The sobsisters made much of her. During the six months preceding the actual trial, the crime became internationally famous.

But nothing new was discovered.

During the thirteen days of the trial, the bewildering story was recounted without any sensational development.

Why should a refined New England spinster suddenly kill her father and stepmother with a hatchet, then boldly "discover" the bodies and summon the police?

The prosecution was unable to give a satisfactory answer. On June 20th, 1893, Lizzie Borden was acquitted by a jury of her peers, after one hour of deliberation.

She retired to her home and lived a life of seclusion for many, many years. The stigma had been erased, but the mystery remained unsolved with her passing.

Only the grave little girls remained, skipping their ropes and solemnly chanting:

> "Lizzie Borden took an axe
> And gave her mother forty whacks.
> When she saw what she had done
> She gave her father forty-one."

4.

That's the story I told Anita—the story you can read wherever famous crimes are chronicled.

She listened without comment, but I could hear the sharp intake of breath as I recounted some singularly significant parallel. *The hot day . . . the barn . . . the fishing sinkers . . . a sudden sleep, a sudden awakening . . . the return to the house . . . discovery of a body . . . took an axe. . . .*

She waited until I had finished before speaking.

"Jim, why do you tell me this? Is it your way of hinting that I—took an axe to my uncle?"

"I'm not hinting anything," I answered. "I was just struck by the amazing similarity of this case and the Lizzie Borden affair."

"What do you think happened, Jim? In the Lizzie Borden case, I mean."

"I don't know," I said slowly. "I was wondering if you had a theory."

Her opal eyes glinted in the shadowed room. "Couldn't it have been the same thing?" she whispered. "You know what I've told you about my dreams. About the incubus."

"Suppose Lizzie Borden had those dreams, too. Suppose an entity emerged from her sleeping brain; an entity that would take up an axe and kill—"

She sensed my protest and ignored it. "Uncle Gideon knew of such things. How the spirit descends upon you in sleep. Couldn't such a presence emerge into the world while she slept and kill her parents? Couldn't such a being creep into the house here while I slept and kill Uncle Gideon?"

I shook my head. "You know the answer I must give you," I said. "And you can guess what the police would say to that. Our only chance now, before calling them, is to find the murder weapon."

We went out into the hall together, and hand in hand we walked through the silent ovens that were the rooms of this old house. Everywhere was dust and desolation. The kitchen alone bore signs of recent occupancy— they had breakfasted there early in the day, Anita said.

26

There was no axe or hatchet to be found anywhere.

It took courage to tackle the cellar. I was almost certain of what we must find. But Anita did not recoil, and we descended the dark stairwell.

The cellar did not yield up a single sharp instrument.

Then we were walking up the stairs to the second floor. The front bedroom was ransacked, then Anita's little room, and at last we stood before the door of Gideon Godfrey's chamber.

"It's locked," I said. "That's funny."

"No," Anita demurred. "He always kept it locked. The key must be downstairs with—him."

"I'll get it," I said. And I did so. When I returned with the rusty key, Anita stood quaking in the hallway.

"I won't go inside with you," she breathed. "I've never been inside his room. I'm afraid. He used to lock himself in and I'd hear sounds late at night—he was praying, but not to God—"

"Wait here, then," I said.

I unlocked the door, opened it, stepped across the threshold.

Gideon Godfrey may have been a madman himself. He may have been a cunning schemer, bent on deluding his niece. But in either case, he did believe in sorcery.

That much was evident from the contents of his room. I saw the books, saw the crudely drawn chalk circles on the floor; literally dozens of them, hastily obliterated and repeated endlessly. There were queer geometric configurations traced in blue chalk upon one of the walls, and candle-drippings covered walls and floors alike.

The heavy, fetid air held a faint, acrid reek of incense. I noted one sharp instrument in the room—a long silver knife lying on a side-table next to a pewter bowl. The knife seemed rusty, and the rust was red. . . .

But it was not the murder weapon, that was certain. I was looking for an axe, and it wasn't here.

I joined Anita in the hall.

"Isn't there anywhere else?" I asked, Another room?"

"Perhaps the barn," she suggested.

"And we didn't really search in the parlor," I added.

"Don't make me go in there again," Anita begged. "Not in the same room where he is. You look there and I'll go through the barn."

We parted at the foot of the stairs. She went out the side entrance and I walked back into the parlor.

I looked behind the chairs, under the sofa. I found nothing. It was hot in there; hot and quiet. My head began to swim.

Heat—silence—and that grinning thing on the floor. I turned away, leaned against the mantel, and stared at my bloodshot eyes in the mirror.

All at once I saw it, standing behind me. It was like a cloud—a black cloud. But it wasn't a cloud. It was a *face*. A face, covered by a black mask of wavering smoke; a mask that leered and pressed closer.

Through heat and silence it came, and I couldn't move. I stared at the swirling, cloudy smoke that shrouded a face.

Then I heard something swish, and I turned.

Anita was standing behind me.

As I grasped her wrists she screamed and fell. I could only stare down at her, stare down as the black cloud over her face disappeared, oozed into air.

The search was over. I'd found the murder weapon, all right; it rested rigidly in her hands—the bloodstained axe!

5.

I carried Anita over to the sofa. She didn't move, and I made no attempt to revive her.

Then I went out into the hall, carrying the axe with me. No sense in taking any chances. I trusted Anita still, but not that thing—not that black mist, swirling up like smoke to take possession of a living brain and make it lust to kill.

Demoniac possession it was; the legend spoken of in ancient books like those in the room of the dead wizard.

I crossed the hall to the little study opposite the parlor. The wall telephone was here; I picked it up and rang the operator.

She got me the Highway Police headquarters. I don't know why I called them, rather than the sheriff. I was in a daze throughout the entire call. I stood there holding the axe in one hand, reporting the murder in a few words.

Questions rose from the other end of the wire; I did not answer them.

"Come on out to the Godfrey place," I said. "There's been a killing."

What else *could* I say?

What would we be telling the police, half an hour from now, when they arrived on the scene?

They wouldn't believe the truth—wouldn't believe that a demon could enter a human body and activate it as an instrument for murder.

But I believed it now. I had seen the fiend peering out of Anita's face when she tried to sneak up behind me with the axe. I had seen the black smoke, the conjuration of a demon lusting for bloody death.

Now I knew that it must have entered her as she slept; made her kill Gideon Godfrey.

Perhaps such a thing had happened to Lizzie Borden. Yes. The eccentric spinster with the over-active imagination, so carefully repressed; the eccentric spinster, sleeping in the barn on that hot summer day—

> *"Lizzie Borden took an axe*
> *And gave her mother forty whacks."*

I leaned back, the verse running through my head.

It was hotter than I had believed possible, and the stillness hinted of approaching storm.

I groped for coolness, felt the cold axeblade in my hand as I leaned the weapon across my lap. As long as I held onto this, we were safe. The fiend was foiled, now. Wherever that presence lurked, it must be raging, for it could not take possession.

Oh, that was madness! The heat was responsible, surely. Sunstroke caused Anita to kill her uncle. Sunstroke brought on her babblings about an incubus and dreams. Sunstroke impelled that sudden, murderous attack upon me before the mirror.

Sympathetic hallucination accounted for my image of a face veiled by a black mist. It had to be that way. The police would say so, doctors would say so.

> *"When she saw what she had done*
> *She gave her father forty-one."*

Police. Doctors. Lizzie Borden. The heat. The cool axe. Forty whacks. . . .

6.

The first crash of thunder awakened me. For a moment I thought the police had arrived, then realized that the heat-storm was breaking. I blinked and rose from the armchair. Then I realized that something was *missing*.

The axe no longer rested across my lap.

It wasn't on the floor. It wasn't visible anywhere. The axe had disappeared again!

"Anita," I gasped. I knew without conscious formulation of thought how it must have happened. She had awakened while I slept—come in here and stolen the axe from me.

What a fool I had been to sleep!

I might have guessed it . . . while she was unconscious, the lurking demon had another chance to gain

30

possession. That was it; the demon had entered into Anita again.

I faced the door, stared at the floor, and saw my confirmation scrawled in a trail of red wetness dotting the carpet and outer hall.

It was blood. Fresh blood.

I rushed across the hall, re-entered the parlor.

Then I gasped, but with relief. For Anita was still lying on the couch, just as I had left her. I wiped the sudden perspiration from my eyes and forehead, then stared again at the red pattern on the floor.

The trail of blood ended beside the couch, all right. But did it lead *to* the couch—or *away* from it?

Thunder roared through the heat. A flicker of lightning seared the shadows of the room as I tried to puzzle it out.

What did it mean? It meant that perhaps Anita was not possessed of a demon now while she slept.

But I had slept, too.

Maybe—maybe the demon had come to *me* when *I* dozed off!

All at once, everything blurred. I was trying to remember. Where was the axe? Where could it possibly be, *now*?

Then the lightning came again and with it the final confirmation—the revelation.

I saw the axe now, crystal-clear—the axe—buried to the hilt in the top of Anita's head!

THE SNAIL WATCHER

By Patricia Highsmith

When Mr. Peter Knoppert began to make a hobby of snail-watching, he had no idea that his handful of specimens would become hundreds in no time. Only two months after the original snails were carried up to the Knoppert study, some thirty glass tanks and bowls, all teeming with snails, lined the walls, rested on the desk and windowsills, and were beginning even to cover the floor. Mrs. Knoppert disapproved strongly, and would no longer enter the room. It smelled, she said, and besides she had once stepped on a snail by accident, a horrible sensation she would never forget. But the more his wife and friends deplored his unusual and vaguely repellent pastime, the more pleasure Mr. Knoppert seemed to find in it.

"I never cared for nature before in my life," Mr. Knoppert often remarked—he was a partner in a brokerage firm, a man who had devoted all his life to the science of finance—"but snails have opened my eyes to the beauty of the animal world."

If his friends commented that snails were not really animals, and their slimy habitats hardly the best example of the beauty of nature, Mr. Knoppert would

32

tell them with a superior smile that they simply didn't know all that *he* knew about snails.

And it was true. Mr. Knoppert had witnessed an exhibition that was not described, certainly not adequately described, in any encyclopaedia or zoology book that he had been able to find. Mr. Knoppert had wandered into the kitchen one evening for a bite of something before dinner, and had happened to notice that a couple of snails in the china bowl on the drainboard were behaving very oddly. Standing more or less on their tails, they were weaving before each other for all the world like a pair of snakes hypnotized by a flute player. A moment later, their faces came together in a kiss of voluptuous intensity. Mr. Knoppert bent closer and studied them from all angles. Something else was happening: a protuberance like an ear was appearing on the right side of the head of either snail. His instinct told him that he was watching a sexual activity of some sort.

The cook came in and said something to him, but Mr. Knoppert silenced her with an impatient wave of his hand. He couldn't take his eyes from the enchanted little creatures in the bowl.

When the earlike excrescences were precisely together rim to rim, a whitish rod like another small tentacle shot out from one ear and arched over toward the ear of the other snail. Mr. Knoppert's first surmise was dashed when a tentacle sallied from the other snail, too. Most peculiar, he thought. The two tentacles withdrew, then shot forth again, one after the other, and then as if they had found some invisible mark, remained fixed in the other snail. Mr. Knoppert peered intently closer. So did the cook.

"Did you ever see anything like this?" Mr. Knoppert asked.

"No. They must be fighting," the cook said indifferently and went away.

33

That was a sample of the ignorance on the subject of snails that he was later to discover everywhere.

Mr. Knoppert continued to observe the pair of snails for nearly an hour, until first the ears, then the rods withdrew, and the snails themselves relaxed their attitudes and paid no further attention to each other. But by that time, a different pair of snails had begun a flirtation, and were slowly rearing themselves to get into a position for kissing. Mr. Knoppert told the cook that the snails were not to be served that evening. He took the whole bowl of them up to his study. And snails were never again served in the Knoppert household.

That night, he searched his encyclopaedias and a few general science books he happened to possess, but there was absolutely nothing on snails' breeding habits, though the oyster's dull reproductive cycle was described in detail. Perhaps it hadn't been a mating he had seen after all, Mr. Knoppert decided after a day or two. His wife Edna told him either to eat the snails or get rid of them—it was at this time she stepped on a snail that had crawled out onto the floor—and Mr. Knoppert might have, if he hadn't come across a certain sentence in Darwin's *Origin of Species* on a page given to gastropoda. The sentence was in French, a language Mr. Knoppert did not know, but the word *sensualité* made him tense like a bloodhound that has suddenly found the scent. He was in the public library at the time, and laboriously he translated the sentence with the aid of a French-English dictionary. It was a statement of less than a hundred words, saying that snails manifested a sensuality in their mating that was not to be found anywhere in the animal kingdom. That was all. It was from the notebook of Henri Fabre. Obviously, Darwin had decided not to translate it for the average reader, but to leave it in its original language for the scholarly few who really cared. Mr. Knoppert considered himself one of the scholarly few now, and his round, pink face beamed with self-esteem.

He had learned that his snails were the fresh water type that laid their eggs in sand or earth, so he put moist earth and a little saucer of water into a big wash-pan and transferred his snails into it. Then he waited for something to happen. Not even another mating happened. He picked up the snails one by one and looked at them, without seeing anything suggestive of pregnancy. But one snail he couldn't pick up. The shell might have been glued to the earth. Mr. Knoppert suspected the snail had buried its head in the ground to die. Two more days went by, and on the morning of the third, Mr. Knoppert found a spot of crumbly earth where the snail had rested. Curious, he investigated the crumbles with a match stem, and to his delight discovered a pit full of shiny new eggs. Snail eggs! He hadn't been wrong. Mr. Knoppert called his wife and the cook to look at them. The eggs looked very much like big caviar, only they were white instead of black or red.

"Well, naturally they have to breed some way," was his wife's comment.

Mr. Knoppert couldn't understand her lack of interest. He had to go look at the eggs every hour that he was at home. He looked at them every morning to see if any change had taken place, and the eggs were his last thought every night before he went to bed. Moreover, another snail was now digging a pit. And another pair of snails was mating! The first batch of eggs turned a grayish color, and minuscule spirals of future shells became discernible on their surfaces. Mr. Knoppert's anticipation rose to higher pitch. At last a morning arrived when he looked down into the egg pit and saw the first tiny moving head, the first stubby little antennae uncertainly exploring its nest. Mr. Knoppert was as happy as the father of a new child. Every one of the thirty or more eggs in the pit came miraculously to life. He had seen the entire reproductive cycle evolve to a successful conclusion. And the fact that no one, at least

35

no one that he knew of, was acquainted with a fraction of what he knew, lent his knowledge a thrill of discovery, the piquancy of the esoteric. Mr. Knoppert made notes on successive matings and egg hatchings. He narrated snail biology to sometimes fascinated, more often shocked friends and guests, until his wife squirmed with embarrassment.

"But where is it going to stop, Peter? If they keep on reproducing at this rate, they'll take over the house!" his wife told him after fifteen or twenty pits had hatched.

"There's no stopping nature," he replied good-humoredly. "They've only taken over the study. There's plenty of room there."

So more and more glass tanks and bowls were moved in. Mr. Knoppert went to the market and chose several of the more lively looking snails, and also a pair he found mating, unobserved by the rest of the world. More and more egg pits appeared in the dirt floors of the tanks, and out of each pit crept finally from thirty to forty baby snails, transparent as dewdrops, gliding up rather than down the strips of fresh lettuce that Mr. Knoppert was quick to give all the pits as edible ladders for them. Matings went on so often that he no longer bothered to watch them. But the thrill of seeing the white caviar become shells and start to move—that never diminished however often he witnessed it.

His colleagues in the brokerage office noticed a new zest for life in Peter Knoppert. He became more daring in his moves, more brilliant in his calculations, became in fact a little vicious in his outlook, but he brought money in for his company. By unanimous vote, his basic salary was raised from forty to sixty thousand per year. When anyone congratulated him on first achievements, Mr. Knoppert was quick to give all the credit to his snails and the beneficial relaxation he derived from watching them.

He spent all his evenings with his snails in the room that was no longer a study but a kind of aquarium.

36

He loved to strew the tanks with fresh lettuce and pieces of boiled potatoes and beets, then turn on the sprinkler system that he had installed in the tanks to simulate natural rainfall. Then all the snails would liven up and begin eating, mating, or merely gliding with obvious pleasure through the shallow water. Mr. Knoppert often let a snail climb onto his forefinger—he fancied his snails enjoyed this human contact—and he would feed it a piece of lettuce by hand, would observe the snail from all sides, finding as much aesthetic satisfaction as another man might have from contemplating a Japanese print.

By now, Mr. Knoppert did not allow anyone to set foot in his study. Too many snails had the habit of crawling around on the floor, of going to sleep glued to chair bottoms and to the backs of books on the shelves. Snails spent most of their time sleeping, especially the older snails. But there were enough less indolent snails who preferred love-making. Mr. Knoppert estimated that about a dozen pairs of snails must be kissing all the time. And certainly there was a multitude of baby and adolescent snails. They were impossible to count. But Mr. Knoppert did count the snails sleeping and creeping on the ceiling alone, and arrived at something between eleven and twelve hundred. The tanks, the bowls, the underside of his desk and the bookshelves must surely have held fifty times that number. Some of them had been up there for weeks, and he was afraid they were not taking in enough nourishment. But of late he had been a little too busy, and too much in need of the tranquility that he got simply from sitting in the study in his favorite chair.

During the month of June, he was so busy, he often worked late in the evening at his office over the reports that were piling in at the end of the fiscal year. He made calculations, spotted a half dozen possibilities of gain, and reserved the most daring, the least obvious moves for his private operations. By this time next year, he thought, he should be three or four times as well off as now. He saw his bank account multiplying as easily and rapidly as his snails. He told his wife this, and she was overjoyed. She even forgave him the appropriation of the study, and the stale, fishy smell that was spreading throughout the whole upstairs.

"Still, I do wish you'd take a look just to see if anything's happening, Peter," she said to him rather anxiously one morning. "A tank might have overturned or something, and I wouldn't want the rug to be ruined. You haven't been in the study for nearly a week, have you?"

Mr. Knoppert hadn't been in for nearly two weeks. He didn't tell his wife that the rug was pretty much ruined already. "I'll go up tonight," he said.

But it was three more days before he found time. He went in one evening just before bedtime and was surprised to find the floor absolutely covered with snails, with three or four layers of snails. He had difficulty closing the door without mashing any. The dense clusters of snails in the corners made the room look positively round, as if he stood inside some huge, conglomerate stone. Mr. Knoppert gazed around him with his mouth open in astonishment. They had not only covered every surface, but thousands of snails hung down into the room from the chandelier in a grotesque coagulation.

Mr. Knoppert felt for the back of a chair to steady himself. He felt only a lot of shells under his hand. He had to smile a little: there were snails in the chair seat, piled up on one another like a lumpy cushion. He really must do something about the ceiling, and immediately. He took an umbrella from the corner, brushed some of the snails off it, and cleared a place on his desk to stand on. The umbrella tore the wallpaper, and then the weight of the snails pulled down a long strip that hung almost to the floor. Mr. Knoppert felt suddenly frus-

38

trated and angry. The sprinklers would make them move. He pulled the lever.

The sprinklers came on in all the tanks, and the seething activity of the entire room increased at once. Mr. Knoppert slid his feet along the floor, through the tumbling snails that made a sound like pebbles on a beach, and directed a couple of the sprinklers at the ceiling. That was a mistake, he saw at once. The softened paper began to tear, and he dodged one slowly falling mass only to be hit by a swinging festoon of snails, really hit quite a stunning blow on the side of the head. He went down on one knee, dazed. He should open a window, he thought, the air was stifling. And there were snails crawling over his shoes and up his trousers legs. He shook his feet irritably. He was just going to the door, intending to call for one of the servants to help him, when the chandelier fell on him. Mr. Knoppert sat down heavily on the floor. He saw now that he couldn't possibly get the window open, because the snails were fastened thick and deep over the windowsill. For a moment, he felt he couldn't get up, felt as if he were suffocating. It was not only the smell of the room, but everywhere he looked long wall-paper strips covered with snails blocked his vision as if he were in a prison.

"Edna!" he called, and was amazed at the muffled, ineffective sound of his voice. The room might have been soundproof.

He crawled to the door, heedless of the sea of snails he crushed under hands and knees. He could not get the door open. There were so many snails on it, crossing and recrossing the crack of the door on all four sides, they actually resisted his strength.

"Edna!" A snail crawled into his mouth. He spat it out in disgust. Mr. Knoppert tried to brush the snails off his arms. But for every hundred he dislodged, four hundred seemed to slide upon him and fasten to him again, as if they deliberately sought him out as the only

CHICKAMAUGA

By *Ambrose Bierce*

One sunny autumn afternoon a child strayed away from
its rude home in a small field and entered a forest unobserved. It was happy in a new sense of freedom from
control, happy in the opportunity of exploration and
adventure; for this child's spirit, in bodies of its ancestors, had for many thousands of years been trained to
memorable feats of discovery and conquest—victories
in battles whose critical moments were centuries, whose
victors' camps were cities of hewn stone. From the
cradle of its race it had conquered its way through two
continents, and passing a great sea, had penetrated a
third, there to be born to war and dominion as a heri-
tage.

The child was a boy aged about six years, the son of a
poor planter. In his younger manhood the father had been
a soldier, had fought against naked savages, and followed the flag of his country into the capital of a
civilized race to the far South. In the peaceful life of a
planter the warrior-fire survived; once kindled, it is
never extinguished. The man loved military books and
pictures, and the boy had understood enough to make
himself a wooden sword, though even the eye of his
father would hardly have known it for what it was. This

41

weapon he now bore bravely, as became the son of an heroic race, and pausing now and again in the sunny spaces of the forest assumed, with some exaggeration, the postures of aggression and defense that he had been taught by the engraver's art. Made reckless by the ease with which he overcame invisible foes attempting to stay his advance, he committed the common enough military error of pushing the pursuit to a dangerous extreme, until he found himself upon the margin of a wide but shallow brook, whose rapid waters barred his direct advance against the flying foe that had crossed with illogical ease. But the intrepid victor was not to be baffled; the spirit of the race which had passed the great sea burned unconquerable in that small breast and would not be denied. Finding a place where some boulders in the bed of the stream lay but a step or a leap apart, he made his way across and fell again upon the rear-guard of his imaginary foe, putting all to the sword.

Now that the battle had been won, prudence required that he withdraw to his base of operations. Alas! like many a mightier conqueror, and like one, the mightiest, he could not

"curb the lust for war,
Nor learn that tempted Fate will leave the loftiest star."

Advancing from the bank of the creek he suddenly found himself confronted with a new and more formidable enemy: in the path that he was following sat, bolt upright, with ears erect and paws suspended before it, a rabbit! With a startled cry the child turned and fled, he knew not in what direction, calling with inarticulate cries for his mother, weeping, stumbling, his tender skin cruelly torn by branches, his little heart beating hard with terror—breathless, blind with tears—lost in the forest! Then, for more than an hour, he wandered with erring feet through the tangled undergrowth, till at last,

42

overcome by fatigue, he lay down in a narrow space between two rocks, within a few yards of the stream, and still grasping his toy sword, no longer a weapon but a companion, sobbed himself to sleep. The wood birds sang merrily above his head; the squirrels, whisking their bravery of tail, ran barking from tree to tree, unconscious of the pity of it, and somewhere far away was a strange muffled thunder, as if the partridges were drumming in celebration of nature's victory over the son of her immemorial enslavers. And back at the little plantation, where white men and black were hastily searching the fields and hedges in alarm, a mother's heart was breaking for her missing child.

Hours passed, and then the little sleeper rose to his feet. The chill of the evening was in his limbs, the fear of the gloom in his heart. But he had rested, and he no longer wept. With some blind instinct which impelled to action he struggled through the undergrowth about him and came to a more open ground—on his right the brook, to the left a gentler acclivity studded with infrequent trees; over all, the gathering gloom of twilight. A thin, ghostly mist rose along the water. It frightened and repelled him; instead of recrossing, in the direction whence he had come, he turned his back upon it, and went forward toward the dark enclosing wood. Suddenly he saw before him a strange moving object which he took to be some large animal—a dog, a pig—he could not name it; perhaps it was a bear. He had seen pictures of bears, but knew of nothing to their discredit and had vaguely wished to meet one. But something in form or movement of this object—something in the awkwardness of its approach—told him that it was not a bear, and curiosity was stayed by fear. He stood still, and as it came slowly on gained courage every moment, for he saw that at least it had not the long, menacing ears of the rabbit. Possibly his impressionable mind was half conscious of something familiar in its shambling, awkward gait. Before it had approached near enough to resolve his doubts, he saw that it was followed by another and another. To right and to left were many more; the whole open space about him was alive with them—all moving toward the brook.

They were men. They crept upon their hands and knees. They used their hands only, dragging their legs. They used their knees only, their arms hanging idle at their sides. They strove to rise to their feet, but fell prone in the attempt. They did nothing naturally, and nothing alike, save only to advance foot by foot in the same direction. Singly, in pairs and in little groups, they came on through the gloom, some halting now and again while others crept slowly past them, then resuming their movement. They came by dozens and by hundreds; as far on either hand as one could see in the deepening gloom they extended, and the black wood behind them appeared to be inexhaustible. The very ground seemed in motion toward the creek. Occasionally one who had paused did not again go on, but lay motionless. He was dead. Some, pausing, made strange gestures with their hands, erected their arms and lowered them again, clasped their heads; spread their palms upward, as men are sometimes seen to do in public prayer.

Not all of this did the child note; it is what would have been noted by an elder observer; he saw little but that these were men, yet crept like babies. Being men, they were not terrible, though unfamiliarly clad. He moved among them freely, going from one to another and peering into their faces with childish curiosity. All their faces were singularly white and many were streaked and gouted with red. Something of this—something too, perhaps, in their grotesque attitudes and movements— reminded him of the painted clown whom he had seen last summer in the circus, and he laughed as he watched them. But on and ever on they crept, these maimed and bleeding men, as heedless as he of the dramatic contrast between his laughter and their own ghastly gravity.

To him it was a merry spectacle. He had seen his father's Negroes creep upon their hands and knees for his amusement—had ridden them so, "making believe" they were his horses. He now approached one of these crawling figures from behind and with an agile movement mounted it astride. The man sank upon his breast, recovered, flung the small boy fiercely to the ground as an unbroken colt might have done, then turned upon him a face that lacked a lower jaw—from the upper teeth to the throat was a great red gap fringed with hanging shreds of flesh and splinters of bone. The unnatural prominence of nose, the absence of chin, the fierce eyes, gave this man the appearance of a great bird of prey crimsoned in throat and breast by the blood of its quarry. The man rose to his knees, the child to his feet. The man shook his fist at the child; the child, terrified at last, ran to a tree near by, got upon the farther side of it, and took a more serious view of the situation. And so the clumsy multitude dragged itself slowly and painfully along in hideous pantomime— moved forward down the slope like a swarm of great black beetles, with never a sound of going—in silence profound, absolute.

Instead of darkening, the haunted landscape began to brighten. Through the belt of trees beyond the brook shone a strange red light, the trunks and branches of the trees making a black lacework against it. It struck the creeping figures and gave them monstrous shadows, which caricatured their movements on the lit grass. It fell upon their faces, touching their whiteness with a ruddy tinge, accentuating the stains with which so many of them were freaked and maculated. It sparkled on buttons and bits of metal in their clothing. Instinctively the child turned toward the growing splendour and moved down the slope with his horrible companions; in a few moments had passed the foremost of the throng —not much of a feat, considering his advantages. He placed himself in the lead, his wooden sword still in

45

hand, and solemnly directed the march, conforming his pace to theirs and occasionally turning as if to see that his forces did not straggle. Surely such a leader never before had such a following.

Scattered about upon the ground now slowly narrowing by the encroachment of this awful march to water were certain articles to which, in the leader's mind, were coupled no significant associations: an occasional blanket, tightly rolled lengthwise, doubled and the ends bound together with a string; a heavy knapsack here, and there a broken rifle—such things, in short, as are found in the rear of retreating troops, the "spoor" of men flying from their hunters. Everywhere near the creek, which here had a margin of lowland, the earth was trodden into mud by the feet of men and horses. An observer of better experience in the use of his eyes would have noticed that these footprints pointed in both directions; the ground had been twice passed over —in advance and in retreat. A few hours before, these desperate, stricken men, with their more fortunate and now distant comrades, had penetrated the forest in thousands. Their successive battalions, breaking into swarms and reforming in lines, had passed the child on every side—had almost trodden on him as he slept. The rustle and murmur of their march had not awakened him. Almost within a stone's throw of where he lay they had fought a battle; but all unheard by him were the roar of the musketry, the shock of the cannon, "the thunder of the captains and the shouting." He had slept through it all, grasping his little wooden sword with perhaps a tighter clutch in unconscious sympathy with his martial environment, but as heedless of the grandeur of the struggle as the dead who had died to make the glory.

The fire beyond the belt of woods on the farther side of the creek, reflected to earth from the canopy of its own smoke, was now suffusing the whole landscape. It transformed the sinuous line of mist to the vapour of gold. The water gleamed with dashes of red, and red, too, were many of the stones protruding above the surface. But that was blood; the less desperately wounded had stained them in crossing. On them, too, the child now crossed with eager steps; he was going to the fire. As he stood upon the farther bank he turned about to look at the companions of his march. The advance was arriving at the creek. The stronger had already drawn themselves to the brink and plunged their faces into the flood. Three or four who lay without motion appeared to have no heads. At this the child's eyes expanded with wonder; even his hospitable understanding could not accept a phenomenon implying such vitality as that. After slaking their thirst these men had not had the strength to back away from the water, nor to keep their heads above it. They were drowned. In rear of these, the open spaces of the forest showed the leader as many formless figures of his grim command as at first; but not nearly so many were in motion. He waved his cap for their encouragement and smilingly pointed with his weapon in the direction of the guiding light—a pillar of fire to this strange exodus.

Confident of the fidelity of his forces, he now entered the belt of woods, passed through it easily in the red illumination, climbed a fence, ran across a field, turning now and again to coquet with his responsive shadow, and so approached the blazing ruin of a dwelling. Desolation everywhere. In all the wide glare not a living thing was visible. He cared nothing for that; the spectacle pleased, and he danced with glee in imitation of the wavering flames. He ran about, collecting fuel, but every object that he found was too heavy for him to cast in from the distance to which the heat limited his approach. In despair he flung in his sword—a surrender to the superior forces of nature. His military career was at an end.

Shifting his position, his eyes fell upon some outbuildings which had an oddly familiar appearance, as if he had dreamed of them. He stood considering them with wonder, when suddenly the entire plantation, with its enclosing forest, seemed to turn as if upon a pivot. His little world swung half around; the points of the compass were reversed. He recognized the blazing building as his own home!

For a moment he stood stupefied by the power of the revelation, then ran with stumbling feet, making a half-circuit of the ruin. There, conspicuous in the light of the conflagration, lay the dead body of a woman—the white face turned upward, the hands thrown out and clutched full of grass, the clothing deranged, the long dark hair in tangles and full of clotted blood. The greater part of the forehead was torn away, and from the jagged hole the brain protruded, overflowing the temple, a frothy mass of grey, crowned with clusters of crimson bubbles—the work of a shell.

The child moved his little hands, making wild, uncertain gestures. He uttered a series of inarticulate and indescribable cries—something between the chattering of an ape and the gobbling of a turkey—a startling, soulless, unholy sound, the language of a devil. The child was a deaf-mute.

Then he stood motionless, with quivering lips, looking down upon the wreck.

a Prussian air of authority. The monster's body did not move, but slowly—with the jerking motion of a badly operating machine—the creature's arm came up to shoulder height and stopped.

"This monster, built from pieces from the dead, cannot die, und if a piece gets too worn out I simply stitch on a new piece with the secret formula passed down from father to son from my great-great-grandfather. It cannot die nor feel pain—as you see—"

This time the gasp was even louder and some of the audience turned away while others watched with eager eyes. The barker had taken a foot-long and wickedly sharp needle, and had pushed it firmly through the monster's biceps until it protruded on both sides. No blood stained it and the creature made no motion, as though completely unaware that anything had been done to its flesh.

". . . impervious to pain, extremes of heat and cold, and possessing the strength of ten men . . ."

Behind him the voice droned on, but Dan Bream had had enough. He had seen the performance three times before, which was more than satisfactory for what he needed to know, and if he stayed in the tent another minute he would melt. The exit was close by and he pushed through the gaping, pallid audience and out into the humid dusk. It wasn't much cooler outside. Life borders on the unbearable along the shores of the Gulf of Mexico in August, and Panama City, Florida, was no exception. Dan headed for the nearest air conditioned beer joint and sighed with relief as the chill atmosphere closed around his steaming garments. The beer bottle frosted instantly with condensation as did the heavy glass stein, cold from the freezer. The first big swallow cut a path straight down to his stomach. He took the beer over to one of the straight-backed wooden booths, wiped the table off with a handful of paper napkins and flopped onto the bench. From the inner pocket of his jacket he took some folded sheets

50

of yellow copy paper, now slightly soggy, and spread them before him. After adding some lines to the scribbled notes he stuffed them back into his jacket and took a long pull on his beer.

Dan was halfway through his second bottle when the barker, who called himself Frankenstein the Fifth, came in. His stage personality had vanished along with the frock coat and monocle, and the Prussian haircut now looked like a common crew cut.

"You've got a great act," Dan called out cheerfully, and waved the man over. "Will you join me for a drink?"

"Don't mind if I do," Frankenstein answered in the pure nasal vowels of New York City, the German accent apparently having disappeared along with the monocle. "And see if they have a Schlitz or a Bud or anything beside the local swamp water."

He settled into the booth while Dan went for the beers, and groaned when he saw the labels on the bottles.

"At least it's cold," he said, shaking salt into his to make it foam, then half drained the stein in a long deep swallow. "I noticed you out there in front of the clems for most of the shows today. Do you like the act—or you a carny buff?"

"It's a good act. I'm a newsman, name's Dan Bream."

"Always pleased to meet the Press, Dan. Publicity is the life of show business, as the man said. I'm Stanley Arnold: call me Stan."

"Then Frankenstein is just your stage name?"

"What else? You act kinda dim for a reporter, are you sure—?" He waved away the Press card that Dan pulled from his breast pocket. "No, I believe you, Dan, but you gotta admit the question was a little on the rube side. I bet you even think that I have a real monster in there!"

"Well, you must admit that he looks authentic. The

51

skin stitched together that way, those plugs in his head—"

"Held on with spirit gum and the embroidery is drawn on with eyebrow pencil. That's show business for you, an illusion. But I'm happy to hear that the act even looked real to an experienced reporter like yourself. What paper did you say you were with?"

"No paper, the news syndicate. I caught your act about six months ago and became interested. Did a little checking when I was in Washington, then followed you down here. You don't really want me to call you Stan, do you? Stein might be closer. After all—Victor Frankenstein *is* the name on your naturalization papers."

"Tell me more," Frankenstein said in a voice suddenly cold and emotionless.

Dan riffled through the yellow sheets. "Yes . . . here it is, from the official records. Frankenstein, Victor—born in Geneva, arrived in the U.S. in 1938, and more of the same."

"The next thing you'll be telling me is that my monster *is* real!" Frankenstein smiled, but only with his mouth.

"I'm betting that it is. No yogi training or hypnotism or such can make a man as indifferent to pain as that thing is—and as terribly strong. I want the whole story, the truth for a change!"

"Do you . . .?" Frankenstein asked in a cold voice and for a long moment the air filled with tension. Then he laughed and clapped the reporter on the arm. "All right, Dan—I'll give it to you. You are a persistent devil and a good reporter and it is the least you deserve. But first you must get us some more drinks, something a measurable degree stronger than this execrable beer." His New York accent had disappeared as easily as had his German one; he spoke English now with skill and perfection without any recognizable regional accent.

Dan gathered their empty glasses. "It'll have to be beer—this is a dry country."

"Nonsense! This is America, the land that raises its hands in horror at the foreign conception of double-think yet practises it with an efficiency that sets the Old World to shame. Bay County may be officially dry but the law has many itchy palms, and under that counter you will find a reasonable supply of a clear liquid that glories in the name of White Mule and is reputed to have a kick of the same magnitude as its cognate beast. If you are still in doubt you will see a framed federal liquor license on the far wall, legitimatizing this endeavor in the eyes of the national government. Simply place a five-dollar-bill on the bar, say Mountain Dew, and do not expect any change."

When they both had enjoyed their first sips of the corn likker Victor Frankenstein lapsed into a friendly mood.

"Call me Vic, Dan. I want us to be friends. I'm going to tell you a story that few have heard before, a story that is astounding but true. True—mark that word—not a hodge-podge of distortions and half-truths and outright ignorance like that vile book produced by Mary Godwin. Oh how my father ever regretted meeting that woman and, in a moment of weakness, confiding in her the secret of some of his original lines of research . . ."

"Just a minute," Dan broke in. "You mentioned the truth, but I can't swallow this guff. Mary Wollstone-craft Shelly wrote *Frankenstein; or, The Modern Prometheus* in 1818. Which would make you and your father so old . . ."

"Please, Dan—no interruptions. I mentioned my father's researches, in the plural you will note, all of them devoted to the secrets of life. The Monster, as it has come to be called, was just one of his works. Longevity was what he was interested in, and he did live to a very, very old age, as will I. I will not stretch your credulity any further at this moment by mentioning the year of my birth, but will press on. That Mary Godwin. She and the poet were living together at this pe-

53

riod, they had not married as yet, and this permitted my father to hope that Mary might one day find him not unattractive, since he was quite taken by her. Well, you can easily imagine the end. She made notes of everything he told her—then discarded him and used the notes to construct her despicable book. Her errors are legion, listen . . ." He leaned across the booth and once again clapped Dan on the shoulder in a hearty way. It was an intimate gesture that the reporter didn't particularly enjoy, but he didn't complain. Not as long as the other kept talking.

"Firstly she made papa a Swiss; he used to tear his hair out at the thought, since ours is a good old Bavarian family with a noble and ancient lineage. Then she had him attending the University of Ingolstadt in *Ingolstadt*—when every schoolboy knows that it was moved to Landshut in 1800. And father's personality, what crimes she committed there! In this libellous volume he is depicted as a weeping and ineffectual man, when in reality he was a tower of strength and determination. And if this isn't enough, she completely misunderstood the meaning of his experiments. Her jim-crack collection of cast-off parts put together to make an artificial man is ludicrous. She was so carried away by the legends of Talos and the Golem that she misinterpreted my father's work and cast it into that ancient mold. Father did not construct an artificial man, he reactivated a *dead* man! That is the measure of his genius! He travelled for years in the darkest reaches of the African jungle, learning the lore of the creation of the zombie. He regularized the knowledge and improved upon it until he had surpassed all of his aboriginal teachers. Raise the dead, that is what he could do. That was his secret—and how can it be kept a secret in the future, Mr. Dan Bream?"

With these last words Victor Frankenstein's eyes opened wide and an unveiled light seemed to glow in their depths. Dan pulled back instinctively, then re-

54

laxed. He was in no danger here in this brightly lit room with men on all sides of them.

"Afraid, Dan? Don't be." Victor smiled and reached out and patted Dan on the shoulder once again.

"What was that?" Dan asked, startled at the tiny brief pain in his shoulder.

"Nothing—nothing but this," Frankenstein smiled again, but the smile had changed subtly and no longer contained any humor. He opened his hand to reveal a small hypodermic needle, its plunger pushed down and its barrel empty.

"Remain seated," he said quietly when Dan started to rise, and Dan's muscles relaxed and he sat back down, horrified.

"What have you done to me?"

"Very little—the injection is harmless. A simple little hypnotic drug, the effect of which wears off in a few hours. But until then you will not have much will of your own. So you will sit and hear me out. Drink some beer though, we don't want you to be thirsty."

Horrified, Dan was a helpless onlooker, as, of its own volition, his hand raised and poured a measure of beer down his throat.

"Now concentrate. Dan, think of the significance of my statement. The so-called Frankenstein monster is no stitched up collection of scraps, but a good honest zombie. A dead man who can walk but not talk, obey but not think. Animate—but still dead. Poor old Charley is one, the creature whom you watched going through his act on the platform. But Charley is just about worn out. Since he is dead he cannot replace the body cells that are destroyed during the normal wear and tear of the day. Why the fellow is like an animated pincushion from the act, holes everywhere. His feet—terrible, not a toe left, keep breaking off when he walks too fast. I think it's time to retire Charley. He has had a long life, and a long death. Stand up, Dan."

55

In spite of his mind saying *No! No!* Dan rose slowly to his feet.

"Aren't you interested in what Charley used to do before he became a sideshow monster? You should be, Dan. Old Charley was a reporter—just like you. And he ran across what he thought was a good story. Like you, he didn't realize the importance of what he had discovered and talked to me about it. You reporters are a very inquisitive bunch. I must show you my scrapbook, it's simply filled with Press cards. Before you die of course. You wouldn't be able to appreciate it afterwards. Now come along."

Dan walked after him, into the hot night, screaming inside in a haze of terror, yet walking quietly and silently down the street.

FEVER DREAM

By Ray Bradbury

They put him between fresh, clean, laundered sheets and there was always a newly squeezed glass of thick orange juice on the table under the dim pink lamp. All Charles had to do was call and Mom or Dad would stick their heads into his room to see how sick he was. The acoustics in the room were fine; you could hear the toilet gargling its porcelain throat of mornings, you could hear rain tap the roof or sly mice run in the secret walls. If you were very alert, sickness wasn't too bad.

He was fifteen, Charles was. It was mid-September, with the land beginning to burn with autumn. He lay in the bed for three days before the terror overtook him.

His hand began to change. His right hand. He looked at it and it was hot and sweating there on the counterpane, alone. It fluttered, it moved a bit. Then it lay there, changing color.

That afternoon the doctor came again and tapped his thin chest like a drum. "How are you?" asked the doctor, smiling. "I know, don't tell me: 'My *cold* is fine, Doctor; but *I* feel lousy!' Ha!" He laughed at his own oft-repeated joke.

57

Charles lay there and for him that terrible and ancient jest was becoming a reality. The joke fixed itself in his mind. His mind touched and drew away from it in a pale terror. The doctor did not know how cruel he was with his jokes! "Doctor," whispered Charles, lying flat and colorless. "My *hand*, it doesn't *belong* to me any more. This morning it *changed* into something else. I want you to change it back, Doctor, Doctor!"

The doctor showed his teeth and patted his hand. "It looks fine to me, son. You just had a little fever-dream."

"But, it changed, Doctor, oh, Doctor," cried Charles, pitifully holding up his pale wild hand. "It *did*."

The doctor winked. "I'll give you a pink pill for that." He popped a tablet onto Charles' tongue. "Swallow."

"Will it make my hand change back and become *me*, again!"

"Yes, yes."

The house was silent when the doctor drove off down the road in his carriage under the quiet, blue September sky. A clock ticked far below in the kitchen world. Charles lay looking at his hand.

It did not change back. It was still—something else.

The wind blew outside. Leaves fell against the cool window.

At four o'clock his other hand changed. It seemed almost to become a fever, a chemical, a virus. It pulsed and shifted, cell by cell. It beat like a warm heart. The fingernails turned blue and then red. It took about an hour for it to change and when it was finished it looked just like any ordinary hand. But it was not ordinary. It no longer was him any more. He lay in a fascinated horror and then fell into an exhausted sleep.

Mother brought the soup up at six. He wouldn't touch it. "I haven't any hands," he said, eyes shut.

"Your hands are perfectly good," said Mother.

"No," he wailed. "My hands are gone. I feel like I

58

have stumps. Oh, Mama, Mama, hold me, hold me, I'm scared!"

She had to feed him herself.

"Mama," he said. "Get the doctor, please again. I'm so sick."

"The doctor'll be here tonight at eight," she said, and went out.

At seven, with night dark and close around the house, Charles was sitting up in bed when he felt the thing happening to first one leg and then the other. "Mama! Come quick!" he screamed.

But when Mama came the thing was no longer happening.

When she went downstairs, he simply lay without fighting as his legs beat and beat, grew warm, red hot, and the room filled with the warmth of his feverish change. The glow crept up from his toes to his ankles and then to his knees.

"May I come in?" The doctor smiled in the doorway.

"Doctor!" cried Charles. "Hurry, take off my blankets!"

The doctor lifted the blankets tolerantly. "There you are. Whole and healthy. Sweating, though. A little fever. I told you not to move around, bad boy." He pinched the moist pink cheek. "Did the pills help? Did your hand change back?"

"No, no, now it's my other hand and my legs!"

"Well, well, I'll have to give you three more pills, one for each limb, eh, my little peach?" laughed the doctor.

"Will they help me? Please, please. What've I *got*?"

"A mild case of scarlet fever, complicated by a slight cold."

"Is it a germ that lives and has more little germs in me?"

"Yes."

"Are you *sure* it's scarlet fever? You haven't taken any tests!"

"I guess I know a certain fever when I see one," said the doctor, checking the boy's pulse with cool authority.

Charles lay there, not speaking until the doctor was crisply packing his black kit. Then, in the silent room, the boy's voice made a small, weak pattern, his eyes alight with remembrance. "I read a book once. About petrified trees, wood turning to stone. About how trees fell and rotted and minerals got in and built up and they look just like trees, but they're not, they're stone." He stopped. In the quiet warm room his breathing sounded.

"Well?" asked the doctor.

"I've been thinking," said Charles, after a time. "Do germs ever get big. I mean, in biology class they told us about one-celled animals, amoebas and things, and how, millions of years ago they got together until there was a bunch and they made the first body. And more and more cells got together and got bigger and then finally maybe there was a fish and finally here *we* are, and all we are is a bunch of cells that decided to get together to help each other out. Isn't that right?" Charles wet his feverish lips.

"What's all this about?" the doctor bent over him.

"I've got to tell you this, Doctor, oh, I've got to," he cried. "What would happen, oh just pretend, please pretend, that, just like in the old days, a lot of microbes got together and wanted to make a bunch, and re-produced and made *more*—"

His white hands were on his chest now, crawling toward his throat.

"And they decided to *take over* a person!" cried Charles.

"Take over a person?"

"Yes, *become* a person. Me, my hands, my feet! What if a disease somehow knew how to kill a person and yet live after him?

60

He screamed.

The hands were on his neck.

The doctor moved forward, shouting.

At nine o'clock the doctor was escorted out to his carriage by the mother and father who handed him up his bag. They conversed in the cool night wind for a few minutes. "Just be sure his hands are kept strapped to his legs," said the doctor. "I don't want him hurting himself."

"Will he be all right, Doctor?" The mother held to his arm a moment.

He patted her shoulder. "Haven't I been your family physician for thirty years? It's the fever, he imagines things."

"But those bruises on his throat, he almost choked himself."

"Just you keep him strapped, he'll be all right in the morning."

The horse and carriage moved off down the dark September road.

At three in the morning, Charles was still awake in his small black room. The bed was damp under his head and his back. He was very warm. Now he no longer had any arms or legs, and his body was beginning to change. He did not move on the bed but looked at the vast blank ceiling spaces with insane concentration. For awhile he had screamed and thrashed but now he was weak and hoarse from it, and his mother had gotten up a number of times to soothe his brow with a wet towel. Now he was silent, his hands strapped to his legs.

He felt the walls of his body change, the organs shift, the lungs catch fire like burning bellows of pure alcohol. The room was lighted up as with the flickerings of a hearthplace.

Now he had no body. It was all gone. It was under

him but it was filled with a vast pulse of some burning, lethargic drug. It was as if a guillotine had neatly lopped off his head and his head lay shining on a midnight pillow while the body, below, still alive, belonged to somebody else. The disease had eaten his body and from the eating had reproduced itself in feverish duplicate. There were the little hand-hairs and the fingernails and the scars and the toenails and the tiny mole on his right hip, all done again in perfect fashion.

I am dead, he thought. I've been killed, and yet I live. My body is dead, it is all disease and nobody will know. I will walk around and it will not be me, it will be something else. I will be something all bad, all evil, so big and so evil it's hard to understand or think about. Something that will buy shoes and drink water and get married some day maybe and do more evil in the world than has ever been done.

Now the warmth was stealing up his neck, into his cheeks, like a hot wine. His lips burned, his eyelids, like leafs, caught fire. His nostrils breathed out blue flame, faintly, faintly.

This will be all, he thought. It'll take my head and my brain and fix each eye and every tooth and all the marks in my brain, and every hair and every wrinkle in my ears, and there'll be nothing left of me.

He felt his brain fill with a boiling mercury. He felt his left eye clench in upon itself and, like a snail, withdraw, shift. He was blind in his left eye. It no longer belonged to him. It was enemy territory. His tongue was gone, cut out. His left cheek was numbed, lost. His left ear stopped hearing. It belonged to someone else now. This thing that was being born, this mineral thing replacing the wooden log, this disease replacing healthy animal cell.

He tried to scream and he was able to scream loud and high and sharply in the room, just as his brain flooded down, his right eye and right ear were cut out,

62

he was blind and deaf, all fire, all terror, all panic, all death.

His scream stopped before his mother ran through the door to his side.

It was a good, clear morning with a brisk wind that helped carry doctor, horse and carriage along the road to halt before the house. In the window above, the boy stood, fully dressed. He did not wave when the doctor waved and called, "What's this? Up? My God!"

The doctor almost ran upstairs. He came gasping into the bedroom.

"What are you doing out of bed?" he demanded of the boy. He tapped his thin chest, took his pulse and temperature. "Absolutely amazing! Normal! Normal, by God!"

"*I* shall never be sick again in my life," declared the boy quietly, standing there, looking out the wide window. "Never."

"I hope not. Why, you're looking fine, Charles!"

"Doctor?"

"Yes, Charles?"

"Can I go to school *now*?" asked Charles.

"Tomorrow will be time enough. You sound positively eager."

"I am. I like school. All the kids. I want to play with them and wrestle with them and spit on them and play with the girls' pigtails and shake the teachers' hands and rub my hands on all the cloaks in the cloakroom, and I want to grow up and travel and shake hands with people all over the world and be married and have lots of children and go to libraries and handle books and—*all* of that I want to!" said the boy, looking off into the September morning. "What's the name you called me?"

"What?" The doctor puzzled. "I called you nothing but Charles."

"It's better than no name at all, I guess," Charles shrugged.

"I'm glad you want to go back to school," said the doctor.

"I really anticipate it," smiled the boy. "Thank you for your help doctor. Shake hands?"

"Glad to." They shook hands gravely and the clear wind blew through the open window. They shook hands for almost a minute, Charles smiling up at the old man and thanking him.

Laughing, Charles raced him downstairs and out to his carriage, where father and mother joined him for the happy farewell. And while the doctor was telling his parents that Charles was "fit as a fiddle," the boy reached over with his left hand and barely touched a number of red ants that were racing wildly about the floorboard of the carriage. From the corners of his shining eyes, while Dad joked with the doctor, Charles saw the ants hesitate, quiver, and lie still on the floorboard. They were dead.

"Goodbye!" The doctor drove off.

"School days, school days, dear old golden rule days," sang Charles, running back to the house.

The parents beamed. "It's good to have him well again. He's *so* looking forward to school!"

Charles condescended to giving them both a big hug and kiss.

"I love you," he said.

THE OTHER CELIA

By Theodore Sturgeon

If you live in a cheap enough rooming house and the
doors are made of cheap enough pine, and the locks
are old-fashioned single-action jobs and the hinges are
loose, and if you have a hundred and ninety lean pounds
to operate with, you can grasp the knob, press the door
sidewise against its hinges, and slip the latch. Further,
you can lock the door the same way when you come
out.

Slim Walsh lived in, and was, and had, and did these
things partly because he was bored. The company doctors had laid him up—not off, up—for three weeks
(after his helper had hit him just over the temple with
a fourteen-inch crescent wrench) pending some more
X-rays. If he was going to get just sick-leave pay, he
wanted to make it stretch. If he was going to get a big
fat settlement—all to the good; what he saved by living
in this firetrap would make the money look even better.
Meanwhile, he felt fine and had nothing to do all day.

"Slim isn't dishonest," his mother used to tell Children's Court some years back. "He's just curious."

She was perfectly right.

Slim was constitutionally incapable of borrowing
your bathroom without looking into your medicine

65

chest. Send him into your kitchen for a saucer and when he came out a minute later, he'd have inventoried your refrigerator, your vegetable bin, and (since he was six feet three inches tall) he would know about a moldering jar of maraschino cherries in the back of the top shelf that you'd forgotten about.

Perhaps Slim, who was not impressed by his impressive size and build, felt that a knowledge that you secretly use hair-restorer, or are one of those strange people who keeps a little mound of unmated socks in your second drawer, gave him a kind of superiority. Or maybe security is a better word. Or maybe it was an odd compensation for one of the most advanced cases of gawking, gasping shyness ever recorded.

Whatever it was, Slim liked you better if, while talking to you, he knew how many jackets hung in your closet, how old that unpaid phone bill was, and just where you'd hidden those photographs. On the other hand, Slim didn't insist on knowing bad or even embarrassing things about you. He just wanted to know things about you, period.

His current situation was therefore a near-paradise. Flimsy doors stood in rows, barely sustaining vacuum on aching vacuum of knowledge; and one by one they imploded at the nudge of his curiosity. He touched nothing (or if he did, he replaced it carefully) and removed nothing, and within a week he knew Mrs. Koyper's roomers far better than she could, or cared to. Each secret visit to the rooms gave him a starting point; subsequent ones taught him more. He knew not only what these people had, but what they did, where, how much, *for* how much, and how often. In almost every case, he knew why as well.

Almost every case. Celia Sarton came.

Now, at various times, in various places, Slim had found strange things in other people's rooms. There was an old lady in one shabby place who had an electric train under her bed; used it, too. There was an old spinster in this very building who collected bottles, large and small, of any value or capacity, providing they were round and squat and with long necks. A man on the second floor secretly guarded his desirables with the unloaded .25 automatic in his top bureau drawer, for which he had a half-box of .38 cartridges.

There was a (to be chivalrous) girl in one of the rooms who kept fresh cut flowers before a photograph on her night-table—or, rather, before a frame in which were stacked eight photographs, one of which held the stage each day. Seven days, eight photographs: Slim admired the system. A new love every day and, predictably, a different love on successive Wednesdays. And all of them movie stars.

Dozens of rooms, dozens of imprints, marks, impressions, overlays, atmospheres of people. And they needn't be odd ones. A woman moves into a room, however standardized; the instant she puts down her dusting powder on top of the flush tank, the room is *hers*. Something stuck in the ill-fitting frame of a mirror, something draped over the long-dead gas jet, and the samest of rooms begins to shrink toward its occupant as if it wished, one day, to be a close-knit, form-fitting, individual integument as intimate as a skin.

But not Celia Sarton's room.

Slim Walsh got a glimpse of her as she followed Mrs. Koyper up the stairs to the third floor. Mrs. Koyper, who hobbled, slowed any follower sufficiently to afford the most disinterested witness a good look, and Slim was anything but disinterested. Yet for days he could not recall her clearly. It was as if Celia Sarton had been—not invisible, for that would have been memorable in itself—but translucent or, chameleonlike, drably re-radiating the drab wall color, carpet color, woodwork color.

She was—how old? Old enough to pay taxes. How tall? Tall enough. Dressed in . . . whatever women cover

67

themselves with in their statistical thousands. Shoes, hose, skirt, jacket, hat.

She carried a bag. When you go to the baggage window at a big terminal, you notice a suitcase here, a steamer-trunk there; and all around, high up, far back, there are rows and ranks and racks of luggage not individually noticed but just *there*. This bag, Celia Sarton's bag, was one of them.

And to Mrs. Koyper, she said—she said—She said whatever is necessary when one takes a cheap room; and to find her voice, divide the sound of a crowd by the number of people in it.

So anonymous, so unnoticeable was she that, aside from being aware that she left in the morning and returned in the evening, Slim let two days go by before he entered her room; he simply could not remind himself about her. And when he did, and had inspected it to his satisfaction, he had his hand on the knob, about to leave, before he recalled that the room was, after all, occupied. Until that second, he had thought he was giving one of the vacancies the once-over. (He did this regularly; it gave him a reference-point.)

He grunted and turned back, flicking his gaze over the room. First he had to assure himself that he was in the right room, which, for a man of his instinctive orientations, was extraordinary. Then he had to spend a moment of disbelief in his own eyes, which was all but unthinkable. When that passed, he stood in astonishment, staring at the refutation of everything his— hobby—had taught him about people and the places they live in.

The bureau drawers were empty. The ashtray was clean. No toothbrush, toothpaste, soap. In the closet, two wire hangers and one wooden one covered with dirty quilted silk, and nothing else. Under the grime-gray dresser scarf, nothing. In the shower stall, the medicine chest, nothing and nothing again, except what Mrs. Koyper had grudgingly installed.

Slim went to the bed and carefully turned back the faded coverlet. Maybe she had slept in it, but very possibly not; Mrs. Koyper specialized in unironed sheets of such a ground-in gray that it wasn't easy to tell. Frowning, Slim put up the coverlet again and smoothed it.

Suddenly he struck his forehead, which yielded him a flash of pain from his injury. He ignored it. "The bag!"

It was under the bed, shoved there, not hidden there. He looked at it without touching it for a moment, so that it could be returned exactly. Then he hauled it out.

It was a black gladstone, neither new nor expensive, of that nondescript rusty color acquired by untended leatherette. It had a worn zipper closure and was not locked. Slim opened it. It contained a cardboard box, crisp and new, for a thousand virgin sheets of cheap white typewriter paper surrounded by a glossy bright blue band bearing a white diamond with the legend: *Nonpareil the writers friend 15% cotton fiber trade mark registered.*

Slim lifted the paper out of the box, looked under it, riffled a thumbful of the sheets at the top and the same from the bottom, shook his head, replaced the paper, closed the box, put it back into the bag and restored everything precisely as he had found it. He paused again in the middle of the room, turning slowly once, but there was simply nothing else to look at. He let himself out, locked the door, and went silently back to his room.

He sat down on the edge of his bed and at last protested, "Nobody *lives* like that!"

His room was on the fourth and topmost floor of the old house. Anyone else would have called it the worst room in the place. It was small, dark, shabby and remote and it suited him beautifully.

Its door had a transom, the glass of which had many

times been painted over. By standing on the foot of his bed, Slim could apply one eye to the peephole he had scratched in the paint and look straight down the stairs to the third-floor landing. On this landing, hanging to the stub of one of the ancient gas jets, was a cloudy mirror surmounted by a dust-mantled gilt eagle and surrounded by a great many rococo carved flowers. By careful propping with folded cigarette wrappers, innumerable tests and a great deal of silent mileage up and down the stairs, Slim had arranged the exact tilt necessary in the mirror so that it covered the second floor landing as well. And just as a radar operator learns to translate glowing pips and masses into aircraft and weather, so Slim became expert at the interpretation of the fogged and distant image it afforded him. Thus he had the comings and goings of half the tenants under surveillance without having to leave his room.

It was in this mirror, at twelve minutes past six, that he saw Celia Sarton next, and as he watched her climb the stairs, his eyes glowed.

The anonymity was gone. She came up the stairs two at a time, with a gait like bounding. She reached the landing and whirled into her corridor and was gone, and while a part of Slim's mind listened for the way she opened the door (hurriedly, rattling the key against the lock-plate, banging the door open, slamming it shut), another part studied a mental photograph of her face.

What raised its veil of the statistical ordinary was its set purpose. Here were eyes only superficially interested in cars, curbs, stairs, doors. It was as if she had projected every important part of herself into that empty room of hers and waited there impatiently for her body to catch up. There was something in the room, or something she had to do there, which she could not, would not, wait for. One goes this way to a beloved after a long parting, or to a deathbed in the last, precipitous

70

moments. This was not the arrival of one who wants, but of one who needs.

Slim buttoned his shirt, eased his door open and sidled through it. He poised a moment on his landing like a great moose sensing the air before descending to a waterhole, and then moved downstairs.

Celia Sarton's only neighbor in the north corridor— the spinster with the bottles—was settled for the evening; she was of very regular habits and Slim knew them well.

Completely confident that he would not be seen, he drifted to the girl's door and paused.

She was there, all right. He could see the light around the edge of the ill-fitting door, could sense that difference between an occupied room and an empty one, which exists however silent the occupant might be. And this one *was* silent. Whatever it was that had driven her into the room with such headlong urgency, whatever it was she was doing (*had* to do) was being done with no sound or motion that he could detect.

For a long time—six minutes, seven—Slim hung there, open-throated to conceal the sound of his breath. At last, shaking his head, he withdrew, climbed the stairs, let himself into his own room and lay down on the bed, frowning.

He could only wait. Yet he *could* wait. No one does any single thing for very long. Especially a thing not involving movement. In an hour, in two—

It was five. At half-past eleven, some faint sound from the floor below brought Slim, half-dozing, twisting up from the bed and to his high peephole in the transom. He saw the Sarton girl come out of the corridor slowly, and stop, and look around at nothing in particular, like someone confined too long in a ship's cabin who has emerged on deck, not so much for the lungs' sake, but for the eyes'. And when she went down the stairs, it was easily and without hurry, as if (again) the important part of her was in the room. But the some-

71

thing was finished with for now and what was ahead of her wasn't important and could wait.

Standing with his head on his own doorknob, Slim decided that he, too, could wait. The temptation to go straight to her room was, of course, large, but caution also loomed. What he had tentatively established as her habit patterns did not include midnight exits. He could not know when she might come back and it would be foolish indeed to jeopardize his hobby—not only where it included her, but all of it—by being caught. He sighed, mixing resignation with anticipatory pleasure, and went to bed.

Less than fifteen minutes later, he congratulated himself with a sleepy smile as he heard her slow footsteps mount the stairs below. He slept.

There was nothing in the closet, there was nothing in the ashtray, there was nothing in the medicine chest nor under the dresser scarf. The bed was made, the dresser drawers were empty, and under the bed was the cheap gladstone. In it was a box containing a thousand sheets of typing paper surrounded by a glossy blue band. Without disturbing this, Slim riffled the sheets, once at the top, once at the bottom. He grunted, shook his head and then proceeded, automatically but meticulously, to put everything back as he had found it.

"Whatever it is the girl does at night," he said glumly, "it leaves tracks like it makes noise."

He left.

The rest of the day was unusually busy for Slim. In the morning he had a doctor's appointment, and in the afternoon he spent hours with a company lawyer who seemed determined to (a) deny the existence of any head injury and (b) prove to Slim and the world that the injury must have occurred years ago. He got absolutely nowhere. If Slim had another characteristic as consuming and compulsive as his curiosity, it was his shyness; these two could stand on one another's shoulders, though, and still look upward at Slim's stubbornness. It served its purpose. It took hours, however, and it was after seven when he got home.

He paused at the third-floor landing and glanced down the corridor. Celia Sarton's room was occupied and silent. If she emerged around midnight, exhausted and relieved, then he would know she had again raced up the stairs to her urgent, motionless task, whatever it was . . . and here he checked himself. He had long ago learned the uselessness of cluttering up his busy head with conjectures. A thousand things might happen; in each case, only one would. He would wait, then, and could.

And again, some hours later, he saw her come out of her corridor. She looked about, but he knew she saw very little; her face was withdrawn and her eyes wide and unguarded. Then, instead of going out, she went back into her room.

He slipped downstairs half an hour later and listened at her door, and smiled. She was washing her lingerie at the hand-basin. It was a small thing to learn, but he felt he was making progress. It did not explain why she lived as she did, but indicated how she could manage without so much as a spare handkerchief.

Oh, well, maybe in the morning.

In the morning, there was no maybe. He found it, he found it, though he could not know what it was he'd found. He laughed at first, not in triumph but wryly, calling himself a clown. Then he squatted on his heels in the middle of the floor (he would not sit on the bed, for fear of leaving wrinkles of his own on those Mrs. Koyper supplied) and carefully lifted the box of paper out of the suitcase and put it on the floor in front of him.

Up to now, he had contented himself with a quick riffle of the blank paper, a little at the top, a little at the bottom. He had done just this again, without removing the box from the suitcase, but only taking the top off and tilting up the banded ream of *Nonpareil-the-writers-friend*. And almost in spite of itself, his quick eye had caught the briefest flash of pale blue.

Gently, he removed the band, sliding it off the pack of paper, being careful not to slit the glossy finish. Now he could freely riffle the pages, and when he did, he discovered that all of them except a hundred or so, top and bottom, had the same rectangular cut-out, leaving only a narrow margin all the way around. In the hollow space thus formed, something was packed.

He could not tell what the something was, except that it was pale tan, with a tinge of pink, and felt like smooth untextured leather. There was a lot of it, neatly folded so that it exactly fitted the hole in the realm of paper.

He puzzled over it for some minutes without touching it again, and then, scrubbing his fingertips against his shirt until he felt that they were quite free of moisture and grease, he gently worked loose the top corner of the substance and unfolded a layer. All he found was more of the same.

He folded it down flat again to be sure he could, and then brought more of it out. He soon realized that the material was of an irregular shape and almost certainly of one piece, so that folding it into a tight rectangle required care and great skill. Therefore he proceeded very slowly, stopping every now and then to fold it up again, and it took him more than an hour to get enough of it out so that he could identify it.

Identify? It was completely unlike anything he had ever seen before.

It was a human skin, done in some substance very like the real thing. The first fold, the one which had been revealed at first, was an area of the back, which was why it showed no features. One might liken it to a balloon, except that a deflated balloon is smaller in every dimension than an inflated one. As far as Slim could judge, this was life-sized—a little over five feet long and proportioned accordingly. The hair was peculiar, looking exactly like the real thing until flexed, and then revealing itself to be one piece.

It had Celia Sarton's face.

Slim closed his eyes and opened them, and found that it was still true. He held his breath and put forth a careful, steady forefinger and gently pressed the left eyelid upward. There was an eye under it, all right, light blue and seemingly moist, but flat.

Slim released the breath, closed the eye and sat back on his heels. His feet were beginning to tingle from his having knelt on the floor for so long.

He looked all around the room once, to clear his head of strangeness, and then began to fold the thing up again. It took a while, but when he was finished, he knew he had it right. He replaced the typewriter paper in the box and the box in the bag, put the bag away and at last stood in the middle of the room in the suspension which overcame him when he was deep in thought.

After a moment of this, he began to inspect the ceiling. It was made of stamped tin, like those of many old-fashioned houses. It was grimy and flaked and stained; here and there, rust showed through, and in one or two places, edges of the tin sheets had sagged. Slim nodded to himself in profound satisfaction, listened for a while at the door, let himself out, locked it and went upstairs.

He stood in his own corridor for a minute, checking the position of doors, the hall window, and his accurate orientation of the same things on the floor below. Then he went into his own room.

His room, though smaller than most, was one of the few in the house which was blessed with a real closet instead of rickety off-the-floor wardrobe. He went into it and knelt, and grunted in satisfaction when he found how loose the ancient, unpainted floorboards were. By removing the side baseboard, he found it possible to get to the air-space between the fourth floor and the third-floor ceiling.

He took out boards until he had an opening perhaps fourteen inches wide, and then, working in almost total silence, he began cleaning away dirt and old plaster. He did this meticulously, because when he finally pierced the tin sheeting, he wanted not one grain of dirt to fall into the room below. He took his time and it was late in the afternoon when he was satisfied with his preparations and began, with his knife on the tin.

It was thinner and softer than he had dared to hope; he almost overcut on the first try. Carefully he squeezed the sharp steel into the little slot he had cut, lengthening it. When it was somewhat less than an inch long, he withdrew all but the point of the knife and twisted it slightly, moved it a sixteenth of an inch and twisted again, repeating this all down the cut until he had widened it enough for his purposes.

He checked the time, then returned to Celia Sarton's room for just long enough to check the appearance of his work from that side. He was very pleased with it. The little cut had come through a foot from the wall over the bed and was a mere pencil line lost in the baroque design with which the tin was stamped and the dirt and rust that marred it. He returned to his room and sat down to wait.

He heard the old house coming to its evening surge of life, a voice here, a door there, footsteps on the stairs. He ignored them all as he sat on the edge of his bed, hands folded between his knees, eyes half closed, immobile like a machine fueled, oiled, tuned and ready, lacking only the right touch on the right control. And like that touch, the faint sound of Celia Sarton's footsteps moved him.

To use his new peephole, he had to lie on the floor half in and half out of the closet, with his head in the hole, actually below floor level. With this, he was perfectly content, any amount of discomfort being well

76

worth his trouble—an attitude he shared with many another ardent hobbyist, mountain-climber or speleologist, duck-hunter or bird-watcher.

When she turned on the light, he could see her splendidly, as well as most of the floor, the lower third of the door and part of the washbasin in the bathroom.

She had come in hurriedly, with that same agonized haste he had observed before. At the same second she turned on the light, she had apparently flung her handbag toward the bed; it was in mid-air as the light appeared. She did not even glance its way, but hastily fumbled the old gladstone from under the bed, opened it, removed the box, opened it, took out the paper, slipped off the blue band and removed the blank sheets of paper which covered the hollowed-out ream.

She scooped out the thing hidden there, shaking it once like a grocery clerk with a folded paper sack, so that the long limp thing straightened itself out. She arranged it carefully on the worn linoleum of the floor, arms down at the side, legs slightly apart, face up, neck straight. Then she lay down on the floor, too, head-to-head with the deflated thing. She reached up over her head, took hold of the collapsed image of herself about the region of the ears, and for a moment did some sort of manipulation of it against the top of her own head.

Slim heard faintly a sharp, chitinous click, like the sound one makes by snapping the edge of a thumbnail against the edge of a fingernail.

Her hands slipped to the cheeks of the figure and she pulled at the empty head as if testing a connection. The head seemed now to have adhered to hers.

Then she assumed the same pose she had arranged for this other, letting her hands fall wearily to her sides on the floor, closing her eyes.

For a long while, nothing seemed to be happening, except for the odd way she was breathing, very deeply but very slowly, like the slow-motion picture of someone panting, gasping for breath after a long hard run. After perhaps ten minutes of this, the breathing became shallower and even slower, until, at the end of a half hour, he could detect none at all.

Slim lay there immobile for more than an hour, until his body shrieked protest and his head ached from eyestrain. He hated to move, but move he must. Silently he backed out of the closet, stood up and stretched. It was a great luxury and he deeply enjoyed it. He felt moved to think over what he had just seen, but clearly and consciously decided not to—not yet, anyway.

When he was unkinked, again, he crept back into the closet, put his head in the hole and his eye to the slot.

Nothing had changed. She still lay quiet, utterly relaxed, so much so that her hands had turned palm upward.

Slim watched and he watched. Just as he was about to conclude that this was the way the girl spent her entire nights and that there would be nothing more to see, he saw a slight and sudden contraction about the solar plexus, and then another. For a time, there was nothing more, and then the empty thing attached to the top of her head began to fill.

And Celia Sarton began to empty.

Slim stopped breathing until it hurt and watched in total astonishment.

Once it started, the process progressed swiftly. It was as if something passed from the clothed body of the girl to this naked empty thing. The something, whatever it might be, had to be fluid, for nothing but a fluid would fill a flexible container in just this way, or make a flexible container slowly and evenly flatten out like this. Slim could see the fingers, which had been folded flat against the palms, inflate and move until they took on the normal relaxed curl of a normal hand. The elbows shifted a little to lie more normally against the body. And yes, it was a body now.

78

The other one was not a body any more. It lay foolishly limp in its garments, its sleeping face slightly distorted by its flattening. The fingers fell against the palms by their own limp weight. The shoes thumped quietly on their sides, heels together, toes pointing in opposite directions.

The exchange was done in less than ten minutes and then the newly filled body moved.

It flexed its hands tentatively, drew up its knees and stretched its legs out again, arched its back against the floor. Its eyes flickered open. It put up its arms and made some deft manipulation at the top of its head. Slim heard another version of the soft-hard click and the now-empty head fell flat to the floor.

The new Celia Sarton sat up and sighed and rubbed her hands slightly over her body, as if restoring circulation and sensation to a chilled skin. She stretched as comfortingly and luxuriously as Slim had a few minutes earlier. She looked rested and refreshed.

At the top of her head, Slim caught a glimpse of a slit through which a wet whiteness showed, but it seemed to be closing. In a brief time, nothing showed there but a small valley in the hair, like a normal parting.

She sighed again and got up. She took the clothed thing on the floor by the neck, raised it and shook twice to make the clothes fall away. She tossed it to the bed and carefully picked up the clothes and deployed them about the room, the undergarments in the washbasin, the dress and slip on a hanger in the wardrobe.

Moving leisurely but with purpose, she went into the bathroom and, except from her shins down, out of Slim's range of vision. There he heard the same faint domestic sounds he had once detected outside her door, as she washed her underclothes. She emerged in due course, went to the wardrobe for some wire hangers and took them into the bathroom. Back she came with the underwear folded on the hangers, which she hooked to the

79

top of the open wardrobe door. Then she took the deflated integument which lay crumpled on the bed, shook it again, rolled it up into a ball and took it into the bathroom.

Slim heard more water-running and sudsing noises, and, by ear, followed the operation through a soaping and two rinses. Then she came out again, shaking out the object, which had apparently just been wrung, pulled it through a wooden clothes-hanger, arranged it creaselessly depending from the crossbar of the hanger with the bar about at its waistline, and hung it with the others on the wardrobe door.

Then she lay down on the bed, not to sleep or to read or even to rest—she seemed very rested—but merely to wait until it was time to do something else.

By now, Slim's bones were complaining again, so he wormed noiselessly backward out of his lookout point, got into his shoes and jacket, and went out to get something to eat. When he came home an hour later and looked, her light was out and he could see nothing. He spread his overcoat carefully over the hole in the closet so no stray light from his room would appear in the little slot in the ceiling, closed the door, read a comic book for a while, and went to bed.

The next day, he followed her. What strange occupation she might have, what weird vampiric duties she might disclose, he did not speculate on. He was doggedly determined to gather information first and think later.

What he found out about her daytime activities was, if anything, more surprising than any wild surmise. She was a clerk in a small five-and-ten on the East Side. She ate in the store's lunch bar at lunchtime—a green salad and a surprising amount of milk—and in the evening stopped at a hot-dog stand and drank a small container of milk, though she ate nothing.

Her steps were slowed by then and she moved wearily, speeding up only when she was close to the rooming house, and then apparently all but overcome with eagerness to get home and . . . into something more comfortable. She was watched in this process, and Slim, had he disbelieved his own eyes the first time, must believe them now.

So it went for a week, three days of which Slim spent in shadowing her, every evening in watching her make her strange toilet. Every twenty-four hours, she changed bodies, carefully washing, drying, folding and putting away the one she was not using.

Twice during the week, she went out for what was apparently a constitutional and nothing more—a half-hour around midnight, when she would stand on the walk in front of the rooming house, or wander around the block.

At work, she was silent but not unnaturally so; she spoke, when spoken to, in a small, unmusical voice. She seemed to have no friends; she maintained her aloofness by being uninteresting and by seeking no one out and by needing no one. She evinced no outside interests, never going to the movies or to the park. She had no dates, not even with girls. Slim thought she did not sleep, but lay quietly in the dark waiting for it to be time to get up and go to work.

And when he came to think about it, as ultimately he did, it occurred to Slim that within the anthill in which we all live and have our being, enough privacy can be exacted to allow for all sorts of strangeness in the members of society, providing the strangeness is not permitted to show. If it is a man's pleasure to sleep upsidedown like a bat, and if he so arranges his life that no one ever sees him sleeping, or his sleeping-place, why, batlike he may sleep all the days of his life.

One need not, by these rules, even *be* a human being. Not if the mimicry is good enough. It is a measure of Slim's odd personality to report that Celia Sarton's ways did not frighten him. He was, if anything, less disturbed by her now than he'd been before he had begun to spy on her. He knew what she did in her room and how she lived. Before, he had not known. Now he did. This made him much happier.

He was, however, still curious.

His curiosity would never drive him to do what another man might—to speak to her on the stairs or on the street, get to know her and more about her. He was too shy for that. Nor was he moved to report to anyone the odd practice he watched each evening. It wasn't his business to report. She was doing no harm as far as he could see. In his cosmos, everybody had a right to live and make a buck if they could.

Yet his curiosity, its immediacy taken care of, did undergo a change. It was not in him to wonder what sort of being this was and whether its ancestors had grown up among human beings, living with them in caves and in tents, developing and evolving along with *homo sap* until it could assume the uniform of the smallest and most invisible of wage-workers. He would never reach the conclusion that in the fight for survival, a species might discover that a most excellent characteristic for survival among human beings might be not to fight them but to join them.

No, Slim's curiosity was far simpler, more basic and less informed than any of these conjectures. He simply changed the field of his wonderment from *what* to *what if?*

So it was that on the eighth day of this survey, a Tuesday, he went again to her room, got the bag, opened it, removed the ream of paper, slid the blue band off, removed the covering sheets, took out the second Celia Sarton, put her on the bed and then replaced paper, blue band, box-cover, box, and bag just as he had found them. He put the folded thing under his shirt and went out, carefully locking the door behind him in his special way, and went upstairs to his room. He put his prize under the four clean shirts in his bottom drawer and sat down to await Celia Sarton's homecoming.

She was a little late that night—twenty minutes, perhaps. The delay seemed to have increased both her fatigue and her eagerness; she burst in feverishly, moved with the rapidity of near-panic. She looked drawn and pale and her hands shook. She fumbled the bag from under the bed, snatched out the box and opened it, contrary to her usual measured movements, by inverting it over the bed and dumping out its contents.

When she saw nothing there but sheets of paper, some with a wide rectangle cut from them and some without, she froze. She crouched over the bed without moving for an interminable two minutes. Then she straightened up slowly and glanced about the room. Once she fumbled through the paper, but resignedly, without hope. She made one sound, a high, sad whimper, and, from that moment on, was silent.

She went to the window slowly, her feet dragging, her shoulders slumped. For a long time, she stood looking out at the city, its growing darkness, its growing colonies of lights, each a symbol of life and life's usages. Then she drew down the blind and went back to the bed.

She stacked the papers there with loose uncaring fingers and put the heap of them on the dresser. She took off her shoes and placed them neatly side by side on the floor by the bed. She lay down in the same utterly relaxed pose she affected when she made her change, hands down and open, legs a little apart.

Her face looked like a death-mask, its tissues sunken and sagging. It was flushed and sick-looking. There was a little of the deep regular breathing, but only a little. There was a bit of the fluttering contractions at the midriff, but only a bit. Then—nothing.

Slim backed away from the peephole and sat up. He felt very bad about this. He had been only curious; he hadn't wanted her to get sick, to die. For he was sure she had died. How could he know what sort of sleep-surrogate an organism like this might require, or what might be the results of a delay in changing? What could he know of the chemistry of such a being? He had thought vaguely of slipping down the next day while she was out and returning her property. Just to see. Just to know *what if*. Just out of curiosity.

Should he call a doctor?

She hadn't. She hadn't even tried, though she must have known much better than he did how serious her predicament was (Yet if a species depended for its existence on secrecy, it would be species-survival to let an individual die undetected.) Well, maybe not calling a doctor meant that she'd be all right, after all. Doctors would have a lot of silly questions to ask. She might even tell the doctor about her other skin, and if Slim was the one who had fetched the doctor, Slim might be questioned about that.

Slim didn't want to get involved with anything. He just wanted to know things.

He thought, "I'll take another look."

He crawled back into the closet and put his head in the hole. Celia Sarton, he knew instantly, would not survive this. Her face was swollen, her eyes protruded, and her purpled tongue lolled far—too far—from the corner of her mouth. Even as he watched, her face darkened still more and the skin of it crinkled until it looked like carbon paper which has been balled up tight and then smoothed out.

The very beginnings of an impulse to snatch the thing she needed out of his shirt drawer and rush it down to her died within him, for he saw a wisp of smoke emerge from her nostrils and then—

Slim cried out, snatched his head from the hole, bumping it cruelly, and clapped his hands over his eyes. Put the biggest size flash-bulb an inch from your nose,

84

and fire it, and you might get a flare approaching the one he got through his little slot in the tin ceiling.

He sat grunting in pain and watching, on the insides of his eyelids, migrations of flaming worms. At last they faded and he tentatively opened his eyes. They hurt and the after-image of the slot hung before him, but at least he could see.

Feet pounded on the stairs. He smelled smoke and a buried, oily unpleasant something which he could not identify. Someone shouted. Someone hammered on a door. Then someone screamed and screamed.

It was in the papers next day. Mysterious, the story said. Charles Fort, in *Lo!,* had reported many such cases and there had been others since—people burned to a crisp by a fierce heat which had nevertheless not destroyed clothes or bedding, while leaving nothing for autopsy. This was, said the paper, either an unknown kind of heat or heat of such intensity and such brevity that it would do such a thing. No known relatives, it said. Police mystified—no clues or suspects.

Slim didn't say anything to anybody. He wasn't curious about the matter any more. He closed up the hole in the closet that same night, and the next day, after he read the story, he used the newspaper to wrap up the thing in his shirt drawer. It smelled pretty bad and, even that early, was too far gone to be unfolded. He dropped it into a garbage can on the way to the lawyer's office on Wednesday.

They settled his lawsuit that afternoon and he moved.

THE OVAL PORTRAIT

By Edgar Allan Poe

The château into which my valet had ventured to make forcible entrance, rather than permit me, in my desperately wounded condition, to pass a night in the open air, was one of those piles of commingled gloom and grandeur which have so long frowned among the Apennines, not less in fact than in the fancy of Mrs. Radcliffe. To all appearance it had been temporarily and very lately abandoned. We established ourselves in one of the smallest and least sumptuously furnished apartments. It lay in a remote turret of the building. Its decorations were rich, yet tattered and antique. Its walls were hung with tapestry and bedecked with manifold and multiform armorial trophies, together with an unusually great number of very spirited modern paintings in frames of rich golden arabesque. In these paintings, which depended from the walls not only in their main surfaces, but in very many nooks which the bizarre architecture of the château rendered necessary—in these paintings my incipient delirium, perhaps, had caused me to take deep interest; so that I bade Pedro to close the heavy shutters of the room—since it was already night,—to light the tongues of a tall candelabrum which stood by the head of my bed, and to throw open far and wide the fringed curtains of black velvet which enveloped the bed itself. I wished all this done that I might resign myself, if not to sleep, at least alternatively to the contemplation of these pictures, and the perusal of a small volume which had been found upon the pillow, and which purported to criticise and describe them.

Long, long I read—and devoutly, devoutly I gazed. Rapidly and gloriously the hours flew by and the deep midnight came. The position of the candelabrum displeased me, and outreaching my hand with difficulty, rather than disturb my slumbering valet, I placed it so as to throw its rays more fully upon the book.

But the action produced an effect altogether unanticipated. The rays of the numerous candles (for there were many) now fell within a niche of the room which had hitherto been thrown into deep shade by one of the bedposts. I thus saw in vivid light a picture all unnoticed before. It was the portrait of a young girl just ripening into womanhood. I glanced at the painting hurriedly, and then closed my eyes. Why I did this was not at first apparent even to my own perception. But while my lids remained thus shut, I ran over in mind my reason for so shutting them. It was an implusive movement to gain time for thought—to make sure that my vision had not deceived me—to calm and subdue my fancy for a more sober and more certain gaze. In a very few moments I again looked fixedly at the picture.

That I now saw aright I could not and would not doubt; for the first flashing of the candles upon that canvas had seemed to dissipate the dreamy stupor which was stealing over my senses, and to startle me at once into waking life.

The portrait, I have already said, was that of a young girl. It was a mere head and shoulders, done in what is technically called a *vignette* manner; much in the style of the favourite heads of Sully. The arms, the bosom, and even the ends of the radiant hair melted imperceptibly into the vague yet deep shadow which formed the background of the whole. The frame was oval, richly gilded and filigreed in *Moresque*. As a thing of art, nothing could be more admirable than the painting itself. But it could have been neither the execution of the work, nor the immortal beauty of the countenance, which had so suddenly and so vehemently moved me. Least of all, could it have been that my fancy, shaken from its half slumber, had mistaken the head for that of a living person. I saw at once that the peculiarities of the design, of the *vignetting,* and of the frame, must have instantly dispelled such idea—must have prevented even its momentary entertainment. Thinking earnestly upon these points, I remained, for an hour perhaps, half sitting, half reclining, with my vision riveted upon the portrait. At length, satisfied with the true secret of its effect, I fell back within the bed. I had found the spell of the picture in an absolute *life-likeliness* of expression, which, at first startling, finally confounded, subdued, and appalled me. With deep and reverent awe I replaced the candelabrum in its former position. The cause of my deep agitation being thus shut from view, I sought eagerly the volume which discussed the paintings and their histories. Turning to the number which designated the oval portrait, I read the vague and quaint words which follow:

"She was a maiden of rarest beauty, and not more lovely than full of glee. And evil was the hour when she saw, and loved, and wedded the painter. He, passionate, studious, austere, and having already a bride in his Art: she a maiden of rarest beauty, and not more lovely than full of glee; all light and smiles, and frolicsome as the young fawn; loving and cherishing all things; hating only the Art which was her rival; dreading only the palette and brushes and other untoward instruments which deprived her of the countenance of her lover. It was thus a terrible thing for this lady to hear the painter speak of his desire to portray even his young bride. But she was humble and obedient, and sat meekly for many weeks in the dark high turret-chamber where the light dripped upon the pale canvas only from overhead. But he, the painter, took glory in his work, which went on from hour to hour, and from day to day. And he was a passionate, and wild, and moody man, who became lost in reveries; so that he *would* not see that the light which fell so ghastly in that lone turret withered the health and the spirits of his bride, who pined visibly to all but him. Yet she smiled on and still on, uncomplainingly, because she saw that the painter (who had high renown) took a fervid and burning pleasure in his task, and wrought day and night to depict her who so loved him, yet who grew daily more dispirited and weak. And in sooth some who beheld the portrait spoke of its resemblance in low words, as of a mighty marvel, and a proof not less of the power of the painter than of his deep love for her whom he depicted so surpassingly well. But at length, as the labour drew nearer to its conclusion, there were admitted none into the turret; for the painter had grown wild with the ardour of his work, and turned his eyes from the canvas rarely, even to regard the countenance of his wife. And he *would* not see that the tints which he spread upon the canvas were drawn from the cheeks of her who sat beside him. And when many weeks had passed, and but little remained to do, save one brush upon the mouth and one tint upon the eye, the spirit of the lady flickered up as the flame within the socket of the lamp. And then the brush was given, and then the tint was placed; and, for one moment, the painter stood entranced before the work which he had wrought; but in the next, while he yet gazed, he grew tremulous and very pallid, and aghast, and crying with a loud voice, 'This is indeed *Life* itself!' turned suddenly to regard his beloved:—*She was dead!*"

THE MONSTER-MAKER

By William C. Morrow

A young man of refined appearance, but evidently suffering great mental distress, presented himself one morning at the residence of a singular old man, who was known as a surgeon of remarkable skill. The house was a queer and primitive brick affair, entirely out of date, and tolerable only in the decayed part of the city in which it stood. It was large, gloomy, and dark, and had long corridors and dismal rooms; and it was absurdly large for the small family—man and wife—that occupied it. The house described, the man is portrayed —but not the woman. He could be agreeable on occasion, but, for all that, he was but animated mystery. His wife was weak, wan, reticent, evidently miserable, and possibly living a life of dread or horror—perhaps witness of repulsive things, subject of anxieties, and victim of fear and tyranny; but there is a great deal of guessing in these assumptions. He was about sixty-five years of age and she about forty. He was lean, and bald, with thin, smooth-shaven face, and very keen eyes; kept always at home, and was slovenly. The man was strong, the woman weak; he dominated, she suffered.

Although he was a surgeon of rare skill, his practice

was almost nothing, for it was a rare occurrence that the few who knew of his ability were brave enough to penetrate the gloom of his home, and when they did so it was with deaf ear turned to sundry ghoulish stories that were whispered concerning him. These were, in great part, but exaggerations of his experiments in vivisection; he was devoted to the science of surgery.

The young man who presented himself on the morning just mentioned was a handsome fellow, yet of evident weak character and unhealthy temperament—sensitive, and easily exalted or depressed. A single glance convinced the surgeon that his visitor was seriously affected in mind, for there was never a bolder skull-grin of melancholia, fixed and irremediable.

A stranger would not have suspected any occupancy of the house. The street door—old, warped, and blistered by the sun—was locked, and the small, faded-green window-blinds were closed. The young man rapped at the door. No answer. He rapped again. Still no sign. He examined a slip of paper, glanced at the number on the house, and then, with the impatience of a child, he furiously kicked the door. There were signs of numerous other such kicks. A response came in the shape of a shuffling footstep in the hall, a turning of the rusty key, and a sharp face that peered through a cautious opening in the door.

"Are you the doctor?" asked the young man.

"Yes, yes! Come in," briskly replied the master of the house.

The young man entered. The old surgeon closed the door and carefully locked it. "This way," he said, advancing to a rickety flight of stairs. The young man followed. The surgeon led the way up the stairs, turned into a narrow, musty-smelling corridor at the left, traversed it, rattling the loose boards under his feet, at the farther end opened a door at the right, and beckoned his visitor to enter. The young man found himself in a pleasant room, furnished in antique fashion and with hard simplicity.

"Sit down," said the old man, placing a chair so that its occupant should face a window that looked out upon a dead wall about six feet from the house. He threw open the blind, and a pale light entered. He then seated himself near his visitor and directly facing him, and with a searching look, that had all the power of a microscope, he proceeded to diagnosticate the case.

"Well?" he presently asked.

The young man shifted uneasily in his seat.

"I—I have come to see you," he finally stammered, "because I'm in trouble."

"Ah!"

"Yes; you see, I—that is—I have given it up."

"Ah!" There was pity added to sympathy in the ejaculation.

"That's it. Given it up," added the visitor. He took from his pocket a roll of banknotes, and with the utmost deliberation he counted them out upon his knee. "Five thousand dollars," he calmly remarked. "That is for you. It's all I have; but I presume—I imagine—no; that is not the word—*assume*—yes; that's the word—assume that five thousand—is it really that much? Let me count." He counted again. "That five thousand dollars is a sufficient fee for what I want you to do."

The surgeon's lips curled pityingly—perhaps disdainfully also. "What do you want me to do?" he carelessly inquired.

The young man rose, looked around with a mysterious air, approached the surgeon, and laid the money across his knee. Then he stopped and whispered two words in the surgeon's ear.

These words produced an electric effect. The old man started violently; then, springing to his feet, he caught his visitor angrily, and transfixed him with a look that was as sharp as a knife. His eyes flashed, and he opened his mouth to give utterance to some harsh imprecation, when he suddenly checked himself. The anger left his face, and only pity remained. He relinquished his grasp, picked up the scattered notes, and, offering them to the visitor, slowly said:

"I do not want your money. You are simply foolish. You think you are in trouble. Well, you do not know what trouble is. Your only trouble is that you have not a trace of manhood in your nature. You are merely insane—I shall not say pusillanimous. You should surrender yourself to the authorities, and be sent to a lunatic asylum for proper treatment."

The young man keenly felt the intended insult, and his eyes flashed dangerously.

"You old dog—you insult me thus!" he cried. "Grand airs, these, you give yourself! Virtuously indignant, old murderer, you! Don't want my money, eh? When a man comes to you himself and wants it done, you fly into a passion and spurn his money; but let an enemy of his come and pay you, and you are only too willing. How many such jobs have you done in this miserable old hole? It is a good thing for you that the police have not run you down, and brought spade and shovel with them. Do you know what is said of you? Do you think you have kept your windows so closely shut that no sound has ever penetrated beyond them? Where do you keep your infernal implements?"

He had worked himself into a high passion. His voice was hoarse, loud, and rasping. His eyes, bloodshot, started from their sockets. His whole frame twitched, and his fingers writhed. But he was in the presence of a man infinitely his superior. Two eyes, like those of a snake, burned two holes through him. An overmastering, inflexible presence confronted one weak and passionate. The result came.

"Sit down," commanded the stern voice of the surgeon.

It was the voice of father to child, of master to slave.

The fury left the visitor, who, weak and overcome, fell upon a chair.

Meanwhile, a peculiar light had appeared in the old surgeon's face, the dawn of a strange idea; a gloomy ray, strayed from the fires of the bottomless pit; the baleful light that illumines the way of the enthusiast. The old man remained a moment in profound abstraction, gleams of eager intelligence bursting momentarily through the cloud of sombre meditation that covered his face. Then broke the broad light of a deep, impenetrable determination. There was something sinister in it, suggesting the sacrifice of something held sacred. After a struggle, mind had vanquished conscience.

Taking a piece of paper and a pencil, the surgeon carefully wrote answers to questions which he peremptorily addressed to his visitor, such as his name, age, place of residence, occupation, and the like, and the same inquiries concerning his parents, together with other particular matters.

"Does any one know you came to this house?" he asked.

"No."

"You swear it?"

"Yes."

"But your prolonged absence will cause alarm and lead to search."

"I have provided against that."

"How?"

"By depositing a note in the post, as I came along, announcing my intention to drown myself."

"The river will be dragged."

"What then?" asked the young man, shrugging his shoulders with careless indifference. "Rapid undercurrent, you know. A good many are never found."

There was a pause.

"Are you ready?" finally asked the surgeon.

"Perfectly." The answer was cool and determined.

The manner of the surgeon, however, showed much

94

perturbation. The pallor that had come into his face at the moment his decision was formed became intense. A nervous tremulousness came over his frame. Above it all shone the light of enthusiasm.

"Have you a choice in the method?" he asked.

"Yes; extreme anaesthesia."

"With what agent?"

"The surest and quickest."

"Do you desire any—any subsequent disposition?"

"No; only nullification; simply a blowing out, as of a candle in the wind; a puff—then darkness, without a trace. A sense of your own safety may suggest the method. I leave it to you."

"No delivery to your friends?"

"None whatever."

Another pause.

"Did you say you are quite ready?" asked the surgeon.

"Quite ready."

"And perfectly willing?"

"Anxious."

"Then wait a moment."

With this request the old surgeon rose to his feet and stretched himself. Then with the stealthiness of a cat he opened the door and peered into the hall, listening intently. There was no sound. He softly closed the door and locked it. Then he closed the window-blinds and locked them. This done, he opened a door leading into an adjoining room, which, though it had no window, was lighted by means of a small skylight. The young man watched closely. A strange change had come over him. While his determination had not one whit lessened, a look of great relief came into his face, displacing the haggard, despairing look of a half-hour before. Melancholic then, he was ecstatic now.

The opening of the second door disclosed a curious sight. In the centre of the room, directly under the skylight, was an operating-table, such as is used by demonstrators of anatomy. A glass case against the wall held surgical instruments of every kind. Hanging in another case were human skeletons of various sizes. In sealed jars, arranged on shelves, were monstrosities of divers kinds preserved in alcohol. There were also, among innumerable articles scattered about the room, a manikin, a stuffed cat, a desiccated human heart, plaster casts of various parts of the body, numerous charts, and a large assortment of drugs and chemicals. There was also a lounge, which could be opened to form a couch. The surgeon opened it and moved the operating-table aside, giving its place to the lounge.

"Come in," he called to his visitor.

The young man obeyed without the least hesitation.

"Take off your coat."

He complied.

"Lie down on that lounge."

In a moment the young man was stretched at full length, eyeing the surgeon. The latter undoubtedly was suffering under great excitement, but he did not waver; his movements were sure and quick. Selecting a bottle containing a liquid, he carefully measured out a certain quantity. While doing this he asked: "Have you ever had any irregularity of the heart?"

"No."

The answer was prompt, but it was immediately followed by a quizzical look in the speaker's face.

"I presume," he added, "you mean by your question that it might be dangerous to give me a certain drug. Under the circumstances, however, I fail to see any relevancy in your question."

This took the surgeon aback; but he hastened to explain that he did not wish to inflict unnecessary pain, and hence his question.

He placed the glass on a stand, approached his visitor, and carefully examined his pulse.

"Wonderful!" he exclaimed.

"Why?"

"It is perfectly normal."

"Because I am wholly resigned. Indeed, it has been long since I knew such happiness. It is not active, but infinitely sweet."

"You have no lingering desire to retract?"

"None whatever."

"Take this," he said, kindly.

The young man partially raised himself and took the glass in his hand. He did not show the vibration of a single nerve. He drank the liquid, draining the last drop. Then he returned the glass with a smile.

"Thank you," he said; "you are the noblest man that lives. May you always prosper and be happy! You are my benefactor, my liberator. Bless you, bless you! You reach down from your seat with the gods and lift me up into glorious peace and rest. I love you—I love you with all my heart!"

These words, spoken earnestly in a musical, low voice, and accompanied with a smile of ineffable tenderness, pierced the old man's heart. A suppressed convulsion swept over him; intense anguish wrung his vitals; perspiration trickled down his face. The young man continued to smile.

"Ah, it does me good!" said he.

The surgeon, with a strong effort to control himself, sat down upon the edge of the lounge and took his visitor's wrist, counting the pulse.

"How long will it take?" the young man asked.

"Ten minutes. Two have passed." The voice was hoarse.

"Ah, only eight minutes more! . . . Delicious, delicious! I feel it coming . . . What was that? . . . Ah, I understand. Music. . . . Beautiful! . . . Coming, coming. . . . Is that—that—water? . . . Trickling? Dripping? Doctor!"

"Well?"

"Thank you, . . . thank you. . . . Noble man, . . . my saviour; . . . my bene . . . bene . . . factor. . . .

Trickling . . . trickling . . . Dripping, dripping. . . . Doctor!"

"Well?"

"Doctor!"

"Past hearing," muttered the surgeon.

"Doctor!"

"And blind."

Response was made by a firm grasp of the hand.

"Doctor!"

"And numb."

"Doctor!"

The old man watched and waited.

"Dripping, . . . dripping."

The last drop had run. There was a sigh, and nothing more.

The surgeon laid down the hand.

"The first step," he groaned, rising to his feet; then his whole frame dilated. "The first step—the most difficult, yet the simplest. A providential delivery into my hands of that for which I have hungered for forty years. No withdrawal now! It is possible, because scientific; rational, but perilous. If I succeed—*if?* I *shall* succeed. I *will* succeed. . . . And after success—what? . . . Yes; what? Publish the plan and the result? The gallows. . . . So long as *it* shall exist, . . . and *I exist,* the gallows. That much. . . . But how account for its presence? Ah, that pinches hard! I must trust to the future."

He tore himself from the reverie and started.

"I wonder if *she* heard or saw anything."

With that reflection he cast a glance upon the form on the lounge, and then left the room, locked the door, locked also the door of the outer room, walked down two or three corridors, penetrated to a remote part of the house, and rapped at a door. It was opened by his wife. He, by this time, had regained complete mastery over himself.

"I thought I heard some one in the house just now," he said, "but I can find no one."

"I heard nothing."

He was greatly relieved.

"I did hear some one knock at the door less than an hour ago," she resumed, "and heard you speak, I think. Did he come in?"

"No."

The woman glanced at his feet and seemed perplexed.

"I am almost certain," she said, "that I heard footfalls in the house, and yet I see that you are wearing slippers."

"Oh, I had on my shoes then!"

"That explains it," said the woman, satisfied; "I think the sound you heard must have been caused by rats."

"Ah, that was it!" exclaimed the surgeon. Leaving, he closed the door, reopened it, and said, "I do not wish to be disturbed to-day." He said to himself, as he went down the hall, "All is clear there."

He returned to the room in which his visitor lay, and made a careful examination.

"Splendid specimen!" he softly exclaimed; "every organ sound, every function perfect; fine, large frame; well-shaped muscles, strong and sinewy; capable of wonderful development—if given opportunity. . . . I have no doubt it can be done. Already I have succeeded with a dog—a task less difficult than this, for in a man the cerebrum overlaps the cerebellum, which is not the case with a dog. This gives a wide range for accident, with but one opportunity in a lifetime! In the cerebrum, the intellect and the affections; in the cerebellum, the senses and the motor forces; in the medulla oblongata, control of the diaphragm. In these two latter lie all the essentials of simple existence. The cerebrum is merely an adornment; that is to say, reason and the affections are almost purely ornamental. I have already proved it. My dog, with its cerebrum removed, was idiotic, but it retained its physical senses to a certain degree."

While thus ruminating he made careful preparations. He moved the couch, replaced the operating-table under the skylight, selected a number of surgical instruments, prepared certain drug-mixtures, and arranged water, towels, and all the accessories of a tedious surgical operation. Suddenly he burst into laughter.

"Poor fool!" he exclaimed. "Paid me five thousand dollars to kill him! Didn't have the courage to snuff his own candle! Singular, singular, the queer freaks these madmen have! You thought you were dying, poor idiot! Allow me to inform you, sir, that you are as much alive at this moment as ever you were in your life. But it will be all the same to you. You shall never be more conscious than you are now; and for all practical purposes, so far as they concern you, you are dead henceforth, though you shall live. By the way, how should you feel *without a head*? Ha, ha, ha! . . . But that's a sorry joke."

He lifted the unconscious form from the lounge and laid it upon the operating-table.

About three years afterwards the following conversation was held between a captain of police and a detective:

"She may be insane," suggested the captain.

"I think she is."

"And yet you credit her story!"

"I do."

"Singular!"

"Not at all. I myself have learned something."

"What!"

"Much, in one sense; little, in another. You have heard those queer stories of her husband. Well, they are all nonsensical—probably with one exception. He is generally a harmless old fellow, but peculiar. He has performed some wonderful surgical operations. The people in his neighborhood are ignorant, and they fear him and wish to be rid of him; hence they tell a great many lies about him, and they come to believe their own stories. The one important thing that I have

100

learned is that he is almost insanely enthusiastic on the subject of surgery—especially experimental surgery; and with an enthusiast there is hardly such a thing as a scruple. It is this that gives me confidence in the woman's story."

"You say she appeared to be frightened?"

"Doubly so—first, she feared that her husband would learn of her betrayal of him; second, the discovery itself has terrified her."

"But her report of this discovery is very strange," argued the captain. "He conceals everything from her. She is merely guessing."

"In part—yes; in other part—no. She heard the sounds distinctly, though she did not see clearly. Horror closed her eyes. What she thinks she saw is, I admit, preposterous; but she undoubtedly saw something extremely frightful. There are many peculiar little circumstances. He has eaten with her but few times during the last three years, and nearly always carries his food to his private rooms. She says that he either consumes an enormous quantity, throws much away, or is feeding something that eats prodigiously. He explains this to her by saying that he has animals with which he experiments. This is not true. Again, he always keeps the door to these rooms carefully locked; and not only that, but he has the doors doubled and otherwise strengthened, and has heavily barred a window that looks from one of the rooms upon a dead wall a few feet distant."

"What does it mean?" asked the captain.

"A prison."

"For animals, perhaps."

"Certainly not."

"Why!"

"Because, in the first place, cages would have been better; in the second place, the security that he has provided is infinitely greater than that required for the confinement of ordinary animals."

"All this is easily explained: he has a violent lunatic under treatment."

"I had thought of that, but such is not the fact."

"How do you know?"

"By reasoning thus: He has always refused to treat cases of lunacy; he confines himself to surgery; the walls are not padded, for the woman has heard sharp blows upon them; no human strength, however morbid, could possibly require such resisting strength as has been provided; he would not be likely to conceal a lunatic's confinement from the woman; no lunatic could consume all the food that he provides; so extremely violent mania as these precautions indicate could not continue three years; if there is a lunatic in the case it is very probable that there should have been communication with some one outside concerning the patient, and there has been none; the woman has listened at the keyhole and has heard no human voice within; and last, we have heard the woman's vague description of what she saw."

"You have destroyed every possible theory," said the captain, deeply interested, "and have suggested nothing new."

"Unfortunately, I cannot; but the truth may be very simple, after all. The old surgeon is so peculiar that I am prepared to discover something remarkable."

"Have you suspicions?"

"I have."

"Of what?"

"A crime. The woman suspects it."

"And betrays it?"

"Certainly, because it is so horrible that her humanity revolts; so terrible that her whole nature demands of her that she hand over the criminal to the law; so frightful that she is in mortal terror; so awful that it has shaken her mind."

"What do you propose to do?" asked the captain.

"Secure evidence. I may need help."

"You shall have all the men you require. Go ahead,

but be careful. You are on dangerous ground. You would be a mere plaything in the hands of that man."

Two days afterwards the detective again sought the captain.

"I have a queer document," he said, exhibiting torn fragments of paper, on which there was writing. "The woman stole it and brought it to me. She snatched a handful out of a book, getting only a part of each of a few leaves."

These fragments, which the men arranged as best they could, were (the detective explained) torn by the surgeon's wife from the first volume of a number of manuscript books which her husband had written on one subject,—the very one that was the cause of her excitement. "About the time that he began a certain experiment three years ago," continued the detective, "he removed everything from the suite of two rooms containing his study and his operating-room. In one of the bookcases that he removed to a room across the passage was a drawer, which he kept locked, but which he opened from time to time. As is quite common with such pieces of furniture, the lock of the drawer is a very poor one; and so the woman, while making a thorough search yesterday, found a key on her bunch that fitted this lock. She opened the drawer, drew out the bottom book of a pile (so that its mutilation would more likely escape discovery), saw that it might contain a clew, and tore out a handful of the leaves. She had barely replaced the book, locked the drawer, and made her escape when her husband appeared. He hardly ever allows her to be out of his sight when she is in that part of the house."

The fragments read as follows: ". . . the motory nerves. I had hardly dared to hope for such a result, although inductive reasoning had convinced me of its possibility, my only doubt having been on the score of my lack of skill. Their operation has been only slightly impaired, and even this would not have been the case had the operation been performed in infancy, before the intellect had sought and obtained recognition as an essential part of the whole. Therefore I state, as a proved fact, that the cells of the motory nerves have inherent forces sufficient to the purpose of those nerves. But hardly so with the sensory nerves. These latter are, in fact, an offshoot of the former, evolved from them by natural (though not essential) heterogeneity, and to a certain extent are dependent on the evolution and expansion of a contemporaneous tendency, that developed into mentality, or mental function. Both of these latter tendencies, these evolvements, are merely refinements of the motory system, and not independent entities; that is to say, they are the blossoms of a plant that propagates from its roots. The motory system is the first . . . nor am I surprised that such prodigious muscular energy is developing. It promises yet to surpass the wildest dreams of human strength. I account for it thus: The powers of assimilation had reached their full development. They had formed the habit of doing a certain amount of work. They sent their products to all parts of the system. As a result of my operation the consumption of these products was reduced fully one-half; that is to say, about one-half of the demand for them was withdrawn. But force of habit required the production to proceed. This production was strength, vitality, energy. Thus double the usual quantity of this strength, this energy, was stored in the remaining . . . developed a tendency that did surprise me. Nature, no longer suffering the distraction of extraneous interferences, and at the same time being cut in two (as it were), with reference to this case, did not fully adjust herself to the new situation, as does a magnet, which, when divided at the point of equilibrium, renews itself in its two fragments by investing each with opposite poles; but, on the contrary, being severed from laws that theretofore had controlled her, and possessing still that mysterious tendency to develop into something more potential and complex, she blindly (having lost her lantern) pushed her demands for material that would secure this development, and as blindly used it when it was given her. Hence this marvellous voracity, this insatiable hunger, this wonderful ravenousness; and hence also (there being nothing but the physical part to receive this vast storing of energy) this strength that is becoming almost hourly herculean, almost daily appalling. It is becoming a serious . . . narrow escape to-day. By some means, while I was absent, it unscrewed the stopper of the silver feeding-pipe (which I have already herein termed 'the artificial mouth'), and, in one of its curious antics, allowed all the chyle to escape from its stomach through the tube. Its hunger then became intense—I may say furious. I placed my hands upon it to push it into a chair, when, feeling my touch, it caught me, clasped me around the neck, and would have crushed me to death instantly had I not slipped from its powerful grasp. Thus I always had to be on my guard. I have provided the screw stopper with a spring catch, and . . . usually docile when not hungry; slow and heavy in its movements, which are, of course, purely unconscious; any apparent excitement in movement being due to local irregularities in the blood-supply of the cerebellum, which, if I did not have it enclosed in a silver case that is immovable, I should expose and . . ."

The captain looked at the detective with a puzzled air.

"I don't understand it at all," said he.

"Nor I," agreed the detective.

"What do you purpose to do?"

"Make a raid."

"Do you want a man?"

"Three. The strongest men in your district."

"Why, the surgeon is old and weak!"

"Nevertheless. I want three strong men; and for that matter, prudence really advises me to take twenty."

At one o'clock the next morning a cautious, scratching sound might have been heard in the ceiling of the surgeon's operating-room. Shortly afterwards the skylight sash was carefully raised and laid aside. A man peered into the opening. Nothing could be heard.

"That is singular," thought the detective.

He cautiously lowered himself to the floor by a rope, and then stood for some moments listening intently. There was a dead silence. He shot the slide of a darklantern, and rapidly swept the room with the light. It was bare, with the exception of a strong iron staple and ring, screwed to the floor in the centre of the room, with a heavy chain attached. The detective then turned his attention to the outer room; it was perfectly bare. He was deeply perplexed. Returning to the inner room, he called softly to the men to descend. While they were thus occupied he re-entered the outer room and examined the door. A glance sufficed. It was kept closed by a spring attachment, and was locked with a strong spring-lock that could be drawn from inside.

"The bird has just flown," mused the detective. "A singular accident! The discovery and proper use of this thumb-bolt might not have happened once in fifty years, if my theory is correct."

By this time the men were behind him. He noiselessly drew the spring-bolt, opened the door, and looked out into the hall. He heard a peculiar sound. It was as though a gigantic lobster was floundering and scrambling in some distant part of the old house. Accompanying this sound was a loud, whistling breathing, and frequent rasping gasps.

These sounds were heard by still another person—the surgeon's wife; for they originated very near her rooms, which were a considerable distance from her husband's. She had been sleeping lightly, tortured by fear and harassed by frightful dreams. The conspiracy into which she had recently entered, for the destruction of her husband, was a source of great anxiety. She constantly suffered from the most gloomy forebodings, and lived in an atmosphere of terror. Added to the natural horror of her situation were those countless sources of fear which a fright-shaken mind creates and then magnifies. She was, indeed, in a pitiable state, having been driven first by terror to desperation, and then to madness.

Startled thus out of fitful slumber by the noise at her door, she sprang from her bed to the floor, every terror that lurked in her acutely tense mind and diseased imagination starting up and almost overwhelming her. The idea of flight—one of the strongest of all instincts —seized upon her, and she ran to the door, beyond all control of reason. She drew the bolt and flung the door wide open, and then fled wildly down the passage, the appalling hissing and rasping gurgle ringing in her ears apparently with a thousandfold intensity. But the passage was in absolute darkness, and she had not taken a half-dozen steps when she tripped upon an unseen object on the floor. She fell headlong upon it, encountering in it a large, soft, warm substance that writhed and squirmed, and from which came the sounds that had awakened her. Instantly realizing her situation, she uttered a shriek such as only an unnamable terror can inspire. But hardly had her cry started the echoes in the empty corridor when it was suddenly stifled. Two prodigious arms had closed upon her and crushed the life out of her.

The cry performed the office of directing the detective and his assistants, and it also aroused, the old surgeon, who occupied rooms between the offices and the object of their search. The cry of agony pierced him to the marrow, and a realization of the cause of it burst upon him with frightful force.

"It has come at last!" he gasped, springing from his bed.

Snatching from a table a dimly-burning lamp and a long knife which he kept at hand for three years, he dashed into the corridor. The four officers had already started forward, but when they saw him emerge they halted in silence. In that moment of stillness the surgeon paused to listen. He heard the hissing sound and the clumsy floundering of a bulky, living object in the direction of his wife's apartments. It evidently was advancing towards him. A turn in the corridor shut out the view. He turned up the light, which revealed a ghastly pallor in his face.

"Wife!" he called.

There was no response. He hurriedly advanced, the four men following quietly. He turned the angle of the corridor, and ran so rapidly that by the time the officers had come in sight of him again he was twenty steps away. He ran past a huge, shapeless object, sprawling, crawling, and floundering along, and arrived at the body of his wife.

He gave one horrified glance at her face, and staggered away. Then a fury seized him. Clutching the knife firmly, and holding the lamp aloft, he sprang toward the ungainly object in the corridor. It was then that the officers, still advancing cautiously, saw a little more clearly, though still indistinctly, the object of the surgeon's fury, and the cause of the look of unutterable anguish in his face. The hideous sight caused them to pause. They saw what appeared to be a man, yet evidently was not a man; huge, awkward, shapeless; a squirming, lurching, stumbling mass, completely naked. It raised its broad shoulders. *It had no head,* but instead of it a small metallic ball surmounting its massive neck.

"Devil!" exclaimed the surgeon, raising the knife.

"Hold, there!" commanded a stern voice.

The surgeon quickly raised his eyes and saw the four officers, and for a moment fear paralyzed his arm.

"The police!" he gasped.

Then, with a look of redoubled fury, he sent the knife to the hilt into the squirming mass before him.

108

The wounded monster sprang to his feet and wildly threw its arms about, meanwhile emitting fearful sounds from a silver tube through which it breathed. The surgeon aimed another blow, but never gave it. In his blind fury he lost his caution, and was caught in an iron grasp. The struggling threw the lamp some feet toward the officers, and it fell to the floor, shattered to pieces. Simultaneously with the crash the oil took fire, and the corridor was filled with flame. The officers could not approach. Before them was the spreading blaze, and secure behind it were two forms struggling in a fearful embrace. They heard cries and gasps, and saw the gleaming of a knife.

The wood in the house was old and dry. It took fire at once, and the flames spread with great rapidity. The four officers turned and fled, barely escaping with their lives. In an hour nothing remained of the mysterious old house and its inmates but a blackened ruin.

COME AND GO MAD

By Fredric Brown

1

He had known it, somehow, when he had awakened that morning. He knew it more surely now, staring out of the editorial room window into the early afternoon sunlight slanting down among the buildings to cast a pattern of light and shadow. He knew that soon, perhaps even today, something important was going to happen. Whether good or bad he did not know, but he darkly suspected. And with reason; there are few good things that may unexpectedly happen to a man, things, that is, of lasting importance. Disaster can strike from innumerable directions, in amazingly diverse ways.

A voice said, "Hey, Mr. Vine," and he turned away from the window, slowly. That in itself was strange for it was not his manner to move slowly; he was a small, volatile man, almost cat-like in the quickness of his reactions and his movements.

But this time something made him turn slowly from the window, almost as though he never again expected to see that chiaroscuro of an early afternoon.

He said, "Hi, Red."

The freckled copy boy said, "His Nibs wants to see ya."

"Now?"

"Naw. Atcher convenience. Sometime next week, maybe. If yer busy, give him an apperntment."

He put his fist against Red's chin and shoved, and the copy boy staggered back in assumed distress.

He got up out of his chair and went over to the water cooler. He pressed his thumb on the button and water gurgled into the paper cup.

Harry Wheeler sauntered over and said, "Hiya, Nappy. What's up? Going on the carpet?"

He said, "Sure, for a raise."

He drank and crumpled the cup, tossing it into the waste basket. He went over to the door marked Private and went through it.

Walter J. Candler, the managing editor, looked up from the work on his desk and said affably, "Sit down, Vine. Be with you in a moment," and then looked down again.

He slid into the chair opposite Candler, worried a cigarette out of his shirt pocket and lighted it. He studied the back of the sheet of paper of which the managing editor was reading the front. There wasn't anything on the back of it.

The M. E. put the paper down and looked at him. "Vine, I've got a screwy one. You're good on screwy ones."

He grinned slowly at the M. E. He said, "If that's a compliment, thanks."

"It's a compliment, all right. You've done some pretty tough things for us. This one's different. I've never yet asked a reporter to do anything I wouldn't do myself. *I* wouldn't do this, so I'm not asking you to."

The M. E. picked up the paper he'd been reading and then put it down again without even looking at it. "Ever hear of Ellsworth Joyce Randolph?"

"Head of the asylum? Hell yes, I've met him. Casually."

"How'd he impress you?"

111

He was aware that the managing editor was staring at him intently, that it wasn't too casual a question. He parried. "What do you mean? In what way? You mean is he a good Joe, is he a good politician, has he got a good bedside manner for a psychiatrist, or what?"

"I mean, how sane do you think he is?"

He looked at Candler and Candler wasn't kidding. Candler was strictly deadpan.

He began to laugh, and then he stopped laughing. He leaned forward across Candler's desk. "Ellsworth Joyce Randolph," he said. "You're talking about Ellsworth Joyce Randolph?"

Candler nodded. "Dr. Randolph was in here this morning. He told a rather strange story. He didn't want me to print it. He did want me to check on it, to send our best man to check on it. He said if we found it was true we could print it in hundred and twenty line type in red ink." Candler grinned wryly. "We could, at that."

He stumped out his cigarette and studied Candler's face. "But the story itself is so screwy you're not sure whether Dr. Randolph himself might be insane?"

"Exactly."

"And what's tough about the assignment?"

"The doc says a reporter could get the story only from the inside."

"You mean, go in as a guard or something?"

Candler said, "Something."

"Oh."

He got up out of the chair and walked over to the window, stood with his back to the managing editor, looking out. The sun had moved hardly at all. Yet the shadow pattern in the streets looked different, obscurely different. The shadow pattern inside himself was different, too. This, he knew, was what had been going to happen. He turned around. He said, "No. Hell no."

Candler shrugged imperceptibly. "Don't blame you. I haven't even asked you to. I wouldn't do it myself."

He asked, "What does Ellsworth Joyce Randolph think is going on inside this nuthouse? It must be something pretty screwy if it made you wonder whether Randolph himself is sane."

"I can't tell you that, Vine. Promised him I wouldn't, whether or not you took the assignment."

"You mean—even if I took the job I still wouldn't know what I was looking for?"

"That's right. You'd be prejudiced. You wouldn't be objective. You'd be looking for something, and you might think you found it whether it was there or not. Or you might be so prejudiced against finding it that you'd refuse to recognize it if it bit you in the leg."

He strode from the window over to the desk and banged his fist down on it.

He said, "God damn it Candler, why *me*? You know what happened to me three years ago."

"Sure. Amnesia."

"Sure, amnesia. Just like that. But I haven't kept it any secret that I never got *over* that amnesia. I'm thirty years old—or am I? My memory goes back three years. Do you know what it feels like to have a blank wall in your memory only three years back?

"Oh, sure, I know what's on the other side of that wall. I know because everybody tells me. I know I started here as a copy boy ten years ago. I know where I was born and when and I know my parents are both dead. I know what they look like—because I've seen their pictures. I know I didn't have a wife and kids, because everybody who knew me told me I didn't. Get that part—everybody who knew me, not everybody I knew. I didn't know anybody.

"Sure, I've done all right since then. After I got out of the hospital—and I don't even remember the accident that put me there—I did all right back here because I still knew how to write news stories, even though I had to learn everybody's name all over again. I wasn't any worse off than a new reporter starting cold

113

on a paper in a strange city. And everybody was as helpful as hell."

Candler raised a placating hand to stem the tide. He said, "Okay, Nappy. You said no, and that's enough. I don't see what all that's got to do with this story, but all you had to do was say no. So forget about it."

The tenseness hadn't gone out of him. He said, "You don't see what *that's* got to do with the story? You ask —or, all right, you don't ask, you suggest—that I get myself certified as a madman, go into an asylum as a patient. When—how much confidence does anyone have in his own mind when he can't remember going to school, can't remember the first time he met any of the people he works with every day, can't remember starting on the job he works at, can't remember—anything back of three years before?"

Abruptly he struck the desk again with his fist, and then looked foolish about it. He said, "I'm sorry. I didn't mean to get wound up about it like that."

Candler said, "Sit down."

"The answer's still no."

"Sit down, anyway."

He sat down and fumbled a cigarette out of his pocket, got it lighted.

Candler said, "I didn't even mean to mention it, but I've got to now. Now that you talked that way. I didn't know you felt like that about your amnesia. I thought that was water under the bridge.

"Listen, when Dr. Randolph asked me what reporter we had that could best cover it, I told him about you. What your background was. He remembered meeting you, too, incidentally. But he hadn't known you'd had amnesia."

"Is that why you suggested me?"

"Skip that till I make my point. He said that while you were there, he'd be glad to try one of the newer, milder forms of shock treatment on you, and that it might restore your lost memories. He said it would be worth trying."

"He didn't say it would work."

"He said it might; that it wouldn't do any harm."

He stubbed out the cigarette from which he'd taken only three drags. He glared at Candler. He didn't have to say what was in his mind; the managing editor could read it.

Candler said, "Calm down, boy. Remember I didn't bring it up until you yourself started in on how much that memory-wall bothered you. I wasn't saving it for ammunition. I mentioned it only out of fairness to you, after the way you talked."

"Fairness!"

Candler shrugged. "You said no. I accepted it. Then you started raving at me and put me in a spot where I had to mention something I'd hardly thought of at the time. Forget it. How's that graft story coming? Any new leads?"

"You going to put someone else on the asylum story?"

"No. You're the logical one for it."

"What *is* the story? It must be pretty woolly if it makes you wonder if Dr. Randolph is sane. Does he think his patients ought to trade places with his doctors, or what?"

He laughed. "Sure, you can't tell me. That's really beautiful double bait. Curiosity—and hope of knocking down that wall. So what's the rest of it? If I say yes instead of no, how long will I be there, under what circumstances? What chance have I got of getting out again? How do I get in?"

Candler said slowly, "Vine, I'm not sure any more I want you to try it. Let's skip the whole thing."

"Let's not. Not until you answer my questions, anyway."

"All right. You'd go in anonymously, so there

115

wouldn't be any stigma attached if the story wouldn't work out. If it does, you can tell the whole truth—including Dr. Randolph's collusion in getting you in and out again. The cat will be out of the bag, then."

"You might get what you want in a few days—and you wouldn't stay on it more than a couple of weeks in any case."

"How many at the asylum would know who I was and what I was there for, besides Randolph?"

"No one." Candler leaned forward and held up four fingers of his left hand. He pointed to the first. "Four people would have to be in on it. You." He pointed to one finger. "Me." A second. "Dr. Randolph." The third finger. "And one other reporter from here."

"Not that I'd object, but why the other reporter?"

"Intermediary. In two ways. First, he'll go with you to some psychiatrist; Randolph will recommend one you can fool comparatively easily. He'll be your brother and request that you be examined and certified. You convince the psychiatrist you're nuts and he'll certify you. Of course it takes two doctors to put you away, but Randolph will be the second. Your alleged brother will want Randolph for the second one."

"All this under an assumed name?"

"If you prefer. Of course, there's no real reason why it should be."

"That's the way I feel about it. Keep it out of the papers, of course. Tell everybody around here—except my—hey, in that case we couldn't make up a brother. But Charlie Doerr, in Circulation, is my first cousin and my nearest living relative. He'd do, wouldn't he?"

"Sure. And he'd have to be intermediary the rest of the way, then. Visit you at the asylum and bring back anything you have to send back."

"And if, in a couple of weeks, I've found nothing, you'll spring me?"

Candler nodded. "I'll pass the word to Randolph; he'll interview you and pronounce you cured, and you're out. You come back here, and you've been on vacation. That's all."

"What kind of insanity should I pretend to have?"

He thought Candler squirmed a little in his chair. Candler said, "Well—wouldn't this Nappy business be a natural? I mean, paranoia is a form of insanity which, Dr. Randolph told me, hasn't any physical symptoms. It's just a delusion supported by a systematic framework of rationalization. A paranoiac can be sane in every way except one."

He watched Candler and there was a faint twisted grin on his lips. "You mean I should think I'm Napoleon?"

Candler gestured slightly. "Choose your own delusion. But—isn't that one a natural? I mean, the boys around the office always kidding you and calling you Nappy. And—" He finished weakly, "—and everything."

And then Candler looked at him squarely. "Want to do it?"

He stood up. "I think so. I'll let you know for sure tomorrow morning after I've slept on it, but unofficially —yes. Is that good enough?"

Candler nodded.

He said, "I'm taking the rest of the afternoon off; I'm going to the library to read up on paranoia. Haven't anything else to do anyway. And I'll talk to Charlie Doerr this evening. Okay?"

"Fine. Thanks."

He grinned at Candler. He leaned across the desk. He said, "I'll let you in on a little secret, now that things have gone this far. Don't tell anyone. I *am* Napoleon!"

It was a good exit line, so he went out.

2

He got his hat and coat and went outside, out of the

117

air-conditioning and into the hot sunlight. Out of the quiet madhouse of a newspaper office after deadline, into the quieter madhouse of the streets on a sultry July afternoon.

He tilted his panama back on his head and ran his handkerchief across his forehead. Where was he going? Not to the library to bone up on paranoia; that had been a gag to get off for the rest of the afternoon. He'd read everything the library had on paranoia—and on allied subjects—over two years ago. He was an expert on it. He could fool any psychiatrist in the country into thinking that he was sane—or that he wasn't.

He walked north to the park and sat down on one of the benches in the shade. He put his hat on the bench beside him and mopped his forehead again.

He stared out at the grass, bright green in the sunlight, at the pigeons with their silly head-bobbing method of walking, at a red squirrel that came down one side of a tree, looked about him and scurried up the other side of the same tree.

And he thought back to the wall of amnesia of three years ago.

The wall that hadn't been a wall at all. The phrase intrigued him: A wall at all. Pigeons on the grass, alas. A wall at all.

It wasn't a wall at all; it was a shift, an abrupt change. A line had been drawn between two lives. Twenty-seven years of a life before the accident. Three years of life since the accident.

They were not the same life.

But no one knew. Until this afternoon he had never even hinted the truth—if it *was* the truth—to anyone. He'd used it as an exit line in leaving Candler's office, knowing Chandler would take it as a gag. Even so, one had to be careful; use a gag-line like that often, and people begin to wonder.

The fact that his extensive injuries from that accident had included a broken jaw was probably responsible for the fact that today he was free and not in an asylum. That broken jaw—it had been in a cast when he'd returned to consciousness forty-eight hours after his car had run head-on into a truck ten miles out of town—had prevented him from talking for three weeks.

And by the end of three weeks, despite the pain and the confusion that had filled them, he'd had a chance to think things over. He'd invented the wall. The amnesia, the convenient amnesia that was so much more believable than the truth as he knew it.

But *was* the truth as he knew it?

That was the haunting ghost that had ridden him for three years now, since the very hour when he had awakened to whiteness in a white room and a stranger, strangely dressed, had been sitting beside a bed the like of which had been in no field hospital he'd ever heard of or seen. A bed with an overhead framework. And when he looked from the stranger's face down at his own body, he saw that one of his legs and both of his arms were in casts and that the cast of the leg stuck upward at an angle, a rope running over a pulley holding it so.

He'd tried to open his mouth to ask where he was, what had happened to him, and that was when he had discovered the cast on his jaw.

He'd stared at the stranger, hoping the latter would have sense enough to volunteer the information and the stranger had grinned at him and said, "Hi, George. Back with us, huh? You'll be all right."

And there was something strange about the language —until he placed what it was. English. Was he in the hands of the English? And it was a language, too, which he knew little of, yet he understood the stranger perfectly. And why did the stranger call him George?

Maybe some of the doubt, some of the fierce bewilderment, showed in his eyes, for the stranger leaned closer to the bed. He said, "Maybe you're still confused, George. You were in a pretty bad smashup. You

119

ran that coupe of yours head-on into a gravel truck. That was two days ago, and you're just coming out of it for the first time. You're all right, but you'll be in the hospital for a while, till all the bones you busted knit. Nothing seriously wrong with you."

And then waves of pain had come and swept away the confusion, and he had closed his eyes.

Another voice in the room said, "We're going to give you a hypo, Mr. Vine," but he hadn't dared open his eyes again. It was easier to fight the pain without seeing.

There had been the prick of a needle in his upper arm. And pretty soon there'd been nothingness.

When he came back again—twelve hours later, he learned afterwards—it had been to the same white room, the same strange bed, but this time there was a woman in the room, a woman in a strange white costume standing at the foot of the bed studying a paper that was fastened to a piece of board.

She had smiled at him when she saw that his eyes were open. She said, "Good morning, Mr. Vine. Hope you're feeling better. I'll tell Dr. Holt that you're back with us."

She went away and came back with a man who was also strangely dressed, in roughly the same fashion as had been the stranger who had called him George.

The doctor looked at him and chuckled. "Got a patient, for once, who can't talk back to me. Or even write notes." Then his face sobered. "Are you in pain, though? Blink once if you're not, twice if you are."

The pain wasn't really very bad this time, and he blinked once. The doctor nodded with satisfaction. "That cousin of yours," he said, "has kept calling up. He'll be glad to know you're going to be back in shape to—well, to listen if not to talk. Guess it won't hurt you to see him a while this evening."

The nurse rearranged his bedclothing and then,

mercifully, both she and the doctor had gone, leaving him alone to straighten out his chaotic thoughts.

Straighten them out? That had been three years ago, and he hadn't been able to straighten them out yet:

The startling fact that they'd spoken English and that he'd understood that barbaric tongue perfectly, despite his slight previous knowledge of it. How could an accident have made him suddenly fluent in a language which he had known but slightly?

The startling fact that they'd called him by a different name. "George" had been the name used by the man who'd been beside his bed last night. "Mr. Vine," the nurse had called him. George Vine, an English name, surely.

But there was one thing a thousand times more startling than either of those: It was what last night's stranger (Could he be the "cousin" of whom the doctor had spoken?) had told him about the accident. "You ran that coupe of yours head-on into a gravel truck."

The amazing thing, the contradictory thing, was that he *knew* what a coupe was and what a truck was. Not that he had any recollection of having driven either, of the accident itself, or of anything beyond that moment when he'd been sitting in the tent after Lodi—but—but how could a picture of a coupe, something driven by a gasoline engine, arise to his mind when such a concept had never been *in* his mind before.

There was that mad mingling of two worlds—the one sharp and clear and definite. The world he'd lived his twenty-seven years of life in, in the world into which he'd been born twenty-seven years ago, on August 15th, 1769, in Corsica. The world in which he'd gone to sleep—it seemed like last night—in his tent at Lodi, as General of the Army in Italy, after his first important victory in the field.

And then there was this disturbing world into which he had awakened, this white world in which people

121

spoke an English—now that he thought of it—which was different from the English he had heard spoken at Brienne, in Valence, at Toulon, and yet which he understood perfectly, which he knew instinctively that he could speak if his jaw were not in a cast. This world in which people called him George Vine, and in which, strangest of all, people used words that he did not know, could not conceivably know, and yet which brought pictures to his mind.

Coupe, truck. They were both forms of—the word came to his mind unbidden—automobiles. He concentrated on what an automobile was and how it worked, and the information was there. The cylinder block, the pistons driven by explosions of gasoline vapor, ignited by a spark of electricity from a generator—

Electricity. He opened his eyes and looked upward at the shaded light in the ceiling, and he knew, somehow, that it was an *electric* light, and in a general way he knew what electricity was.

The Italian Galvani—yes, he'd read of some experiments of Galvani, but they hadn't encompassed anything practical such as a light like that. And staring at the shaded light, he visualized behind it water power running dynamos, miles of wire, motors running generators. He caught his breath at the concept that came to him out of his own mind, or part of his own mind.

The faint, fumbling experiments of Galvani with their weak currents and kicking frogs' legs had scarcely foreshadowed the unmysterious mystery of that light up in the ceiling; and that was the strangest thing yet; part of his mind found it mysterious and another part took it for granted and understood in a general sort of way how it all worked.

Let's see, he thought, the electric light was invented by Thomas Alva Edison somewhere around—Ridiculous; he'd been going to say around 1900, and it was now only 1796!

And then the really horrible thing came to him and he tried—painfully, in vain—to sit up in bed. It *had* been 1900, his memory told him, and Edison had died in 1931— And a man named Napoleon Bonaparte had died a hundred and ten years before that, in 1821.

He'd nearly gone insane then.

And, sane or insane, only the fact that he could not speak had kept him out of a madhouse; it gave him time to think things out, time to realize that his only chance lay in pretending amnesia, in pretending that he remembered nothing of life prior to the accident. They don't put you in a madhouse for amnesia. They tell you who you are, let you go back to what they tell you your former life was. They let you pick up the threads and weave them, while you try to remember.

Three years ago he'd done that. Now, tomorrow, he was going to go to a psychiatrist and say that he was— Napoleon!

3

The slant of the sun was greater. Overhead a big bird of a plane droned by and he looked up at it and began laughing, quietly to himself—not the laughter of madness. True laughter because it sprang from the conception of Napoleon Bonaparte riding in a plane like that and from the overwhelming incongruity of that idea.

It came to him then that he'd never ridden in a plane, that he remembered. Maybe George Vine had; at some time in the twenty-seven years of life George Vine had spent, he must have. But did that mean that *he* had ridden in one? That was a question that was part of the big question.

He got up and started to walk again. It was almost five o'clock; pretty soon Charlie Doerr would be leaving the paper and going home for dinner. Maybe he'd better phone Charlie and be sure he'd be home this evening.

He headed for the nearest bar and phoned; he got Charlie just in time. He said, "This is George. Going to be home this evening?"

"Sure, George. I was going to a poker game, but I called it off when I learned you'd be around."

"When you learned—Oh, Candler talked to you?"

"Yeah. Say, I didn't know you'd phone me or I'd have called Marge, but how about coming out for dinner? It'll be all right with her; I'll call her now if you can."

He said, "Thanks, no, Charlie. Got a dinner date. And say, about that card game; you can go. I can get there about seven and we won't have to talk all evening; an hour'll be enough. You wouldn't be leaving before eight anyway."

Charlie said, "Don't worry about it; I don't much want to go anyway, and you haven't been out for a while. So I'll see you at seven, then."

From the phone booth, he walked over to the bar and ordered a beer. He wondered why he'd turned down the invitation to dinner; probably because, subconsciously, he wanted another couple of hours by himself before he talked to anyone, even Charlie and Marge.

He sipped his beer slowly, because he wanted to make it last; he had to stay sober tonight, plenty sober. There was still time to change his mind; he'd left himself a loop-hole, however small. He could still go to Candler in the morning and say he'd decided not to do it.

Over the rim of his glass he stared at himself in the back-bar mirror. Small, sandy-haired, with freckles on his nose, stocky. The small and stocky part fitted all right; but the rest of it! Not the remotest resemblance.

He drank another beer slowly, and that made it half past five.

124

He wandered out again and walked, this time toward town. He walked past the *Blade* and looked up to the third floor and at the window he'd been looking out of when Candler had sent for him. He wondered if he'd ever sit by that window again and look out across a sunlit afternoon.

Maybe. Maybe not.

He thought about Clare. Did he want to see her tonight?

Well, no, to be honest about it, he didn't. But if he disappeared for two weeks or so without having even said good-bye to her, then he'd have to write her off his books; she wouldn't like that.

He'd better.

He stopped in at a drug store and called her home. He said, "This is George, Clare. Listen, I'm being sent out of town tomorrow on an assignment; don't know how long I'll be gone. One of those things that might be a few days or a few weeks. But could I see you late this evening, to say so-long?"

"Why sure, George. What time?"

"It might be after nine, but not much after. That be okay? I'm seeing Charlie first, on business; may not be able to get away before nine."

"Of course, George. Any time."

He stopped in at a hamburger stand, although he wasn't hungry, and managed to eat a sandwich and a piece of pie. That made it a quarter after six and, if he walked, he'd get to Charlie's at just about the right time. So he walked.

Charlie met him at the door. With finger on his lips, he jerked his head backward toward the kitchen where Marge was wiping dishes. He whispered, "I didn't tell Marge, George. It'd worry her."

He wanted to ask Charlie why it would, or should, worry Marge, but he didn't. Maybe he was a little afraid of the answer. It would have to mean that Marge was worrying about him already, and that was a bad

125

sign. He thought he'd been carrying everything off pretty well for three years now.

Anyway, he couldn't ask because Charlie was leading him into the living room and the kitchen was within easy earshot, and Charlie was saying, "Glad you decided you'd like a game of chess, George. Marge is going out tonight; movie she wants to see down at the neighborhood show. I was going to that card game out of self-defense, but I didn't want to."

He got the chessboard and men out of the closet and started to set up a game on the coffee table.

Marge came in with a tray bearing tall cold glasses of beer and put it down beside the chessboard. She said, "Hi, George. Hear you're going away a couple of weeks."

He nodded. "But I don't know where. Candler—the managing editor—asked me if I'd be free for an out of town assignment and I said sure, and he said he'd tell me about it tomorrow."

Charlie was holding out clenched hands, a pawn in each, and he touched Charlie's left hand and got white. He moved pawn to king's fourth and, when Charlie did the same, advanced his queen's pawn.

Marge was fussing with her hat in front of the mirror. She said, "If you're not here when I get back, George, so long and good luck."

He said, "Thanks, Marge. 'Bye."

He made a few more moves before Marge came over, ready to go, kissed Charlie good-bye and then kissed him lightly on the forehead. She said, "Take care of yourself, George."

For a moment his eyes met her pale blue ones and he thought, she *is* worrying about me. It scared him a little.

After the door had closed behind her, he said, "Let's not finish the game, Charlie. Let's get to the brass tacks, because I've got to see Clare about nine. Dunno

126

how long I'll be gone, so I can't very well not say good-bye to her."

Charlie looked up at him. "You and Clare serious, George?"

"I don't know."

Charlie picked up his beer and took a sip. Suddenly his voice was brisk and business-like. He said, "All right, let's sit on the brass tacks. We've got an appointment for eleven o'clock tomorrow morning with a guy named Irving, Dr. J. E. Irving, in the Appleton Block. He's a psychiatrist; Dr. Randolph recommended him.

"I called him up this afternoon after Candler had talked to me; Candler had already phoned Randolph. My story was this: I gave my right name. I've got a cousin who's been acting queer lately and whom I wanted him to talk to. I didn't give the cousin's name. I didn't tell him in what way you'd been acting queer; I ducked the question and said I'd rather have him judge for himself without prejudice. I said I'd talked you into talking to a psychiatrist and that the only one I knew of was Randolph; that I'd called Randolph who said he didn't do much private practice and recommended Irving. I told him I was your nearest living relative.

"That leaves the way open to Randolph for the second name on the certificate. If you can talk Irving into thinking you're really insane and he wants to sign you up, I can insist on having Randolph, whom I wanted in the first place. And this time, of course, Randolph will agree."

"You didn't say a thing about what kind of insanity you suspected me of having?"

Charlie shook his head. He said, "So, anyway, neither of us goes to work at the *Blade* tomorrow. I'll leave home the usual time so Marge won't know anything, but I'll meet you downtown—say, in the lobby of the Christina—at a quarter of eleven. And if you can convince Irving that you're committable—if that's the word

127

—we'll get Randolph right away and get the whole thing settled tomorrow."

"And if I change my mind?"

"Then I'll call the appointment off. That's all. Look, isn't that all there is to talk over? Let's play this game of chess out; it's only twenty after seven."

He shook his head. "I'd rather talk, Charlie. One thing you forgot to cover, anyway. After tomorrow. How often you coming to see me to pick up bulletins for Candler?"

"Oh, sure, I forgot that. As often as visiting hours will permit—three times a week. Monday, Wednesday, Friday afternoons. Tomorrow's Friday, so if you get in, the first time I'll be able to see you is Monday."

"Okay. Say, Charlie, did Candler even hint to you at what the story is that I'm supposed to get in there?"

Charlie Doerr shook his head slowly. "Not a word. What is it? Or is it too secret for you to talk about?

He stared at Charlie, wondering. And suddenly he felt that he couldn't tell the truth; that he didn't know either. It would make him look too silly. It hadn't sounded so foolish when Candler had given the reason —*a* reason, anyway—for not telling him, but it would sound foolish now.

He said, "If he didn't tell you, I guess I'd better not either, Charlie." And since that didn't sound too convincing, he added, "I promised Candler I wouldn't."

Both glasses of beer were empty by then, and Charlie took them into the kitchen for refilling.

He followed Charlie, somehow preferring the informality of the kitchen. He sat a-straddle on a kitchen chair, leaning his elbows on the back of it, and Charlie leaned against the refrigerator.

Charlie said, "Prosit!" and they drank, and then Charlie asked, "Have you got your story ready for Doc Irving?"

He nodded. "Did Candler tell you what I'm to tell him?"

"You mean, that you're Napoleon?" Charlie chuckled. Did that chuckle quite ring true? He looked at Charlie, and he knew that what he was thinking was completely incredible. Charlie was square and honest as they came. Charlie and Marge were his best friends; they'd been his best friends for three years that he knew of. Longer than that, a hell of a lot longer, according to Charlie. But beyond those three years—that was something else again.

He cleared his throat because the words were going to stick a little. But he had to ask, he had to be sure. "Charlie, I'm going to ask you a hell of a question. Is this business on the up and up?"

"Huh?"

"It's a hell of a thing to ask. But—look, you and Candler don't think I'm crazy, do you? You didn't work this out between you to get me put away—or anyway examined—painlessly, without my knowing it was happening, till too late, did you?"

Charlie was staring at him. He said, "Jeez, George, you don't think I'd do a thing like that, do you?"

"No, I don't. But—you could think it was for my own good, and you might on that basis. Look, Charlie, if it *is* that, if you *think* that, let me point out that this isn't fair. I'm going up against a psychiatrist tomorrow to lie to him, to try to convince him that I have delusions. Not to be honest with him. And that would be unfair as hell, to me. You see that, don't you, Charlie?"

Charlie's face got a little white. He said slowly, "Before God, George, it's nothing like that. All I know about this is what Candler and you have told me."

"You think I'm sane, fully sane?"

Charlie licked his lips. He said, "You want it straight?"

"Yes."

"I never doubted it, until this moment. Unless—

129

well, amnesia is a form of mental aberration, I suppose, and you've never got over that, but that isn't what you mean, is it?"

"No."

"Then, until right now—George, that sounds like a persecution complex, if you really meant what you asked me. A conspiracy to get you to— Surely you can see how ridiculous it is. What possible reason would either Candler or I have to get you to lie yourself into being committed?"

He said, "I'm sorry, Charlie. It was just a screwy momentary notion. No, I don't think that, of course." He glanced at his wrist watch. "Let's finish that chess game, huh?"

"Fine. Wait till I give us a refill to take along."

He played carelessly and managed to lose within fifteen minutes. He turned down Charlie's offer of a chance for revenge and leaned back in his chair.

He said, "Charlie, ever hear of chessmen coming in red and black?"

"N-no. Either black and white, or red and white, any I've ever seen. Why?"

"Well—" He grinned. "I suppose I oughtn't to tell you this after just making you wonder whether I'm really sane after all, but I've been having recurrent dreams recently. No crazier than ordinary dreams except that I've been dreaming the same things over and over. One of them is something about a game between the red and the black; I don't even know whether it's chess. You know how it is when you dream; things seem to make sense whether they do or not. In the dream, I don't wonder whether the red-and-black business is chess or not; I know, I guess, or seem to know. But the knowledge doesn't carry over. You know what I mean?"

"Sure. Go on."

"Well, Charlie, I've been wondering if it just might

130

have something to do with the other side of that wall of amnesia I've never been able to cross. This is the first time in my—well, not in my life, maybe, but in the three years I remember of it, that I've had recurrent dreams. I wonder if—if my memory may not be trying to get through.

"Did I ever have a set of red and black chessmen, for instance? Or, in any school I went to, did they have intramural basketball or baseball between red teams and black teams, or—or anything like that?"

Charlie thought for a long moment before he shook his head. "No," he said. "Nothing like that. Of course there's red and black in roulette—rouge et noir. And it's the two colors in a deck of playing cards."

"No, I'm pretty sure it doesn't tie in with cards or roulette. It's not—not like that. It's a game *between* the red and the black. They're the players, somehow. Think hard, Charlie; not about where you might have run into that idea, but where *I* might have."

He watched Charlie struggle and after a while he said, "Okay, don't sprain your brain, Charlie. Try this one. *The brightly shining.*"

"The brightly shining what?"

"Just that phrase, *the brightly shining.* Does it mean anything to you, at all?"

"No."

"Okay," he said. "Forget it."

4

He was early and he walked past Clare's house, as far as the corner and stood under the big elm there, smoking the rest of his cigarette, thinking bleakly.

There wasn't anything to think about, really; all he had to do was say good-bye to her. Two easy syllables. And stall off her questions as to where he was going, exactly how long he'd be gone. Be quiet and casual and unemotional about it, just as though they didn't mean anything in particular to each other.

It *had* to be that way. He'd known Clare Wilson a year and a half now, and he'd kept her dangling that long; it wasn't fair. This had to be the end, for her sake. He had about as much business asking a woman to marry him as—as a madman who thinks he's Napoleon!

He dropped his cigarette and ground it viciously into the walk with his heel, then went back to the house, up on the porch, and rang the bell.

Clare herself came to the door. The light from the hallway behind her made her hair a circlet of spun gold around her shadowed face.

He wanted to take her into his arms so badly that he clenched his fists with the effort it took to keep his arms down.

Stupidly, he said, "Hi, Clare. How's everything?"

"I don't know, George. How *is* everything? Aren't you coming in?"

She'd stepped back from the doorway to let him past and the light was on her face now, sweetly grave. She knew something was up, he thought; her expression and the tone of her voice gave that away.

He didn't want to go in. He said, "It's such a beautiful night, Clare. Let's take a stroll."

"All right, George." She came out onto the porch. "It is a fine night, such beautiful stars." She turned and looked at him. "Is one of them yours?"

He started a little. Then he stepped forward and took her elbow, guiding her down the porch steps. He said lightly, "All of them are mine. Want to buy any?"

"You wouldn't *give* me one? Just a teeny little dwarf star, maybe? Even one that I'd have to use a telescope to see?"

They were out on the sidewalk then, out of hearing of the house, and abruptly her voice changed, the playful note dropped from it, and she asked another question, "What's wrong, George?"

He opened his mouth to say nothing was wrong, and then closed it again. There wasn't any lie that he could tell her, and he couldn't tell her the truth, either. Her asking of that question, in that way, should have made things easier; it made them more difficult.

She asked another, "You mean to say good-bye for —for good, don't you, George?"

He said, "Yes," and his mouth was very dry. He didn't know whether it came out as an articulate monosyllable or not, and he wetted his lips and tried again. He said, "Yes, I'm afraid so, Clare."

"Why?"

He couldn't make himself turn to look at her, he stared blindly ahead. He said, "I—I can't tell you, Clare. But it's the only thing I can do. It's best for both of us."

"Tell me one thing, George. Are you really going away? Or was that just—an excuse?"

"It's true. I'm going away; I don't know for how long. But don't ask me where, please. I can't tell you that."

"Maybe I can tell you, George. Do you mind if I do?"

He minded all right; he minded terribly. But how could he say so? He didn't say anything, because he couldn't say yes, either.

They were beside the park now, the little neighborhood park that was only a block square and didn't offer much in the way of privacy, but which did have benches. And he steered her—or she steered him; he didn't know which—into the park and they sat down on a bench. There were other people in the park, but not too near. Still he hadn't answered her question.

She sat very close to him on the bench. She said, "You've been worried about your mind, haven't you George?"

"Well—yes, in a way, yes, I have."

133

"And your going away has something to do with that, hasn't it? You're going somewhere for observation or treatment, or both?"

"Something like that. It's not as simple as that, Clare, and I—I just can't tell you about it."

She put her hand on his hand, lying on his knee. She said, "I knew it was something like that, George. And I don't ask you to tell me anything about it.

"Just—just don't say what you meant to say. Say so-long instead of good-bye. Don't even write me, if you don't want to. But don't be noble and call everything off here and now, for my sake. At least wait until you've been wherever you're going. Will you?"

He gulped. She made it sound so simple when actually it was so complicated. Miserably he said, "All right, Clare. If you want it that way."

Abruptly she stood up. "Let's get back, George."

He stood beside her. "But it's early."

"I know, but sometimes— Well, there's a psychological moment to end a date, George. I know that sounds silly, but after what we've said, wouldn't it be —uh—anticlimactic—to—"

He laughed a little. He said, "I see what you mean."

They walked back to her home in silence. He didn't know whether it was happy or unhappy silence; he was too mixed up for that.

On the shadowed porch, in front of the door, she turned and faced him. "George," she said. Silence.

"Oh, damn you, George; quit being so *noble* or whatever you're being. Unless, of course, you *don't* love me. Unless this is just an elaborate form of—of runaround you're giving me. Is it?"

There were only two things he could do. One was run like hell. The other was what he did. He put his arms around her and kissed her, hungrily.

When that was over, and it wasn't over too quickly, he was breathing a little hard and not thinking too

134

clearly, for he was saying what he hadn't meant to say at all, "I love you, Clare. I love you; I love you."

And she said, "I love you, too, dear. You'll come back to me, won't you?" And he said, "Yes. *Yes.*"

It was four miles or so from her home to his rooming house, but he walked, and the walk seemed to take only seconds.

He sat at the window of his room, with the light out, thinking, but the thoughts went in the same old circles they'd gone in for three years.

No new factor had been added except that now he was going to stick his neck out, miles out. Maybe, just maybe, this thing was going to be settled one way or the other.

Out there, out his window, the stars were bright diamonds in the sky. Was one of them his star of destiny? If so, he was going to follow it, follow it even into the madhouse if it led there. Inside him was a deeply rooted conviction that this wasn't accident, that it wasn't coincidence that had led to his being asked to tell the truth under guise of falsehood.

His star of destiny.

Brightly shining? No, the phrase from his dreams did not refer to that; it was not an adjective phrase, but a noun. *The brightly shining?* What was *the brightly shining?*

And the red and the black? He'd thought of everything Charlie had suggested, and other things, too. Checkers, for instance. But it was not that.

The red and the black.

Well, whatever the answer was, he was running fullspeed toward it now, not away from it.

After a while he went to bed, but it was a long time before he went to sleep.

5

Charlie Doerr came out of the inner office marked

Private and put his hand out. He said, "Good luck, George. The doc's ready to talk to you now."

He shook Charlie's hand and said, "You might as well run along. I'll see you Monday, first visiting day."

"I'll wait here," Charlie said. "I took the day off work anyway, remember? Besides, maybe you won't have to go."

He dropped Charlie's hand, and stared into Charlie's face. He said slowly, "What do you mean, Charlie—maybe I won't have to go."

"Why—" Charlie looked puzzled. "Why, maybe he'll tell you you're all right, or just suggest regular visits to see him until you're straightened out, or—" Charlie finished weakly, "—or something."

Unbelievingly, he stared at Charlie. He wanted to ask, am I crazy or are you, but that sounded crazy to ask under the circumstances. But he had to be sure, sure that Charlie just hadn't let something slip from his mind; maybe he'd fallen into the role he was supposed to be playing when he talked to the doctor just now. He asked, "Charlie, don't you remember that—" And even of that question the rest seemed insane for him to be asking, with Charlie staring blankly at him. The answer was in Charlie's face; it didn't have to be brought to Charlie's lips.

Charlie said again, "I'll wait, of course. Good luck, George."

He looked into Charlie's eyes and nodded, then turned and went through the door marked Private. He closed it behind him, meanwhile studying the man who had been sitting behind the desk and who had risen as he entered. A big man, broad shouldered, iron gray hair.

"Dr. Irving?"

"Yes, Mr. Vine. Will you be seated, please?"

He slid into the comfortable, padded armchair across the desk from the doctor.

"Mr. Vine," said the doctor, "a first interview of this

136

sort is always a bit difficult. For the patient, I mean. Until you know me better, it will be difficult for you to overcome a certain natural reticence in discussing yourself. Would you prefer to talk, to tell things your own way, or would you rather I asked questions?"

He thought that over. He'd had a story ready, but those few words with Charlie in the waiting room had changed everything.

He said, "Perhaps you'd better ask questions."

"Very well." There was a pencil in Dr. Irving's hand and paper on the desk before him. "Where and when were you born?"

He took a deep breath. "To the best of my knowledge, in Corsica on August 15th, 1769. I don't actually remember being born, of course. I do remember things from my boyhood on Corsica, though. We stayed there until I was ten, and after that I was sent to school at Brienne."

Instead of writing, the doctor was tapping the paper lightly with the tip of the pencil. He asked, "What month and year is this?"

"August, 1947. Yes, I know that should make me a hundred and seventy-some years old. You want to know how I account for that. I don't. Nor do I account for the fact that Napoleon Bonaparte died in 1821."

He leaned back in the chair and crossed his arms, staring up at the ceiling. "I don't attempt to account for the paradoxes or the discrepancies. I recognize them as such. But according to my own memory, and aside from logic pro or con, I was Napoleon for twenty-seven years. I won't recount what happened during that time; it's all down in the history books.

"But in 1796, after the battle of Lodi, while I was in charge of the armies in Italy, I went to sleep. As far as I knew, just as anyone goes to sleep anywhere, any time. But I woke up—with no sense whatever of duration, by the way—in a hospital in town here, and

I was informed that my name was George Vine, that the year was 1944, and that I was twenty-seven years old.

"The twenty-seven years old part checked, and that was all. Absolutely all. I have no recollection of any parts of George Vine's life, prior to his—my—waking up in the hospital after the accident. I know quite a bit about his early life now, but only because I've been told.

"I know when and where he was born, where he went to school, and when he started work at the *Blade*. I know when he enlisted in the army and when he was discharged—late in 1943—because I developed a trick knee after a leg injury. Not in combat, incidentally, and there wasn't any 'psycho-neurotic' on my—his—discharge."

The doctor quit doodling with the pencil. He asked, "You've felt this way for three years—and kept it a secret?"

"Yes, I had time to think things over after the accident, and yes, I decided then to accept what they told me about my identity. They'd have locked me up, of course. Incidentally, I've *tried* to figure out an answer. I've studied Dunne's theory of time—even Charles Fort!" He grinned suddenly. "Ever read about Casper Hauser?"

Dr. Irving nodded.

"Maybe he was playing smart the way I did. And I wonder how many other amnesiacs pretended they didn't know what happened prior to a certain date—rather than admit they had memories at obvious variance with the facts."

'Dr. Irving said slowly, "Your cousin informs me that you were a bit—ah—'hipped' was his word—on the subject of Napoleon before your accident. How do you account for that?"

"I've told you I don't account for any of it. But I

138

can verify that fact, aside from what Charlie Doerr says about it. Apparently I—the George Vine I, if I was ever George Vine—was quite interested in Napoleon, had read about him, made a hero of him, and had talked about him quite a bit. Enough so that the fellows he worked with at the *Blade* had nicknamed him 'Nappy.'"

"I notice you distinguish between yourself and George Vine. Are you or are you not he?"

"I have been for three years. Before that—I have no recollection of being George Vine. I don't think I was. I think—as nearly as I think anything—that *I*, three years ago, woke up in George Vine's body."

"Having done what for a hundred and seventy some years?"

"I haven't the faintest idea. Incidentally, I don't doubt that this *is* George Vine's body, and with it I inherited his knowledge—except his personal memories. For example, I knew how to handle his job at the newspaper, although I didn't remember any of the people I worked with there. I have his knowledge of English, for instance, and his ability to write. I knew how to operate a typewriter. My handwriting is the same as his."

"If you think that you are not Vine, how do you account for that?"

He leaned forward. "I think part of me *is* George Vine, and part of me isn't. I think some transference has happened which is outside the run of ordinary human experience. That doesn't necessarily mean that it's supernatural—not that I'm insane. *Does it?*"

Dr. Irving didn't answer. Instead, he asked, "You kept this secret for three years, for understandable reasons. Now, presumably for other reasons, you decide to tell. What are the other reasons? What has happened to change your attitude?"

It was the question that had been bothering him.

He said slowly, "Because I don't believe in coincidence. Because something in the situation itself has

139

changed. Because I'm tired of pretending. Because I'm willing to risk imprisonment as a paranoiac to find out the truth."

"What in the situation has changed?"

"Yesterday it was suggested—by my employer—that I feign insanity for a practical reason. And the very kind of insanity which I have, if any. Surely, I will admit the possibility that I'm insane. But I can only operate on the theory that I'm not. You know that you're Dr. Willard E. Irving; you can only operate on that theory—but how do you *know* you are? Maybe you're insane, but you can only act as though you're not."

"You think your employer is part of a plot—ah—against you? You think there is a conspiracy to get you into a sanitarium?"

"I don't know. Here's what has happened since yesterday noon." He took a deep breath. Then he plunged. He told Dr. Irving the whole story of his interview with Candler, what Candler had said about Dr. Randolph, about his talk with Charlie Doerr last night and about Charlie's bewildering about-face in the waiting room.

When he was through he said, "That's all." He looked at Dr. Irving's expressionless face with more curiosity than concern, trying to read it. He added, quite casually, "You don't believe me, of course. You think I'm insane."

He met Irving's eyes squarely. He said, "You have no choice—unless you would choose to believe I'm telling you an elaborate set of lies to convince you I'm insane. I mean, as a scientist and as a psychiatrist, you cannot even admit the possibility that the things I believe—*know*—are objectively true. Am I not right?"

"I fear that you are. So?"

"So go ahead and sign your commitment. I'm going to follow this thing through. Even to the detail of having Dr. Ellsworth Joyce Randolph sign the second one."

"You make no objection?"

"Would it do any good if I did?"

"On one point, yes, Mr. Vine. If a patient has a prejudice against—or a delusion concerning—one psychiatrist, it is best not to have him under that particular psychiatrist's care. If you think Dr. Randolph is concerned in a plot against you, I would suggest that another one be named."

He said softly, "Even if I choose Randolph?"

Dr. Irving waved a deprecating hand, "Of course, if both you and Mr. Doerr prefer—"

"We prefer."

The iron gray head nodded gravely. "Of course you understand one thing; if Dr. Randolph and I decide you should go to the sanitarium, it will not be for custodial care. It will be for your recovery through treatment."

He nodded.

Dr. Irving stood. "You'll pardon me a moment? I'll phone Dr. Randolph."

He watched Dr. Irving go through a door to an inner room. He thought; there's a phone on his desk right there; but he doesn't want me to overhear the conversation.

He sat there very quietly until Irving came back and said, "Dr. Randolph is free. And I phoned for a cab to take us there. You'll pardon me again? I'd like to speak to your cousin, Mr. Doerr."

He sat there and didn't watch the doctor leave in the opposite direction for the waiting room. He could have gone to the door and tried to catch words in the low-voiced conversation, but he didn't. He just sat there until he heard the waiting room door open behind him and Charlie's voice said, "Come on, George. The cab will be waiting downstairs by now."

They went down in the elevator and the cab was there. Dr. Irving gave the address.

In the cab, about half way there, he said, "It's a beautiful day," and Charlie cleared his throat and said,

141

"Yeah, it is." The rest of the way he didn't try it again and nobody said anything.

6

He wore gray trousers and a gray shirt, open at the collar and with no necktie that he might decide to hang himself with. No belt, either, for the same reason, although the trousers buttoned snugly enough around the waist that there was no danger of them falling off. Just as there was no danger of his falling out any of the windows; they were barred.

He was not in a cell, however; it was a large ward on the third floor. There were seven other men in the ward. His eyes ran over them. Two were playing checkers, sitting on the floor with the board on the floor between them. One sat in a chair, staring fixedly at nothing; two leaned against the bars of one of the open windows, looking out and talking casually and sanely. One read a magazine. One sat in a corner, playing smooth arpeggios on a piano that wasn't there at all.

He stood leaning against the wall, watching the other seven. He'd been here two hours now; it seemed like two years.

The interview with Dr. Ellsworth Joyce Randolph had gone smoothly; it had been practically a duplicate of his interview with Irving. And quite obviously, Dr. Randolph had never heard of him before.

He'd expected that, of course.

He felt very calm, now. For a while, he'd decided, he wasn't going to think, wasn't going to worry, wasn't even going to feel.

He strolled over and stood watching the checker game.

It was a sane checker game; the rules were being followed.

One of the men looked up and asked, "What's your name?" It was a perfectly sane question; the only thing

142

wrong with it was that the same man had asked the same question four times now within the two hours he'd been here.

He said, "George Vine."

"Mine's Bassington, Ray Bassington. Call me Ray. Are you insane?"

"No."

"Some of us are and some of us aren't. He is." He looked at the man who was playing the imaginary piano. "Do you play checkers?"

"Not very well."

"Good. We eat pretty soon now. Anything you want to know, just ask me."

"How do you get out of here? Wait, I don't mean that for a gag, or anything. Seriously, what's the procedure?"

"You go in front of the board once a month. They ask you questions and decide if you go or stay. Sometimes they stick needles in you. What you down for?"

"Down for? What do you mean?"

"Feeble-minded, manic-depressive, dementia praecox, involutional melancholia—"

"Oh, paranoia, I guess."

"That's bad. Then they stick needles in you."

A bell rang somewhere.

"That's dinner," said the other checker player. "Ever try to commit suicide? Or kill anyone?"

"No."

"They'll let you eat at an A table then, with knife and fork."

The door of the ward was being opened. It opened outward and a guard stood outside and said, "All right." They filed out, all except the man who was sitting in the chair staring into space.

"How about him?" he asked Ray Bassington.

"He'll miss a meal tonight. Manic-depressive, just going into the depressive stage. They let you miss one

143

meal; if you're not able to go to the next they take you and feed you. You a manic-depressive?"

"No."

"You're lucky. It's hell when you're on the down-swing. Here, through this door."

It was a big room. Tables and benches were crowded with men in gray shirts and gray trousers, like his. A guard grabbed his arm as he went through the door-way and said, "There. That seat."

It was right beside the door. There was a tin plate, messy with food, and a spoon beside it. He asked, "Don't I get a knife and fork? I was told—"

The guard gave him a shove toward the seat. "Ob-servation period, seven days. Nobody gets silverware till their observation period's over. Siddown."

He sat down. No one at his table had silverware. All the others were eating, several of them noisily and messily. He kept his eyes on his own plate, unappetiz-ing as that was. He toyed with his spoon and managed to eat a few pieces of potato out of the stew and one or two of the chunks of meat that were mostly lean.

The coffee was in a tin cup and he wondered why until he realized how breakable an ordinary cup would be and how lethal could be one of the heavy mugs cheap restaurants use.

The coffee was weak and cool; he couldn't drink it.

He sat back and closed his eyes. When he opened them again there was an empty plate and an empty cup in front of him and the man at his left was eating very rapidly. It was the man who'd been playing the non-existent piano.

He thought, if I'm here long enough, I'll get hungry enough to eat that stuff. He didn't like the thought of being there that long.

After a while a bell rang and they got up, one table at a time on signals he didn't catch, and filed out. His group had come in last; it went out first.

Ray Bassington was behind him on the stairs. He said, "You'll get used to it. What'd you say your name is?"

"George Vine."

Bassington laughed. The door shut on them from the outside.

He saw it was dark outside. He went over to one of the windows and stared out through the bars. There was a single bright star that showed just above the top of the elm tree in the yard. *His* star? Well, he'd followed it here. A cloud drifted across it.

Someone was standing beside him. He turned his head and saw it was the man who'd been playing piano. He had a dark, foreign-looking face with intense black eyes; just then he was smiling, as though at a secret joke.

"You're new here, aren't you? Or just get put in this ward, which?"

"New. George Vine's the name."

"Baroni. Musician. Used to be, anyway. Now—let it go. Anything you want to know about the place?"

"Sure. How to get out of it."

Baroni laughed, without particular amusement but not bitterly either. "First, convince them you're all right again. Mind telling what's wrong with you—or don't you want to talk about it? Some of us mind, others don't."

He looked at Baroni, wondering which way he felt. Finally he said, "I guess I don't mind. I—think I'm Napoleon."

"Are you?"

"Am I what?"

"*Are* you Napoleon? If you aren't, that's one thing. Then maybe you'll get out of here in six months or so. If you really *are*—that's bad. You'll probably die here."

"Why? I mean, if I *am,* then I'm sane and—"

"Not the point. Point's whether they think you're

145

sane or not. Way they figure, if you think you're Napoleon you're not sane. Q. E. D. You stay here."

"Even if I tell them I'm convinced I'm George Vine?"

"They've worked with paranoia before. And that's what they've got you down for, count on it. And any time a paranoiac gets tired of a place, he'll try to lie his way out of it. They weren't born yesterday. They know that."

"In general yes, but how—"

A sudden cold chill went down his spine. He didn't have to finish the question. *They stick needles in you—* It hadn't meant anything when Ray Bassington had said it.

The dark man nodded. "Truth serum," he said. "When a paranoiac reaches the stage where he's cured *if* he's telling the truth, they make sure he's telling it before they let him go."

He thought, what a beautiful trap it had been that he'd walked into. He'd probably die here, now.

He leaned his head against the cool iron bars and closed his eyes. He heard footsteps walking away from him and knew he was alone.

He opened his eyes and looked out into blackness; now the clouds had drifted across the moon, too.

Clare, he thought; *Clare.*

A trap.

But—if there was a trap, there must be a trapper.

He was sane or he was insane. If he was sane, he'd walked into a trap, and *if there was a trap, there must be a trapper, or trappers.*

If he was insane—

God, let it be that he *was* insane. That way everything made such sweetly simple sense, and someday he might be out of here, he might go back to working for the *Blade,* possibly even with a memory of all the years he'd worked there. Or that George Vine had worked there.

That was the catch. *He* wasn't George Vine.

And there was another catch. He *wasn't* insane.
The cool iron of the bars against his forehead.

After a while he heard the door open and looked around. Two guards had come in. A wild hope, reasonless, surged up inside him. It didn't last.

"Bedtime, you guys," said one of the guards. He looked at the manic-depressive sitting motionless on the chair and said, "Nuts. Hey, Bassington, help me get this guy in."

The other guard, a heavy-set man with hair close-cropped like a wrestler's, came over to the window.

"You. You're the new one in here. Vine, ain't it?"

He nodded.

"Want trouble, or going to be good?" Fingers of the guard's right hand clenched, the fist went back.

"Don't want trouble. Got enough."

The guard relaxed a little. "Okay, stick to that and you'll get along. Vacant bunk's in there." He pointed. "One on the right. Make it up yourself in the morning. Stay in the bunk and mind your own business. If there's any noise or trouble here in the ward, we come in and take care of it. Our own way. You wouldn't like it."

He didn't trust himself to speak, so he just nodded. He turned and went through the door of the cubicle to which the guard had pointed. There were two bunks in there; the manic-depressive who'd been on the chair was lying flat on his back on the other, staring blindly up at the ceiling through wide-open eyes. They'd pulled his slippers off, leaving him otherwise dressed.

He turned to his own bunk, knowing there was nothing on earth he could do for the other man, no way he could reach him through the impenetrable shell of blank misery which is the manic-depressive's intermittent companion.

He turned down a gray sheet-blanket on his own bunk and found under it another gray sheet-blanket atop a hard but smooth pad. He slipped off his shirt

147

and trousers and hung them on a hook on the wall at the foot of his bed. He looked around for a switch to turn off the light overhead and couldn't find one. But, even as he looked, the light went out.

A single light still burned somewhere in the ward room outside, and by it he could see to take his shoes and socks off and get into the bunk.

He lay very quietly for a while, hearing only two sounds, both faint and seeming far away. Somewhere in another cubicle off the ward someone was singing quietly to himself, a wordless monody; somewhere else someone else was sobbing. In his own cubicle, he couldn't hear even the sound of breathing from his room mate.

Then there was a shuffle of bare feet and someone in the open doorway said, "George Vine."

He said, "Yes?"

"Shhh, not so loud. This is Bassington. Want to tell you about that guard; I should have warned you before. Don't ever tangle with him."

"I didn't."

"I heard; you were smart. He'll slug you to pieces if you give him half a chance. He's a sadist. A lot of guards are; that's why they're bughousers; that's what they call themselves, bughousers. If they get fired one place for being too brutal they get on at another one. He'll be in again in the morning; I thought I'd warn you."

The shadow in the doorway was gone.

He lay there in the dimness, the almost-darkness, feeling rather than thinking. Wondering. Did mad people ever know that they were mad? Could they tell? Was every one of them sure, as he was sure——?

That quiet, still thing lying in the bunk near his, inarticulately suffering, withdrawn from human reach into a profound misery beyond the understanding of the sane——

"Napoleon Bonaparte!"

A clear voice, but had it been within his mind, or

148

from without? He sat up on the bunk. His eyes pierced the dimness, could discern no form, no shadow, in the doorway.

He said, "Yes?"

7

Only then, sitting up on the bunk and having answered "Yes," did he realize the name by which the voice had called him.

"Get up. Dress."

He swung his legs out over the edge of the bunk, stood up. He reached for his shirt and was slipping his arms into it before he stopped and asked, "Why?"

"To learn the truth."

"Who are you?" he asked.

"Do not speak aloud. I can hear you. I am within you and without. I have no name."

"Then *what* are you?" He said it aloud, without thinking.

"An instrument of The Brightly Shining."

He dropped the trousers he'd been holding. He sat down carefully on the edge of the bunk, leaned over and groped around for them.

His mind groped, too. Groped for he knew not what. Finally he found a question—*the* question. He did ask it aloud this time; he thought it, concentrated on it as he straightened out his trousers and thrust his legs in them.

"Am I mad?"

The answer—*No*—came clear and sharp as a spoken word, but had it been spoken? Or was it a sound that was only in his mind?

He found his shoes and pulled them on his feet. As he fumbled the laces into some sort of knots, he thought, "Who—what—is The Brightly Shining?"

"The Brightly Shining is *that which is Earth*. It is the intelligence of our planet. It is one of three intelligences in the solar system, one of many in the universe. Earth is one; it is called The Brightly Shining."

"I do not understand," he thought.

"You will. Are you ready?"

He finished the second knot. He stood up. The voice said, "Come. Walk silently."

It was as though he was being led through the almost-darkness, although he felt no physical touch upon him; he saw no physical presence beside him. But he walked confidently, although quietly on tiptoe, knowing he would not walk into anything nor stumble. Through the big room that was the ward, and then his out-stretched hand touched the knob of a door.

He turned it gently and the door opened inward. Light blinded him. The voice said, "Wait," and he stood immobile. He could hear sound—the rustle of paper, the turn of a page—outside the door, in the lighted corridor.

Then from across the hall came the sound of a shrill scream. A chair scraped and feet hit the floor of the corridor, walking away toward the sound of the scream. A door opened and closed.

The voice said, "Come," and he pulled the door open the rest of the way and went outside, past the desk and the empty chair that had been just outside the door of the ward.

Another door, another corridor. The voice said, "Wait," the voice said, "Come"; this time a guard slept. He tiptoed past. Down steps.

He thought the question, "Where am I going?"

"Mad," said the voice.

"But you said I wasn't—" He'd spoken aloud and the sound startled him almost more than had the answer to his last question. And in the silence that followed the words he'd spoken there came—from the bottom of the stairs and around the corner—the sound of a buzzing switchboard, and someone said, "Yes? . . .

Okay, Doctor, I'll be right up." Footsteps and the closing of an elevator door.

He went down the remaining stairs and around the corner and he was in the front main hall. There was an empty desk with a switchboard beside it. He walked past it and to the front door. It was bolted and he threw the heavy bolt.

He went outside, into the night.

He walked quietly across cement, across gravel; then his shoes were on grass and he didn't have to tiptoe any more. It was as dark now as the inside of an elephant; he felt the presence of trees nearby and leaves brushed his face occasionally, but he walked rapidly, confidently and his hand went forward just in time to touch a brick wall.

He reached up and he could touch the top of it; he pulled himself up and over it. There was broken glass on the flat top of the wall; he cut his clothes and his flesh badly, but he felt no pain, only the wetness of blood and the stickiness of blood.

He walked along a lighted road, he walked along dark and empty streets, he walked down a darker alley. He opened the back gate of a yard and walked to the back door of a house. He opened the door and went in. There was a lighted room at the front of the house; he could see the rectangle of light at the end of a corridor. He went along the corridor and into the lighted room.

Someone who had been seated at a desk stood up. Someone, a man, whose face he knew but whom he could not—

"Yes," said the man, smiling, "you know me, but you do not know me. Your mind is under partial control and your ability to recognize me is blocked out. Other than that and your analgesia—you are covered with blood from the glass on the wall, but you don't feel any pain—your mind is normal and you are sane."

151

"What's it all about?" he asked. "Why was I brought here?"

"Because you are sane. I'm sorry about that, because you can't be. It is not so much that you retained memory of your previous life, after you'd been moved. That happens. It is that you somehow know something of what you shouldn't—something of The Brightly Shining, and of the Game between the red and the black. For that reason—"

"For that reason, what?" he asked.

The man he knew and did not know smiled gently. "For that reason you must know the rest, so that you will know nothing at all. For everything will add to nothing. The truth will drive you mad."

"That I do not believe."

"Of course you don't. If the truth were conceivable to you, it would not drive you mad. But you cannot remotely conceive the truth."

A powerful anger surged up within him. He stared at the familiar face that he knew and did not know, and he stared down at himself; at the torn and bloody gray uniform, at his torn and bloody hands. The hands hooked like claws with the desire to kill—someone, the someone, whoever it was, who stood before him.

He asked, "What are you?"

"I am the instrument of The Brightly Shining."

"The same which led me here, or another?"

"One is all, all is one. Within the whole and its parts, there is no difference. One instrument is another and the red is the black and the black is the white and there is no difference. The Brightly Shining is the soul of Earth. I use *soul* as the nearest word in your vocabulary."

Hatred was almost a bright light. It was almost something that he could lean into, lean his weight against.

He asked, "What is The Brightly Shining?" He made the words a curse in his mouth.

"Knowing will make you mad. You want to know?"

"Yes." He made a curse out of that simple, sibilant syllable.

The lights were dimming. Or was it his eyes? The room was becoming dimmer, and at the same time receding. It was becoming a tiny cube of dim light, seen from afar and outside, from somewhere in the distant dark, ever receding, turning into a pin-point of light, and within that point of light ever the hated Thing, the man—or was it a man?—standing beside the desk.

Into the darkness, into space, up and apart from the earth—a dim sphere in the night, a receding sphere outlined against the spangled blackness of eternal space, occulting the stars, a disk of black.

It stopped receding, and time stopped. It was as though the clock of the universe stood still. Beside him, out of the void, spoke the voice of the instrument of The Shining One.

"Behold," it said. "The Being of Earth."

He beheld. Not as though an outward change was occurring, but an inward one, as though his senses were being changed to enable him to perceive something hitherto unseeable.

The ball that was Earth began to glow. Brightly to shine.

"You see the intelligence that rules Earth," said the voice. "The sum of the black and the white and the red, that are one, divided only as the lobes of a brain are divided, the trinity that is one."

The glowing ball and the stars behind it faded, and the darkness became deeper darkness and then there was dim light, growing brighter, and he was back in the room with the man standing at the desk.

"You saw," said the man whom he hated. "But you do not understand. You ask, *what* you have seen, *what* is The Brightly Shining? It is a group intelligence, the true intelligence of Earth, one intelligence among three in the Solar system, one among many in the Universe.

"What then, is man? Men are pawns, in games of—

153

to you—unbelievable complexity, between the red and the black, the white and the black, for amusement. Played by one part of an organism against another part, to while away an instant of eternity. There are vaster games, played between galaxies. Not with man.

"Man is a parasite peculiar to Earth, which tolerates his presence for a little while. He exists nowhere else in the cosmos, and he does not exist here for long. A little while, a few chessboard wars, which he thinks he fights himself— You begin to understand."

The man at the desk smiled.

"You want to know of yourself. Nothing is less important. A move was made, before Lodi. The opportunity was there for a move of the red; a stronger, more ruthless personality was needed; it was a turning point in history—which means in the game. Do you understand now? A pinch-hitter was put in to become Emperor."

He managed two words. "And then?"

"The Brightly Shining does not kill. You had to be put somewhere, some time. Long later a man named George Vine was killed in an accident; his body was still usable. George Vine had not been insane, but he had had a Napoleonic complex. The transference was amusing."

"No doubt." Again it was impossible to reach the man at the desk. The hatred itself was a wall between them. "Then George Vine is dead?"

"Yes. And you, because you knew a little too much, must go mad so that you will know nothing. Knowing the truth will drive you mad."

"No!"

The instrument smiled.

8

The room, the cube of light, dimmed; it seemed to tilt.

Still standing, he was going over backward, his position becoming horizontal instead of vertical.

His weight was on his back and under him was the soft-hard smoothness of his bunk, the roughness of a gray sheet blanket. And he could move; he sat up.

Had he been dreaming? Had he really been outside the asylum? He held up his hands, touched one to the other, and they were wet with something sticky. So was the front of his shirt and the thighs and knees of his trousers.

And his shoes were on.

The blood was there from climbing the wall. And now the analgesia was leaving, and pain was beginning to come into his hands, his chest, his stomach and his legs. Sharp biting pain.

He said aloud, *"I am not mad. I am not mad."* Was he screaming it?

A voice said, "No. Not yet." Was it the voice that had been here in the room before? Or was it the voice of the man who had stood in the lighted room? Or had both been the same voice?

It said, "Ask, 'What is man?'"

Mechanically, he asked it.

"Man is a blind alley evolution, who came too late to compete, who has always been controlled and played with by The Brightly Shining, which was old and wise before man walked erect.

"Man is a parasite upon a planet populated before he came, populated by a Being that is one and many, a billion cells but a single mind, a single intelligence, a single will—as is true of every other populated planet in the universe.

"Man is a joke, a clown, a parasite. He is nothing; he will be less."

"Come and go mad."

He was getting out of bed again; he was walking. Through the doorway of the cubicle, along the ward. To the door that led to the corridor; a thin crack of

155

light showed under it. But this time his hand did not reach out for the knob. Instead he stood there facing the closed door, and it began to glow; slowly it became light and visible.

As though from somewhere an invisible spotlight played upon it, the door became a visible rectangle in the surrounding blackness; as brightly visible as the crack under it.

The voice said, "You see before you a cell of your ruler, a cell unintelligent in itself, yet a tiny part of a unit which is intelligent, one of a million units which make up *the* intelligence which rules the earth—and you. And which earth-wide intelligence is one of a million intelligences which rules the universe."

"The *door*? I don't—"

The voice spoke no more; it had withdrawn, but somehow inside his mind was the echo of silent laughter.

He leaned closer and saw what he was meant to see. An ant was crawling up the door.

His eyes followed it, and numbering horror crawled apace, up his spine. A hundred things that had been told and shown him suddenly fitted into a pattern, a pattern of sheer horror. The black, the white, the red; the black ants, the white ants, the red ants; the players with men, separate lobes of a single group brain, the intelligence that was one. Man an accident, a parasite, a pawn; a million planets in the universe inhabited each by an insect race that was a single intelligence for the planet—and all the intelligences together were the single cosmic intelligence that was—*God!*

The one-syllable word wouldn't come.

He went mad, instead.

He beat upon the now-dark door with his bloody hands, with his knees, his face, with himself, although already he had forgotten why, had forgotten what he wanted to crush.

He was raving mad—dementia praecox, not paranoia

—when they released his body by putting it in a strait jacket, released it from frenzy to quietude.

He was quietly mad—paranoia, not dementia praecox—when they released him as sane eleven months later.

Paranoia, you see, is a peculiar affliction; it has no physical symptoms, it is merely the presence of a fixed delusion. A series of metrazol shocks had cleared up the dementia praecox and left only the fixed delusion that he was George Vine, a reporter.

The asylum authorities thought he was, too, so the delusion was not recognized as such and they released him and gave him a certificate to prove he was sane.

He married Clare; he still works at the *Blade*—for a man named Candler. He still plays chess with his cousin, Charlie Doerr. He still sees—for periodic checkups—both Dr. Irving and Dr. Randolph.

Which of them smiles inwardly? What good would it do you to know? Yes it was, is, one of those four.

It doesn't matter. Don't you understand? Nothing matters!

THE SURVIVOR

By H. P. Lovecraft and August Derleth

"Certain houses, like certain persons, manage somehow to proclaim at once their character for evil.
Perhaps it is the aroma of evil deeds committed under a particular roof, long after the actual doers have
passed away, that makes the gooseflesh come and the
hair rise. Something of the original passion of the
evil-doer, and of the horror felt by his victim, enters
the heart of the innocent watcher, and he becomes
suddenly conscious of tingling nerves, creeping skin,
and a chilling of the blood . . ."

—ALGERNON BLACKWOOD

I had never intended to speak or write again of the
Charriere house, once I had fled Providence on that
shocking night of discovery—there are memories which
every man would seek to suppress, to disbelieve, to
wipe out of existence—but I am forced to set down
now the narrative of my brief acquaintance with the
house on Benefit Street, and my precipitate flight there-
from, lest some innocent person be subjected to in-
dignity by the police in an effort to explain the horrible
discovery the police have made at last—that same
ghastly horror it was my lot to look upon before any

158

other human eye—and what I saw was surely far more terrible than what remained to be seen after all these years, the house having reverted to the city, as I had known it would.

While it is true that an antiquarian might be expected to know considerably less about some ancient avenues of human research than about old houses, it is surely conceivable that one who is steeped in the processes of research among the habitations of the human race might occasionally encounter a more abstruse mystery than the date of an ell or the source of a gambrel roof and find it possible to come to certain conclusions about it, no matter how incredible, how horrible or frightening or even—yes, damnable! In those quarters where antiquarians gather, the name of Alijah Atwood is not entirely unknown; modesty forbids me to say more, but it is surely permissible to point out that anyone sufficiently interested to look up references will find more than a few paragraphs about me in those directories devoted to information for the antiquary.

I came to Providence, Rhode Island, in 1930, intending to make only a brief visit and then to go on to New Orleans. But I saw the Charriere house on Benefit Street, and was drawn to it as only an antiquarian would be drawn to any unusual house isolated in a New England street of a period not its own, a house clearly of some age, and with an indefinable aura that both attracted and repelled.

What was said about the Charriere house—that it was haunted—was no more than what was said about many an old, abandoned dwelling in the old world as well as in the new, and even, if I can depend on the solemn articles in the *Journal of American Folklore,* about the primitive dwellings of American Indians, Australian bush-people, the Polynesians, and many others. Of ghosts I do not wish to write; suffice it to say that there have been within the circle of my experience

159

certain manifestations which have lent themselves to no scientific explanation, though I am rational enough to believe that there is such explanation to be found, once man chances upon the proper interpretation through the correct scientific approach.

In that sense, surely the Charriere house was not haunted. No spectre passed among its rooms rattling its chain, no voice moaned at midnight, no sepulchral figure appeared at the witching hour to warn of approaching doom. But that there was an aura about the house—one of evil? of terror? of hideous, eldritch things?—none could deny; and had I been born a less insensitive clod, I have no doubt that the house would have driven me forth raving out of mind. Its aura was less tangible than others I have known, but it suggested that the house concealed unspeakable secrets, long hidden from human perception. Above all else, it conveyed an overpowering sense of age—of centuries not alone of its own being, but far, far in the past, when the world was young, which was curious indeed, for the house, however old, was less than three centuries of age.

I saw it first as an antiquarian, delighted to discover set in a row of staid New England houses a house which was manifestly of a seventeenth-century Quebec style, and thus so different from its neighbors as to attract immediately the eye of any passerby. I had made many visits to Quebec, as well as to other old cities of the North American continent, but on this first visit to Providence, I had not come primarily in search of ancient dwellings, but to call upon a fellow antiquarian of note, and it was on my way to his home on Barnes Street that I passed the Charriere house, observed that it was not tenanted, and resolved to lease it for my own. Even so, I might not have done so, had it not been for the curious reluctance of my friend to speak of the house, and, indeed, his seeming unwillingness that I go near the place. Perhaps I do him an injustice in retrospect, for he, poor fellow, was even then on his death-bed, though neither of us knew it; so it was at his bed-side I sat, and not in his study, and it was there that I asked about the house, describing it unmistakably, for, of course, I did not then know its name or anything about it.

A man named Charriere had owned it—a French surgeon, who had come down from Quebec. But who had built it, Gamwell did not know; it was Charriere he had known. "A tall, rough-skinned man—I saw little of him, but no one saw more. He had retired from practice," said Gamwell. He had lived there—and pre-sumably older members of his family, though Gamwell could not say as to this—for as long as Gamwell had known the house. Dr. Charriere had lived a reclusive life, and had died, according to notice duly published in the Providence *Journal,* in 1927, three years ago. Indeed, the date of Dr. Charriere's death was the only date that Gamwell could give me; all else was shrouded in vagueness. The house had not been rented more than once; there had been a brief occupation by a profession-al man and his family, but they had left it after a month, complaining of its dampness and the smells of the old house; since then it had stood empty, but it could not be torn down, for Dr. Charriere had left in his will a considerable sum of money to keep the property off the tax-delinquent list for a long enough time—some said twenty years—to guarantee that the house would be standing there if and when heirs of the surgeon ap-peared to lay claim to it, the doctor having written vaguely of a nephew in French Indo-China, on military service. All attempts to find the nephew had proved futile, and now the house was being permitted to stand until the period specified in the will of Dr. Charriere had expired.

"I think of leasing it," I told Gamwell.

Ill though he was, my fellow antiquarian raised him-self up on one elbow in protest. "A passing whim, Atwood—let it pass. I have heard disquieting things of the house."

"What things?" I asked him bluntly.

But of these things he would not speak; he only shook his head feebly and closed his eyes.

"I hope to examine it tomorrow," I went on.

"It offers nothing you could not find in Quebec, believe me," said Gamwell.

But, as I have set forth, his curious opposition served only to augment my desire to examine the house at close range. I did not mean to spend a lifetime there, but only to lease it for a half year or so, and make it a base of operations, while I went about the countryside around the city as well as the lanes and byways of Providence in search of the antiquities of that region. Gamwell did surrender at last the name of the firm of lawyers in whose hands the Charriere will had been placed, and when I made application to them, and overcame their own lack of enthusiasm, I became master of the old Charriere house for a period of not more than six months, and less, if I so chose.

I took possession of the house at once, though I was somewhat nonplussed to discover that, while running water had been put in, electricity had not. I found among the furnishings of the house—these had been left in each room, exactly as at the death of Dr. Charriere—a half dozen lamps of various shapes and ages, some of them apparently dating back a century or more, with which to light my way. I had expected to find the house cobwebbed and dusty, but I was surprised to learn that this was not the case, though I had not understood that the lawyers—the firm of Baker & Greenbaugh—had undertaken to care for the house during the half century it was to stand, short of someone's appearing to lay claim to it as the sole survivor of Dr. Charriere and his line.

The house was all I had hoped for. It was heavily timbered, and in some of the rooms paper had begun

162

to peel from the plaster, while in others the plaster itself had never been covered with paper, and shone yellow with age on the wall. Its rooms were irregular—appearing to be either quite large or very small. It was of two storeys, but the upper floor had not been much used. The lower or ground floor, however, abounded in evidence of its one-time occupant, the surgeon, for one room of it had manifestly served him as a laboratory of some kind, and an adjoining room as a study, for both had the look of having been but recently abandoned in the midst of some inquiry or research, quite as if the occupation of the house by its brief tenant—*post-mortem* Charriere—had not touched upon these rooms. And perhaps it had not, for the house was large enough to permit of habitation without disturbing them, both laboratory and study being at the back of the house, opening out upon a garden, now much overgrown with shrubs and trees, a garden of some size, since the house occupied a frontage of over three lots in width, and in depth reached to a high stone wall which was but a lot removed from the street in its rear.

Dr. Charriere had evidently been in the midst of some work when his hour had struck, and I confess its nature intrigued me at once, for it was plainly no ordinary one. The inquiry was not alone a study of man, for there were strange, almost cabalistic drawings, resembling physiological charts, of various kinds of saurians, though the most prominent among them were of the order *Loricata* and the genera *Crocodylus* and *Osteolaemus*, though there were also recognizable drawings of *Gavialis, Tomistoma, Gaiman,* and *Alligator,* with a lesser number being speculative sketches of earlier members of this reptilian order reaching back to the Jurassic period. Yet even this facinating glimpse of the surgeon's odd vein of inquiry would not have stimulated any really genuine delving into his affairs had it not been for the antiquarian mystery of the house.

The Charriere house impressed me at once as having

been the product of its age, save for the later introduction of waterworks. I had all along assumed that
Dr. Charriere himself had built it; Gamwell had nowhere in our somewhat elliptical conversation given me
to understand otherwise; nor had he, for that matter,
mentioned the surgeon's age at his death. Presuming
it to be a well-rounded eighty years, then it was certainly not he who had built the house, for internal evidence spoke clearly of its origin in the vicinity of the
year 1700!—or over two centuries before Dr. Charriere's death. It seemed to me, therefore, that the house
only bore the name of its most recent long-time tenant,
and not that of its builder; it was the pursuit of this
problem which brought me to several disturbing facts
which bore no relationship, seemingly, to credible facts.

For one thing, the year of Dr. Charriere's birth was
nowhere in evidence. I sought out his grave—it was,
strangely, on his own property; he had obtained permission to be buried in his garden, not far from a
gracious old well which stood, roofed over, with bucket
and all still as it had stood, doubtless, for almost as
long as the house had been standing—with a view to
examine its headstone for the date of his birth, but, to
my disappointment and chagrin, his stone bore only
his name—Jean-François Charriere—his calling: Surgeon—his places of residence of professional occupation—Bayonne: Paris: Pondicherry: Quebec: Providence—and the year of his death: 1927. No more. This
was enough only to further me on my quest, and forthwith I started to make inquiry by letter of acquaintances in various places where research might be done.

Within a fortnight, the results of my inquiries were
at hand. But, far from being in any way satisfied, I was
more perplexed than ever. I had made my first inquiry
of a correspondent in Bayonne, presuming that, since
this was first mentioned on the stone, Charriere might
have been born in that vicinity. I had next inquired in
Paris, then of a friend in London, who might have

access to information in British archives pertaining to India, and then in Quebec. What did I glean from all this correspondence but a riddling sequence of dates? A Jean-François Charriere had indeed been born in Bayonne—but in the year *1636!* The name was not unknown in Paris, either, for a seventeen-year-old lad of that name had studied under the Royalist exile, Richard Wiseman, in 1653 and for three years thereafter. At Pondicherry—and later, too, on the Coromandel Coast of India—one Dr. Jean-François Charriere, surgeon in the French army, had been on duty from 1674 onward. And in Quebec, the earliest record of Dr. Charriere was in 1691; he had practiced in that city for six years, and had then left the city for an unknown destination.

I was left, patently, with but one conclusion: that the said Dr. Jean-François Charriere, born in Bayonne, 1636, last known to have been in Quebec the very year of the erection of the Charriere house on Benefit Street, was a forebear of the same name as the late surgeon who had last occupied the house. But if so, there was an absolute lacuna between that time in 1697 and the lifetime of the last occupant of the house, for there was nowhere any account of the family of that earlier Jean-Françoise Charriere; if there had been a Madame Charriere, if there had been children—as assuredly there must have been for the line to continue to the present century—there was no record of them. It was not impossible that the elderly gentleman who had come down from Quebec might have been of single status upon his arrival in Providence, and might have married thereafter. He would then have been sixty-one years of age. Yet a search of the appropriate registry failed to reveal any record of such a marriage, and I was left more bewildered than ever, though, as an antiquarian, I was fully aware of the difficulties of discovering facts and I was not at that time too discouraged to continue my inquiries.

I took a new line, and approached the firm of Baker & Greenbaugh for information about the late Dr. Charriere. Here an even more curious rebuff awaited me, for when I inquired about the appearance of the French surgeon, both the lawyers were forced to admit that they had never laid eyes on him. All their instructions had come by letter, together with cheques of generous figures; they had acted for Dr. Charriere approximately six years before his death, and thereafter; before that time, they had not been retained by Dr. Charriere.

I inquired then about his "nephew," since the existence of a nephew implied, at least, that there had at one time been a sister or brother to Charriere. But here, too, I was rebuffed; Gamwell had misinformed me, for Charriere had not specifically identified him as a nephew, but only as "the sole male survivor of my line"; this survivor had only been presumed to have been a nephew, and all search for him had come to naught, though there was that in Dr. Charriere's will which implied that the said "sole male survivor" would not need to be sought, but would make application to the firm of Baker & Greenbaugh either in person or by letter in such terms as to be unmistakable. Mystery there was, certainly; the lawyers did not deny it, but it was understood, also, that they had been well rewarded for their trust, too well to permit of any betrayal of it save in such casual terms as they had related to me. After all, as one of the lawyers sensibly pointed out, only three years had elapsed since the death of Dr. Charriere, and there was still ample time for the survivor to present himself.

Failing in this line of inquiry, I again called on my old friend, Gamwell, who was still abed, and now noticeably weaker. His attending physician, whom I encountered on the way out, now for the first time intimated that old Gamwell might not rise again, and cautioned me not to excite him, or to tire him with too many questions. Nevertheless, I was determined to

166

ferret out what I could about Charriere, though I was not entirely prepared for the keen scrutiny to which I was subjected by Gamwell, quite as if he had expected that less than three weeks' residence in the Charriere house should have altered my very appearance.

After the amenities had been exchanged, I turned to the subject about which I had come; explaining that I had found the house so interesting, I desired to know more of its late tenant. Gamwell had mentioned seeing him.

"But that was years ago," said Gamwell. "He's been dead three years. Let me see—1907, I think."

I was astounded. "But that was twenty years before he died!" I protested.

Nevertheless, Gamwell insisted, that was the year.

And how had he looked? I pressed the question upon him.

Disappointingly, senility and illness had encroached upon the old man's once fine mind.

"Take a newt, grow him a little, teach him to walk on his hind legs, and dress him in elegant clothes," Gamwell said. "I give you Dr. François Charriere. Except that his skin was rough, almost horny. A cold man. He lived in another world."

"How old was he?" I asked then. "Eighty?"

"Eighty?" He was contemplative. "When I first saw him—I was but twenty, then—he looked no older. And twenty years ago—my good Atwood—he had not changed a jot. He seemed eighty the first time. Was it the perspective of my youth? Perhaps. He seemed eighty in 1907. And died twenty years later."

"A hundred, then."

"It might well have been."

But Gamwell, too, was dissatisfying. Once again there was nothing definite, nothing concrete, no single fact—only an impression, a memory, of someone, I felt, Gamwell had disliked for no reason he could name.

Perhaps some professional jealousy he did not care to name biased his judgment.

I next sought the neighbors, but I found them for the most part younger people who had little memory of Dr. Charriere, except as someone whom they wished elsewhere, for he had an abominable traffic in lizards and the like, and none knew what diabolic experiments he performed in his laboratory. Only one among them was of advanced age; this was an old woman, a Mrs. Hepzibah Cobbett, who lived in a little two-storey house directly behind the Charriere garden wall, and I found her much enfeebled, in a wheel chair, guarded over by her daughter, a hawk-nosed woman whose cold blue eyes looked at me askance from behind her pince-nez. Yet the old woman spoke, starting to life at mention of Dr. Charriere's name, realizing that I lived in the house.

"Ye'll not live there long, mark my words. It's a devil's house," she said with some spirit that degenerated rapidly into a senile cackling. "Many's the time I've laid eyes on him. A tall man, bent like a sickle, with a wee tuft of beard like a goat's whisker on his chin. And what was it that crawled about at his feet I could not see? A long, black thing, too big for a snake —though 'twas snakes I thought of every time I set eyes on Dr. Charriere. And what was it screamed that night? And what barked at the wall?—a fox, indeed, I know a fox and a dog too. Like the yawping of a seal. I've seen things, I tell ye, but nobody'll believe a poor old woman with one foot in her grave. And ye—ye won't either, for none does."

What was I to make of this? Perhaps the daughter was right when she said, as she showed me out, "You must overlook mother's ramblings. She has an arteriosclerotic condition which occasionally makes her sound quite weak-minded." But I did not think old Mrs. Cobbett weak-minded, for her eyes snapped and sparkled when she talked, quite as if she were enjoying a secret joke of proportions so vast that its very outlines escaped

168

her keeper, the grim daughter who hovered ever near.

Disappointment seemed to await me at every turn. All avenues of information yielded little more together than any one had yielded. Newspaper files, library, records—all that was to be found was the date of the erection of the house: 1697, and the date of the death of Dr. Jean-François Charriere. If any other Charriere had died in the city's history, there was no mention of him. It was inconceivable that death had stricken all the other members of the Charriere family, predeceasing the late tenant of the house on Benefit Street, away from Providence, and yet it must have been so, for there was no other feasible explanation.

Yet there was one additional fact—a likeness of Dr. Charriere which I discovered in the house; though no name was appended to it where it hung in a remote and almost inaccessible corner of an upstairs room, the initials J.F.C. identified it beyond reasonable doubt. It was the likeness of a thin-faced ascetic, wearing a straggly goatee; his face was distinguished by high cheekbones, sunken cheeks, and dark, blazing eyes. His aspect was gaunt and sepulchral.

Thus, in the absence of other avenues of information, I was driven once again to the papers and books left in Dr. Charriere's study and laboratory. Hitherto, I had been much away from the house, in the pursuit of my inquiry into Dr. Charriere's background; but now I was as much confined to the house as I had previously been away from it. Perhaps it was because of this confinement that I began to grow more keenly aware of the aura of the house—both in a psychic and a physical sense. That unhappy professional man and his family who had remained here but a month and then left because of the smells abounding had perhaps conditioned me to *smell* the house, and now, for the first time, I did indeed become sharply cognizant of various aromas and musks, some of them typical of old houses, but others completely alien to me. The dominant one, however, was identifiable; it was a musk I had encountered several times before—in zoos, swamps, along stagnant pools—almost a miasma which suggested most strongly the presence of reptiles. It was not impossible that reptiles had found their way through the city to the haven of the garden behind the Charriere house, but it was incredible that they should have persisted in such numbers as to taint the very air of the place. Yet, seek as I might, I could find no source of this reptilian musk, inside or out, though I fancied once that it emanated from the well, which was doubtless a result of an allusory conviction.

The musk persisted, and it was especially strong whenever rain fell, or fog formed, or dew lay on the grass, as might have been expected, moisture heightening all odors. The house was moist, too; its short-lived tenantry had been explained in part by this, and in this, certainly, the renter had not been in error. I found it often unpleasant, but not disturbing—not half so disturbing as other aspects of the house.

Indeed, it was as if my invasion of the study and laboratory had stirred the old house to protest, for certain hallucinations began to occur with annoying regularity. There was, for one, the curious barking sound which seemed to emanate from the garden late at night. And, for another, the illusion that an oddly bent, reptilian figure haunted the darkness of the garden outside the study windows. These and other illusions persisted—and I, in turn, persisted in looking upon them as hallucinatory—until that fateful night when, after hearing a distinct sound as of someone bathing in the garden, I woke from my sleep convinced that I was not alone in the house, and, putting on my dressing-robe and slippers, I lit a lamp and hurried to the study.

What I saw there must certainly have been inspired by the nature of my inquiry into the late Dr. Charriere's papers; that it was a figment of a nightmare, I could not doubt at the moment, though I caught but a faint

170

glimpse of the invader; for there was an invader in the study, and he made off with certain papers belonging to the Charriere estate, but as I saw him in the brief glimpse I had of him in the wan yellow light of the lamp held overhead and partially blinding me he seemed to glisten, he shone blackly, and he seemed to be wearing a skin-tight suit of some rough, black material. I saw him for only an instant, before he leapt through the open window into the darkness of the garden; I would have followed then, had it not been for the disquieting things I saw in the light of the lamp.

Where the invader had stood there were the irregular marks of feet—of wet feet—and more, of feet which were oddly broad, the toes of which were so long-nailed as to leave the marks of those nails before each toe; and where he had bent above the papers there was the same wetness; and over all there hung the powerful reptilian musk I had begun to accept as an integral part of the house, so powerful, indeed, that I almost reeled and fainted.

But my interest in the papers transcended fear or curiosity. At that time, the only rational explanation which occurred to me was that one of the neighbors, who had some animus against the Charriere house and were constantly agitating to have it torn down, must have come from swimming to invade the study. Farfetched, yes, certainly. But could any other explanation readily account for what I saw? I am inclined to think not.

As for the papers, certain of them were undeniably gone. Fortunately, these were the very ones I had finished with; I had put them into a neat pile, though many were not consecutive. I could not imagine why anyone would have wanted to take them, unless someone other than myself were interested in Dr. Charrriere, perhaps with a view to laying claim to the house and property; for these papers were painstaking notes about the longevity of crocodiles and alligators, as well as of

171

related reptiles. It had already begun to be plainly evident to me that the late doctor had been studying reptilian longevity with almost obsessive devotion, and with a view, clearly, to learning how man might lengthen his own life. If the secrets of reptilian longevity had been revealed to Dr. Charriere, there was nothing in his papers thus far to show that it had, though I had come upon two or three disquieting suggestions of "operations" performed—on whom was not set down—with a view to increasing the life span of the subject.

True, there was one variant vein of notes in what I assumed to be Dr. Charriere's handwriting, treated as a related subject, but, to me, one at variance from the more or less scientific inquiry into the long life of reptiles. This was a sequence of cryptic references to certain mythological creatures, particularly one named "Cthulhu," and another named "Dagon," who were evidently deities of the sea in some ancient mythology completely unknown to me; and suggestions of long-lived creatures (or people?) who served these ancient Gods, named the "Deep Ones," evidently amphibious creatures living in the depths of the seas. Among these notes were photographs of a singularly hideous monolithic statue, of a distinctly saurian cast of feature, labeled "E. coast Hivaoa Is., Marquesas. Object of worship?" and of a totem pole of the North-west Coast Indians of a disturbingly similar workmanship, also reptilian in aspect, this one being marked, "Kwakiutl Indian totem. Quatsino Sound. Sim. t. erected by Tlingit Inds." These curious notes existed as if to show that Dr. Charriere was not averse to examining rites of ancient sorceries and primitive religious beliefs in an effort to bring about some earnestly desired goal.

What that goal might be was soon evident enough. Dr. Charriere had not been interested in the study of longevity for its sake alone; no, he had also wished to prolong his own life. And there were certain upsetting hints in the writings he had left behind him to suggest that in part, at least, he had succeeded beyond his wildest dreams. This was a disturbing discovery to make because it recalled again the curious history of that first Jean-François Charriere, also a surgeon, about whose later years and death there was fully as much mystery as there was about the birth and early years of the late Dr. Jean-François Charriere, who died in Providence in 1927.

The events of that night, though not frightening me too badly, did result in my purchasing a powerful Luger pistol in a second-hand shop, as well as a new flashlight; the lamp had impeded me in the night, which a flashlight would not do in similar circumstances. If indeed I had a visitor from among the neighbors, I could be sure that the papers he had taken would no more than whet his appetite, and sooner or later he would return. Against that contingency I meant to be fully prepared, and if again I caught a marauder in the study of the house I had leased, I would not hesitate to shoot if my demand to stop where he was were not heeded. I hoped, however, that I would not have occasion to use the weapon in such a manner.

On the next night I resumed my study of Dr. Charriere's books and papers. The books had surely at one time belonged to his forebears, for many of them dated back through the centuries; among them was a book translated into the French from the English of R. Wiseman, testifying to some connection between the Dr. Jean-François Charriere who had studied in Paris under Wiseman, and that other surgeon of similar name who had, until recently, lived in Providence, Rhode Island.

They were en masse a singular hodge-podge of books. They seemed to be in every known language, from French to Arabic. Indeed, I could not hope to translate a majority of the titles, though I could read French and had some smattering of the other Romance languages. I had at that time no understanding of the

173

meaning of such a title as *Unaussprechlichen Kulten,* by von Junzt, though I suspected that it was akin to the Count d'Erlette's *Cules des Goules,* since it stood next to that book on the shelf. But then, books on zoological subjects stood beside weighty tomes about ancient cultures; they bore such titles as *An Inquiry Into the Relationship of the Peoples of Polynesia and the Indian Cultures of the South American Continent, with Special Reference to Peru; The Pnakotic Manuscripts, De Furtivis Literarum Notis,* by Giambattista Porta; Thicknesse's *Kryptographik;* the *Daemonolatreia* of Remigius; Banfort's *The Saurian Age;* a file of the Aylesbury, Massachusetts, *Transcript;* another of the Arkham, Massachusetts, *Gazette*—and the like. Some of these books were certainly of immense value, for many of them dated as far back as from 1670 to 1820, and, though all showed much wear from use, all were still in relatively good condition.

These books, however, meant comparatively little to me. In retrospect, I am constrained to believe that, had I examined them more attentively, I might have learned even more than I did; but there is a saying that too much knowledge of such matters men are better off without knowing is even more damning than too little. I soon gave over my examination of the books because I discovered, pressed in among them on the shelves, what seemed at first glance to be a diary or journal, but was, on closer examination, manifestly a notebook, for the entries dated too far back to have encompassed Dr. Charriere's span of years. Yet all were written in a crabbed, tiny script, which was most certainly the late surgeon's, and, despite the age of the first pages, all had been written by the same hand, suggesting that Dr. Charriere had set down these notes in a kind of rough chronology, very probably from some earlier draft. Nor were they jottings alone; some were illustrated with crude drawings which were nevertheless effective, as

174

are on many occasions the primitive paintings of un-
tutored artists.

Thus, upon the very first page of the hand-bound
manuscript, I came upon this entry. "1851. Arkham.
Aseph Goade, D.O." and with it a drawing, presumably
of the said Aseph Goade, emphasizing certain aspects
of his features, which were batrachian in essence, for
they were distinguished by an abnormally wide mouth,
with peculiar leathery lips, a very low brow, strangely
webbed eyes, and a generally squat physiognomy, giving them a distinctly and unmistakably froglike appearance. This drawing took up the majority of the page,
and the jotting accompanying it I assumed to be a nota-
tion of an encounter—evidently in research, for it could
hardly have been in the flesh—with a sub-human type
—(could the "D.O." have been a reference to the
"Deep Ones," mention of which I had previously encountered?), which, doubtless, Dr. Charriere looked
upon as a verification of the trend of his research, a
trend to support a belief he probably held that some
kinship with batrachia, and hence very probably also
saurians, could be traced.

To that end, too, there were other jottings. Most of
them were so vague—perhaps purposely so—as to
seem to me at that first examination of them virtually
meaningless. What was I to make of a page like this,
for instance?

"1857. St Augustine. Henry Bishop. Skin very scaly,
but not ichthyic. Said to be 107 years old. No dete-
riorative process. All senses still keen. Ancestry uncertain, but Polynesian trade in background.

"1861. Charleston. Balacz family. Crusted hands.
Double jaw construction. Entire family manifesting
similar stigmata. Anton 117 years old. Anna 109.
Unhappy away from water.

"1863. Innsmouth. Marsh, Waite, Eliot, Gilman families. Captain Obed Marsh a trader in Polynesia, married to a Polynesian woman. All bearing facial characteristics similar to Aseph Goade's. Much secretive living. Women seldom seen in streets, but at night much swimming—entire families, all the rest of the town keeping to their houses, swimming out to Devil Reef. Relationship to D.O. very marked. Considerable traffic between Innsmouth and Ponape. Some dark religious worship.

"1871. Jed Price, carnival entertainer. Billed as 'Alligator Man.' Appears in pool of alligators. Saurian look. Long lantern jaw. Said to have pointed teeth, but whether real or filed unable to determine."

This was the general tenor of the jottings in the book. Their range was continental—there were notes referring to Canada and Mexico as well as the eastern seaboard of North America. From then, Dr. Jean-François Charriere began to emerge as a man obsessed with a strange compulsion—to establish proof of the longevity of certain human beings seemingly bearing some kinship to saurian or batrachian ancestors.

Admittedly, the weight of the evidence gathered, could one have accepted it all as fact, rather than as wishfully colored accounts of people with some marked physical defect, seemed to lend to Dr. Charriere and his belief a strange and provocative corroboration. Yet the surgeon had not often gone beyond the realm of pure conjecture. What he sought seemed to be the connecting link among the various instances which had come to his notice. He had sought this link in three bodies of lore. The most familiar of these was the *Vodu* legendry of Negro culture. Next to it, in familiarity, stood the animal worship of ancient Egypt. Finally, and most important, according to the surgeon's notes, was a completely alien culture which was as old as earth, nay, older, involving ancient Elder Gods and their terrible, unceasing conflict with equally primeval Old Ones who bore such names as Cthulhu, Hastur, Yog-Sothoth, Shub-Niggurath, and Nyarlathotep, and who were served in turn by such curious beings as the Tcho-Tcho People, the Deep Ones, the Shantaks, the Abominable Snow Men, and others, some of whom appeared to have been a sub-order of human being, but others of which were either definite mutations or not human at all. All this fruit of Dr. Charriere's research was fascinating, but in no case had he adduced a definite, provable link. There were certain saurian references in the *Vodu* cult; there were similar connections to the religious culture of ancient Egypt; and there were many obscure and tantalizing suggestions connecting the saurians to the Cthulhu myth-pattern, ranging far deeper into the past than *Crocodylus* and *Gavialis,* embracing *Tyrannosaurus* and *Brontosaurus, Megalosaurus* and other Mesozoic reptilia.

In addition to these interesting notes, there were diagrams of what seemed to be very odd operations, the nature of which I did not fully comprehend at that time. These were apparently copied out of ancient texts, particularly one given frequently as source, entitled *De Vermis Myteriis,* by Ludvig Prinn, another of those obscure references completely foreign to me. The operations themselves suggested a *raison d'être* too astounding to accept on face; one of them, for instance, was designed to stretch the skin, consisting of many incisions made to "permit growth." Yet another was a simple cross-incision made at the base of the spine for the purpose of "extension of the tail-bone." What these fantastic diagrams suggested was too horrible to contemplate, yet it was part and parcel, surely, of the strange research conducted for so many years by Dr. Charriere, whose seclusion was thus readily explicable, since his was a project which could only be conducted

177

in secret lest it bring down upon him the scorn and laughter of his fellow scientists.

Among these papers there were also certain references set down in such a manner that I could not doubt they were the experiences of the narrator. Yet, for all that these antedated 1850, in some cases by decades, they were unmistakably in Dr. Charriere's handwriting, so that—excepting always the possibility that he had transcribed the experiences of someone else—it was evident that he was more than an octogenarian at the time of his death, indeed, far more, so much more that the very anticipation of it made me uneasy, and cast my thoughts back to that other Dr. Charriere who had gone before him.

The sum total of Dr. Charriere's credo amounted to a strongly hypothetical conviction that a human being could, by means of certain operations, together with other unusual practices of a macabre nature, take upon himself something of the longevity that characterized the sauria; that as much as a century and a half, perhaps even two centuries, could be added to a man's life span; and, beyond that, given a period of semiconscious torpor in some moist place, which would amount to a kind of gestation, the individual could emerge again, somewhat altered in aspect, true, to begin another lenthy span of life, which would, by virtue of the physiological *changes* which had taken place in him, be of necessity somewhat altered from his previous mode of existence. To support this conviction, Dr. Charriere had amassed only a number of legendary tales, certain data of a kindred nature, and highly speculative accounts of curious human mutations known to have existed in the past two hundred and ninety-one years— a figure which later assumed far more meaning, when I realized that this was the exact span of time from the year of the birth of that earlier Dr. Charriere to the date of the later surgeon's death. Nowhere in all this material was there anything resembling a concrete line of scientific research, with adducible proof—only hints, vague intimations, hideous suggestions—sufficient, in truth, to fill a casual reader with horrible doubts and terrible, half-formed convictions, but not nearly enough to warrant the sober interest of any genuine scholar.

How much farther I would have gone into Dr. Charriere's research, I do not know.

Had it not been for the occurrence of *that* which sent me screaming in horror from that house on Benefit Street, it was possible that I would have gone much farther instead of leaving house and contents to be claimed by a survivor who, I know now, will never come, thus leaving the house to fall to its ultimate destruction by the city.

It was while I was contemplating these "findings" of Dr. Charriere that I became aware of being under scrutiny, that manifestation people are fond of calling the "sixth sense." Unwilling to turn, I did the next best thing; I opened my pocket-watch, set it up before me, and used the inside of the highly polished case as a kind of mirror to reflect the windows behind me. And there I saw, dimly reflected, a horrible travesty of a human face, which so startled me that I turned to view for myself that which I had seen mirrored. But there was nothing at the pane, save the shadow of movement. I rose, put out the light, and hastened to the window. Did I then see a tall, curiously bent figure, crouched and shuffling in an awkward gait into the darkness of the garden? I believed that I did, but I was not given to folly enough to venture out in pursuit. Whoever it was would come again, even as he had come the previous night.

Accordingly, I settled back to watch, a score of possible explanations crowding upon my mind. As the source of my nocturnal visitor, I confess I put at the head of the list the neighbors who had long opposed the continued standing of the house of Dr. Charriere. It was possible that they meant to frighten me away,

179

unaware of the shortness of my lease; it was also possible that there was something in the study they wanted, though this was far-fetched, in view of the time they had had to search the house during its long period of unoccupancy. Certainly the truth of the matter never once occurred to me; I am not by nature any more skeptical than an antiquarian might be expected to be; but the true identity of my visitor did not, I confess, suggest itself to me despite all the curious interlocking circumstances which might have conveyed a greater meaning to a less scientific mind than my own.

As I sat there in the dark, I was more than ever impressed with the aura of the old house. The very darkness seemed alive, but incredibly remote from the life of Providence which swirled all around it. The interior darkness was filled instead with the psychic residue of years—the persistent smell of moisture, accompanied by that musk so commonly associated with reptilian quarters at the zoo; the smell of old wood, old limestone, of which the cellar walls were composed, the odor of decay, for the centuries had begun to deteriorate both wood and stone. And there was something more—the vaporous hint of an animal presence, which seemed indeed to grow stronger with every passing moment.

I sat there well over an hour, before I heard any untoward sound.

Then it was indistinguishable. At first I thought it a bark, akin to that sound made by alligators; but then I thought it rather less a figment of my perfervid imagination than the actual sound of a door closing. Yet it was some time before another sound smote upon my ears—a rustling of papers. Astonishing as it was, an intruder had actually found his way into the study before my very eyes without being seen! I turned on the flashlight, which was directed at the desk I had left.

What I saw was incredible, horrible. It was not a man who stood there, but a travesty of a man. I know that for one cataclysmic moment I thought consciousness would leave me; but a sense of urgency coupled with an awareness of acute danger swept over me, and without a moment's hesitation, I fired four times, at such a range that I knew each shot had found harbor in the body of the bestial thing that leaned over Dr. Charriere's desk in that darkened study.

Of what followed I have, mercifully, only the vaguest memory. A wild thrashing about—the escape of the invader—my own uncertain pursuit. I had struck him, certainly, for a trail of blood led from the study to the windows through which he had gone, tearing away glass and frame in one. Outside, the light of my flash gleamed on the drops of blood, so that I had no difficulty following them. Even without this to follow, the strong musk pervading the night air would have enabled me to trace whoever had gone ahead.

I was led—not away from the house—but deeper into the garden, straight to the curb of the well behind the house. And over the curb *into the well,* where I saw for the first time in the glow of the flashlight the cunningly fashioned steps which led down into that dark maw. So great was the discharge of blood at the well-curb, that I was confident I had mortally wounded the intruder. It was that confidence which impelled me to follow, despite the manifest danger.

Would that I had turned at the well-curb and gone away from that accursed place! For I followed down the rungs of the ladder set into the well-wall—not to the water below, as I had first thought I might be led— but to an aperture opening into a tunnel in the well-wall, leading even deeper into the garden. Compelled now by a burning desire to know the nature of my victim, I pushed into this tunnel, unmindful of the damp earth which stained my clothes, with my light thrust before me, and my weapon in instant readiness. Up ahead I could see a kind of hollowed out cavern—not any larger than enough to permit a man to kneel upright—and in the center of my flashlight glow stood a casket, at sight of which I hesitated momentarily, for I recognized the direction of the tunnel away from the well led toward the grave of Dr. Charriere.

But I had come too far to retreat.

The smell in this narrow opening was almost indescribable. Pervading every part of the tunnel was the nauseatingly strong musk of reptiles; indeed, it lay so thickly in the air that I had to force myself to press on toward the casket. I came up to it and saw that it lay uncovered. The trail of blood led to the edge of the casket and into it. Impelled by burning curiosity and a half-formed fear of what I might find, I rose to my knees and forced the light tremblingly into the casket.

. . .

It may well be charged that after so many years my memory is no longer to be relied upon. But what I saw there was imprinted indelibly on my memory. For there in the glow of my light, lay a newly-dead being, the implications of whose existence overwhelmed me with horror. This was the thing I had killed. Half-man, half-saurian, it was a ghastly travesty upon what had once been a human being. Its clothes were split and torn by the horrible mutations of the flesh, by the crusted skin which had burst its bonds, its hands and unshod feet were flat, powerful in appearance, claw-like. I gazed in speechless terror at the shuddersome tail-like appendage which pushed bluntly out from the base of the spine, at the terribly elongated, crocodilian jaw, to which still grew a tuft of hair, like a goat's beard. . . .

All this I saw before a merciful unconsciousness overcame me,—*for I had seen enough to recognize what lay in that coffin—him who had lain there in a cataleptic torpor since 1927, waiting his turn to come back in frightfully altered form to live again—Dr. Jean-François Charriere, surgeon, born in Bayonne in 1636, "died" in Providence in 1927—and I knew that the survivor of whom he had written in his will was none other than himself, born again, renewed by a hellish knowledge of long-forgotten, eldritch rites more ancient than mankind, as old as that early vernal earth on which great beasts fought and tore!*

THE ANCESTOR

By H. P. Lovecraft and August Derleth

1

When my cousin, Ambrose Perry, retired from the active practice of medicine, he was still a comparatively young man, ruddy and vigorous and in his fifties. He had had a very lucrative practice in Boston, and, though he was fond of his work, he was somewhat more given to the development of certain of his theories, which—and he was an individualist in this—he did not inflict upon his colleagues, whom, truth to tell, he was inclined to look down upon as too bound by the most orthodox methods, and too timid to venture forth upon experiments of their own without the sanction of the American Medical Association. He was a cosmopolitan in every sense of the word, for he had studied extensively in Europe—in Vienna, at the Sorbonne, at Heidelberg—and he had traveled widely, but for all that he was content to lose himself in wild country in Vermont, when at last he chose retirement to climax his brilliant career.

He went into virtual seclusion at his home, which he had built in the middle of a dense wood, and outfitted with as complete a laboratory as money could buy. No one heard from him, and for three years not a word of his activities reached the public prints or the private correspondence of his relatives and friends. It was thus with considerable surprise that I received a letter from him—I found it waiting on my return from a sojourn in Europe—asking me to come and spend some time with him, if possible. I replied regretfully that I had now to set about finding a position for myself, and expressed my pleasure at hearing from him and the hope that some day I might be able to avail myself of his invitation, which was as kind as it was unexpected. His answer came by return mail, offering me a handsome emolument if I would accept the position of secretary —by which, I was certain, he meant me to do everything about the house as well as take notes.

Perhaps my motivation was as much curiosity as the attractiveness of the remuneration, which was generous; I accepted as quickly, almost fearful lest he withdraw his offer, and within a week I presented myself at my cousin's rambling house, built in the Pennsylvania Dutch farm manner, though of but one storey with sharply pointed gables and deeply pitched roofs. I had had some difficulty finding it, even after receiving my cousin's explicit instructions, for he was at least ten miles from the nearest village, which was a hamlet called Tyburn, and his house was set so far back from the little-traveled road, and had so slight a lane leading up to it, that I was constrained to believe for some time that I had traveled past it in my eagerness to arrive at the hour I had promised.

An alert German shepherd dog guarded the premises, but, though he was chained, he was not at all vicious, for apart from watching me intently, he neither growled nor made any move in my direction when I went up to the door and rang the bell. My cousin's appearance, however, shocked me, for he was thin and gaunt; the hale, ruddy man I had last seen almost four years ago had vanished, and in his place stood a mere travesty of his former self. His hearty vigor, too, seemed sadly diminished, though his handshake was firm and strong, and his eyes no less keen.

"Welcome, Henry," he cried at sight of me. "Even Ginger seems to have accepted you without so much as a bark."

At the mention of his name, the dog came bounding forward, as far as his long chain would reach, tail wagging.

"But come in. You can always put your car up later on."

I did as I was bidden and found the interior of his house very masculine, almost severe in its appointments. A meal was on the table, and I learned that, far from expecting me to do other than serve as his "secretary," my cousin had a cook and a handyman, who lived above his garage, and had no intention whatsoever that I should do more than take down such notes as he intended to give me, and to file the results of his experiments. For he was experimenting; he made so much clear at once, though he said nothing of the nature of his experiments, and all during our meal, in the course of which I met both Edward and Meta Reed, the couple who took care of the house and grounds, he asked only about myself, what I had been doing, what I hoped to do—at thirty, he reminded me, there was considerably less time to dawdle about deciding on one's future—and occasionally, though only as my own answers to his questions brought up their names, about other members of the family, who were, as always, widely scattered. Yet I felt that he asked about me only to satisfy the amenities of the situation, and without any real interest, though he did once hint that if only I could turn to medicine for a career, he might be persuaded to see me through college in pursuit of my degree. But all this, I felt sure, was only the superficiality, the politeness of the moment, representing those aspects of our first meeting in some years which were to be got over with at the earliest opportunity; there was, moreover, that in his manner which suggested a suppressed impatience at this subject he himself had initiated, an impatience with me for my preoccupation with his questions, and at himself for having so far yielded to the conventionalities of the situation as to have asked questions about matters in which he was plainly not interested at all.

The Reeds, man and wife, who were both in their sixties, were subdued. They made little conversation, not only because Mrs. Reed both cooked and served her dinner, but because they were plainly accustomed to carrying on an existence apart from their employer's, for all that they ate at his table. They were both greying, yet they managed to look far more youthful than Ambrose, and they showed none of the signs of the physical deterioration which had come upon my cousin. The meal went on with only the dialogue between Ambrose and myself to break the silence; the Reeds partook of the meal not in subservience, but with a mask of indifference, though I did notice, two or three times, that quick, sharp glances passed from one to the other of them at something my cousin said, but that was all.

It was not until we had retired to Ambrose's study that he touched upon the subject closest to his thoughts. My cousin's study adjoined his laboratory, which was at the rear of the house; the kitchen and large dining and living room combination came next, and the bedrooms, curiously, were at the front of the house; once in the cozy study, Ambrose relaxed, his voice filled with the tremor of excitement.

"You will never guess the direction my experiments have taken since I left practice, Henry," he began, "and I dare to wonder at my temerity in telling you. Were it not, indeed that I need someone to set down these amazing facts, I would not do so. But now that I am on the road to success, I must think of posterity. I have, in short, made successful efforts to recapture all my past, down to the most minute nooks and crannies of human memory, and I am now further convinced that, by the same methods, I can extend this perceptive process to *hereditary* memory and re-create the events of man's heredity. I see your expression—you doubt me."

"On the contrary, I am astounded at the possibilities in it," I answered, quite truthfully—though I failed to admit that a stab of alarm possessed me simultaneously.

"Ah, good, good! I sometimes think that, because of the means I must use to induce the state of mind necessary to this ceaseless probing of past time, I have gravely disappointed the Reeds, for they look upon all experimentation on human beings as fundamentally un-Christian and treading upon forbidden ground."

I wanted to ask what means he had reference to, but I knew that in good time he would tell me if he had a mind to; if he had not, no question of mine would bring the answer. And presently he came to it.

"I have found that a combination of drugs and music, at a time when the body is half-starved, induces the mood and makes it possible to cast back in time and sharpen all the faculties to such a degree that memory is regained. I can tell you, Henry, I have achieved the most singular and remarkable results; I have actually gone back to memory of the womb, incredible as it may seem."

He spoke with great intensity; his eyes shone, his voice trembled. Plainly, he was exhilarated beyond ordinary stimulation by his dreams of success. This had been one of his goals when he was still in practice; now he had used his considerable means to further his ambition to achieve success in this, and he seemed to have accomplished something. So much I was ready to admit, however cautiously, for his experiments explained his appearance—drugs and starvation could easily account for his gauntness, which was in fact a kind of emaciation—he had starved himself so frequently and so steadily that he had not only lost his excess weight but had reduced beyond the point of wisdom and health. Furthermore, as I sat listening to him, I could not help observing that he had all the aspects of fanaticism, and I knew that no demur I could offer would affect him in the slightest or bring about any deviation whatsoever in his direction. He had his eyes fixed on this strange goal, and he would permit nothing and no one to deflect him from it.

"But you will have the task of transcribing my shorthand notes, Henry," he went on, less intensely. "For, of course, I have kept them—some of them written in a trance-like state, quite as if I were possessed by some spirit guide, which is an absurdity, naturally. They range backward in time to just before my birth, and I am now engaged in probing ancestral memory. You shall see how far I have got when you have had time to examine and transcribe such data as I have set down."

With that, my cousin turned to other matters, and soon excused himself, vanishing into his laboratory.

2

It took me fully a fortnight to assimilate and copy Ambrose's notes, which were more extensive than he had led me to believe, and also disturbingly revelatory. I had already come to look upon Ambrose as extremely quixotic, but now I was convinced that a strong vein of aberration was manifest in his make-up as well, for the relentless driving of himself to achieve an end which was incapable of proof, for the most part, and promised no boon to mankind even if his goal were reached, seemed to me to border on irrational fanaticism. He was not interested so much for the information he might obtain in this incessant probing of memory as he was in the experiment for its sake alone, and what was most disturbing about it was the patent evidence that his experiment, which might at first have had only the proportions of a hobby, was becoming obsessive, to such an extent that all other matters were relegated to second place—not excluding his health.

At the same time, I was forced to admit that the material the notes contained was often deeply surprising. There was no question but that my cousin had found some way to tap the stream of memory; he had established beyond doubt that everything that happened to a human being was registered in some compartment of the brain, and that it needed but the proper bridge to its place of storage in memory to bring it to consciousness once more. By recourse to drugs and music, he had gone back into the past to such a degree that his notes, as finally put together, constituted an exact biography which was in no way complicated by the glossing over of wish-fulfillment dreams, the enchantment of distance, or the ego-gratifications which always play a part in adjustment of the individual personality to life's disappointments which have dealt blows to the ego.

My cousin's course so far was undeniably fascinating. For the immediately past years, his notes mentioned many people we knew in common; but soon the two decades between us began to become obvious and his memory concerned strangers to me and events in which I had no part, even indirectly. The notes were especially revealing in what they conveyed of my cousin's dominant thoughts during his youth and early manhood—in their cryptic references to the themes which were constantly uppermost in his thoughts.

"Argued vehemently with de Lesseps about the primal source. The chimpanzee linkage too recent. Primal fish?" So he wrote of his days at the Sorbonne. And, at Vienna—" 'Man did not always live in trees'— so says von Wiedersen. Agreed. Presumably he swam. What role, if any, did man's ancestors have in the age of the brontosaur?" Such notes as these, including many far more detailed, were interspersed with the daily record of his years, mingling with accounts of parties, romances, an adolescent duel, differences with his parents, and the like—all the assorted trivia of one man's life. This subject appeared to hold my cousin's interest with an astonishing consistency; his more recent years, of course, were filled with it, but it recurred all the way through his life from the age of nine onward, when on one occasion he had asked our grandfather to explain the family tree and demanded to know what was beyond the registered beginnings of the line.

There was, too, in these notes, certain evidence of how much he was taxing himself in this obsessive experiment, for his handwriting had undergone a marked decrease in legibility from the time he had first begun to chronicle his memories to the present; that is, as he went backward through time to his earliest years—and indeed, into the place of darkness which was the womb, for he had accomplished this return, if his notes were not a skillful fabrication—his script grew steadily more illegible, quite as if there were a change in degrees with the change in the age of his memories, which was as fantastic a concept as, I felt then, my cousin's belief that he could reach back into ancestral and hereditary memory, both involving the memory of his forebears for many generations, and presumably transmitted in the genes and chromosomes from which he had sprung.

To a very large extent, however, I suspended judgment while I was putting his notes in order, and there was no mention of the notes, except for the help I asked once or twice when I could not decipher a word in Ambrose's script. Read over, when at last it was completed, the transcript was impressive and cogent, and I handed it to my cousin at last with mixed feelings and not without some suspension of belief.

"Are you convinced?" he asked me.

"As far as you have gone, yes," I admitted.

"You shall see," he replied imperturbably.

I undertook to remonstrate with him about the diligence with which he pursued this dream of his. In the two weeks it had taken me to assimilate and copy his notes, he had plainly driven himself beyond the bounds of reason. He had taken so little food and had slept so little that he had grown noticeably thinner and more haggard than he had been on the day of my arrival. He had been secluded in his laboratory day and night, for long hours at a time; indeed, on many occasions in that fortnight there were but three of us at the table for meals—Ambrose had not come out of the laboratory. His hands had a tendency to tremble, and there was a hint of palsy too about his mouth, while his eyes burned with the fire of the fanatic, to whom all else but the goal of his fanaticism had ceased to exist.

The laboratory was out of bounds for me. Though my cousin had no objection to showing me about the extensive laboratory, he required the utmost solitude when he was conducting his experiments. Nor had he any intention of setting down exactly what drugs he had recourse to—though I had reason to believe that *Cannabis indica,* or Indian hemp, commonly known as hashish, was one of them—in the punishment he inflicted on his body in pursuit of his wild dream to recapture his ancestral and hereditary memory, a goal he sought daily and often nightly, as well, without surcease, so much so that I saw him with increasing rarity, though he sat for a long time with me on the night I finally gave him the transcript of his notes tracing the course of his life through his recaptured memory, going over each page with me, making certain small corrections and additions, striking out a few passages here and there, and, in general, improving the narrative as I had transcribed it. A retyping was obviously necessary, but what then, if I were not to attend him in the actual course of his experiments?

But my cousin had yet another sheaf of notes ready for me when the retyping was finished. And this time the notes were not of his own memories, but ranged back through time; they were the memories of his parents, his grandparents, of his forebears even before them—not specific, as were his own, but only general, yet enough to convey an amazing picture of the family before his own generation. They were memories of great cataclysms, of major events of history, of the earth in its youth; they were such re-creations of time past as I would have thought impossible for one man to set down. Yet here they were, undeniably, impressive and unforgettable, an accomplishment by any standard. I was convinced that they were a skillful fabrication, yet I dared not pass judgment on Ambrose, whose fanatical belief brooked no doubt. I copied them as carefully as I copied his earlier notes, and in but a few days I finished and handed the new transcript to him.

"You need not doubt me, Henry," he said, smiling grimly. "I see it in your eyes. What would I have to gain by making a false record? I am not prone to self-deception."

"I am not qualified to judge, Ambrose. Perhaps not even to believe or disbelieve."

"That is well enough put," agreed my cousin.

I pressed him to tell me what I must do next, but he suggested that I wait on his pleasure. I might take time to explore the woods or roam the fields on the far side of the road, until he had more work ready for me. I planned to take his suggestion and explore the adjoining woods, but this was never to be done, for other events intervened. That very night I was set in a different direction, providing a decided change from the routine of my cousin's increasingly difficult notes, for in the middle of the night Reed came to awaken me and tell me that Ambrose wanted me in his laboratory.

I dressed and went down at once.

I found Ambrose stretched out on an operating table, clad in the worn mouse-colored dressing-gown he usually wore. He was in a semi-conscious state, yet not so far gone that he failed to recognize me.

"Something's happened to my hands," he said with

193

effort. "I'm going under. Will you take down anything I may say?"

"What is it?" I asked.

"A temporary nerve block, perhaps. A muscular cramp. I don't know. They'll be all right tomorrow."

"All right," I said. "I'll take down anything you may say."

I took his pad and pencil and sat waiting.

The atmosphere of the laboratory, ill-lit with but one low red light near the operating table, was eerie. My cousin looked far more like a corpse than a man under the influence of drugs. Moreover, there was playing in one corner an electric phonograph, so that the low, discordant strains of Stravinsky's *Le Sacre du Printemps* flowed through the room and took possession of it. My cousin lay perfectly still, and for a long time not a sound escaped him; he had sunk into the deep drugged sleep in which he carried on his experiment, and I could not have awakened him had I tried.

Perhaps an hour elapsed before he began to speak, and then he spoke so disjointedly that I was hard put to it to catch his words.

"Forest sunk into earth," he said. "Great ones fighting, tearing. Run, run. . . ." And again, "New trees for old. Footprint ten feet across. We live in cave, cold, damp, fire. . . ."

I put down everything he said insofar as I could catch his muttered words, for his hints were of great beasts that roamed the face of his land and fought and tore, walking through forests as though they were of grass, seeking out and devouring mankind, the dwellers in caves and holes under the surface of the earth.

But the effort of driving himself back so far into the past was a singular strain on my cousin Ambrose, and, when at last he came back to consciousness that night, he shuddered, directing me to turn off the phonograph, and muttered something about "degenerative tissues" curiously allied to "my dreams—my memories," and

194

announced that we would all rest for a while before he resumed his experiments.

3

It is possible that if my cousin could have been persuaded to rest his experiment on the admitted probability of ultimate success, and taken care of himself, he might have avoided the consequences of pushing himself beyond the boundaries mortal man was meant to go. But he did not do so; indeed, he scorned my every suggestion, and reminded me that he was the doctor, not I. My retort that like all doctors, he was more careless of himself as patient than he would have been of anyone else fell on deaf ears. Yet even I could not have foreseen what was to take place, though Ambrose's vague hint about "degenerative tissues" ought to have lent direction to my contemplation of the harm he was doing to himself by the addiction to drugs which had made him their victim.

For a week he rested.

Then he resumed his experiments, and soon I was once more putting his notes into typescript. But this time his notes were increasingly difficult to decipher; his script was indeed deteriorating, even as he had hinted, and, moreover, their subject was often very difficult to follow, though it was evident that Ambrose had gone far back in time. The possibility remained, of course, and was strong, that my cousin had fallen victim to a kind of self-hypnosis, and that, far from experiencing any such memory as he chronicled, he was reproducing from the memory of books he had read the salient aspects of the lives of ancient cave- and tree-dwellers; yet there were disturbingly clear indications from time to time that the observations he made were not made from any printed text or the memory of such a text, though I had no way of seeking out such possible sources for my cousin's bizarre chroniclings.

I saw Ambrose increasingly seldom, but on the rare occasions when I did see him, I could not avoid noticing the alarming degree to which he had yielded to drugs and starvation; his emaciation was complicated by certain repellent signs of degeneration. He tended to slaver at his food and his eating habits became so deplorable that Mrs. Reed was pointedly absent from the table at more than one occasion; though, because of Ambrose's growing dislike of leaving his laboratory, we were not often more than three at table.

I do not remember just when the drastic alteration in Ambrose's habits came about, but I believe I had been at the house just over two months. Now that I think back to it, it seems to me that events were signalled by Ginger, my cousin's dog, which began to act up most restlessly. Whereas hitherto he had been a singularly well-behaved dog, now he began to bark often at night, and by day he whined and moved about house and yard with an air of alarm. Mrs. Reed said of him, "That dog smells or hears something he don't like." Perhaps she spoke truly, for all that I paid little attention.

It was about this time that my cousin elected to remain in his laboratory all together, instructing me to leave his food on a tray outside the laboratory door. I took issue with him, but he would neither open the door nor come out, and very often he left his food stand for some time before he took it in, so that Mrs. Reed made ever less attempts to serve him hot food, for most of the time it had grown cold by the time he took it in. Curiously, none of us ever saw Ambrose take his food; the tray might stand for an hour, two hours, even three—then suddenly it would be gone, only to be replaced later by an empty tray.

His eating habits also underwent a change; though he had formerly been a heavy coffee drinker, he now spurned it, returning his cup untouched so many times that Mrs. Reed no longer troubled to serve it. He

seemed to grow ever more partial to simpler foods—
meat, potatoes, lettuce, bread—and was not attracted
to salads or most casserole dishes. Sometimes his empty
tray contained notes, but these were growing fewer and
farther between, and such as there were I found almost
impossible to transcribe, for in his handwriting now, as
well as in the content of his notes, there was the same
distressing deterioration. He seemed to have difficulty
properly holding a pencil, and his lines were scrawled
in large letters over all the sheets of paper without any
sense of order, though this was not entirely unexpected
in one heavily dosed with drugs.

The music which welled forth from the laboratory
was even more primitive. Ambrose had obtained certain records of ethnic music—Polynesian, ancient Indian, and the like—and it was these he now played to
the exclusion of all else. These were weird sounds, indeed, and peculiarly trying in endless repetition, however interesting they were at first hearing, and they
prevailed with monotonous insistence, night and day,
for over a week, when one night the phonograph began
to manifest every indication of having run down or
worn out, and then abruptly stopped, it was not thereafter heard again.

It was at about this time that the notes ceased to
appear, and, concomitant with this development, there
were two others. The dog, Ginger, erupted into frantic
barking during the night, at fairly regular intervals, as
if someone were invading the property; I got up once
or twice, and once I did think I saw some unpleasantly
large animal scuttling into the woods, but nothing came
of this; it was gone by the time I had got outside, and,
however wild this portion of Vermont was, it was not
bear country, nor, for that matter, was there any likeli-
hood of encountering in the woods anything larger or
more dangerous than a deer. The other development
was more disturbing; Mrs. Reed noticed it first, and
called my attention to it—a pervasive and highly repel-

lent musk, clearly an animal odor, which seemed to emanate from the laboratory.

Could my cousin somehow have brought an animal in from the woods through the back door of the laboratory, which opened out upon the woods? This was always a possibility, but, in truth, I knew of no animal which might give out so powerful a musk. Efforts to question Ambrose from this side of the door were of no avail; he resolutely refused to make any answer, and even the threat of the Reeds that they would leave, unable any longer to work in such a stench, did not move him. After three days of it, the Reeds departed with their belongings, and I was left alone to take care of Ambrose and his dog.

In the shock of discovery, the exact sequence of events thereafter is no longer very clear. I know that I determined to reach my cousin by one way or other, though all my pleadings remained unanswered. I lightened my burdens as much as possible by unchaining the dog that morning, and letting him roam. I made no attempt to undertake the various tasks Reed had performed, but spent my time going to and from the laboratory door. I had long ago given up trying to look into the laboratory from the outside, for its windows were high rectangles parallel to the roof, and, like the single window in the door, they were covered over so as to make it impossible to look in upon any experiment under way inside.

Though my cajolery and pleadings had no effect on Ambrose, I knew that ultimately he must eat, and that, if I withheld food from him, he would finally be forced to come out of the laboratory. So for all of one day I set no food before his door; I sat grimly watching for him to appear, despite the almost nauseating animal musk which invaded the house from behind the laboratory door. But he did not appear. Determinedly, I continued to keep my vigil at the door, fighting sleep, which was not difficult, for in the quiet of the night I was aware of peculiarly disturbing movements within the laboratory—awkward, shuffling sounds, as if some large creature were crawling about,—combined with a guttural mewing sound, as if some mute animal were trying to speak. Several times I called out, and as often I tried the laboratory door anew, but it still resisted my efforts, being not only locked, but also barred by some heavy object.

I decided that, if this refusal to serve my cousin the food to which he had become accustomed did not bring him out, I would tackle the outer door of the laboratory in the morning, and force it by whatever means I could devise. I was now in a state of high alarm, since Ambrose's persistent silence seemed wholly unlike him.

But this decision had hardly been made, when I was aware of the frantic excitement of the dog. This time, unhampered by the chain which had hitherto bound him, he streaked along one side of the house and made for the woods, and in a moment I heard the furious snarling and growling which always accompanied an attack.

Momentarily forgetting my cousin, I made for the nearest door, snatching up my flashlight as I ran, and, running outside, I was on my way to the woods when I stopped short, I had come around the corner of the house, in view of the back of the laboratory—and I saw that the door to the laboratory stood open.

Instantly I turned and ran into the laboratory.

All was dark inside. I called my cousin's name. There was no response. With the flashlight I found the switch and turned up the light.

The sight that met my eyes startled me profoundly. When last I had been in the laboratory, it had been a conspicuously neat and trim room—yet now it was in a shocking state. Not only were the impedimenta of my cousin's experiments tipped over and broken, but there were scattered over instruments and floor fragments of partly decayed food—some that was clearly recogniz-

199

able as having come prepared, but also a disturbing amount of wild food—remains of partially-consumed rabbits, squirrels, skunks, woodchucks, and birds. Above all, the laboratory bore the nauseatingly repellent odor of a primal animal's abode—the scattered instruments bespoke civilization, but the smell and sight of the place were of subhuman life.

Of my cousin Ambrose there was no sign.

I recalled the large animal I had seen faintly in the woods, and the first thought that came to mind was that somehow the creature had broken into the laboratory and made off with Ambrose, the dog in pursuit. I acted on the thought, and ran from the laboratory to the place in the woods from which still came the throaty, animal sounds of a lethal battle which ended only as I came running up. Ginger stepped back, panting, and my light fell upon the kill.

I do not know how I managed to return to the house, to call the authorities, even to think coherently for five minutes at a time, so great was the shock of discovery. For in that one cataclysmic moment, I understood everything that had taken place—I knew why the dog barked so frantically in the night when the "thing" had gone to feed, I understood the source of that horrible animal musk. I realized that what had happened to my cousin was inevitable.

For the thing that lay below Ginger's bloody jaws was a subhuman caricature of a man, a hellish parody of primal growth, with horrible malformations of face and body, giving off an all-pervasive and wholly charnel musk—but it was clad in the rags of my cousin's mouse-colored dressing-gown, and it wore on its wrist my cousin's watch.

By some unknown primal law of nature, in sending his memory back to that prehuman era, into man's hereditary past, Ambrose had been trapped in that period of evolution, and his body had retrograded to the level of man's pre-human existence on the earth.

He had gone nightly to forage for food in the woods, maddening the already alarmed dog; and it was by my hand that he had come to this horrible end—for I had unchained Ginger and made it possible for Ambrose to come to his death at the jaws of his own dog!

THE MORTAL IMMORTAL

By Mary Shelley

July 16, 1833.—This is a memorable anniversary for me; on it I complete my three hundred and twenty-third year!

The Wandering Jew?—certainly not. More than eighteen centuries have passed over his head. In comparison with him, I am a very young Immortal.

Am I, then, immortal? This is a question which I have asked myself, by day and night, for now three hundred and three years, and yet cannot answer it. I detected a grey hair amidst my brown locks this very day—that surely signifies decay. Yet it may have remained concealed there for three hundred years—for some persons have become entirely whiteheaded before twenty years of age.

I will tell my story, and my reader shall judge for me. I will tell my story, and so contrive to pass some few hours of a long eternity, become so wearisome to me. For ever! Can it be? to live for ever! I have heard of enchantments, in which the victims were plunged into a deep sleep, to awake, after a hundred years, as fresh as ever: I have heard of the Seven Sleepers—thus to be immortal would not be so burdensome: but, oh! the weight of never-ending time—the tedious passage of the still-succeeding hours! How happy was the fabled Nourjahad!—But to my task.

All the world has heard of Cornelius Agrippa. His memory is as immortal as his arts have made me. All the world has also heard of his scholar, who, unawares, raised the foul fiend during his master's absence, and was destroyed by him. The report, true or false, of this accident, was attended with many inconveniences to the renowned philosopher. All his scholars at once deserted him—his servants disappeared. He had no one near him to put coals on his ever-burning fires while he slept, or attend to the changeful colours of his medicines while he studied. Experiment after experiment failed, because one pair of hands was insufficient to complete them: the dark spirits laughed at him for not being able to retain a single mortal in his service.

I was then very young—very poor—and very much in love. I had been for about a year the pupil of Cornelius, though I was absent when this accident took place. On my return, my friends implored me not to return to the alchymist's abode. I trembled as I listened to the dire tale they told; I required no second warning; and when Cornelius came and offered me a purse of gold if I would remain under his roof, I felt as if Satan himself tempted me. My teeth chattered—my hair stood on end;—I ran off as fast as my trembling knees would permit.

My failing steps were directed whither for two years they had every evening been attracted,—a gently bubbling spring of pure living water, beside which lingered a dark-haired girl, whose beaming eyes were fixed on the path I was accustomed each night to tread. I cannot remember the hour I did not love Bertha; we had been neighbours and playmates from infancy,—her parents, like mine, were of humble life, yet respectable, —our attachment had been a source of pleasure to them. In an evil hour, a malignant fever carried off both her father and mother, and Bertha became an

203

orphan. She would have found a home beneath my paternal roof, but, unfortunately, the old lady of the near castle, rich, childless, and solitary, declared her intention to adopt her. Henceforth Bertha was clad in silk—inhabited a marble palace—and was looked on as being highly favoured by fortune. But in her new situation among her new associates, Bertha remained true to the friend of her humbler days; she often visited the cottage of my father, and when forbidden to go thither, she would stray towards the neighbouring wood, and meet me beside its shady fountain.

She often declared that she owed no duty to her new protectress equal in sanctity to that which bound us. Yet still I was too poor to marry, and she grew weary of being tormented on my account. She had a haughty but an impatient spirit, and grew angry at the obstacles that prevented our union. We met now after an absence, and she had been sorely beset while I was away; she complained bitterly, and almost reproached me for being poor. I replied hastily,—

"I am honest, if I am poor!—were I not, I might soon become rich!"

This exclamation produced a thousand questions. I feared to shock her by owning the truth, but she drew it from me; and then casting a look of disdain on me, she said,—

"You pretend to love, and you fear to face the Devil for my sake!"

I protested that I had only dreaded to offend her;—while she dwelt on the magnitude of the reward that I should receive. Thus encouraged—shamed by her—led on by love and hope, laughing at my late fears, with quick steps and a light heart, I returned to accept the offers of the alchymist, and was instantly installed in my office.

A year passed away. I became possessed of no insignificant sum of money. Custom had banished my fears. In spite of the most painful vigilance, I had never detected the trace of a cloven foot; nor was the studious silence of our abode ever disturbed by demoniac howls. I still continued my stolen interviews with Bertha, and Hope dawned on me—Hope—but not perfect joy: for Bertha fancied that love and security were enemies, and her pleasure was to divide them in my bosom. Though true of heart, she was somewhat of a coquette in manner; and I was jealous as a Turk. She slighted me in a thousand ways, yet would never acknowledge herself to be in the wrong. She would drive me mad with anger, and then force me to beg her pardon. Sometimes she fancied that I was not sufficiently submissive, and then she had some story of a rival, favoured by her protectress. She was surrounded by silk-clad youths—the rich and gay. What chance had the sad-robed scholar of Cornelius compared with these?

On one occasion, the philosopher made such large demands upon my time, that I was unable to meet her as I was wont. He was engaged in some mighty work, and I was forced to remain, day and night, feeding his furnaces and watching his chemical preparations. Bertha waited for me in vain at the fountain. Her haughty spirit fired at this neglect; and when at last I stole out during the few short minutes allotted to me for slumber, and hoped to be consoled by her, she received me with disdain, dismissed me in scorn, and vowed that any man should possess her hand rather than he who could not be in two places at once for her sake. She would be revenged! And truly she was. In my dingy retreat I heard that she had been hunting, attended by Albert Hoffer. Albert Hoffer was favoured by her protectress, and the three passed in cavalcade before my smoky window. Methought that they mentioned my name; it was followed by a laugh of derision, as her dark eyes glanced contemptuously towards my abode.

Jealousy, with all its venom and all its misery, entered my breast. Now I shed a torrent of tears, to think that I should never call her mine; and, anon, I imprecated a thousand curses on her inconstancy. Yet, still I must stir the fires of the alchymist, still attend on the changes of his unintelligible medicines.

Cornelius had watched for three days and nights, nor closed his eyes. The progress of his alembics was slower than he expected: in spite of his anxiety, sleep weighed upon his eyelids. Again and again he threw off drowsiness with more than human energy; again and again it stole away his senses. He eyed his crucibles wistfully. "Not ready yet," he murmured; "will another night pass before the work is accomplished? Winzy, you are vigilant—you are faithful—you have slept, my boy—you slept last night. Look at that glass vessel. The liquid it contains is of a soft rose-colour: the moment it begins to change its hue, awaken me—till then I may close my eyes. First, it will turn white, and then emit golden flashes; but wait not till then; when the rose-colour fades, rouse me." I scarcely heard the last words, muttered, as they were, in sleep. Even then he did not quite yield to nature. "Winzy, my boy," he again said, "do not touch the vessel—do not put it to your lips; it is a philtre—a philtre to cure love; you would not cease to love your Bertha—beware to drink!"

And he slept. His venerable head sunk on his breast, and I scarce heard his regular breathing. For a few minutes I watched the vessels—the rosy hue of the liquid remained unchanged. Then my thoughts wandered—they visited the fountain, and dwelt on a thousand charming scenes never to be renewed—never! Serpents and adders were in my heart as the word "Never!" half formed itself on my lips. False girl!—false and cruel! Never more would she smile on me as that evening she smiled on Albert. Worthless, detested woman! I would not remain unrevenged—she should see Albert expire at her feet—she should die beneath my vengeance. She had smiled in disdain and triumph —she knew my wretchedness and her power. Yet what power had she?—the power of exciting my hate—my utter scorn—my—oh, all but indifference! Could I attain that—could I regard her with careless eyes, transferring my rejected love to one fairer and more true, that were indeed a victory!

A bright flash darted before my eyes. I had forgotten the medicine of the adept; I gazed on it with wonder: flashes of admirable beauty, more bright than those which the diamond emits when the sun's rays are on it, glanced from the surface of the liquid; an odour the most fragrant and grateful stole over my sense; the vessel seemed one globe of living radiance, lovely to the eye, and most inviting to the taste. The first thought, instinctively inspired by the grosser sense, was, I will —I must drink. I raised the vessel to my lips. "It will cure me of love—of torture!" Already I had quaffed half of the most delicious liquor ever tasted by the palate of man, when the philosopher stirred. I started —I dropped the glass—the fluid flamed and glanced along the floor, while I felt Cornelius's grip at my throat, as he shrieked aloud, "Wretch! you have destroyed the labour of my life!"

The philosopher was totally unaware that I had drunk any portion of his drug. His idea was, and I gave a tacit assent to it, that I had raised the vessel from curiosity, and that, frightened at its brightness, and the flashes of intense light it gave forth, I had let it fall. I never undeceived him. The fire of the medicine was quenched—the fragrance died away—he grew calm, as a philosopher should under the heaviest trials, and dismissed me to rest.

I will not attempt to describe the sleep of glory and bliss which bathed my soul in paradise during the remaining hours of that memorable night. Words would be faint and shallow types of my enjoyment, or of the gladness that possessed my bosom when I woke. I trod air—my thoughts were in heaven. Earth appeared heaven, and my inheritance upon it was to be one trace of delight. "This it is to be cured of love," I thought;

"I will see Bertha this day, and she will find her lover cold and regardless; too happy to be disdainful, yet how utterly indifferent to her!"

The hours danced away. The philosopher, secure that he had once succeeded, and believing that he might again, began to concoct the same medicine once more. He was shut up with his books and drugs, and I had a holiday. I dressed myself with care; I looked in an old but polished shield, which served me for a mirror; methought my good looks had wonderfully improved. I hurried beyond the precincts of the town, joy in my soul, the beauty of heaven and earth around me. I turned my steps towards the castle—I could look on its lofty turrets with lightness of heart, for I was cured of love. My Bertha saw me afar off, as I came up the avenue. I know not what sudden impulse animated her bosom, but at the sight, she sprung with a light fawn-like bound down the marble steps, and was hastening towards me. But I had been perceived by another person. The old high-born hag, who called herself her protectress, and was her tyrant, had seen me also; she hobbled, panting, up the terrace; a page, as ugly as herself, held up her train, and fanned her as she hurried along, and stopped my fair girl with a "How, now, my bold mistress? whither so fast? Back to your cage—hawks are abroad!"

Bertha clasped her hands—her eyes were still bent on my approaching figure. I saw the contest. How I abhorred the old crone who checked the kind impulses of my Bertha's softening heart. Hitherto, respect for her rank had caused me to avoid the lady of the castle; now I disdained such trivial consideration. I was cured of love, and lifted above all human fears; I hastened forwards, and soon reached the terrace. How lovely Bertha looked! her eyes flashing fire, her cheeks glowing with impatience and anger, she was a thousand times more graceful and charming than ever. I no longer loved—oh no! I adored—worshipped—idolized her!

She had that morning been persecuted, with more than usual vehemence, to consent to an immediate marriage with my rival. She was reproached with the encouragement that she had shown him—she was threatened with being turned out of doors with disgrace and shame. Her proud spirit rose in arms at the threat; but when she remembered the scorn that she had heaped upon me, and how, perhaps, she had thus lost one whom she now regarded as her only friend, she wept with remorse and rage. At that moment I appeared. "Oh, Winzy!" she exclaimed, "take me to your mother's cot; swiftly let me leave the detested luxuries and wretchedness of this noble dwelling—take me to poverty and happiness."

I clasped her in my arms with transport. The old dame was speechless with fury, and broke forth into invective only when we were far on our road to my natal cottage. My mother received the fair fugitive, escaped from a gilt cage to nature and liberty, with tenderness and joy; my father, who loved her, welcomed her heartily; it was a day of rejoicing, which did not need the addition of the celestial potion of the alchymist to steep me in delight.

Soon after this eventful day, I became the husband of Bertha. I ceased to be the scholar of Cornelius, but I continued his friend. I always felt grateful to him for having, unawares, procured me that delicious draught of a divine elixir, which, instead of curing me of love (sad cure! solitary and joyless remedy for evils which seem blessings to the memory), had inspired me with courage and resolution, thus winning for me an inestimable treasure in my Bertha.

I often called to mind that period of trance-like inebriation with wonder. The drink of Cornelius had not fulfilled the task for which he affirmed that it had been prepared, but its effects were more potent and blissful than words can express. They had faded by degrees, yet they lingered long—and painted life in hues of splendour. Bertha often wondered at my lightness of heart and unaccustomed gaiety; for, before, I had been rather serious, or even sad, in my disposition. She loved me the better for my cheerful temper, and our days were winged by joy.

Five years afterwards I was suddenly summoned to the bedside of the dying Cornelius. He had sent for me in haste, conjuring my instant presence. I found him stretched on his pallet, enfeebled even to death; all of life that yet remained animated his piercing eyes, and they were fixed on a glass vessel, full of a roseate liquid.

"Behold," he said, in a broken and inward voice, "the vanity of human wishes! a second time my hopes are about to be crowned, a second time they are destroyed. Look at that liquor—you remember five years ago I prepared the same, with the same success;—then, as now, my thirsting lips expected to taste the immortal elixir—you dashed it from me! and at present it is too late."

He spoke with difficulty, and fell back on his pillow. I could not help saying,—

"How, revered master, can a cure for love restore you to life?"

A faint smile gleamed across his face as I listened earnestly to his scarcely intelligible answer.

"A cure for love and for all things—the Elixir of Immortality. Ah! if now I might drink, I should live for ever!"

As he spoke, a golden flash gleamed from the fluid; a well-remembered fragrance stole over the air; he raised himself, all weak as he was—strength seemed miraculously to re-enter his frame—he stretched forth his hand—a loud explosion startled me—a ray of fire shot up from the elixir, and the glass vessel which contained it was shivered to atoms! I turned my eyes towards the philosopher; he had fallen back—his eyes were glassy—his features rigid—he was dead!

But I lived, and was to live for ever! So said the

unfortunate alchymist, and for a few days I believed his words. I remembered the glorious intoxication that had followed my stolen draught. I reflected on the change I had left in my frame—in my soul. The bounding elasticity of the one—the buoyant lightness of the other. I surveyed myself in a mirror, and could perceive no change in my features during the space of the five years which had elapsed. I remembered the radiant hues and grateful scent of that delicious beverage— worthy the gift it was capable of bestowing—I was, then, IMMORTAL!

A few days after I laughed at my credulity. The old proverb, that "a prophet is least regarded in his own country," was true with respect to me and my defunct master. I loved him as a man—I respected him as a sage—but I derided the notion that he could command the powers of darkness, and laughed at the superstitious fears with which he was regarded by the vulgar. He was a wise philosopher, but had no acquaintance with any spirits but those clad in flesh and blood. His science was simply human; and human science, I soon persuaded myself, could never conquer nature's laws so far as to imprison the soul for ever within its carnal habitation. Cornelius had brewed a soul-refreshing drink—more inebriating than wine—sweeter and more fragrant than any fruit: it possessed probably strong medicinal powers, imparting gladness to the heart and vigour to the limbs; but its effects would wear out; already were they diminished in my frame. I was a lucky fellow to have quaffed health and joyous spirits, and perhaps long life, at my master's hands; but my good fortune ended there: longevity was far different from immortality.

I continued to entertain this belief for many years. Sometimes a thought stole across me—Was the alchymist indeed deceived? But my habitual credence was, that I should meet the fate of all the children of Adam at my appointed time—a little late, but still at a natural age. Yet it was certain that I retained a wonderfully youthful look. I was laughed at for my vanity in consulting the mirror so often, but I consulted it in vain—my brow was untrenched—my cheeks—my eyes—my whole person continued as untarnished as in my twentieth year.

I was troubled. I looked at the faded beauty of Bertha—I seemed more like her son. By degrees our neighbours began to make similar observations, and I found at last that I went by the name of the Scholar bewitched. Bertha herself grew uneasy. She became jealous and peevish, and at length she began to question me. We had no children; we were all in all to each other; and though, as she grew older, her vivacious spirit became a little allied to ill-temper, and her beauty sadly diminished, I cherished her in my heart as the mistress I had idolized, the wife I had sought and won with such perfect love.

At last our situation became intolerable: Bertha was fifty—I twenty years of age. I had, in very shame, in some measure adopted the habits of a more advanced age; I no longer mingled in the dance among the young and gay, but my heart bounded along with them while I restrained my feet; and a sorry figure I cut among the Nestors of our village. But before the time I mentioned, things were altered—we were universally shunned; we were—at least, I was—reported to have kept up an iniquitous acquaintance with some of my former master's supposed friends. Poor Bertha was pitied, but deserted. I was regarded with horror and detestation.

What was to be done? we sat by our winter fire—poverty had made itself felt, for none would buy the produce of my farm; and often I had been forced to journey twenty miles, to some place where I was not known, to dispose of our property. It is true, we had saved something for an evil day—that day was come.

We sat by our lone fireside—the old-hearted youth

and his antiquated wife. Again Bertha insisted on knowing the truth; she recapitulated all she had ever heard said about me, and added her own observations. She conjured me to cast off the spell; she described how much more comely grey hairs were than my chestnut locks; she descanted on the reverence and respect due to age—how preferable to the slight regard paid to mere children: could I imagine that the despicable gifts of youth and good looks outweighed disgrace, hatred, and scorn? Nay, in the end I should be burnt as a dealer in the black art, while she, to whom I had not deigned to communicate any portion of my good fortune, might be stoned as my accomplice. At length she insinuated that I must share my secret with her, and bestow on her like benefits to those I myself enjoyed, or she would denounce me—and then she burst into tears.

Thus beset, methought it was the best way to tell the truth. I revealed it as tenderly as I could, and spoke only of a *very long life,* not of immortality—which representation, indeed, coincided best with my own ideas. When I ended, I rose and said,—

"And now, my Bertha, will you denounce the lover of your youth?—You will not, I know. But it is too hard, my poor wife, that you should suffer from my ill-luck and the accursed arts of Cornelius. I will leave you—you have wealth enough, and friends will return in my absence. I will go; young as I seem, and strong as I am, I can work and gain my bread among strangers, unsuspected and unknown. I loved you in youth; God is my witness that I would not desert you in age, but that your safety and happiness require it."

I took my cap and moved towards the door; in a moment Bertha's arms were round my neck, and her lips were pressed to mine. "No, my husband, my Winzy," she said, "you shall not go alone—take me with you; we will remove from this place, and, as you say, among strangers we shall be unsuspected and safe. I am not so very old as quite to shame you, my Winzy;

and I daresay the charm will soon wear off, and, with the blessing of God, you will become more elderly-looking, as is fitting; you shall not leave me."

I returned the good soul's embrace heartily. "I will not, my Bertha; but for your sake I had not thought of such a thing. I will be your true, faithful husband while you are spared to me, and do my duty by you to the last."

The next day we prepared secretly for our emigration. We were obliged to make great pecuniary sacrifices—it could not be helped. We realised a sum sufficent, at least, to maintain us while Bertha lived; and, without saying adieu to any one, quitted our native country to take refuge in a remote part of western France.

It was a cruel thing to transport poor Bertha from her native village, and the friends of her youth, to a new country, new language, new customs. The strange secret of my destiny rendered this removal immaterial to me; but I compassioned her deeply, and was glad to perceive that she found compensation for her misfortunes in a variety of little ridiculous circumstances. Away from all tell-tale chroniclers, she sought to decrease the apparent disparity of our ages by a thousand feminine arts—rouge, youthful dress, and assumed juvenility of manner. I could not be angry. Did not I myself wear a mask? Why quarrel with hers, because it was less successful? I grieved deeply when I remembered that this was my Bertha, whom I had loved so fondly and won with such transport—the dark-eyed, dark-haired girl, with smiles of enchanting archness and a step like a fawn—this mincing, simpering, jealous old woman. I should have revered her grey locks and withered cheeks; but thus!—It was my work, I knew; but I did not the less deplore this type of human weakness.

Her jealousy never slept. Her chief occupation was to discover that, in spite of outward appearances, I was myself growing old. I verily believe that the poor soul loved me truly in her heart, but never had woman so tormenting a mode of displaying fondness. She would discern wrinkles in my face and decrepitude in my walk, while I bounded along in youthful vigour, the youngest looking of twenty youths. I never dared address another woman. On one occasion, fancying that the belle of the village regarded me with favouring eyes, she brought me a grey wig. Her constant discourse among her acquaintances was, that though I looked so young, there was ruin at work within my frame; and she affirmed that the worst symptom about me was my apparent health. My youth was a disease, she said, and I ought at all times to prepare, if not for a sudden and awful death, at least to awake some morning white-headed and bowed down with all the marks of advanced years. I let her talk—I often joined in her conjectures. Her warnings chimed in with my never-ceasing speculations concerning my state, and I took an earnest, though painful, interest in listening to all that her quick wit and excited imagination could say on the subject.

Why dwell on these minute circumstances? We lived on for many long years. Bertha became bedridden and paralytic; I nursed her as a mother might a child. She grew peevish, and still harped upon one string—of how long I should survive her. It has ever been a source of consolation to me, that I performed my duty scrupulously towards her. She had been mine in youth, she was mine in age; and at last, when I heaped the sod over her corpse, I wept to feel that I had lost all that really bound me to humanity.

Since then how many have been my cares and woes, how few and empty my enjoyments! I pause here in my history—I will pursue it no further. A sailor without rudder or compass, tossed on a stormy sea—a traveller lost on a widespread heath, without landmark or stone to guide him—such have I been: more lost, more hopeless than either. A nearing ship, a gleam from some far cot, may save them; but I have no beacon except the hope of death.

Death! mysterious, ill-visaged friend of weak humanity! Why alone of all mortals have you cast me from your sheltering fold? Oh, for the peace of the grave! the deep silence of the iron-bound tomb! that thought would cease to work in my brain, and my heart beat no more with emotions varied only by new forms of sadness!

Am I immortal? I return to my first question. In the first place, is it not more probable that the beverage of the alchymist was fraught rather with longevity than eternal life? Such is my hope. And then be it remembered, that I only drank *half* of the potion prepared by him. Was not the whole necessary to complete the charm? To have drained half the Elixir of Immortality is but to be half-immortal—my For-ever is thus truncated and null.

But again, who shall number the years of the half of eternity? I often try to imagine by what rule the infinite may be divided. Sometimes I fancy age advancing upon me. One grey hair I have found. Fool! do I lament? Yes, the fear of age and death often creeps coldly into my heart; and the more I live, the more I dread death, even while I abhor life. Such an enigma is man—born to perish—when he wars, as I do, against the established laws of his nature.

But for this anomaly of feeling surely I might die: the medicine of the alchymist would not be proof against fire—sword—and the strangling waters. I have gazed upon the blue depths of many a placid lake, and the tumultuous rushing of many a mighty river, and have said, peace inhabits those waters; yet I have turned my steps away, to live yet another day. I have asked myself, whether suicide would be a crime in one to whom thus only the portals of the other world could be opened. I have done all, except presenting myself as a soldier or duellist, an objection of destruction to my

—no, *not* my fellow-mortals, and therefore I have shrunk away. They are not my fellows. The inextinguishable power of life in my frame, and their ephemeral existence, places us wide as the poles asunder. I could not raise a hand against the meanest or the most powerful among them.

Thus I have lived on for many a year—alone, and weary of myself—desirous of death, yet never dying—a mortal immortal. Neither ambition nor avarice can enter my mind, and the ardent love that gnaws at my heart, never to be returned—never to find an equal on which to expend itself—lives there only to torment me.

This very day I conceived a design by which I may end all—without self-slaughter, without making another man a Cain—an expedition, which mortal frame can never survive, even endued with the youth and strength that inhabits mine. Thus I shall put my immortality to the test, and rest for ever—or return, the wonder and benefactor of the human species.

Before I go, a miserable vanity has caused me to pen these pages. I would not die, and leave no name behind. Three centuries have passed since I quaffed the fatal beverage; another year shall not elapse before, encountering gigantic dangers—warring with the powers of frost in their home—beset by famine, toil, and tempest—I yield this body, too tenacious a cage for a soul which thirsts for freedom, to the destructive elements of air and water; or, if I survive, my name shall be recorded as one of the most famous among the sons of men; and, my task achieved, I shall adopt more resolute means, and, by scattering and annihilating the atoms that compose my frame, set at liberty the life imprisoned within, and so cruelly prevented from soaring from this dim earth to a sphere more congenial to its immortal essence.

DR. HEIDEGGER'S EXPERIMENT

By Nathaniel Hawthorne

That very singular man, old Dr. Heidegger, once invited four venerable friends to meet him in his study. There were three white-bearded gentlemen, Mr. Medbourne, Colonel Killigrew, and Mr. Gasgoigne, and a withered gentle-woman, whose name was the Widow Wycherly. They were all melancholy old creatures, who had been unfortunate in life, and whose greatest misfortune it was, that they were not long ago in their graves. Mr. Medbourne, in the vigour of his age, had been a prosperous merchant, but had lost his all by a frantic speculation, and was now little better than a mendicant. Colonel Killigrew had wasted his best years, and his health and substance, in the pursuit of sinful pleasures, which had given birth to a brood of pains, such as the gout, and divers other torments of soul and body. Mr. Gascoigne was a ruined politician, a man of evil fame, or at least had been so, till time had buried him from the knowledge of the present generation, and made him obscure instead of infamous. As for the Widow Wycherly, tradition tells us that she was a great beauty in her day; but, for a long while past, she had lived in deep seclusion, on account of certain scandalous stories, which had prejudiced the gentry of the town against her. It is a circumstance worth mentioning, that each of these three old gentlemen, Mr. Medbourne, Colonel Killigrew, and Mr. Gascoigne, were early lovers of the Widow Wycherly, and had once been on the point of cutting each other's throats for her sake. And before proceeding further, I will merely hint, that Dr. Heidegger and all his four guests were sometimes thought to be a little beside themselves; as is not infrequently the case with old people, when worried either by present troubles or woeful recollections.

"My dear old friends," said Dr. Heidegger, motioning them to be seated. "I am desirous of your assistance in one of those little experiments with which I amuse myself here in my study."

If all stories were true, Dr. Heidegger's study must have been a very curious place. It was a dim, old-fashioned chamber, festooned with cobwebs, and besprinkled with antique dust. Around the walls stood several oaken bookcases, the lower shelves of which were filled with rows of gigantic folios, and black-letter quartos, and the upper with little parchment-covered duodecimos. Over the central bookcase was a bronze bust of Hippocrates, with which, according to some authorities, Dr. Heidegger was accustomed to hold consultations, in all difficult cases of his practice. In the obscurest corner of the room stood a tall and narrow oaken closet, with its door ajar, within which doubtfully appeared a skeleton. Between two of the bookcases hung a looking-glass, presenting its high and dusty plate within a tarnished gilt frame. Among many wonderful stories related of this mirror, it was fabled that the spirits of all the doctor's deceased patients dwelt within its verge, and would stare him in the face whenever he looked thitherward. The opposite side of the chamber was ornamented with the full-length portrait of a young lady, arrayed in the faded magnificence of silk, satin, and brocade, and with a visage as faded as the dress. Above half a century ago, Dr. Heidegger had been on the point of marriage with this young lady; but, being affected with some slight disorder, she had swallowed one of her lover's prescriptions, and died on the bridal evening. The greatest curiosity of the study remains to be mentioned; it was a ponderous folio volume, bound in black leather, with massive silver clasps. There were no letters on the back, and nobody could tell the title of the book. But it was well known to be a book of magic; and once, when a chambermaid had lifted it, merely to brush away the dust, the skeleton had rattled in its closet, the picture of the young lady had stepped one foot upon the floor, and several ghastly faces had peeped forth from the mirror; while the brazen head of Hippocrates frowned, and said— "Forbear!"

Such was Dr. Heidegger's study. On the summer afternoon of our tale, a small round table, as black as ebony, stood in the centre of the room, sustaining a cut-glass vase, of beautiful form and elaborate workmanship. The sunshine came through the window, between the heavy festoons of two faded damask curtains, and fell directly across this vase; so that a mild splendour was reflected from it on the ashen visages of the five old people who sat around. Four champagne glasses were also on the table.

"My dear old friends," repeated Dr. Heidegger, "may I reckon on your aid in performing an exceedingly curious experiment?"

Now Dr. Heidegger was a very strange old gentleman, whose eccentricity had become the nucleus for a thousand fantastic stories. Some of these fables, to my shame be it spoken, might possibly be traced back to mine own veracious self; and if any passages of the present tale should startle the reader's faith, I must be content to bear the stigma of a fiction-monger.

When the doctor's four guests heard him talk of his proposed experiment, they anticipated nothing more wonderful than the murder of a mouse in an air-pump, or the examination of a cobweb by the microscope, or some similar nonsense, with which he was constantly in the habit of pestering his intimates. But without waiting for a reply, Dr. Heidegger hobbled across the chamber, and returned with the same ponderous folio, bound in black leather, which common report affirmed to be a book of magic. Undoing the silver clasps, he opened the volume, and took from among its black-letter pages a rose, or what was once a rose, though now the green leaves and crimson petals had assumed one brownish hue, and the ancient flower seemed ready to crumble to dust in the doctor's hands.

"This rose," said Dr. Heidegger, with a sigh, "this same withered and crumbling flower, blossomed five and fifty years ago. It was given me by Sylvia Ward, whose portrait hangs yonder; and I meant to wear it in my bosom at our wedding. Five and fifty years it has been treasured between the leaves of this old volume. Now, would you deem it possible that this rose of half a century could ever bloom again?"

"Nonsense!" said the Widow Wycherly, with a peevish toss of her head. "You might as well ask whether an old woman's wrinkled face could ever bloom again."

"See!" answered Dr. Heidegger.

He uncovered the vase, and threw the faded rose into the water which it contained. At first, it lay lightly on the surface of the fluid, appearing to imbibe none of its moisture. Soon, however, a singular change began to be visible. The crushed and dried petals stirred, and assumed a deepening tinge of crimson, as if the flower were reviving from a deathlike slumber; the slender stalk and twigs of foliage became green; and there was the rose of half a century, looking as fresh as when Sylvia Ward had first given it to her lover. It was scarcely full blown; for some of its delicate red leaves curled modestly around its moist bosom, within which two or three dewdrops were sparkling.

221

"That is certainly a very pretty deception," said the doctor's friends; carelessly, however, for they had witnessed greater miracles at a conjurer's show; "pray how was it effected?"

"Did you never hear of the 'Fountain of Youth'?" asked Dr. Heidegger, "which Ponce de Leon, the Spanish adventurer, went in search of, two or three centuries ago?"

"But did Ponce de Leon ever find it?" said the Widow Wycherly.

"No," answered Dr. Heidegger, "for he never sought it in the right place. The famous Fountain of Youth, if I am rightly informed, is situated in the southern part of the Floridian peninsula, not far from Lake Macaco. Its source is overshadowed by several gigantic magnolias, which, though numberless centuries old, have been kept as fresh as violets, by the virtues of this wonderful water. An acquaintance of mine, knowing my curiosity in such matters, has sent me what you see in the vase."

"Ahem!" said Colonel Killigrew, who believed not a word of the doctor's story; "and what may be the effect of this fluid on the human frame?"

"You shall judge for yourself, my dear colonel," replied Dr. Heidegger; "and all of you, my respected friends, are welcome to so much of this admirable fluid as may restore to you the bloom of youth. For my own part, having had much trouble in growing old, I am in no hurry to grow young again. With your permission, therefore, I will merely watch the progress of the experiment."

While he spoke, Dr. Heidegger had been filling the four champagne glasses with the water of the Fountain of Youth. It was apparently impregnated with an effervescent gas, for little bubbles were continually ascending from the depths of the glasses, and bursting in silvery spray at the surface. As the liquor diffused a pleasant perfume, the old people doubted not that it possessed cordial and comfortable properties; and, though utter sceptics as to its rejuvenescent power, they were inclined to swallow it at once. But Dr. Heidegger besought them to stay a moment.

"Before you drink, my respectable old friends," said he, "it would be well that, with the experience of a lifetime to direct you, you should draw up a few general rules for your guidance, in passing a second time through the perils of youth. Think what a sin and shame it would be, if, with your peculiar advantages, you should not become patterns of virtue and wisdom to all the young people of the age!"

The doctor's four venerable friends made him no answer, except by a feeble and tremulous laugh; so very ridiculous was the idea, that, knowing how closely repentance treads behind the steps of error, they should ever go astray again.

"Drink, then," said the doctor, bowing: "I rejoice that I have so well selected the subjects of my experiment."

With palsied hands, they raised the glasses to their lips. The liquor, if it really possessed such virtues as Dr. Heidegger imputed to it, could not have been bestowed on four human beings who needed it more woefully. They looked as if they had never known what youth or pleasure was, but had been the offspring of Nature's dotage, and always the grey, decrepit, sapless, miserable creatures, who now sat stooping round the doctor's table, without life enough in their souls or bodies to be animated even by the prospect of growing young again. They drank off the water, and replaced their glasses on the table.

Assuredly there was an almost immediate improvement in the aspect of the party, not unlike what might have been produced by a glass of generous wine, together with a sudden glow of cheerful sunshine, brightening over all their visages at once. There was a healthful suffusion on their cheeks, instead of the ashen hue that had made them look so corpse-like. They gazed at one another, and fancied that some magic power had really begun to smooth away the deep and sad inscriptions which Father Time had been so long engraving on their brows. The Widow Wycherly adjusted her cap, for she felt almost like a woman again.

"Give us more of this wonderful water!" cried they, eagerly. "We are younger—but we are still too old! Quick—give us more!"

"Patience, patience!" quoth Dr. Heidegger, who sat watching the experiment, with philosophic coolness. "You have been a long time growing old. Surely, you might be content to grow young in half an hour! But the water is at your service."

Again he filled their glasses with the liquor of youth, enough of which still remained in the vase to turn half the old people in the city to the age of their own grandchildren. While the bubbles were yet sparkling on the brim, the doctor's four guests snatched their glasses from the table, and swallowed the contents at a single gulp. Was it delusion? even while the draught was passing down their throats, it seemed to have wrought a change on their whole systems. Their eyes grew clear and bright; a dark shade deepened among their silvery locks; they sat around the table, three gentlemen of middle age, and a woman hardly beyond her buxom prime.

"My dear widow, you are charming!" cried Colonel Killigrew, whose eyes had been fixed upon her face, while the shadows of age were flitting from it like darkness from the crimson daybreak.

The fair widow knew of old that Colonel Killigrew's compliments were not always measured by sober truth; so she started up and ran to the mirror, still dreading that the ugly visage of an old woman would meet her gaze. Meanwhile, the three gentlemen behaved in such a manner, as proved that the water of the Fountain of Youth possessed some intoxicating qualities; unless, indeed, their exhilaration of spirits were merely a lightsome dizziness, caused by the sudden removal of the weight of years. Mr. Gascoigne's mind seemed to run on political topics, but whether relating to the past, present, or future, could not easily be determined, since the same ideas and phrases have been in vogue these fifty years. Now he rattled forth full-throated sentences about patriotism, national glory, and the people's right; now he muttered some perilous stuff or other, in a sly and doubtful whisper, so cautiously that even his own conscience could scarely catch the secret; and now, again, he spoke in measured accents, and a deeply deferential tone, as if a royal ear were listening to his well-turned periods. Colonel Killigrew all this time had been trolling forth a jolly bottle song, and ringing his glass in symphony with the chorus, while his eyes wandered toward the buxom figure of the Widow Wycherly. On the other side of the table, Mr. Medbourne was involved in a calculation of dollars and cents, with which was strangely intermingled a project for supplying the East Indies with ice, by harnessing a team of whales to the polar icebergs.

As for the Widow Wycherly, she stood before the mirror curtseying and simpering to her own image, and greeting it as the friend whom she loved better than all the world beside. She thrust her face close to the glass, to see whether some long-remembered wrinkle or crow's foot had indeed vanished. She examined whether the snow had so entirely melted from her hair, that the venerable cap could be safely thrown aside. At last, turning briskly away, she came with a sort of dancing step to the table.

"My dear old doctor," cried she, "pray favour me with another glass!"

"Certainly, my dear madam, certainly!" replied the complaisant doctor; "see! I have already filled the glasses."

There, in fact, stood the four glasses, brimful of this wonderful water, the delicate spray of which, as it effervesced from the surface, resembled the tremulous glitter of diamonds. It was now so nearly sunset, that the chamber had grown duskier than ever; but a mild and moonlike splendour gleamed from within the vase, and rested alike on the four guests, and on the doctor's venerable figure. He sat in a high-backed, elaborately-carved, oaken arm-chair, with a grey dignity of aspect that might have well befitted that very Father Time, whose power had never been disputed, save by this fortunate company. Even while quaffing the third draught of the Fountain of Youth, they were almost awed by the expression of his mysterious visage.

But, the next moment, the exhilarating gush of young life shot through their veins. They were now in the happy prime of youth. Age, with its miserable train of cares, and sorrows, and diseases, was remembered only as the trouble of a dream, from which they had joyously awoke. The fresh gloss of the soul, so early lost, and without which the world's successive scenes had been but a gallery of faded pictures, again threw its enchantment over all their prospects. They felt like new-created beings, in a new-created universe.

"We are young! We are young!" they cried exultingly.

Youth, like the extremity of age, had affected the strongly-marked characteristics of middle life, and mutually assimilated them all. They were a group of merry youngsters, almost maddened with the exuberant frolicsomeness of their years. The most singular effect of their gaiety was an impulse to mock the infirmity and decrepitude of which they had so lately been the victims. They laughed loudly at their old fashioned attire, the wide-skirted coats and flapped waistcoats of the young men, and the ancient cap and gown of the blooming girl. One limped across the floor like a gouty grandfather; one set a pair of spectacles astride of his nose, and pretended to pore over the black-letter pages of the book of magic; a third the venerable dignity of Dr. Heidegger. Then all shouted mirthfully, and leaped

226

about the room. The Widow Wycherly—if so fresh a damsel could be called a widow—tripped up to the doctor's chair, with a mischievous merriment in her rosy face.

"Doctor, you dear old soul," she cried, "get up and dance with me!" And then the four young people laughed louder than ever, to think what a queer figure the poor old doctor would cut.

"Pray excuse me," answered the doctor quietly. "I am old and rheumatic, and my dancing days were over long ago. But either of these gay young gentlemen will be glad of so pretty a partner."

"Dance with me, Clara!" cried Colonel Killigrew.

"No, no, I will be her partner!" shouted Mr. Gascoigne.

"She promised me her hand, fifty years ago!" exclaimed Mr. Medbourne.

They all gathered round her. One caught both her hands in his passionate grasp—another threw his arm about her waist— the third buried his hand among the glossy curls that clustered beneath the widow's cap. Blushing, panting, struggling, chiding, laughing, her warm breath fanning each of their faces by turns, she strove to disengage herself, yet still remained in their triple embrace. Never was there a livelier picture of youthful rivalship, with bewitching beauty for the prize. Yet, by a strange deception, owing to the duskiness of the chamber, and the antique dresses which they still wore, the tall mirror is said to have reflected the figures of the three old grey, withered grandsires, ridiculously contending for the skinny ugliness of a shrivelled grandam.

But they were young: their burning passions proved them so. Inflamed to madness by the coquetry of the girl-widow, who neither granted nor quite withheld her favours, the three rivals began to interchange threatening glances. Still keeping hold of the fair prize, they grappled fiercely at one another's throats. As they struggled to and fro, the table was overturned, and the vase dashed into a thousand fragments. The precious Water of Youth flowed into a bright stream across the floor, moistening the wings of a butterfly which, grown old in the decline of summer, had alighted there to die. The insect fluttered lightly through the chamber, and settled on the snowy head of Dr. Heidegger.

"Come, come, gentlemen!—Come Madame Wycherly," exclaimed the doctor, "I really must protest against this riot."

They stood still, and shivered; for it seemed as if grey Time were calling them back from their sunny youth, far down into the chill and darksome vale of years. They looked at old Dr. Heidegger, who sat in his carved arm-chair, holding the rose of a century, which he had rescued from among the fragments of the shattered vase. At the motion of his hand, the four rioters resumed their seats; the more readily, because their violent exertions had wearied them, youthful though they were.

"My poor Sylvia's rose!" ejaculated Dr. Heidegger, holding it in the light of the sunset clouds; "it appears to be fading again."

And so it was. Even while the party were looking at it, the flower continued to shrivel up, till it became as dry and fragile as when the doctor had first thrown it into the vase. He shook off a few drops of moisture which clung to its petals.

"I love it as well thus, as in its dewy freshness," observed he, pressing the withered rose to his withered lips. While he spoke, the butterfly fluttered down from the doctor's snowy head, and fell upon the floor.

His guests shivered again. A strange chillness, whether of the body or spirit they could not tell, was creeping gradually over them all. They gazed at one another, and fancied that each fleeting moment snatched away a charm, and left a deepening furrow where none had been before. Was it an illusion? Had the changes of a lifetime been crowded into so brief a space, and were they now four aged people, sitting with their old friend, Dr. Heidegger?

"Are we grown old again, so soon?" cried they, dolefully.

In truth, they had. The Water of Youth possessed merely a virtue more transient than that of wine. The delirium which it created had effervesced away. Yes! they were old again. With a shuddering impulse, that showed her a woman still, the widow clasped her skinny hands before her face, and wished that the coffin lid were over it, since it could be no longer beautiful.

"Yes, friends, ye are old again," said Dr. Heidegger; "and lo! the Water of Youth is all lavished on the ground. Well—I bemoan it not; for if the fountain gushed at my doorstep, I would not stoop to bathe my lips in it—no, though its delirium were for years instead of moments. Such is the lesson ye have taught me!"

But the doctor's four friends had taught no such lesson to themselves. They resolved forthwith to make a pilgrimage to Florida, and quaff at morning, noon, and night, from the Fountain of Youth.

BY THESE PRESENTS

By Henry Kuttner

The devil smiled uneasily at James Fenwick.

"It's very irregular," he said. "I'm not at all sure—"

"Do you want my soul or don't you?" James Fenwick demanded.

"Naturally I do," the devil said. "But I'll have to think this over. Under the circumstances I don't exactly see how I could collect."

"All I want is immortality," Fenwick said, with a pleased smile. "I wonder why no one has ever thought of this before. In my opinion it's foolproof. Come, come, now, make up your mind. Do you want to back out?"

"Oh no," the devil said hastily. "It's just that—— Look here, Fenwick, I'm not sure you realize—immortality's a long time, you know."

"Exactly. The question is, will it ever have an end. If it does, you collect my soul. If not——" Fenwick made an airy gesture. "*I* win," he said.

"Oh, it has an end," the devil said, somewhat grimly. "It's just that right now I'd rather not undertake such a long-term investment. You wouldn't care for immortality, Fenwick. Believe me."

Fenwick said, "Ha."

"I don't see why you're so set on immortality," the devil said a little peevishly, tapping the point of his tail on the carpet.

"I'm not," Fenwick told him. "Actually, it's just a byproduct. There happen to be quite a number of things I'd like to do without suffering the consequences, but——"

"I could promise you that," the devil put in eagerly.

"But," Fenwick said, lifting his hand for quiet, "the deal would obviously end right there. Played this way, I get not only an unlimited supply of immunities of all kinds, but I get immortality besides. Take it or leave it my friend."

The devil rose from his chair and began to pace up and down the room, scowling at the carpet. Finally he looked up.

"Very well," he said briskly. "I accept."

"You do?" Fenwick was aware of a slight sinking feeling. Now that it actually came to the point, maybe. . . . He looked uneasily towards the drawn blinds of his apartment. "How will you go about it?" he asked.

"Biochemically," the devil said. Now that he had made up his mind he seemed quite confident. "And with quantum mechanics. Aside from the internal regenerative functions, some space-time alterations will have to be made. You'll become independent of your external environment. Environment is often fatal."

"I'll stay right here, though? Visible, tangible—no tricks?"

"Tricks?" the devil looked wounded. "If there's any trickery, it seems to me you're the offender. No indeed, Fenwick. You'll get value received for your investment. I promise that. You'll become a closed system, like Achilles. Except for the heel. There will have to be a vulnerable point, you see."

"No," Fenwick said quickly. "I won't accept that."

"It can't be helped, I'm afraid. You'll be quite safe inside the closed system from anything outside. And

231

there'll be nothing inside except you. It *is* you. In a way this is in your own interest." The devil's tail lashed upon the carpet. Fenwick regarded it uneasily. "If you wish to put an end to your own life eventually," the devil went on, "I can't protect you against that. Consider, however, that in a few million years you may wish to die."

"That reminds me," Fenwick said. "Tithonus. I'll keep my youth, health, present appearance, all my faculties——"

"Naturally, naturally. I'm not interested in tricking you over terms. What I had in mind was the possibility that boredom might set in."

"Are you bored?"

"I have been in my time," the devil admitted.

"You're immortal?"

"Of course."

"Then why haven't you killed yourself? Or couldn't you?"

"I could," the devil said bleakly. "I did. . . . Now, the terms of our contract. Immortality, youth, health, etc., etc., invulnerability with the single exception of suicide. In return for this service, I shall possess your soul at death."

"Why?" Fenwick asked with sudden curiosity.

The devil looked at him somberly. "In your fall, and in the fall of every soul, I forget my own for a moment." He plucked out of empty air a parchment scroll and a quill pen.

"Our agreement," the devil said.

Fenwick read the scroll carefully. At one point he looked up.

"What's this?" he asked. "I didn't know I was supposed to put up surety."

"I will naturally want some kind of bond," the devil said. "Unless you can find a coguarantor?"

"I'm sure I couldn't," Fenwick said. "Not even in

232

the death house. Well, what kind of security do you want?"

"Certain of your memories of the past," the devil said. "All of them unconscious, as it happens."

Fenwick considered. "I'm thinking about amnesia. I need my memories."

"Not these. Amnesia is concerned with conscious memories. You will never know the structure I want is missing."

"Is it—the soul?"

"No," the devil said calmly. "It is a necessary part of the soul, of course, or it would be of no value to me. But you will keep the essentials until you choose to surrender them to me at your death. I will then combine the two and take possession of your soul. But that will no doubt be a long time from now, and in the meantime you will suffer no inconvenience."

"If I write that into the contract, will you sign?"

The devil nodded.

Fenwick scribbled in the margin and then signed his name with the wet red point of the quill. "Here," he said.

The devil, with a tolerant air, added his name. He then waved the scroll into emptiness.

"Very well," he said. "Now stand up, please. Some glandular readjustment is necessary." His hands sank into Fenwick's breast painlessly, and moved swiftly here and there. "The thyroid . . . and the other endocrines . . . can be reset to regenerate your body indefinitely. Turn round, please."

In the mirror over the fireplace Fenwick saw his red visitor's hand sink softly into the back of Fenwick's head. He felt a sudden dizziness.

"Thalamus and pineal," the devil murmured. "The space-time cognition is subjective . . . and now you're independent of your external environment. One moment, now. There's another slight . . ."

His wrist twisted suddenly and he drew his closed

hand out of Fenwick's head. At the same time Fenwick felt a strange, sudden elation.

"What did you do then?" he asked, turning.

No one stood behind him. The apartment was quite empty. The devil had disappeared.

It could, of course, have been a dream. Fenwick had anticipated this possible skepticism after the event. Hallucinations could occur. He thought he was immortal and invulnerable now. But this is, by common standards, a psychotic delusion. He had no proof.

But he had no doubt, either. Immortality, he thought, is something tangible. An inward feeling of infinite well-being. That glandular readjustment, he thought. My body is functioning now as it never did before, as no one's ever did. I am a self-regenerating, closed system which nothing can injure, not even time.

A curious, welling happiness possessed him. He closed his eyes and summoned up the oldest memories he could command. Sunlight on a porch floor, the buzzing of a fly, warmth and a rocking motion. He was aware of no lack. His mind ranged free in the past. The rhythmic sway and creak of swings in a playground, the echoing stillness of a church. A piano-box clubhouse. The roughness of a washcloth scrubbing his face, and his mother's voice. . . .

Invulnerable, immortal, Fenwick crossed the room, opened a door and went down a short hallway. He walked with a sense of wonderful lightness, of pure pleasure in being alive. He opened a second door quietly and looked in. His mother lay in bed asleep, propped on a heap of pillows.

Fenwick felt very happy.

He moved softly forward, skirting the wheel chair by the bed, and stood looking down. Then he tugged a pillow gently free and lifted it in both hands, to lower it again slowly, at first, towards his mother's face.

Since this is not the chronicle of James Fenwick's

sins, it is clearly not necessary to detail the steps by which he arrived, within five years, at the title of the Worst Man in the World. Sensational newspapers reveled in him. There were, of course, worse men, but being mortal and vulnerable they were more reticent.

Fenwick's behavior was based on an increasing feeling that he was the only permanent object in a transient world. "Their days are as grass," he mused, watching his fellow Satanists as they crowded around an altar with something unpleasant on it. This was early in his career, when he was exploring pure sensation along traditional lines, later discarded as juvenilia.

Meanwhile, perfectly free, and filled with that enduring, delightful sense of well-being. Fenwick experimented with many aspects of living. He left a trail of hung juries and baffled attorneys behind him. "A modern Caligula!" said the New York *News,* explaining to its readers who Caligula had been, with examples. "Are the shocking charges against James Fenwick true?"

But somehow, he could never quite be convicted. Every charge fell through. He was, as the devil had assured him, a closed system within his environment, and his independence of the outer world was demonstrated in many a courtroom. Exactly how the devil managed things so efficiently Fenwick could never understand. Very seldom did an actual miracle have to happen.

Once an investment banker, correctly blaming Fenwick for the collapse of his entire fortune, fired five bullets at Fenwick's heart. The bullets ricocheted. The only witnesses were the banker and Fenwick. Theorizing that his unharmed target was wearing a bulletproof vest, the banker aimed the last bullet at Fenwick's head, with identical results. Later the man tried again, with a knife. Fenwick, who was curious, decided to wait and see what would happen. What happened was that eventually the banker went mad.

Fenwick, who had appropriated his fortune by very direct means, proceeded to increase it. Somehow, he was never convicted of any of the capital charges he incurred. It took a certain technique to make sure that the crimes he committed would always endanger his life if he were arrested for them, but he mastered the method without much difficulty and his wealth and power increased tremendously.

He was certainly notorious. Presently he decided that something was lacking, and began to crave admiration. It was not so easy to achieve. He did not yet possess enough wealth to transcend the mortal judgment of society. That was easily remedied. Ten years after his bargain with the devil, Fenwick was not perhaps the most powerful man in the world, but certainly the most powerful man in the United States. He attained the admiration and the fame he thought he wanted.

And it was not enough. The devil had suggested that in a few million years Fenwick might wish to die, out of sheer boredom. It took only ten years for Fenwick to realize, one summer day, with a little shock of unpleasant surprise, that he did not know what he wanted to do next.

He examined his state of mind with close attention. "Is this boredom?" he asked himself. If so, not even boredom was unpleasant. There was a delightful, sensuous relaxation about it, like floating in a warm summer ocean. In a sense, he was *too* relaxed.

"If this is all there is to immortality," he told himself. "I might as well not have bothered. Pleasant, certainly, but not worth bartering my soul for. There must be things that will rouse me out of this somnolence."

He experimented. The next five years witnessed his meteoric fall from public favor as he tried more and more frantically to break through that placid calm. He couldn't do it. He got no reaction from even the most horrific situations. What others saw with shock and often with horror had no meaning to Fenwick.

With a sense of smothered desperation under the calm he saw that he was beginning to lose contact with

236

the race of man. Humans were mortal, and more and more they seemed to recede into the distance, less real than the solid earth underfoot. In time, he thought, the earth would become less solid, as he watched the slow shifting of the geologic tides.

He turned at last to the realm of the intellect. He took up painting and he dabbled in literature and in some of the sciences. Interesting—up to a point. But always he came before long to a closed door in the mind, beyond which lay only that floating calm which dissolved all interest out of his mind. Something was lacking in him. . . .

The suspicion was slow in forming. It floated almost to the surface and then sank again under the pressure of new experiments. But eventually it broke free into the realm of the conscious.

Early one summer morning Fenwick roused out of a sound sleep and sat straight up in bed as if an invisible hand had pulled him out of slumber.

"Something is missing!" he told himself with great conviction. "But what?" He meditated. "How long has it been gone?" He could not say—at first. The deep, ineradicable calm kept lulling him and it was hard to follow the thought. That calm in itself was part of the trouble. How long had he had it? Obviously, since the day of his pact. What caused it? Well, he had been assuming all these many years that it was simply the physical well-being of perfectly and eternally functioning bodily mechanisms. But what if this were really something more? What if it were an artificially induced dulling of the mind so that he would not suspect a theft had been committed?

A theft? Sitting up in bed among heavy silk sheets, with the June dawn pale outside the windows, James Fenwick suddenly saw the outrageous truth. He struck his knee a resounding blow under the bedclothes.

"My soul!" he cried to the unheeding dawn. "He swindled me! He stole my soul!"

237

The moment the idea took shape it seemed so obvious Fenwick could not understand why it had not been clear from the first. The devil had cunningly and most unfairly anticipated the pay-off by seizing his soul too soon. And if not all of it, then the most important part. Fenwick had actually stood before the mirror and watched him do it. The proof seemed obvious. For something was very definitely missing. He seemed to stand always just inside a closed door in the mind that would not open for him because he lacked the essential something, the lost, the stolen soul. . . .

What good was immortality, without this mysterious something that gave immortality its savor? He was helpless to enjoy the full potentialities of eternal life because he had been robbed of the very key to living.

" 'Certain memories of the past,' is it?" he sneered, remembering the devil's casual description of the thing he wanted for surety. "Never miss them, eh? And all the time it was something out of the very middle of my soul!"

Now he remembered episodes out of folklore and mythology, people in legend who had lacked souls. The Little Mermaid, the Seal Maiden, someone or other in *A Midsummer Night's Dream*—a standard situation in myth, once you considered the question. And those who lacked the souls always yearned to get one at any cost. Nor was it, Fenwick realized, simply ethnocentric thinking on the part of the author. He was in the unique position of knowing this yearning for a soul to be quite valid.

Now that he was aware of his loss, the queer, crippling inward lack tormented him. It had presumably tormented the Little Mermaid and others. Like him, they had had immortality. Being extrahuman they had probably possessed this curious, light-headed, light-hearted freedom which even now interposed a cushion of partial indifference between Fenwick and his loss. Were not the gods supposed to spend their days in just

238

this simple-minded joy, laughing and singing, dancing and drinking endlessly, never weary, never bored?

Up to a point it was wonderful. But once you began to suspect that something had been removed, you lost your taste for the Olympian life and began at all costs to crave a soul. Why? Fenwick couldn't say. He only *knew*. . . .

At this moment the cool summer dawn shimmered between him and the window, and the devil stood before James Fenwick.

Fenwick shuddered slightly.

"The bargain," he said, "was for eternity."

"Yes," the devil said. "Only you can abrogate it."

"Well, I don't intend to," Fenwick told him sharply. "How did you happen to show up at just this moment?"

"I thought I heard my name called," the devil said. "Did you want to speak to me? I seemed to catch a note of despair in your mind. How do you feel? Bored yet? Ready to end it?"

"Certainly not," Fenwick said. "But if I were it's because you swindled me. I want a word with you. What was it you took out of my head in your closed hand the day of our pact?"

"I don't care to discuss it," the devil said, lashing his tail slightly.

"Well, I care," Fenwick cried. "You told me it was only a few unimportant memories I'd never miss."

"And so it was," the devil said, grinning.

"It was my soul!" Fenwick said, striking the bed-clothes angrily. "You cheated me. You collected my soul in advance, and now I can't enjoy the immortality I bought with it. This is out-and-out breach of contract."

"What seems to be the trouble?" the devil asked.

"There must be a great many things I'd enjoy doing, if I had my soul back," Fenwick said. "I could take up music and become a great musician, if I had my soul. I always liked music, and I have eternity to learn

239

in. Or I could study mathematics. I could learn nuclear physics and who knows, with all the time and money and knowledge in the world at my command, there's no limit to the things I could achieve. I could even blow up the world and rob you of all future souls. How would you like that?"

The devil laughed politely and polished his talons on his sleeve.

"Don't laugh," Fenwick said. "It's perfectly true. I could study medicine and prolong human life. I could study politics and economics and put an end to wars and suffering. I could study crime and fill up Hell with new converts. I could do anything—if I had my soul back. But without it—well, everything is too—too peaceful." Fenwick's shoulders sagged disconsolately. "I feel cut off from humanity," he said. "Everything I do is blocked. But I'm calm and carefree. I'm not even unhappy. And yet I don't know what to do next. I—"

"In a word, you're bored," the devil said. "Excuse me if I don't show enough sympathy for your plight."

"In a word, you swindled me," Fenwick said. " I want back my soul."

"I told you exactly what it was I took," the devil said.

"My soul!"

"Not at all," the devil assured him. "I'm afraid I shall have to leave you now."

"Give me back my soul, you swindler!"

"Try and make me do it," the devil said with a broad grin. The first ray of the morning sun shimmered in the cool air of the bedroom, and in the shimmer the devil dissolved and vanished.

"Very well," Fenwick said to the emptiness. "Very well, I will."

He wasted no time about it. Or at least, no more time than his curious, carefree placidity enforced.

"How can I bring pressure on the devil?" he asked

himself. "By blocking him in some way? I don't see how. Well, then, by depriving him of something he values? What does he value? Souls. All souls. *My* soul. Hm-m-m." He frowned pensively. "I could," he reflected, "repent. . . ."

Fenwick thought all day about it. The idea tempted him, and yet of course in a way it was self-defeating. The consequences were unpredictable. Besides, he was not sure how to go about it. To undertake a lifetime of good deeds seemed too boring.

In the evening he went out alone and walked at twilight through the streets, thinking deeply. The people he passed were like transient shadows reflected on the screen of time. They had no significance. The air was sweet and calm, and if it had not been for this sense of nagging injustice, the aimless inability to use the immortality he had paid so high for, he would have felt entirely at peace.

Presently the sound of music penetrated his rapt senses and he looked up to find himself outside the portal of a great cathedral. Shadowy people went up and down the steps. From within deep organ music rolled, the sound of singing emerged, occasional waves of incense were sweet on the air. It was most impressive.

Fenwick thought, "I could go up and embrace the altar and shout out my repentance." He put his foot on the bottom step, but then he hesitated and felt that he could not face it. The cathedral was too impressive. He would feel like such a fool. And yet—

He walked on, undecided. He walked a long way.

Again the sound of music interrupted his thinking. this time he was passing a vacant lot upon which a large revival tent had been pitched. There was a great deal of noise coming out of it. Music pounded wildly through the canvas walls. Men and women were singing and shouting inside.

Fenwick paused, struck by hope. Here at least he

could do his repenting without more than a passing glance. He hesitated briefly and then went in.

It was very noisy, crowded and confused inside. But before Fenwick, an aisle stretched between benches toward an altar, of sorts, with several highly excited people clustered under the uplifted arms of an even more highly excited speaker in an improvised pulpit.

Fenwick started down the aisle.

"How should I phrase this?" he wondered, walking slowly. "Just 'I repent'? Is that enough? Or something like, 'I have sold my soul to the devil and I hereby repudiate the bargain'? Are legal terms necessary?"

He had almost reached the altar when the air shimmered before him and the crimson outlines of the devil appeared very faintly, a mere three-dimensional sketch upon the dusty air.

"I wouldn't do this if I were you," the pale image said.

Fenwick sneered and walked through him.

At this the devil pulled himself together and appeared in full form and color in the aisle, blocking Fenwick's way.

"I wish you wouldn't create scenes like this," the devil said pettishly. "I can't tell you how uncomfortable I feel here. Kindly don't be a fool, Fenwick."

Several people in the crowd cast curious glances at the devil, but no one seemed unduly interested. Most probably thought him a costumed attendant, and those who knew him for what he was may have been accustomed to the sight, or perhaps they expected some such apparition in such a place at such a time. There was no disturbance.

"Out of my way," Fenwick said. "My mind is made up."

"You are cheating," the devil complained. "I can't allow it."

"You cheated," Fenwick reminded him. "Try and stop me."

"I will," the devil said, and reached out both taloned hands. Fenwick laughed.

"I am a system enclosed within itself," he said. "You can't harm me. Remember?"

The devil gnashed his teeth.

Fenwick brushed the crimson form aside and went on.

Behind him the devil said, "Oh, very well, Fenwick. You win."

Relieved, Fenwick turned. "Will you give me back my soul?"

"I'll give you back what I took as surety," the devil said, "but you won't like it."

"Hand it over," Fenwick said. "I don't believe a word you say."

"I am the father of lies," the devil said, "but this time—"

"Never mind," Fenwick said. "Just give me back my soul."

"Not here. I find this very uncomfortable," the devil told him. "Come with me. Don't cringe like that, I merely want to take you to your apartment. We need privacy."

He lifted his crimson hands and sketched a wall around himself and Fenwick. Immediately the pushing crowds, the shouting and tumult faded and the walls of Fenwick's sumptuous apartment rose around them. Slightly breathless, Fenwick crossed the familiar floor and looked out the window. He was indubitably at home again.

"That was clever," he congratulated the devil. "Now give me back my soul."

"I will give you back the part of it I removed," the devil said. "It was not in violation of the contract, but a bargain is a bargain. I think it only fair to warn you, however, that you won't like it."

"No shilly-shallying," Fenwick said. "I don't expect you to admit you cheated."

"You are warned," the devil said.

"Hand it over."

The devil shrugged. He then put his hand into his own chest, groped for a moment, murmuring, "I put it away for safekeeping," and withdrew his closed fist. "Turn around," he said. Fenwick did so. He felt a cool breeze pass through his head from the back. . . .

"Stand still," the devil said from behind. "This will take a moment or two. You are a fool, you know. I expected a better entertainment or I'd never have troubled myself to go through this farce. My poor stupid friend, it was not your soul I took. It was merely unconscious memories, as I said all along."

"Then why," Fenwick demanded, "am I unable to enjoy my immortality? What is it that stops me at the threshold of everything I attempt? I'm tired of living like a god if I have to stop with immortality only, and no real pleasure in it."

"Hold still," the devil said. "There. My dear Fenwick, you are not a god. You're a very limited mortal man. Your own limitations are all that stand in your way. In a million years you could never become a great musician or a great economist or any of the greats you dream of. It simply isn't in you. Immortality has nothing to do with it. Oddly enough—" And here the devil sighed. "Oddly enough, those who make bargains with me never do have the capability to use their gifts. I suppose only inferior minds expect to get something for nothing. Yours is distinctly inferior."

The cool breeze ceased.

"There you are," the devil said. "I have now returned what I took. It was, in Freudian terms, simply your superego."

"Superego?" Fenwick echoed, turning. "I don't quite—"

"Understand?" the devil finished for him, suddenly smiling broadly. "You will. It is the structure of early learning built up in your unconscious mind. It guides your impulses into channels acceptable to society. In a word, my poor Fenwick, I have just restored your conscience. Why did you think you felt so light and carefree without it?"

Fenwick drew breath to reply, but it was too late. The devil had vanished. He stood alone in the room.

Well, no, not entirely alone. There was a mirror over the fireplace and in the mirror he met his own appalled eyes in the instant the superego took up again the interrupted function of the conscience.

A terrible, smashing awareness struck down upon Fenwick like the hand of a punishing God. He knew now what he had done. He remembered his crimes. All of them. Every last terrible, unforgivable, immutable sin he had committed in the past twenty years.

His knees buckled under him. The world turned dark and roared in his ears. Guilt was a burden he could hardly stagger under. The images of the things he had seen and done in the years of his carefree evil were thunder and lightning that shook the brain in his skull. Intolerable anguish roared through his mind and he struck his hands to his eyes to blot out vision, but he could not blot out memory.

Staggering, he turned and stumbled toward his bedroom door. He tore it open, reeled across the room and reached into a bureau drawer. He took out a revolver.

He lifted the revolver, and the devil came in.

WHOSITS DISEASE

By Henry Slesar

There wasn't much substance to the short, pale-eyed man who entered Dr. Cravert's examining room, and there was even less once he shucked padded shoulders, shirt, and tie. His complexion was sallow, his aspect melancholy, and there was a tremor in the heavy-knuckled hands that dangled at the end of stalk-like arms. He was complaining of joint pains, sleeplessness, a buzzing in his left ear and a tic in his right eye, and there was a strange blue rash forming a cummerbund around his naked waist. His name was Herman Kunkle, age 38, and he drove a dairy truck.

"Mmph," Dr. Cravert said professionally. "How long have you had the rash?"

"Three, four weeks," Kunkle sighed. "It doesn't itch or anything. Also, my feet tickle at night."

"Tickle?"

"Yeah, tickle, in the middle of the night. I wake up I'm laughin' so hard."

"We'd better make this a *thorough* examination," Dr. Cravert said grimly.

The physician made good his promise, to the limitation of his diagnostic equipment. Cravert practiced in a downtown area that had been deteriorating for twenty

246

years. By the time the city planners moved in with new construction, he was too old to compete with the Medical Arts center that was part of their blueprint. He had been ambitious once, eager for attention and fame. Now, as he explored the peculiar alterations in Herman Kunkle's body, he felt the touch of the spur again.

"Mr. Kunkle," he said, tapping his reflex hammer against his palm, "Whatever is wrong with you is certainly out of the ordinary. I want you to have a series of x-rays before I reach any definite opinion."

"Couldn't you give me something? Penicillin or something?"

"I can't be sure what's indicated until the diagnosis is complete. It may well be—" He caught his breath. "It may well be a brand-new disease, Mr. Kunkle."

When Kunkle left, dissatisfied, the address of an x-ray laboratory in his pocket, Dr. Cravert took the time between appointments to ponder the problem. It was a long time, and the more he brooded about Kunkle's syndrome, the more convinced he became that he had stumbled across a new breed of cat. One by one, he ticked off possibilities and rejected them. Cravert prided himself on an encyclopedic knowledge of pathology, and his remarkable memory in student days had pushed him to the head of his class. Then, sadly, he had learned that memory and scholastic ability were not the only factors in a physician's success. There was an intuitive mysterious something he lacked; perhaps it was personality. He had been disappointed first, then embittered, and finally resigned to five-dollar fees and transient cases. Kunkle, for instance, had come in off the street. But what was wrong with Kunkle? Back to research.

That night, he spent four hours with his medical books, seeking some forgotten passage. The more he searched, the more his excitement grew. As volume after volume was put aside, he was actually hoping that he would find no description of Kunkle's ailment. He didn't want it to be there. He wanted Kunkle to be an original—*his* original.

By the time the doctor went to bed, he was already composing the learned article in his mind.

"The symptoms of Cravert's Disease are as follows . . ."

Kunkle returned two days later with x-rays in hand. Cravert read the technician's report, and then corroborated it by examining the negatives carefully. There was no doubt of it; x-ray analysis failed to provide any clues to the ailment.

"Well, Doc?" Kunkle said. "What do you see?"

"Nothing abnormal. There's no question that you're suffering from something rare—unique, as a matter of fact. I'd like to make several new tests of your blood, metabolism, and so forth, and then we'll see. By the way," he said, as Kunkle slowly removed his shirt, "you may be interested to know that I'm submitting a report on your case to the medical journals." He chuckled good-naturedly. "You're going to be famous, Mr. Kunkle, the first man to have Cravert's Disease."

"Have what?" Kunkle blinked.

"Cravert's Disease," the doctor said. "That's what I'm calling it. Would you extend your left arm, please?"

"I thought you said you didn't know what it was?"

"No, and that's why I'm giving it a name," Cravert beamed, and took a blood sample. Kunkle watched the procedure dully, his mouth working in the throes of some undefined emotion.

"I don't get it," he said. "How come you're calling it Cravert's Disease?"

"Well, that's my name, Cravert."

"Yeah, but you ain't got the disease, doc, I do."

Cravert laughed, and shook the sample in the test tube. "I know that, Mr. Kunkle, but in these matters that's only standard procedure. A new disease is always named for the discoverer. And that's me."

"You?" Kunkle's jaw stiffened belligerently. "What

do you mean, you? *I'm* the one that discovered it. I *got* it. You oughta call it Kunkle's Disease."

"But that just isn't done. You've heard of Bright's Disease? Hodgkin's Disease? Parkinson's Disease? All those were named for the physician who first diagnosed them."

"I don't *care* about them!" Kunkle said, throwing out his thin arms. It was the first display of animation since his appearance. "It ain't *fair* to call it anything but Kunkle's Disease. I'm the one's got it, I oughta get the credit!"

"Really, Mr. Kunkle—"

"Don't really me!" Kunkle yelled. "You better not call it Cravert's Disease, doc, you ain't got no right!"

"I'm afraid that's not your decision—"

"It ain't, huh?" Kunkle grabbed his shirt and started yanking his arms through the sleeves.

"What do you think you're doing?"

"I'm walking out!" Kunkle said hotly. "That's what I'm doing! I'm finding myself another doctor—"

"You can't do that! I've already started—"

"Nobody says I can't pick any doctor I want! I'll find me somebody who'll call what I got by the right name." He whipped the tie around his thin neck. "Kunkle's Disease!" he shouted, his hands trembling around the fabric. "Herman Kunkle's Disease! You ain't cheatin' me outa *that,* mister!"

His shirttail flopping over his belt, Kunkle stalked out of the examining room. The sound of the slamming door was loud enough to jar the test tube out of Cravert's hand. It dropped to the floor and shattered, and the doctor looked down blankly at the blood splatter on the white tiles.

He was unnerved for the rest of the day. He read and re-read the first page of the article he had planned to submit for publication. His phrases had been only tentative, awaiting the final outcome of his tests; the only firm wording was the title: *A Report on the Dis-*

249

covery of Cravert's Disease. Now the title mocked him.

Angrily, he tore up the page and let the scraps float into the wastebasket. The finality of the gesture pained him; the pain became real, and he helped himself to an analgesic. When the telephone rang, and a patient requested an appointment, he grunted an excuse; he was in no mood to talk to anyone. For the first time since Herman Kunkle brought his blue rash and odd symptoms into his office, he realized how important, how *vital* an opportunity had entered his life. The promised glory of his student days had neared fulfillment; the recognition that had passed him by had been within hypodermic range. Herman Kunkle was more than a patient. He was immortality for him!

That night, in the dingy quiet of his apartment, he made the necessary decision. He telephoned Kunkle.

"Mr. Kunkle? This Dr. Cravert."

"I got nothin' to say to you, doc. I got an appointment at the Medical Arts center tomorrow."

Cravert winced.

"Mr. Kunkle, you're making a mistake. I've already determined the proper treatment for your illness, and you owe it to yourself to let me help you."

"But I ain't got no Cravert's Disease—"

"I didn't say anything about Cravert's Disease. Since you feel so strongly about it, I promise not to call it that."

"You really mean that?" Kunkle said suspiciously.

"I mean it. I still plan to write my paper; I feel that's a duty I owe the profession. But if you wish me to call it Kunkle's Disease, or anything else, I'll do so."

"How do I know that?"

"What?"

"How do I know you'll keep your word?"

Cravert sighed. "I'll put it in writing. I'll post a bond. I'll let you mail the article yourself. I'll do anything you say. Can you return to my office tomorrow?"

There was a pause.

"Okay, doc. As long as you keep your promise."

Kunkle showed up the next day, and, after a complete series of tests and examinations, Dr. Cravert began his first treatment with an intravenous injection.

"And so, gentlemen," Dr. Cravert said turning slowly to encompass the auditorium. "While we of the profession prefer to add new cures to the body of medical knowledge rather than new ailments, our duty is clear. Cravert's Disease is now part of the lexicon of human afflictions. And unfortunately, rare as the affliction may be, it must be described as fatal. At least," he added gravely, "in this particular case."

KING PEST

By Edgar Allan Poe

About twelve o'clock, one night in the month of October, and during the chivalrous reign of the third Edward, two seamen belonging to the crew of the *Free and Easy,* a trading schooner plying between Sluys and the Thames, and then at anchor in that river, were much astonished to find themselves seated in the tap room of an ale-house in the parish of St. Andrew, London—which ale-house bore for sign the portraiture of a "Jolly Tar."

The room, although ill-contrived, smoke-blackened, low-pitched, and in every other respect agreeing with the general character of such places at the period—was nevertheless, in the opinion of the grotesque groups scattered here and there within it, sufficiently well adapted to its purpose.

Of these groups our two seamen formed, I think, the most interesting, if not the most conspicuous.

The one who appeared to be the elder, and whom his companion addressed by the characteristic appellation of "Legs," was at the same time much the taller of the two. He might have measured six feet and a half, and an habitual stoop in the shoulders seemed to have been the necessary consequence of an altitude so enormous. Superfluities in height were, however, more than accounted for by deficiencies in other respects. He was exceedingly thin; and might, as his associates asserted, have answered, when drunk, for a pennant at the mast-head, or, when sober, have served for a jib-boom. But these jests, and others of a similar nature, had evidently produced, at no time, any effect upon the cachinnatory muscles of the tar. With high cheek-bones, a large hawk-nose, retreating chin, fallen underjaw, and huge protruding white eyes, the expression of his countenance, although tinged with a species of dogged indifference to matters and things in general, was not the less utterly solemn and serious beyond all attempts at imitation or description.

The younger seaman was, in all outward appearance, the converse of his companion. His stature could not have exceeded four feet. A pair of stumpy bow legs supported his squat, unwieldy figure, while his unusually short and thick arms, with no ordinary fists at their extremities, swung off dangling from his sides like the fins of a sea-turtle. Small eyes, of no particular colour, twinkled far back in his head. His nose remained buried in the mass of flesh which enveloped his round, full and purple face; and his thick upper-lip rested upon the still thicker one beneath with an air of complacent self-satisfaction, much heightened by the owner's habit of licking them at intervals. He evidently regarded his tall shipmate with a feeling half-wondrous half-quizzical; and stared up occasionally in his face as the red setting sun stares up at the crags of Ben Nevis.

Various and eventful, however, had been the peregrinations of the worthy couple in and about the different tap-houses of the neighbourhood during the earlier hours of the night. Funds, even the most ample, are not always everlasting; and it was with empty pockets our friends had ventured upon the present hostelrie.

At the present period, then, when this history properly commences, Legs, and his fellow, Hugh Tarpaulin, sat, each with both elbows resting upon the large oaken table in the middle of the floor, and with a hand upon either cheek. They were eyeing from behind a huge flagon of unpaid-for "humming-stuff," the portentous words, "No Chalk," which to their indignation and astonishment were scored over the door-way by means of that very mineral whose presence they purported to deny. Not that the gift of deciphering written characters—a gift among the commonality of that day considered little less cabalistical than the art of indicting—could, in strict justice, have been laid to the charge of either disciple of the sea; but there was, to say the truth, a certain twist in the formation of the letters—an indescribable lee-lurch about the whole—which foreboded, in the opinion of both seamen, a long run of dirty weather; and determined them at once, in the allegorical words of Legs himself, to "clew up all sail, and scud before the wind."

Having accordingly disposed of what remained of the ale, and looped up the points of their short doublets, they finally made a bolt for the street. Although Tarpaulin rolled twice into the fireplace, mistaking it for the door, yet their escape was at length happily effected—and half after twelve o'clock found our heroes ripe for mischief, and running for life down a dark alley in the direction of St. Andrew's Stair, hotly pursued by the landlady of the "Jolly Tar."

At the epoch of this eventful tale, and periodically, for many years before and after, all England, but more especially the metropolis, resounded with the fearful cry of "Plague!" The city was in a great measure depopulated—and in those horrible regions, in the vicinity of the Thames, where, amid the dark, narrow, and filthy lanes and alleys, the Demon of Disease was supposed to have had his nativity, Awe, Terror, and Superstition were alone to be found stalking abroad.

By authority of the king such districts were placed *under ban,* and all persons forbidden, under pain of death, to intrude upon their dismal solitude. Yet neither the mandate of the monarch, nor the huge barriers erected at the entrances of the streets, nor the prospect of that loathsome death which, with almost absolute certainty, overwhelmed the wretch whom no peril could deter from the adventure, prevented the unfurnished and untenanted dwellings from being stripped, by the hand of nightly rapine, of every article, such as iron, brass, or lead-work, which could in any manner be turned to a profitable account.

Above all, it was usually found, upon the annual winter opening of the barriers, that locks, bolts, and secret cellars had proved but slender protection to those rich stores of wines and liquors which, in consideration of the risk and trouble of removal, many of the numerous dealers having shops in the neighbourhood had consented to trust, during the period of exile, to so insufficient a security.

But there were very few of the terror-stricken people who attributed these doings to the agency of human hands. Pest-spirits, plague-goblins, and fever-demons were the popular imps of mischief; and tales so blood-chilling were hourly told, that the whole mass of forbidden buildings was, at length, enveloped in terror as in a shroud, and the plunderer himself was often scared away by the horrors his own depredations had created; leaving the entire vast circuit of prohibited district to gloom, silence, pestilence, and death.

It was by one of the terrific barriers already mentioned, and which indicated the region beyond to be under the Pest-ban, that, in scrambling down an alley, Legs and the worthy Hugh Tarpaulin found their progress suddenly impeded. To return was out of the question, and no time was to be lost as their pursuers were close upon their heels. With thorough-bred seamen to clamber up the roughly fashioned plankwork was a trifle; and maddened with the twofold excitement of exercise and liquor, they leaped unhesitatingly down within the enclosure, and holding on their drunken course with shouts and yellings, were soon bewildered in its noisome and intricate recesses.

Had they not, indeed, been intoxicated beyond moral sense, their reeling footsteps must have been palsied by the horrors of their situation. The air was cold and misty. The paving-stones, loosened from their beds, lay in wild disorder amid the tall, rank grass, which sprang up around the feet and ankles. Fallen houses choked up the streets. The most fetid and poisonous smells everywhere prevailed: and by the aid of that ghastly light which, even at midnight, never fails to emanate from a vapoury and pestilential atmosphere, might be discerned lying in the by-paths and alleys, or rotting in the windowless habitations, the carcass of many a nocturnal plunderer arrested by the hand of the plague in the very perpetration of his robbery.

But it lay not in the power of the images, or sensations, or impediments such as these, to stay the course of men, who, naturally brave, and at that time especially, brimful of courage and of "humming-stuff," would have reeled, as straight as their condition might have permitted, undauntedly into the very jaws of Death. Onward—still onward stalked the grim Legs, making the desolate solemnity echo and re-echo with yells like the terrific war-whoop of the Indian; and onward, still onward rolled the dumpy Tarpaulin, hanging on to the doublet of his more active companion, and far surpassing the latter's most strenuous exertions in the way of vocal music, by bull-roarings *in basso,* from the profundity of his stentorian lungs.

They had now evidently reached the stronghold of the pestilence. Their way at every step or plunge grew more noisome and more horrible—the paths more narrow and more intricate. Huge stones and beams falling momently from the decaying roofs above them, gave evidence, by their sullen and heavy descent, of the vast height of the surrounding houses; and while actual exertion became necessary to force a passage through frequent heaps of rubbish, it was by no means seldom that the hand fell upon a skeleton or rested upon a more fleshy corpse.

Suddenly, as the seamen stumbled against the entrance of a tall and ghastly-looking building, a yell more than usually shrill from the throat of the excited Legs, was replied to from within, in a rapid succession of wild, laughter-like, and fiendish shrieks. Nothing daunted at sounds which, of such a nature, at such a time, and in such a place, might have curdled the very blood in hearts less irrevocably on fire, the drunken couple rushed headlong against the door, burst it open, and staggered into the midst of things with a volley of curses.

The room within which they found themselves proved to be the shop of an undertaker; but an open trap-door, in the corner of the floor near the entrance, looked down upon a long range of wine-cellars, whose depths the occasional sound of burst bottles proclaimed to be well stored with their appropriate contents. In the middle of the room stood a table—in the centre of which again arose a huge tub of what appeared to be punch. Bottles of various wines and cordials, together with jugs, pitchers, and flagons of every shape and quality, were scattered profusely upon the board. Around it, upon coffin-tressels, was seated a company of six. This company I will endeavor to delineate one by one.

Fronting the entrance, and elevated a little above his companions, sat a personage who appeared to be the president of the table. His stature was gaunt and tall, and Legs was confounded to behold in him a figure more emaciated than himself. His face was as yellow as saffron—but no feature excepting one alone was sufficiently marked to merit a particular description. This one consisted in a forehead so unusually and hideously lofty, as to have the apperance of a bonnet or crown of flesh superadded upon the natural head. His mouth was puckered and dimpled into an expression of ghastly affability, and his eyes, as indeed the eyes of all at the table, were glazed over with the fumes of intoxication. This gentleman was clothed from head to foot in a richly-embroidered black silk-velvet pall, wrapped negligently around his form after the fashion of a Spanish cloak. His head was stuck full of sable hearse-plumes, which he nodded to and fro with a jaunty and knowing air; and, in his right hand, he held a huge human thigh-bone, with which he appeared to have been just knocking down some member of the company for a song.

Opposite him, and with her back to the door, was a lady of no whit less extraordinary character. Although quite as tall as the person just described, she had no right to complain of his unnatural emaciation. She was evidently in the last stage of dropsy; and her figure resembled nearly that of the huge puncheon of October beer which stood, with the head driven in, close by her side, in a corner of the chamber. Her face was exceedingly round, red, and full; and the same peculiarity, or rather want of peculiarity, attached itself to her countenance, which I before mentioned in the case of the president—that is to say, only one feature of her face was sufficiently distinguished to need a separate characterization: indeed the acute Tarpaulin immediately observed that the same remark might have applied to each individual person of the party, every one of whom seemed to possess a monopoly of some particular portion of physiognomy. With the lady in question this portion proved to be the mouth. Commencing at the right ear, it swept with a terrific chasm to the left—the short pendants which she wore on either auricle continually bobbing into the aperture. She made, however, every exertion to keep her mouth closed and look dignified, in a dress consisting of a newly-starched and ironed shroud coming up close under her chin, with a crimpled ruffle of cambric muslin.

At her right hand sat a diminutive young lady whom she appeared to patronize. This delicate little creature, in the trembling of her wasted fingers, in the livid hue of her lips, and in the slight hectic spot which tinged her otherwise leaden complexion, gave evident indications of a galloping consumption. An air of extreme *haut ton*, however, pervaded her whole appearance; she wore in a graceful and *dégagé* manner, a large and beautiful winding-sheet of the finest Indian lawn; her hair hung in ringlets over her neck; a soft smile played about her mouth; but her nose, extremely long, thin, sinuous, flexible, and pimpled, hung down far below her under-lip, and, in spite of the delicate manner in which she now and then moved it to one side or the other with her tongue, gave to her countenance a somewhat equivocal expression.

Over against her, and upon the left of the dropsical lady, was seated a little puffy, wheezing, and gouty old man, whose cheeks reposed upon the shoulders of their owner, like two huge bladders of Oporto wine. With his arms folded, and with one bandaged leg deposited upon the table, he seemed to think himself entitled to some consideration. He evidently prided himself much upon every inch of his personal appearance, but took more especial delight in calling attention to his gaudy-coloured surtout. This, to say the truth, must have cost him no little money, and was made to fit him exceedingly well—being fashioned from one of the curiously embroidered silken covers appertaining to those glorious escutcheons which, in England and elsewhere, are customarily hung up, in some conspicuous place, upon the dwelling of departed aristocracy.

Next to him, and at the right hand of the president, was a gentleman in long white hose and cotton drawers. His frame shook in a ridiculous manner, with a fit of what Tarpaulin called "the horrors." His jaws, which had been newly shaved, were tightly tied up by a bandage of muslin; and his arms being fastened in a similar way at the wrists, prevented him from helping himself too freely to the liquors upon the table; a precaution rendered necessary, in the opinion of Legs, by the peculiarly sottish and wine-bibbing cast of his visage. A pair of prodigious ears, nevertheless, which it was no doubt found impossible to confine, towered away into the atmosphere of the apartment, and were occasionally pricked up in a spasm at the sound of the drawing of a cork.

Fronting him, sixthly and lastly, was situated a singularly stiff-looking personage, who, being afflicted with paralysis, must, to speak seriously, have felt very ill at ease in his unaccommodating habiliments. He was habited, somewhat uniquely, in a new and handsome mahogany coffin. Its top or head piece pressed upon the skull of the wearer, and extended over it in the fashion of a hood, giving to the entire face an air of indescribable interest. Arm-holes had been cut in the sides for the sake not more of elegance than of convenience; but the dress, nevertheless, prevented its proprietor from sitting as erect as his associates; and as he lay reclining against his tressels, at an angle of forty-five degrees, a pair of huge goggle eyes rolled up their awful whites toward the ceiling in absolute amazement at their own enormity.

Before each of the party lay a portion of a skull, which was used as a drinking-cup. Overhead was suspended a human skeleton, by means of a rope tied round one of the legs and fastened to a ring in the ceiling. The other limb, confined by no such fetter, stuck off from the body at right angles, causing the whole loose and rattling frame to dangle and twirl about at the caprice of every occasional puff of wind which found its way into the apartment. In the cranium of this hideous thing lay a quantity of ignited charcoal, which threw a fitful but vivid light over the entire scene; while coffins, and other wares appertaining to the shop of an undertaker, were piled high up around the room, and against the windows, preventing any ray escaping into the street.

At sight of this extraordinary assembly, and of their still more extraordinary paraphernalia, our two seamen did not conduct themselves with that degree of decorum which might have been expected. Legs, leaning against the wall near which he happened to be standing, dropped his lower jaw still lower than usual, and spread open his eyes to their fullest extent; while Hugh Tarpaulin, stooping down so as to bring his nose upon a level with the table, and spreading out a palm upon either knee, burst into a long, loud, and obstreperous roar of very ill-timed and immoderate laughter.

Without, however, taking offence at behaviour so excessively rude, the tall president smiled very graciously upon the intruders—nodded to them in a dignified manner with his head of sable plumes—and, arising, took each by an arm, and led him to a seat which some others of the company had placed in the meantime for his accommodation. Legs to all this offered not the slightest resistance, but sat down as he was directed; while the gallant Hugh, removing his coffin-tressel from its station near the head of the table, to the vicinity of the little consumptive lady in the winding-sheet, plumped down by her side in high glee and pouring out a skull of red wine, quaffed to their better acquaintance. But at this presumption the stiff gentleman in the coffin seemed exceedingly nettled; and serious consequences might have ensued, had not the president, rapping upon the table with his truncheon, diverted the attention of all present to the following speech:

"It becomes our duty upon the present happy occasion—"

"Avast there!" interrupted Legs, looking very serious, "avast there a bit, I say, and tell us who the devil ye all are, and what business ye have here, rigged off like the foul fiends, and swilling the snug blue ruin stowed away for the winter by my honest shipmate, Will Wimble, the undertaker!"

At this unpardonable piece of ill-breeding, all the original company half-started to their feet, and uttered the same rapid succession of wild fiendish shrieks which had before caught the attention of the seamen. The president, however, was the first to recover his composure, and at length, turning to Legs with great dignity, recommenced:

"Most willingly will we gratify any reasonable curiosity on the part of guests so illustrious, unbidden though they be. Know then that in these dominions I am monarch, and here rule with undivided empire under the title of 'King Pest the First.'

"This apartment, which you no doubt profanely suppose to be the shop of Will Wimble the undertaker—a man whom we know not, and whose plebeian appellation has never before this night thwarted our royal ears —this apartment, I say, is the Dais-Chamber of our Palace, devoted to the councils of our kingdom, and to other sacred and lofty purposes.

"The noble lady who sits opposite is Queen Pest, our Serene Consort. The other exalted personages whom you behold are all of our family, and wear the insignia of the blood royal under the respective titles of 'His Grace the Arch Duke Pest-Iferous'—'His Grace the Duke Pest-Ilential'—'His Grace the Duke Tem-Pest' —'and Her Serene Highness the Arch Duchess Ana-Pest.'

"As regards," continued he, "your demand of the business upon which we sit here in council, we might be pardoned for replying that it concerns *alone,* our own private and regal interest, and is in no manner important to any other than ourselves. But in consideration of those rights to which as guests and strangers you may feel yourselves entitled, we will furthermore explain that we are here this night, prepared by deep

262

research and accurate investigation, to examine, analyse, and thoroughly determine the indefinable spirit —the incomprehensible qualities and nature—of those inestimable treasures of the palate, the wines, ales, and liqueurs of this goodly metropolis: by so doing to advance not more our own designs than the true welfare of that unearthly sovereign whose reign is over us all, whose dominions are unlimited, and whose name is 'Death.' "

"Whose name is Davy Jones!" ejaculated Tarpaulin, helping the lady by his side to a skull of liqueur, and pouring out a second for himself.

"Profane varlet!" said the president, now turning his attention to the worthy Hugh, "profane and execrable wretch!—we have said, that, in consideration of those rights which, even in thy filthy person, we feel no inclination to violate, we have condescended to make reply to thy rude and unreasonable inquiries. We nevertheless, for your unhallowed intrusion upon our councils, believe it our duty to mulct thee and thy companion each in a gallon of Black Strap—having imbibed which to the prosperity of our kingdom—at a single draught—and upon your bended knees—ye shall be forthwith free either to proceed upon your way, or remain and be admitted to the privileges of our table, according to your respective and individual pleasure."

"It would be a matter of utter impossibility," replied Legs, whom the assumptions and dignity of King Pest the First had evidently inspired with some feelings of respect, and who arose and steadied himself by the table as he spoke—"it would, please your majesty, be a matter of utter impossibility to stow away in my hold even one-fourth part of that same liquor which your majesty has just mentioned. To say nothing of the stuffs placed on board in the forenoon by way of ballast, and not to mention the various ales and liqueurs shipped this evening at various seaports, I have, at present, a full cargo of 'humming-stuff' taken in and

263

duty paid for at the sign of the 'Jolly Tar.' You will, therefore, please your majesty, be so good as to take the will for the deed—for by no manner of means either can I or will I swallow another drop—least of all a drop of that villainous bilge-water that answers to the name of 'Black Strap.'"

"Belay that," interrupted Tarpaulin, astonished not more at the length of his companion's speech than at the nature of his refusal—"Belay that, you lubber!—and I say, Legs, none of your palaver. *My* hull is still light, although I confess you yourself seem to be a little top-heavy; and as far as the matter of your share of the cargo, why rather than raise a squall I would find stowage-room for it myself, but—"

"This proceeding," interposed the president, "is by no means in accordance with the terms of the mulct or sentence, which is in its nature Median, and not to be altered or recalled. The conditions we have imposed must be fulfilled to the letter, and that without a moment's hesitation—in failure of which fulfilment we decree that you do here be tied neck and heels together, and duly drowned as rebels in yon hogshead of October beer!"

"A sentence!—a sentence!—a righteous and just sentence!—a glorious decree!—a most worthy and upright and holy condemnation!" shouted the Pest family all together. The king elevated his forehead into innumerable wrinkles; the gouty little old man puffed like a pair of bellows; the lady of the winding-sheet waved her nose to and fro; the gentleman in the cotton drawers pricked up his ears; she of the shroud gasped like a dying fish; and he of the coffin looked stiff and rolled up his eyes.

"Ugh! ugh! ugh!" chuckled Tarpaulin, without heeding the general excitement, "ugh! ugh! ugh!—ugh! ugh! ugh! ugh!—ugh ugh ugh!—I was saying," said he— "I was saying when Mr. King Pest poked in his marlin-spike, that as for the matter of two or three gallons

264

more or less of Black Strap, it was a trifle to a tight sea-boat like myself not overstowed—but when it comes to drinking the health of the Devil (whom God assoilize) and going down upon my marrow-bones to his ill-favoured majesty there, whom I know, as well as I know myself to be a sinner, to be nobody in the whole world but Tim Hurlygurly the stage-player!—why! it's quite another guess sort of a thing, and utterly and altogether past my comprehension."

He was not allowed to finish this speech in tranquility. At the name of Tim Hurlygurly the whole assembly leaped from their seats.

"Treason!" shouted his Majesty King Pest the First.

"Treason!" said the little man with the gout.

"Treason!" screamed the Arch Duchess Ana-Pest.

"Treason!" muttered the gentleman with his jaws tied up.

"Treason!" growled he of the coffin.

"Treason! treason!" shrieked her majesty of the mouth; and seizing by the hinder part of his breeches the unfortunate Tarpaulin, who had just commenced pouring out for himself a skull of liqueur, she lifted him high into the air, and let him fall without ceremony into the huge open puncheon of his beloved ale. Bobbing up and down, for a few seconds, like an apple in a bowl of toddy, he, at length, finally disappeared amid the whirlpool of foam which, in the already effervescent liquor, his struggles easily succeeded in creating.

Not tamely, however, did the tall seaman behold the discomfiture of his companion. Jostling King Pest through the open trap, the valient Legs slammed the door down upon him with an oath, and strode toward the centre of the room. Here tearing down the skeleton which swung over the table, he laid it about him with so much energy and good-will that, as the last glimpses of light died away within the apartment, he succeeded in knocking out the brains of the little gentleman with

265

the gout. Rushing then with all his force against the fatal hogshead full of October ale and Hugh Tarpaulin, he rolled it over and over in an instant. Out poured a deluge of liquor so fierce—so impetuous—so overwhelming—that the room was flooded from wall to wall—the loaded table was overturned—the tressels were thrown upon their backs—the tub of punch into the fire-place—and the ladies into hysterics. Piles of death-furniture floundered about. Jugs, pitchers, and carboys mingled promiscuously in the *mêlée,* and wicker flagons encountered desperately with bottles of junk. The man with the horrors was drowned upon the spot—the little stiff gentleman floated off in his coffin —and the victorious Legs, seizing by the waist the fat lady in the shroud, rushed out with her into the street, and made a bee-line for the *Free and Easy,* followed under easy sail by the redoubtable Hugh Tarpaulin, who, having sneezed three or four times, panted and puffed after him with the Arch Duchess Ana-Pest.

MAYAYA'S LITTLE GREEN MEN

By Harold Lawlor

I have it here in the lower right-hand drawer of my desk, in a pint Mason jar full of alcohol. A gruesome souvenir, some might say, but I look upon it as a talisman. And—who knows?—some day I may go to Trinidad. . . .

Mayaya came unexpectedly, and just in the nick of time. For Peggy had been doing the cooking and cleaning, inefficiently enough, this long week past, and she was on the verge of hysteria that morning.

A rambling, reconverted farmhouse, twenty miles from town, is all very well and beautiful—in the decorator's magazines. But we'd had hell's own time of it trying to keep servants—three batches of them in less than two months. They couldn't stand the isolation, the lack of amusements.

So there were just the three of us now in a house with twelve rooms, two studios, and four baths; my wife Peggy, our three-year-old son Scooter, and myself. The servant-less week had left Peggy a wraith—a somewhat peevish wraith.

"No, no, no!" she said to Scooter, as we were at breakfast that morning in the kitchen. "The oatmeal goes *in* your face, darling, not on it."

Peggy's voice was on the thin edge, and I should have known better. I should have kept my mouth shut. But I said, "You've really exceeded yourself this morning, baby. The coffee is even lousier than yesterday's."

Peggy glared at me, speechless. Then her face broke up, and she laid her head in her arms on the table, and bawled. "If you can do any better," she cried incoherently, "go right ahead! I'm fed up! I'm nearly crazy! Max phoning me this morning that if I don't get the illustrations done for the Nellis book I'll never get another job out of them, so help him. And I'm three weeks behind now. And the bathrooms to be cleaned! And who *wanted* to live in the country, anyway? *You* did!"

"Sh, sh, sh!" For some time I'd been trying to stem the tide. "There, baby, calm down, for the love of Mike. We'll get somebody yet. And, anyway, I'll help—"

"A fat lot of help you are," Peggy sniffed. "You and your darned old soap operas."

"Yes, and where would we be if I didn't get an installment out every day, I'd like to know! You like to eat, don't you?"

"You can't *talk* to me like that!" Peggy cried.

"Oh, can't I?" We stood there glaring at each other, shaping up to a nice battle.

Scooter then added his bit to the general confusion by crying, "Whee!" and shoving his dish of oatmeal onto the linoleum.

"Oh, my God!" Peggy wailed at this last straw. "And I spent all day yesterday scrubbing that blasted—"

Obviously we were badly in need of help. Then the knock came on the kitchen door.

Peggy was in no condition to answer it, with her face all tear-streaked. I handed her my handkerchief sulkily. "Here wipe your face. I don't know which is the bigger baby, you or Scooter. I'll go."

"Oh, shut up," Peggy said mildly.

So I opened the door, and Mayaya was there, smiling.

"Good day," she said softly. "I understand you are in need of domestic help?"

I couldn't help but stare. She was a very superior-looking colored girl. At least I thought she was colored, though she was no darker than well-creamed coffee. And rather beautiful, with unrouged skin, wine-red lips, and dark lustrous eyes. She was an undeniable figure of chic in her plain black coat and hat, and looked totally unlike any household help I'd ever seen before.

Peggy recovered first. "For heaven's sake, Jay, ask her in. You might even roll out the red carpet."

Our visitor laughed huskily, with a sound like muted chimes. "I'm Mayaya," she introduced herself.

"If you can make coffee, you're hired," I said.

Peggy glared at me for this. "And we'll get other servants to help you, just as soon as possible," she enticed.

The girl was already taking off her coat and hat, to our relief. She shooed us gently out of the kitchen, and in less than a half-hour called us to the breakfast room. The china, silver, glassware, were shining—which they certainly hadn't been under Peggy's inexpert ministrations. Scooter was already seated and—miracle!—his face was even clean for a change.

"Pinch me," Peggy whispered. "I don't believe a word of this."

Neither did I. But the coffee was marvelous. I smacked my lips.

"The bacon, the eggs, the muffins!" Peggy was almost delirious. "We've found ourselves a pearl!"

"What'd she say her name was again?" I asked.

"Sounded like she said 'Me-yah-yah' to me."

"Never heard of a name like that."

"Listen," Peggy said intensely. "If she can go on like

this, I don't care if she calls herself Ming Toy Fatima O'Rourke!"

Neither did I. We beamed at each other. Peace was restored. All was right with the world.

We thought.

There was just one small thing troubling me slightly. When Mayaya came in with more muffins—neat, clean, a candy pink *tignon* wrapped around her head—I asked her, "How did you know we were in need of domestic help?"

And that was when she said the strange thing.

She laughed throatily, "Oh, the little green men told me."

The little green men!

Well, we didn't think it so strange at the time. I thought it was just a phrase, a gag, one of those things you say. There was no impudence behind it, and as we were too glad to have her, we weren't really very curious to learn just how she'd known of our desperate need for a servant. So we dismissed the little green men from our minds.

For a while.

Mayaya promised to keep a watchful eye on Scooter, so Peggy went off to her studio, and I went off to mine, and soon lost myself in the fictional woes of Ma Costello and her brood. (Universal Network, 10:45 a.m. It'll tear your heart out.) It was wonderful to be able to work again without stopping to blow Scooter's nose, or having to call up the laundry to bawl them out for ripping my shirts.

At noon I'd got Ma nicely embroiled with a loan shark, and her youngest son threatened with the reformatory (though innocent as an unborn babe), and her oldest daughter's lovable daughter stricken with acute appendicitis, when there was an interruption.

Peggy knocked on my door, and when I opened it she said solemnly, "Spooks!"

"Spooks?"

270

"M-h'm. Come and look."

She led me to the living room, and then stood there eyeing me expectantly. Clearly she expected me to be bowled over. But I couldn't see anything at first.

I blinked, and said, "So what?"

"Well, *look,* dummy! It's clean. And so are the other eleven rooms. And the four baths! Look at the gloss on that piano! Look at the windows, the blinds, the draperies. Spotless!"

I said, "You mean Mayaya did all this? In four hours? Alone?"

"And looked after Scooter besides!"

"It's impossible," I said flatly, knowing Scooter.

"It certainly is," Peggy agreed. "What did I tell you? Spooks!"

It made us just curious enough to ring for Mayaya. When the girl came in—neat, unobtrusive—Peggy cleared her throat. "Mayaya, the house looks beautiful. You couldn't have done this all alone?"

"Oh, no, Mrs. Chase."

Peggy and I looked bewildered. "Well, then, *who* —?"

Mayaya said, "The little green men. They helped me."

I started to laugh. I couldn't help it. After a minute, Peggy began to laugh, too. Mayaya joined in. The three of us stood there laughing like fools. And what we were laughing at, I don't know. Nothing made any sense.

When Mayaya excused herself, and went back to the kitchen, I said to Peggy, "Our pearl is a jewel of the first water, honey, but she's nuts."

"She must be, Jay, do you suppose it's safe to leave Scooter with her? I know she adores him already, but—"

"Well, she doesn't seem to be violent. And, anyway, maybe we're wronging her. Maybe there really *are* some little green men."

"Jay, darling! Don't be a blithering, driveling idiot!"

271

But, nevertheless, Peggy looked thoughtful. And so did I.

Definitely, the little green men were beginning to intrigue us.

But something happened that evening that wasn't funny. At least, we didn't think so. We saw it with our own eyes, and I don't mind telling you I could feel every hair on my scalp itching to stand erect as I watched. Not that it was such a macabre incident. It was just—impossible. Yet it happened.

Peggy, in chartreuse slacks, was sprawled on the floor in front of the fireplace reading a magazine. Scooter was upstairs in bed. Mayaya was in the kitchen washing the dinner dishes. And I was at the piano, picking out with one finger the *Meditation* from Massenet's Thais, which Peggy always claims gives her the colly-wobbles, whatever they are.

She said now, "Jay."

"Um?" I said, absorbed. The artist. I hit A instead of B flat, and winced myself.

"I'm not likely to fall asleep while you're striking all those sour notes," Peggy said tartly, "but it really is stuffy in here. Open a window, will you, there's a lamb?"

"Can't."

"I know they're stuck, ever since the painters finished. But try again, Jay, please."

"Am I Tarzan, the ape? I like to broke my back last night to get 'em open, and—"

I broke off, struck by something in Peggy's expression. She was staring over my shoulder, her mouth open, her eyes wide. I turned to see what she was looking at.

The window behind me was sliding open of itself, easily, silently.

There was absolutely no one near it.

I tell you, it gave me the damnedest sensation in the

small of my back. Like tiny mice scurrying up my spine.

Halfway up, the windows stopped rising. The draperies swayed faintly in the breeze. And I turned at last to look at Peggy, my jaw ajar, like her own.

We stared at each other, speechless. Peggy was the first to regain her voice. She usually is.

She said, "Jay, wasn't that the strangest thing?"

It was the well-known rhetorical question. I didn't bother to answer. Instead I got up and went over to the window. And I'm ashamed to say I was almost afraid to touch it. But at last I put my hands on the sash and tried to shove it down.

I couldn't force it down any more than I could open it the night before. It was stuck fast in its frame, and it stayed stuck, though I shoved and heaved till I was red in the face, using all my strength, and I'm no lightweight.

I gave up at last, and I tell you I *backed* away from the window, never taking my eyes off it. Weakly I sat down on the piano bench. Peggy came over and huddled on it beside me. I put my arm around her, and we sat there gaping at the window as if we were hypnotized.

"Of course, there's one explanation—" I said at last, half in jest.

Peggy nodded, but she wasn't laughing. "The little green men," she whispered.

Well, this couldn't go on forever. On a sudden decision, I rang for Mayaya. She came in presently and stood before us respectfully, her head swathered in a poison-green *tignon*—a strangely exotic figure there in our living-room. She looked at us inquiringly.

I swallowed. "Mayaya, I've been unable to open these windows since the painters finished a week ago. Yet tonight, when Mrs. Chase expressed a wish to have one of them open—one of them opened of itself."

If I had hoped to disconcert her, or expected expres-

273

sions of disbelief or ignorance of the whole thing, I was disappointed.

Mayaya smiled faintly. It was as if she were secretly enchanted, and a little proud. "It might have been the little green men," she said. "They heard—and helped."

"But Mayaya!" I protested. "This is insane. Who—or what—are the little green men?"

"I do not know, Mr. Chase. When I left Trinidad to come to the States, *Maman* said they must accompany me."

"But we can't *see* them!" Peggy broke in.

"Oh, no, Mrs. Chase," Mayaya agreed. "Myself, I have never seen them either. I just know—they are there."

She beamed at us as if everything were reasonably explained. Eliciting information from Mayaya, we found, was like pushing one of those roly-poly toys children play with. You push it down, and think you have it down, and it bounces right back again, leaving you with a horrible feeling of frustration.

I tried again. "But Mayaya, we can't have the house cluttered up with invisible men!" I sounded like a fool, and I knew it, which didn't add to my peace of mind. "It's—it's eerie."

"But they have offered you no harm, Mr. Chase!" Mayaya protested. Her lovely eyes filled mistily. "Of course, if you want me to leave—"

Well, we didn't want her to leave. And in all fairness I have to admit we had no reason to think that Mayaya was laughing up her sleeve at us. It was obvious that she sincerely believed in the little green men.

So Peggy and I both protested we didn't want her to go. And that was the way the interview ended. Mayaya stayed.

And we were stuck with the little green men.

Peggy said, half-hysterically, "So help me, from now on I'll be afraid to take a shower!"

Scooter was next to be touched with the idiocy.

A scream from Peggy next morning brought me to my feet with a jerk. Life in the country, where we'd hoped to find peace, was rapidly becoming a nightmare. Leaving Ma Costello in the middle of a garrulous, valiant speech, her head bloody but still unbowed as it were, I raced for the stairs.

"Jay Chase, will you look at this child? What in the world—!"

Our nearest neighbor, Myles Slavitt, was standing in the hall, and in his arms was Scooter, dripping wet. Now that the initial sensation was over, Scooter seemed a little bored with it all.

"I faw inna fiss-pool," he announced matter-of-factly, albeit with a slightly apprehensive eye on me.

We had no time to question him in the ensuing confusion, while we got him upstairs, and dried him, and called the doctor. When the doctor came, he said there was still a little water in Scooter's lungs, but not much.

"Someone did a little excellent life-saving work, here," the doctor observed, "and got the rest of the water out promptly."

Naturally we thought it had been Slavitt. And though Peggy and I had never liked the man—he was too oleaginous, his manner too ingratiating—still we felt we owed him a debt of gratitude.

The doctor finally left, after putting Scooter to bed.

"And stay there, see?" I said at the door. "I hear you out of that bed inside of an hour, I'll come up and annihilate you."

Scooter smiled at me seraphically. And fell asleep. It had been just another incident in his crowded days.

Slavitt was still waiting downstairs.

Well, Scooter, as it transpired, hadn't fallen into a fishpool. He'd fallen into Myles Slavitt's swimming pool, near the diving board, where the water is twelve feet deep. And thereby hung a tale, according to Slavitt.

He seemed deeply puzzled by it all. "I didn't see him

275

fall in. I was shaving in the upstairs bathroom, and I just happened to look out the window and see the little fella come up for what must have been the second or third time. Now I'm a heavy man, as you can see, and the pool is a long roundabout way from the house. There was no one else in sight. I thought the little fella was a goner, sure. It must have been all of ten minutes before I reached the pool, though I ran as fast as I could."

Peggy shivered, and moved closer to me.

"Well, sir," Slavitt said, bewildered. "When I got there, the kid was sitting on the edge of the pool, dripping wet and coughing a little, but otherwise okay. Now the water is low, and it's a good two-foot reach to grab the edge of the pool from inside. There's an overhang and it's quite a little job for a full-grown man to drag himself up. And the ladder out of the pool is 'way off at the shallow end. Besides, the kid couldn't swim, could he?"

"No," I said. I was feeling kind of peculiar, and doing a little puzzled thinking myself.

Slavitt nodded his head. "Then how did the little fella get out?" he asked triumphantly.

I shook my head slightly at Peggy, who looked as if she were about to speak. I thought I knew what she was going to say, and there was no use letting Slavitt think we were out of our minds.

"Somebody must have pulled him out," I ventured.

"That's just it!" Slavitt said. "There wasn't anybody around at all. Nobody's going to save a kid that size from drowning, and then just walk off and leave him, are they? It don't make sense."

"Well, who pumped the water out of his lungs? You?"

"No. He was all right when I got there, I tell you. Yet somebody must have done it. Who?"

There wasn't any answer. At least, no answer either Peggy or I cared to make to Slavitt.

Well, there was nothing to do but wait for our neighbor to leave, and Scooter to awaken from his nap so that we could question him. In the meantime, we were grateful to Slavitt, so Peggy rang for drinks.

It's strange to remember now that Slavitt's kindly errand of mercy was really the starting point for the tragedy that was to follow.

Mayaya came in with the tray of drinks, neat and trim in her mulberry uniform. She looked the ideal maid, except for the turban of bon-bon yellow in which her head was wrapped.

I didn't like the look that came into Slavitt's face when he saw her, nor the way his eyes followed her as she moved about. I sensed that Mayaya was aware of his gaze, too, and resented it. Peggy was at the far end of the long living room, pouring salted nuts into a silver compote, and after a hasty glance in her direction, Slavitt nodded at Mayaya and said to me:

"Likely looking gal. Colored?"

I said, "Yes," shortly.

Slavitt chuckled, and said too loud, "Dark meat's sweetest, eh?" with a nudge and a leer at me.

It was hard to remember the man was a guest in the house. Peggy heard, and looked up, frowning. Mayaya shot him a venomous glance. I ached to poke him in the nose, but contented myself with changing the subject abruptly.

Myles Slavitt had a thick hide, but even he realized he'd spoken out of turn, and he flushed a little. It was an ugly scene that left us all feeling acutely uncomfortable. Nevertheless the unpleasant glow remained in Slavitt's eyes whenever they rested on Mayaya as she passed through the hall.

I don't like to remember that I was the one who first spoke of the town meeting to be held the following night. For I can't help feeling that in doing so I played right into Slavitt's hand.

God knows why I urged Slavitt to attend. I must

277

have been talking hastily, thoughtlessly, in my attempt to fill the awkward silence that had settled upon us after the man's earlier unpleasant remarks. I wished heartily that the fool would leave.

"My wife and I always go," I said, speaking of the town meeting. "Nothing very important ever comes up, but now that we own property here, we feel it's our duty."

Myles admitted he'd never before gone to any of the meetings, but he more or less promised to put in an appearance the following night.

Peggy and I didn't protest when he finally made a move to leave. I went with him to the hall, and Mayaya was there, holding the door open for him which was unfortunate.

Apparently our stupid neighbor was a man who never learned.

He laid a too-familiar hand on Mayaya's arm, and said, "Those were fine drinks, girl."

Mayaya didn't cower. She bore herself with dignity. But she couldn't resist a glance of appeal at me.

Well, he'd been nice about Scooter, but there are limits to gratitude. I removed Myles' hand from her arm, ungently, and all but shoved him through the door. I'd had enough of him. He blustered a little on the doorstep, but when I stepped through the door, his voice trailed off, and he slunk away.

"Ugh!" Peggy said from the living room archway. "That goon!"

"Let's forget him," I said. "I'm sorry, Mayaya.'

"It's quite all right, Mr. Chase, I understand," she said quietly. "Thank you."

"By the way," I said. "I wish you'd keep a closer watch on Scooter. You know what happened when he wandered away this morning."

"But he didn't wander, Mr. Chase." Mayaya protested softly. "I knew he was gone. And I knew the little green men would watch over him. And you see, they did."

My head was beginning to spin. And I knew Peggy's was, too, judging from the expression on her face.

Scooter was awake when we went up to the nursery, and fidgety to get out of bed. He seemed none the worse for his experience, and was a little restive under our questions.

Yes, he remembered going across the lawn to Slavitt's. Well, no, he didn't think he'd been so *very* naughty, 'zackly. Mayaya had told him he might leave her side. The little green men, she'd said, would watch over him.

Peggy and I exchanged glances over Scooter's head.

And there'd been a leaf floating on the surface of the pool, like a little boat. And, in reaching for it, he'd fallen in. And water got up his nose. And it hadn't been very nice, according to Scooter. He couldn't breathe. And he couldn't see. And finally everything went black, like at night-time.

"I was afraid—just a little bit," he assured us solemnly.

Peggy hugged him. "Of course you were, darling. But now, try to remember—real hard. This is the important part. How did you get *out* of the pool?"

Scooter pushed out his lower lip, and squinted his eyes. He was thinking. He opened his eyes. "The little green men pulled me out!" he announced at last.

"But, darling, are you sure? Did you see them? Actually?"

Well. He was *pretty* sure he'd seen them. But he wasn't *very* sure. And could he get up now please?

It was hopeless. After all, he was only three. It was impossible to tell what he'd actually seen, and what his imagination was prompting him to believe he'd seen, fired as it had been by Mayaya's remarks.

Later, Peggy and I had a private confab behind the closed door of our room.

"I guess there's nothing else for it," I said. "We'll have to let her go before we all wind up batty."

"But Jay, dear, she's so wonderful in every other way."

I raised an eyebrow. "She—or the little green men?"

"Jay! You don't really believe in them, and you know it."

"Do you?"

"Certainly not!" Peggy was indignant. But after a minute, she added thoughtfully, "Still, you have to admit—"

"Oh, for God's sake!" I shouted irritably. "You see? She has us all headed for the nut factory."

"Well, let's wait till the end of the week, at least. I'll have the Nellis illustrations done by then, if I hurry, and—well."

So we left it at that. And there's no use now blaming ourselves for not having fired Mayaya immediately.

We had dismissed Myles Slavitt so completely from our minds that we didn't even notice he wasn't at the town meeting next night.

There was the usual argument about whether or not a traffic signal was needed at First and Main. And Jed Stout was warned sternly again he'd better fix that there hole in the sidewalk in front of his store afore somebody broke their neck—at which Jed looked blank. (He was becoming adept at looking blank by this time.)

Peggy and I left at eleven, a little smug with the sense of a duty conscientiously performed, and highly amused all the way home at Jed Stout's callous unconcern for the necks of his fellow-townsmen. I remember we made an hilarious bet as to whether or not Jed would relent at the next meeting.

Unfortunately, our gaiety wasn't to last.

We'd no sooner turned off the highway onto our private lane, and the house loomed up distinctly before us, than we knew something was radically wrong. Every light in the place was out. Even if Mayaya had retired early, she had instructions to leave the hall light burning. And it wasn't like her to be forgetful.

Peggy grew alarmed at once.

"Jay, hurry!" She sat on the edge of the seat. "I have a feeling—"

I was uncomfortable myself. I stepped on it, and we covered the last mile of private lane in nothing flat. Gravel spit under the tires as we jerked to a stop. We could hear Scooter sobbing softly to himself in the hall, even before we could get the door open. I was all thumbs, and the damned key wouldn't go into the lock, and it didn't help any to have Peggy needling me with, "Oh, hurry *up!*" accompanied by nervous prods in the back.

The door opened at last, and we practically fell over ourselves getting into the hall. I snapped the light on, and Scooter rushed into Peggy's arms, howling.

"Oh, my darling! What's the matter?" Peggy cried.

God, the hall was a sight! There were streaks of blood all over the white marbelized linoleum, the mahogany chairs were overturned, and the Chippendale mirror had been knocked from the walls and lay in fragments.

But Scooter was all right, though terrified.

While Peggy tried to quiet him, I went into the darkened living room, and tripped over something on the floor just beyond the arch. I fumbled for the ceiling light switch, found it. And then I was calling sharply to Peggy, "You stay out there in the hall."

I paid no attention to her startled questions.

Mayaya was lying on the floor before me, face down. I turned her over gently, though there was no real need of gentleness, for she was dead. Apparently she'd been choked to death. There wasn't a scratch on her.

281

Then why all the blood in the hall?

I was mystified.

I switched off the light again, and went to the phone in the hall, to call Doc and the police. When I'd got the two numbers at last, I spoke as quickly and briefly as possible.

Peggy overheard. "You mean—she's been murdered?"

"She certainly didn't strangle herself."

Scooter was still sobbing a little, and babbling of a "great, big man."

"But, Jay, who—?"

I was beginning to think I knew. But Peggy was white and shivering, so I kept my mouth shut about my suspicions. I said instead, "You go upstairs, Peg. I'm going to follow these bloodstains. They seem to lead outside."

"I won't stay in this house with a corpse!" Peggy announced flatly. "I'm coming with you."

I couldn't argue her out of it. And, anyway, she was probably safer near me. Still holding Scooter, she followed me to the car where I got a flashlight.

There were stains all over the doorstep, and the gravel driveway was streaked with them, leading to the left towards Slavitt's place.

Peggy gripped my arm. "Jay! Slavitt! Of course!"

I nodded grimly. I wanted to get my hands on Slavitt before the police came. He'd be too safe with the police.

We started off toward the Slavitt estate, following the bloodstains, but I wasn't quite prepared for what I found.

For I found Slavitt all right. The flash lighted up something just over his lot line. I turned it quickly aside, and said to Peggy, "Stay back here. I'm only going a few steps farther on. Don't let Scooter see, and don't look yourself."

282

I'd had just a glimpse in the momentary glare of the flash, but it had been enough. When I was sure she wouldn't follow, I went ahead gingerly.

He was lying there, face down, and his clothing had been shredded from his body. I needed only one sickened closer glance at the raw, red bleeding mass of pulp to know that he was forever beyond help—or further punishment. God, what a way to die! He'd been literally skinned alive by what must have been hundreds of tiny knives wielded by who knows whose hands.

The hands of the little green men?

Yes. They'd been too late to save Mayaya, but they'd revenged themselves horribly upon Slavitt. I'm positive. For, you see, there was something else.

Peggy took one glance at my face when I reached her side again, and mercifully asked no questions. It wasn't until we were back at the house, waiting for the police, that she noticed how tightly Scooter's hands were clenched.

"Jay, Scooter seems to have something in his hand."

He was still hysterical, pood kid. We had to pry his hand open, for he kept it clenched convulsively. But we took at last from his small moist palm, the tiny lifeless figure of a little green man.

"I found him on the floor," Scooter sobbed. "The big man hurted him, and I picked him up—"

I have it here in the lower right hand drawer of my desk in a pint Mason jar full of alcohol. A gruesome souvenir, some might say, but I look upon it as a talisman. And—who knows?—some day I may go to Trinidad. . . .

FOR THE BLOOD IS THE LIFE

By Francis Marion Crawford

We have dined at sunset on the broad roof of the old
tower, because it was cooler there during the great heat
of summer. Besides, the little kitchen was built at one
corner of the great square platform, which made it
more convenient than if the dishes had to be carried
down the steep stone steps, broken in places and everywhere worn with age. The tower was one of those
places built all down the west coast of Calabria by the
Emperor Charles V early in the sixteenth century, to
keep off the Barbary pirates, when the unbelievers were
allied with Francis I against the Emperor and the
Church. They have gone to ruin, a few still stand in-
tact, and mine is one of the largest. How it came into
my possession ten years ago, and why I spend a part
of each year in it, are matters which do not concern
this tale. The tower stands in one of the loneliest spots
in Southern Italy, at the extremity of a curving rocky
promontory, which forms a small but safe natural har-
bour at the southern extremity of the Gulf of Policastro,
and just north of Cape Scalea, the birthplace of Judas
Iscariot, according to the old local legend. The tower
stands alone on this hooked spur of the rock, and there
is not a house to be seen within three miles of it. When

284

I go there I take a couple of sailors, one of whom is a fair cook, and when I am away it is in charge of a gnome-like little being who was once a miner and who attached himself to me long ago.

My friend, who sometimes visits me in my summer solitude, is an artist by profession, a Scandinavian by birth, and a cosmopolitan by force of circumstances. We had dined at sunset; the sunset glow had reddened and faded again, and the evening purple steeped the vast chain of the mountains that embrace the deep gulf to eastward and rear themselves higher and higher toward the south. It was hot, and we sat at the landward corner of the platform, waiting for the night breeze to come down from the lower hills. The colour sank out of the air, there was a little interval of deep-grey twilight, and a lamp sent a yellow streak from the open door of the kitchen, where the men were getting their supper.

Then the moon rose suddenly above the crest of the promontory, flooding the platform and lighting up every little spur of rock and knoll of grass below us, down to the edge of the motionless water. My friend lighted his pipe and sat looking at a spot on the hill-side. I knew that he was looking at it, and for a long time past I had wondered whether he would ever see anything there that would fix his attention. I knew that spot well. It was clear that he was interested at last, though it was a long time before he spoke. Like most painters, he trusts to his own eyesight, as a lion trusts his strength and a stag his speed, and he is always disturbed when he cannot reconcile what he sees with what he believes that he ought to see.

"It's strange," he said. "Do you see that little mound just on this side of the boulder?"

"Yes," I said, and I guessed what was coming.

"It looks like a grave," observed Holger.

"Very true. It does look like a grave."

"Yes," continued my friend, his eyes still fixed on

285

the spot. "But the strange thing is that I see the body lying on the top of it. Of course," continued Holger, turning his head on one side as artists do, "it must be an effect of light. In the first place, it is not a grave at all. Secondly, if it were, the body would be inside and not outside. Therefore, it's an effect of the moonlight. Don't you see it?"

"Perfectly; I always see it on moonlight nights."

"It doesn't seem to interest you much," said Holger.

"On the contrary, it does interest me, though I am used to it. You're not so far wrong, either. The mound is really a grave."

"Nonsense!" cried Holger, incredulously. "I suppose you'll tell me what I see lying on it is really a corpse!"

"No," I answered, "it's not. I know, because I have taken the trouble to go down and see."

"Then what is it?" asked Holger.

"It's nothing."

"You mean that it's an effect of light, I suppose?"

"Perhaps it is. But the inexplicable part of the matter is that it makes no difference whether the moon is rising or setting, or waxing or waning. If there's moonlight at all, from east or west or overhead, so long as it shines on the grave you can see the outline of the body on top."

Holger stirred up his pipe with the point of his knife, and then used his finger for a stopper. When the tobacco burned well he rose from his chair.

"If you don't mind," he said, "I'll go down and take a look at it."

He left me, crossed the roof, and disappeared down the dark steps. I did not move, but sat looking down until he came out of the tower below. I heard him humming an old Danish song as he crossed the open space in the bright moonlight, going straight to the mysterious mound. When he was ten paces from it, Holger stopped short, made two steps forward, and then three or four backward, and then stopped again. I knew what that meant. He had reached the spot where the Thing ceased to be visible—where, as he would have said, the effect of light changed.

Then he went on till he reached the mound and stood upon it. I could see the Thing still, but it was no longer lying down; it was on its knees now, winding its white arms around Holger's body and looking up into his face. A cool breeze stirred my hair at that moment, as the night wind began to come down from the hills, but it felt like a breath from another world.

The Thing seemed to be trying to climb to its feet, helping itself up by Holger's body while he stood upright, quite unconscious of it and apparently looking toward the tower, which is very picturesque when the moonlight falls upon it on that side.

"Come along!" I shouted. "Don't stay there all night!"

It seemed to me that he moved reluctantly as he stepped from the mound, or else with difficulty. That was it. The Thing's arms were still round his waist, but its feet could not leave the grave. As he came slowly forward it was drawn and lengthened like a wreath of mist, thin and white, till I saw distinctly that Holger shook himself, as a man does who feels a chill. At the same instant a little wail of pain came to me on the breeze—it might have been the cry of the small owl that lives among the rocks—and the misty presence floated swiftly back from Holger's advancing figure and lay once more at its length upon the mound.

Again I felt the cool breeze in my hair, and this time an icy thrill of dread ran down my spine. I remembered very well that I had once gone down there alone in the moonlight; that presently, being near, I had seen nothing; that, like Holger, I had gone and stood upon the mound; and I remembered how, when I came back, sure that there was nothing there, I had felt the sudden conviction that there was something after all if I would only look behind me. I remembered the strong temptation to look back, a temptation I had resisted as unworthy of a man of sense, until, to get rid of it, I had shaken myself just as Holger did.

And now I knew that those white, misty arms had been round me too; I knew it in a flash, and I shuddered as I remembered that I had heard the night owl then too. But it had not been the night owl. It was the cry of the Thing.

I refilled my pipe and poured out a cup of strong southern wine; in less than a minute Holger was seated beside me again.

"Of course there's nothing there," he said, "but it's creepy, all the same. Do you know, when I was coming back I was so sure that there was something behind me that I wanted to turn round and look? It was an effort not to."

He laughed a little, knocked the ashes out of his pipe, and poured himself out some wine. For a while neither of us spoke, and the moon rose higher, and we both looked at the Thing that lay on the mound.

"You might make a story about that," said Holger after a long time.

"There is one," I answered. "If you're not sleepy, I'll tell it to you."

"Go ahead," said Holger, who likes stories.

Old Alario was dying up there in the village behind the hill. You remember him, I have no doubt. They say that he made his money by selling sham jewellery in South Africa, and escaped with his gains when he was found out. Like all those fellows, if they bring anything back with them, he at once set to work to enlarge his house, and as there are no masons here, he sent all the way to Paola for two workmen. They were a rough-looking pair of scoundrels—a Neapolitan who had lost one eye and a Sicilian with an old scar half an inch deep across his left cheek. I often saw them, for on Sundays they used to come down here and fish off the rocks. When Alario caught the fever that killed him the masons were still at work. As he had agreed that part of their pay should be their board and lodging, he made them sleep in the house. His wife was dead, and he had an only son called Angelo, who was a much better sort than himself. Angelo was to marry the daughter of the richest man in the village, and, strange to say, though their marriage was arranged by their parents, the young people were said to be in love with each other.

For that matter, the whole village was in love with Angelo, and among the rest a wild, good-looking creature called Cristina, who was more like a gipsy than any girl I ever saw about here. She had very red lips and very black eyes, she was built like a greyhound, and had the tongue of the devil. But Angelo did not care a straw for her. He was rather a simple-minded fellow, quite different from his old scoundrel of a father, and under what I should call normal circumstances I really believe that he would never have looked at any girl except the nice plump little creature, with a fat dowry, whom his father meant him to marry. But things turned up which were neither normal nor natural.

On the other hand, a very handsome young shepherd from the hills above Maratea was in love with Cristina, who seems to have been quite indifferent to him. Cristina had no regular means of subsistence, but she was a good girl and willing to do any work or go on errands to any distance for the sake of a loaf of bread or a mess of beans, and permission to sleep under cover. She was especially glad when she could get something to do about the house of Angelo's father. There is no doctor in the village, and when the neighbors saw that old Alario was dying they sent Cristina to Scalea to fetch one. That was late in the afternoon, and if they had waited so long, it was because the dying miser refused to allow such extravagance while he was able to speak. But while Cristina was gone matters grew rapidly

289

worse, the priest was brought to the bedside, and when he had done what he could he gave it as his opinion to the bystanders that the old man was dead, and left the house.

You know these people. They have a physical horror of death. Until the priest spoke, the room had been full of people. The words were hardly out of his mouth before it was empty. It was night now. They hurried down the dark steps and out into the street.

Angelo, as I have said, was away, Cristina had not come back—the simple woman-servant who had nursed the sick man fled with the rest, and the body was left alone in the flickering light of the earthen oil lamp.

Five minutes later two men looked in cautiously and crept forward toward the bed. They were the one-eyed Neapolitan mason and his Sicilian companion. They knew what they wanted. In a moment they had dragged from under the bed a small but heavy iron-bound box, and long before anyone thought of coming back to the dead man they had left the house and the village under cover of the darkness. It was easy enough, for Alario's house is the last toward the gorge which leads down here, and the thieves merely went out by the back door, got over the stone wall, and had nothing to risk after that except the possibility of meeting some belated countryman, which was very small indeed, since few of the people used that path. They had a mattock and shovel, and they made their way here without accident.

I am telling you this story as it must have happened, for, of course, there were no witnesses to this part of it. The men brought the box down by the gorge, intending to bury it until they should be able to come back and take it away in a boat. They must have been clever enough to guess that some of the money would be in paper notes, for they would otherwise have buried it on the beach in the wet sand, where it would have been much safer. But the paper would have rotted if they

290

had been obliged to leave it there long, so they dug their hole down there, close to that boulder. Yes, just where the mound is now.

Cristina did not find the doctor in Scalea, for he had been sent for from a place up in the valley, half-way to San Domenico. If she had found him, he would have come on his mule by the upper road, which is smoother but much longer. But Cristina took the short cut by the rocks, which passes about fifty feet above the mound, and goes round that corner. The men were digging when she passed, and she heard them at work. It would not have been like her to go by without finding out what the noise was, for she was never afraid of anything in her life, and, besides, the fishermen sometimes come ashore here at night to get a stone for an anchor or to gather sticks to make a little fire. The night was dark, and Cristina probably came close to the two men before she could see what they were doing. She knew them, of course, and they knew her, and understood instantly that they were in her power. There was only one thing to be done for their safety, and they did it. They knocked her on the head, they dug the hole deep, and they buried her quickly with the iron-bound chest. They must have understood that their only chance of escaping suspicion lay in getting back to the village before their absence was noticed, for they returned immediately, and were found half an hour later gossiping with the man who was making Alario's coffin. He was a crony of theirs, and had been working at the repairs in the old man's house. So far as I have been able to make out, the only persons who were supposed to know where Alario kept his treasure were Angelo and the one woman-servant I have mentioned. Angelo was away; it was the woman who discovered the theft.

It was easy enough to understand why no one else knew where the money was. The old man kept his door locked and the key in his pocket when he was out, and did not let the woman enter to clean the place unless he was there himself. The whole village knew that he had money somewhere, however, and the masons had probably discovered the whereabouts of the chest by climbing in at the window in his absence. If the old man had not been delirious until he lost consciousness, he would have been in frightful agony of mind for his riches. The faithful woman-servant forgot their existence only for a few moments when she fled with the rest, overcome by the horror of death. Twenty minutes had not passed before she returned with the two hideous old hags who are always called in to prepare the dead for burial. Even then she had not at first the courage to go near the bed with them, but she made a pretence of dropping something, went down on her knees as if to find it, and looked under the bedstead. The walls of the room were newly whitewashed down to the floor, and she saw at a glance that the chest was gone. It had been there in the afternoon; it had therefore been stolen in the short interval since she had left the room.

There are no carabineers stationed in the village; there is not so much as a municipal watchman, for there is no municipality. There never was such a place, I believe. Scalea is supposed to look after it in some mysterious way, and it takes a couple of hours to get anybody from there. As the old woman had lived in the village all her life, it did not even occur to her to apply to any civil authority for help. She simply set up a howl and ran through the village in the dark screaming out that her dead master's house had been robbed. Many of the people looked out, but at first no one seemed inclined to help her. Most of them, judging her by themselves, whispered to each other that she had probably stolen the money herself. The first man to move was the father of the girl whom Angelo was to marry; having collected his household, all of whom felt a personal interest in the wealth which was to have come into the family, he declared it to be his opinion that the chest had been stolen by the two journeyman

292

masons who lodged in the house. He headed a search for them, which naturally began in Alario's house and ended in the carpenter's workshop, where the thieves were found discussing a measure of wine with the carpenter over the half-finished coffin, by the light of one earthen lamp filled with oil and tallow. The search party at once accused the delinquents of the crime, and threatened to lock them up in the cellar till the carabineers could be fetched from Scalea. The two men looked at each other for one moment, and then without the slightest hesitation they put out the single light, seized the unfinished coffin between them, using it as a sort of battering ram, dashed upon their assailants in the dark. In a few moments they were beyond pursuit.

That is the end of the first part of the story. The treasure had disappeared, and as no trace of it could be found the people naturally supposed that the thieves had succeeded in carrying it off. The old man was buried and when Angelo came back at last he had to borrow money to pay for the miserable funeral, and had some difficulty in doing so. He hardly needed to be told that in losing his inheritance he had lost his bride. In this part of the world marriages are made on strictly business principles, and if the promised cash is not forthcoming on the appointed day the bride or the bridegroom whose parents have failed to produce it may as well take themselves off, for there will be no wedding. Poor Angelo knew that well enough. His father had been possessed of hardly any land, and now that the hard cash which he had brought from South Africa was gone, there was nothing left but debts for the building materials that were to have been used for enlarging and improving the old house. Angelo was beggared, and the nice plump little creature who was to have been his turned up her nose at him in the most approved fashion. As for Cristina, it was several days before she was missed, for no one remembered that she had been sent to Scalea for the doctor, who had

293

never come. She often disappeared in the same way for days together, when she could find a little work here and there at the distant farms among the hills. But when she did not come back at all, people began to wonder, and at last made up their minds that she had connived with the masons and had escaped with them.

I paused and emptied my glass.

"That sort of thing could not happen anywhere else," observed Holger, filling his everlasting pipe again. "It is wonderful what a natural charm there is about murder and sudden death in a romantic country like this. Deeds that would be simply brutal and disgusting anywhere else become dramatic and mysterious because this is Italy and we are living in a genuine tower of Charles V built against genuine Barbary pirates."

"There's something in that," I admitted. Holger is the most romantic man in the world inside of himself, but he always thinks it necessary to explain why he feels anything.

"I suppose they found the poor girl's body with the box," he said presently.

"As it seems to interest you," I answered, "I'll tell you the rest of the story."

The moon had risen high by this time; the outline of the Thing on the mound was clearer to our eyes than before.

The village very soon settled down to its small, dull life. No one missed old Alario, who had been away so much on his voyages to South Africa that he had never been a familiar figure in his native place. Angelo lived in the half-finished house, and because he had no money to pay the old woman-servant she would not stay with him, but once in a long time she would come and wash a shirt for him for old acquaintance's sake. Besides the house, he had inherited a small patch of ground at some distance from the village; he tried to cultivate it, but he had no heart in the work, for he knew he could never pay the taxes on it and on the house, which would certainly be confiscated by the Government, or seized for the debt of the building material, which the man who had supplied it refused to take back.

Angelo was very unhappy. So long as his father had been alive and rich, every girl in the village had been in love with him; but that was all changed now. It had been pleasant to be admired and courted, and invited to drink wine by fathers who had girls to marry. It was hard to be stared at coldly, and sometimes laughed at because he had been robbed of his inheritance. He cooked his miserable meals for himself, and from being sad became melancholy and morose.

At twilight, when the day's work was done, instead of hanging about in the open space before the church with young fellows of his own age, he took to wandering in lonely places on the outskirts of the village till it was quite dark. Then he slunk home and went to bed to save the expense of a light. But in those lonely twilight hours he began to have strange waking dreams. He was not always alone, for often when he sat on the stump of a tree, where the narrow path turns down the gorge, he was sure that a woman came up noiselessly over the rough stones, as if her feet were bare; and stood under a clump of chestnut trees only half a dozen yards down the path, and beckoned to him without speaking. Though she was in the shadow he knew that her lips were red, and that when they parted a little and smiled at him she showed two small sharp teeth. He knew this at first rather than saw it, and he knew that it was Cristina, and that she was dead. Yet he was not afraid; he only wondered whether it was a dream, for he thought that if he had been awake he should have been frightened.

Besides, the dead woman had red lips, and that could only happen in a dream. Whenever he went near the gorge after sunset she was already there waiting for him, or else she very soon appeared, and he began to be sure that she came a little nearer to him every day. At first he had only been sure of her blood-red mouth, but now each feature grew distinct, and the pale face looked at him with deep and hungry eyes.

It was the eyes that grew dim. Little by little he came to know that some day the dream would not end when he turned away to go home, but would lead him down the gorge out of which the vision rose. She was nearer now when she beckoned to him. Her cheeks were not livid like those of the dead, but pale with starvation, with the furious and unappeased physical hunger of her eyes that devoured him. They feasted on his soul and cast a spell over him, and at last they were close to his own and held him. He could not tell whether her breath was as hot as fire or as cold as ice; he could not tell whether her red lips burned his or froze them, or whether her five fingers on his wrist seared scorching scars or bit his flesh like frost; he could not tell whether he was awake or asleep, whether she was alive or dead, but he knew that she loved him, she alone of all creatures, earthly or unearthly, and her spell had power over him.

When the moon rose high that night the shadow of that Thing was not alone down there upon the mound.

Angelo awoke in the cool dawn, drenched with dew and chilled through flesh, and blood, and bone. He opened his eyes to the faint grey light, and saw the stars shining overhead. He was very weak, and his heart was beating so slowly that he was almost like a man fainting. Slowly he turned his head on the mound as on a pillow, but the other face was not there. Fear seized him suddenly, a fear unspeakable and unknown; he sprang to his feet and fled up the gorge, and he never looked behind him until he reached the door of the house on the outskirts of the village. Drearily he went to his work that day, and wearily the hours dragged themselves after the sun, till at last it touched the sea and sank, and the great sharp hills above Maratea turned purple against the dove-coloured eastern sky.

Angelo shouldered his heavy hoe and left the field. He felt less tired now than in the morning when he had begun to work, but he promised himself that he would go home without lingering by the gorge, and eat the best supper he could get himself, and sleep all night in his bed like a Christian man. Not again would he be tempted down the narrow way by a shadow with red lips and icy breath; not again would he dream that dream of terror and delight. He was near the village now; it was half an hour since the sun had set, and the cracked church bell sent little discordant echoes across the rocks and ravines to tell all good people that the day was done. Angelo stood still a moment where the path forked, where it led toward the village on the left, and down to the gorge on the right, where a clump of chestnut trees overhung the narrow way. He stood still a minute, lifting his battered hat from his head and gazing at the fast-fading sea westward, and his lips moved as he silently repeated the familiar evening prayer. His lips moved, but the words that followed them in his brain lost their meaning and turned into others, and ended in a name that he spoke aloud— Cristina! With the name, the tension of his will relaxed suddenly, reality went out and the dream took him again, and bore him on swiftly and surely like a man walking in his sleep, down, down, by the steep path in the gathering darkness. And as she glided beside him, Cristina whispered strange, sweet things in his ear, which somehow, if he had been awake, he knew that he could not quite have understood; but now they were the most wonderful words he had ever heard in his life. And she kissed him also, but not upon his mouth. He felt her sharp kisses upon his white throat, and he knew that her lips were red. So the wild dream sped on through twilight and darkness and moonrise, and all the glory of the summer's night. But in the chilly dawn he lay as one half dead upon the mound down there, recalling and not recalling, drained of his blood, yet strangely longing to give those red lips more. Then came the fear, the awful nameless panic, the mortal horror that guards the confines of the world we see not, neither know of as we know of other things, but which we feel when its icy chill freezes our bones and stirs our hair with the touch of a ghostly hand. Once more Angelo sprang from the mound and fled up the gorge in the breaking day, but his step was less sure this time, and he panted for breath as he ran; and when he came to the bright spring of water that rises halfway up the hillside, he dropped upon his knees and hands and plunged his whole face in and drank as he had never drunk before—for it was the thirst of the wounded man who has lain bleeding all night long upon the battle-field.

She had him fast now, and he could not escape her, but would come to her every evening at dusk until she had drained him of his last drop of blood. It was in vain that when the day was done he tried to take another turning and to go home by a path that did not lead near the gorge. It was in vain that he made promises to himself each morning at dawn when he climbed the lonely way up from the shore to the village. It was all in vain, for when the sun sank burning into the sea, and the coolness of the evening stole out as from a hiding-place to delight the weary world, his feet turned toward the old way, and she was waiting for him in the shadow under the chestnut trees; and then all happened as before, and she fell to kissing his white throat even as she flitted lightly down the way, winding one arm about him. And as his blood failed, she grew more hungry and more thirsty every day, and every day when he awoke in the early dawn it was harder to rouse himself to the effort of climbing the steep path to the village; and when he went to his work his feet dragged painfully, and there was hardly strength in his arms to wield the heavy hoe. He scarcely spoke to any one now, but the people said he was "consuming himself" for love of the girl he was to have married when he lost his inheritance; and they laughed heartily at the thought, for this is not a very romantic country. At this time, Antonio, the man who stays here to look after the tower, returned from a visit to his people, who live near Salerno. He had been away all the time since before Alario's death and knew nothing of what had happened. He has told me that he came back late in the afternoon and shut himself up in the tower to eat and sleep, for he was very tired. It was past midnight when he awoke, and when he looked out the waning moon was rising over the shoulder of the hill. He looked out toward the mound, and he saw something, and he did not sleep again that night. When he went out again in the morning it was broad daylight, and there was nothing to see on the mound but loose stones and driven sand. Yet he did not go very near it; he went straight up the path to the village and directly to the house of the old priest.

"I have seen an evil thing this night," he said; "I have seen how the dead drink the blood of the living. And the blood is the life."

"Tell me what you have seen," said the priest in reply.

Antonio told him everything he had seen.

"You must bring your book and your holy water tonight," he added. "I will be here before sunset to go down with you, and if it pleases your reverence to sup with me while we wait, I will make ready."

"I will come," the priest answered, "for I have read in old books of these strange beings which are neither quick nor dead, and which lie ever fresh in their graves, stealing out in the dusk to taste life and blood."

Antonio cannot read, but he was glad to see that

the priest understood the business; for, of course, the books must have instructed him as to the best means of quieting the half-living Thing for ever.

So Antonio went away to his work, which consists largely in sitting on the shady side of the tower, when he is not perched upon a rock with a fishing-line catching nothing. But on that day he went twice to look at the mound in the bright sunlight, and he searched round and round it for some hole through which the being might get in and out; but he found none. When the sun began to sink and the air was cooler in the shadows, he went up to fetch the old priest, carrying a little wicker basket with him; and in this they placed a bottle of holy water, and the basin, and sprinkler, and the stole which the priest would need; and they came down and waited in the door of the tower till it should be dark. But while the light still lingered very grey and faint, they saw something moving, just there, two figures, a man's that walked, and a woman's that flitted beside him, and while her head lay on his shoulder she kissed his throat. The priest has told me that, too, and that his teeth chattered and he grasped Antonio's arm. The vision passed and disappeared into the shadow. Then Antonio got the leathern flask of strong liquor, which he kept for great occasions, and poured such a draught as made the old man feel almost young again; and he got the lantern, and his pick and shovel, and gave the priest his stole to put on and the holy water to carry, and they went out together toward the spot where the work was to be done. Antonio says that in spite of the rum his own knees shook together, and the priest stumbled over his Latin. For when they were yet a few yards from the mound the flickering light of the lantern fell upon Angelo's white face, unconscious as if in sleep, and on his upturned throat, over which a very thin red line of blood trickled down into his collar; and the flickering light of the lantern played upon another face that looked up from the feast—upon two deep, dead eyes that saw in spite of death—upon parted lips redder than life itself— upon two gleaming teeth on which glistened a rosy drop. Then the priest, good old man, shut his eyes tight and showered holy water before him, and his cracked voice rose almost to a scream; and then Antonio, who is no coward after all, raised his pick in one hand and the lantern in the other, as he sprang forward, not knowing what the end should be; and then he swears that he heard a woman's cry, and the Thing was gone, and Angelo lay alone on the mound unconscious, with the red line on his throat and the beads of deathly sweat on his cold forehead. They lifted him, half-dead as he was, and laid him on the ground close by; then Antonio went to work, and the priest helped him, though he was old and could not do much; and they dug deep, and at last Antonio, standing in the grave, stooped down with his lantern to see what he might see.

His hair used to be dark brown, with grizzled streaks about the temples; in less than a month from that day he was as grey as a badger. He was a miner when he was young, and most of these fellows have seen ugly sights now and then, when accidents happened, but he had never seen what he saw that night—that Thing which is neither alive nor dead, that Thing that will abide neither above ground nor in the grave. Antonio had brought something with him which the priest had not noticed. He had made it that afternoon—a sharp stake shaped from a piece of tough old driftwood. He had it with him now, and he had his heavy pick, and he had taken the lantern down into the grave. I don't think any power on earth could make him speak of what happened then, and the old priest was too frightened to look in. He says he heard Antonio breathing like a wild beast, and moving as if he were fighting with something almost as strong as himself; and he heard an evil sound also, with blows, as of something violently driven through flesh and bone; and then the most awful sound of all—a woman's shriek, the unearthly scream of a woman neither dead nor alive, but buried deep for many days. And he, the poor old priest, could only rock himself as he knelt there in the sand, crying aloud his prayers and exorcisms to drown these dreadful sounds. Then suddenly a small iron-bound chest was thrown up and rolled over against the old man's knee, and in a moment more Antonio was beside him, his face as white as tallow in the flickering light of the lantern, shovelling the sand and pebbles into the grave with furious haste, and looking over the edge till the pit was half full; and the priest said that there was much fresh blood on Antonio's hands and on his clothes.

I had come to the end of my story. Holger finished his wine and leaned back in his chair.

"So Angelo got his own again," he said. "Did he marry the prim and plump young person to whom he had been betrothed?"

"No; he had been badly frightened. He went to South America, and has not been heard of since."

"And that poor thing's body is there still, I suppose," said Holger. "Is it quite dead yet, I wonder?"

I wonder, too. But whether it be dead or alive, I should hardly care to see it, even in broad daylight. Antonio is as grey as a badger, and he has never been quite the same man since that night.

THE HUMAN CHAIR

By Edogawa Rampo

Oshiko saw her husband off to his work at the Foreign Office at a little past ten o'clock. Then, now that her time was once again her very own, she shut herself up in the study she shared with her husband to resume work on the story she was to submit for the special summer issue of *K*—magazine.

She was a versatile writer with high literary talent and a smooth-flowing style. Even her husband's popularity as a diplomat was overshadowed by hers as an authoress.

Daily she was overwhelmed with letters from readers praising her works. In fact, this very morning, as soon as she sat down before her desk, she immediately proceeded to glance through the numerous letters which the morning mail had brought. Without exception, in content they all followed the same pattern, but prompted by her deep feminine sense of consideration, she always read through each piece of correspondence addressed to her, whether monotonous or interesting.

Taking the short and simple letters first, she quickly noted their contents. Finally she came to one which was a bulky, manuscript-like sheaf of pages. Although she had not received any advance notice that a manuscript

303

was to be sent her, still it was not uncommon for her to receive the efforts of amateur writers seeking her valuable criticism. In most cases these were long-winded, pointless, and yawn-provoking attempts at writing. Nevertheless, she now opened the envelope in her hand and took out the numerous, closely written sheets.

As she had anticipated, it was a manuscript, carefully bound. But somehow, for some unknown reason, there was neither a title nor a by-line. The manuscript began abruptly:

"Dear Madam: . . ."

Momentarily she reflected. Maybe, after all, it was just a letter. Unconsciously her eyes hurried on to read two or three lines, and then gradually she became absorbed in a strangely gruesome narrative. Her curiosity aroused to the bursting point and spurred on by some unknown magnetic force, she continued to read:

Dear Madam: I do hope you will forgive this presumptuous letter from a complete stranger. What I am about to write, Madam, may shock you no end. However, I am determined to lay bare before you a confession—my own—and to describe in detail the terrible crime I have committed.

For many months I have hidden myself away from the light of civilization, hidden, as it were, like the devil himself. In this whole wide world no one knows of my deeds. However, quite recently a queer change took place in my conscious mind, and I just couldn't bear to keep my secret any longer. I simply had to confess!

All that I have written so far must certainly have awakened only perplexity in your mind. However, I beseech you to bear with me and kindly read my communication to the bitter end, because if you do, you will fully understand the strange workings of my mind and the reason why it is to you in particular that I make this confession.

I am really at a loss as to where to begin, for the facts which I am setting forth are all so grotesquely out of the ordinary. Frankly, words fail me, for human words seem utterly inadequate to sketch all the details. But, nevertheless, I will try to lay bare the events in chronological order, just as they happened.

First let me explain that I am ugly beyond description. Please bear this fact in mind; otherwise I fear that if and when you do grant my ultimate request and *do* see me, you may be shocked and horrified at the sight of my face—after so many months of unsanitary living. However, I implore you to believe me when I state that, despite the extreme ugliness of my face, within my heart there has always burned a pure and overwhelming passion!

Next, let me explain that I am a humble workman by trade. Had I been born in a well-to-do family, I might have found the power, with money, to ease the torture of my soul brought on by my ugliness. Or perhaps, if I had been endowed by nature with artistic talents, I might again have been able to forget my bestial countenance and seek consolation in music or poetry. But, unblessed with any such talents, and being the unfortunate creature that I am, I had no trade to turn to except that of a humble cabinet-maker. Eventually my specialty became that of making assorted types of chairs.

In this particular line I was fairly successful, to such a degree in fact that I gained the reputation of being able to satisfy any kind of order, no matter how complicated. For this reason, in woodworking circles I came to enjoy the special privilege of accepting only orders for luxury chairs, with complicated requests for unique carvings, new designs for the back-rest and arm-supports, fancy padding for the cushions and seat—all work of a nature which called for skilled hands and patient trial and study, work which an amateur craftsman could hardly undertake.

The reward for all my pains, however, lay in the sheer delight of creating. You may even consider me a braggart when you hear this, but it all seemed to me to be the same type of thrill which a true artist feels upon creating a masterpiece.

As soon as a chair was completed, it was my usual custom to sit on it to see how it felt, and despite the dismal life of one of my humble profession, at such moments I experienced an indescribable thrill. Giving my mind free rein, I used to imagine the types of people who would eventually curl up in the chair, certainly people of nobility, living in palatial residences, with exquisite, priceless paintings hanging on the walls, glittering crystal chandeliers hanging from the ceilings, expensive rugs on the floor, etc.; and one particular chair, which I imagined standing before a mahogany table, gave me the vision of fragrant Western flowers scenting the air with sweet perfume. Enwrapped in these strange visions, I came to feel that I, too, belonged to such settings, and I derived no end of pleasure from imagining myself to be an influential figure in society.

Foolish thoughts such as these kept coming to me in rapid succession. Imagine, Madam, the pathetic figure I made, sitting comfortably in a luxurious chair of my own making and pretending that I was holding hands with the girl of my dreams. As was always the case, however, the noisy chattering of the uncouth women of the neighborhood and the hysterical shrieking, babbling, and wailing of their children quickly dispelled all my beautiful dreams; again grim reality reared its ugly head before my eyes.

Once back to earth I again found myself a miserable creature, a helpless crawling worm! And as for my beloved, that angelic woman, she too vanished like a mist. I cursed myself for my folly! Why, even the dirty women tending babies in the streets did not so much as bother to glance in my direction. Every time I completed a new chair I was haunted by feelings of utter despair. And with the passing of the months, my long-accumulated misery was enough to choke me.

One day I was charged with the task of making a huge, leather-covered armchair, of a type I had never before conceived, for a foreign hotel located in Yokohama. Actually, this particular type of chair was to have been imported from abroad, but through the persuasion of my employer, who admired my skill as a chair-maker, I received the order.

In order to live up to my reputation as a super-craftsman, I began to devote myself seriously to my new assignment. Steadily I became so engrossed in my labors that at times I even skipped food and sleep. Really, it would be no exaggeration to state that the job became my very life, every fiber of the wood I used semingly linked to my heart and soul.

At last when the chair was completed, I experienced a satisfaction hitherto unknown, for I honestly believed I had achieved a piece of work which immeasurably surpassed all my other creations. As before, I rested the weight of my body on the four legs that supported the chair, first dragging it to a sunny spot on the porch of my workshop. What comfort! What supreme luxury! Not too hard or too soft, the springs seemed to match the cushion with uncanny precision. And as for the leather, what an alluring touch it possessed! This chair not only supported the person who sat in it, but it also seemed to embrace and to hug. Still further, I also noted the perfect reclining angle of the back-support, the delicate puffy swelling of the arm-rests, the perfect symmetry of each of the component parts. Surely, no product could have expressed with greater eloquence the definition of the word "comfort."

I let my body sink deeply into the chair and, caressing the two arm-rests with my hands, gasped with genuine satisfaction and pleasure.

Again my imagination began to play its usual tricks raising strange fancies in my mind. The scene which I imagined now rose before my eyes so vividly that, for a moment, I asked myself if I were not slowly going insane. While in this mental condition, a weird idea suddenly leaped to my mind. Assuredly, it was the whispering of the devil himself. Although it was a sinister idea, it attracted me with a powerful magnetism which I found impossible to resist.

At first, no doubt, the idea found its seed in my secret yearning to keep the chair for myself. Realizing, however, that this was totally out of the question, I next longed to accompany the chair wherever it went. Slowly but steadily, as I continued to nurse this fantastic notion, my mind fell into the grip of an almost terrifying temptation. Imagine, Madam, I really and actually made up my mind to carry out that awful scheme to the end, come what may!

Quickly I took the airmchair apart, and then put it together again to suit my weird purposes. As it was a large armchair, with the seat covered right down to the level of the floor, and furthermore, as the back rest and arm-supports were all large in dimensions, I soon contrived to make the cavity inside large enough to accommodate a man without any danger of exposure. Of course, my work was hampered by the large amount of wooden framework and the springs inside, but with my usual skill as a craftsman I remodeled the chair so that the knees could be placed below the seat, the torso and the head inside the back-rest. Seated thus in the cavity, one could remain perfectly concealed.

As this type of craftsmanship came as second nature to me, I also added a few finishing touches, such as improved acoustics to catch outsides noises and of course a peep-hole cut out in the leather but absolutely unnoticeable. Furthermore, I also provided storage space for supplies, wherein I placed a few boxes of hardtack and a water bottle. For another of nature's needs I also inserted a large rubber bag, and by the time I finished fitting the interior of the chair with these and other unique facilities, it had become quite a habitable place, but not for longer than two or three days at a stretch.

Completing my weird task, I stripped down to my waist and buried myself inside the chair. Just imagine the strange feeling I experienced, Madam! Really, I felt that I had buried myself in a lonely grave. Upon careful reflection I realized that it was indeed a grave. As soon as I entered the chair I was swallowed up by complete darkness, and to everyone else in the world I no longer existed!

Presently a messenger arrived from the dealer's to take delivery of the armchair, bringing with him a large handcart. My apprentice, the only person with whom I lived, was utterly unaware of what had happened. I saw him talking to the messenger.

While my chair was being loaded onto the handcart, one of the cart-pullers exclaimed: "Good God! This chair certainly is heavy! It must weigh a ton!"

When I heard this, my heart leaped to my mouth. However, as the chair itself was obviously an extraordinarily heavy one, no suspicions were aroused, and before long I could feel the vibration of the rattling handcart being pulled along the streets. Of course, I worried incessantly, but at length, that same afternoon, the armchair in which I was concealed was placed with a thud on the floor of a room in the hotel. Later I discovered that it was not an ordinary room, but the lobby.

Now as you may already have guessed long ago, my key motive in this mad venture was to leave my hole in the chair when the coast was clear, loiter around the hotel, and start stealing. Who would dream that a man was concealed inside a chair? Like a fleeting shadow I could ransack every room at will, and by the time any alarm was sounded, I would be safe and sound inside my sanctuary, holding my breath and observing the ridiculous antics of the people outside looking for me.

Possibly you have heard of the hermit crab that is often found on coastal rocks. Shaped like a large spider, this crab crawls about stealthily and, as soon as it hears footsteps, quickly retreats into an empty shell, from which hiding place, with gruesome, hairy front legs partly exposed, it looks furtively about. I was just like this freak monster-crab. But instead of a shell, I had a better shield—a chair which would conceal me far more effectively.

As you can imagine, my plan was so unique and original, so utterly unexpected, that no one was ever the wiser. Consequently, my adventure was a complete success. On the third day after my arrival at the hotel I discovered that I had already taken in quite a haul.

Imagine the thrill and excitement of being able to rob to my heart's content, not to mention the fun derived from observing the people rushing hither and thither only a few inches away under my very nose, shouting: "The thief went this way!" and: "He went that way!" Unfortunately, I do not have the time to describe all my experiences in detail. Rather, allow me to proceed with my narrative and tell you of a far greater source of weird joy which I managed to discover—in fact, what I am about to relate now is the key point of this letter.

First, however, I must request you to turn your thoughts back to the moment when my chair—and I— were both placed in the lobby of the hotel. As soon as the chair was put on the floor all the various members of the staff took turns testing out the seat. After the novelty wore off they all left the room, and then silence reigned, absolute and complete. However, I could not find the courage to leave my sanctum, for I began to imagine a thousand dangers. For what seemed like ages I kept my ears alerted for the slightest sound. After a while I heard heavy footsteps drawing near, evidently from the direction of the corridor. The next moment the unknown feet must have started to tread on heavy carpet, for the walking sound died out completely.

Some time later the sound of a man panting, all out of breath, assailed my ears. Before I could anticipate

what the next development would be, a large, heavy
body like that of a European fell on my knees and
seemed to bounce two or three times before settling
down. With just a thin layer of leather between the seat
of his trousers and my knees, I could almost feel the
warmth of his body. As for his broad, muscular shoulders, they rested flatly against my chest, while his two
heavy arms were deposited squarely on mine. I could
imagine this individual puffing away at his cigar, for
the strong aroma came floating to my nostrils.

Just imagine yourself in my queer position, Madam,
and reflect for a brief moment on the utterly unnatural
state of affairs. As for myself, however, I was utterly
frightened, so much so that I crouched in my dark hide-
out as if petrified, cold sweat running down my armpits.

Beginning with this individual, several people "sat on
my knees" that day, as if they had patiently awaited
their turn. No one, however, suspected even for a fleeting moment that the soft "cushion" on which they were
sitting was actually human flesh with blood circulating
in its veins—confined in a strange world of darkness.

What was it about this mystic hole that fascinated
me so? I somehow felt like an animal living in a totally
new world. And as for the people who lived in the
world outside, I could distinguish them only as people
who made weird noises, breathed heavily, talked,
rustled their clothes, and possessed soft, round bodies.

Gradually I could begin to distinguish the sitters just
by the sense of touch rather than of sight. Those who
were fat felt like large jellyfish, while those who were
specially thin made me feel that I was supporting a
skeleton. Other distinguishing factors consisted of the
curve of the spine, the breadth of the shoulder blades,
the length of the arms, and the thickness of their thighs
as well as the contour of their bottoms. It may seem
strange, but I speak nothing but the truth when I say
that, although all people may seem alike, there are
countless distinguishing traits among all men which can

311

be "seen" merely by the feel of their bodies. In fact, there are just as many differences as in the case of finger-prints or facial contours. This theory, of course, also applies to female bodies.

Usually women are classified in two large categories —the plain and the beautiful. However, in my dark, confined world inside the chair, facial merits or demerits were of secondary importance, being overshadowed by the more meaningful qualities found in the feel of flesh, the sound of the voice, body odor. (Madam, I do hope you will not be offended by the boldness with which I sometimes speak.)

And so, to continue with my narration, there was one girl—the first who ever sat on me—who kindled in my heart a passionate love. Judging solely by her voice, she was European. At the moment, although there was no one else present in the room, her heart must have been filled with happiness, because she was singing with a sweet voice when she came tripping into the room.

Soon I heard her standing immediately in front of my chair, and without giving any warning she suddenly burst into laughter. The very next moment I could hear her flapping her arms like a fish struggling in a net, and then she sat down—on me! For a period of about thirty minutes she continued to sing, moving her body and feet in tempo with her melody.

For me this was quite an unexpected development, for I had always held aloof from all members of the opposite sex because of my ugly face. Now I realized that I was present in the same room with a European girl whom I had never seen, my skin virtually touching hers through a thin layer of leather.

Unaware of my presence, she continued to act with unreserved freedom, doing as she pleased. Inside the chair, I could visualize myself hugging her, kissing her snowy white neck—if only I could remove that layer of leather . . . .

Following this somewhat unhallowed but neverthe-

312

less enjoyable experience, I forgot all about my original intentions of committing robbery. Instead, I seemed to be plunging headlong into a new whirlpool of maddening pleasure.

Long I pondered: "Maybe I was destined to enjoy this type of existence." Gradually the truth seemed to dawn on me. For those who were as ugly and as shunned as myself, it was assuredly wiser to enjoy life inside a chair. For in this strange, dark world I could hear and touch all desirable creatures.

Love in a chair! This may seem altogether too fantastic. Only one who has actually experienced it will be able to vouch for the thrills and the joys it provides. Of course, it is a strange sort of love, limited to the senses of touch, hearing, and smell, a love burning in a world of darkness.

Believe it or not, many of the events that take place in this world are beyond full understanding. In the beginning I had intended only to perpetrate a series of robberies, and then flee. Now, however, I became so attached to my "quarters" that I adjusted them more and more to permanent living.

In my nocturnal prowling I always took the greatest of precautions, watching each step I took, hardly making a sound. Hence there was little danger of being detected. When I recall, however, that I spent several months inside the chair without being discovered even once, it indeed surprises even me.

For the better part of each day I remained inside the chair, sitting like a contortionist with my arms folded and knees bent. As a consequence I felt as if my whole body was paralyzed. Furthermore, as I could never stand up straight, my muscles became taut and inflexible, and gradually I began to crawl instead of walk to the washroom. What a madman I was! Even in the face of all these sufferings I could not persuade myself to abandon my folly and leave that weird world of sensuous pleasure.

In the hotel, although there were several guests who stayed for a month or even two, making the place their home, there was always a constant inflow of new guests, and an equal exodus of the old. As a result I could never manage to enjoy a permanent love. Even now, as I bring back to mind all my "love affairs," I can recall nothing but the touch of warm flesh.

Some of the women possessed the firm bodies of ponies; others seemed to have the slimy bodies of snakes; and still others had bodies composed of nothing but fat, giving them the bounce of a rubber ball. There were also the unusual exceptions who seemed to have bodies made only of sheer muscle, like artistic Greek statues. But notwithstanding the species or types, one and all had a special magnetic allure quite distinctive from the others, and I was perpetually shifting the object of my passions.

At one time, for example, an internationally famous dancer came to Japan and happened to stay at this same hotel. Although she sat in my chair only on one single occasion, the contact of her smooth, soft flesh against my own afforded me a hitherto unknown thrill. So divine was the touch of her body that I felt inspired to a state of positive exaltation. On this occasion, instead of my carnal instincts being aroused, I simply felt like a gifted artist being caressed by the magic wand of a fairy.

Strange, eerie episodes followed in rapid succession. However, as space prohibits, I shall refrain from giving a detailed description of each and every case. Instead, I shall continue to outline the general course of events.

One day, several months following my arrival at the hotel, there suddenly occurred an unexpected change in the shape of my destiny. For some reason the foreign proprietor of the hotel was forced to leave for his homeland, and as a result the management was transferred to Japanese hands.

Originating from this change in proprietorship, a new

policy was adopted, calling for a drastic retrenchment in expenditures, abolishment of luxurious fittings, and other steps to increase profits through economy. One of the first results of this new policy was that the management put all the extravagant furnishings of the hotel up for auction. Included in the list of items for sale was my chair.

When I learned of this new development, I immediately felt the greatest of disappointments. Soon, however, a voice inside me advised that I should return to the natural world outside—and spend the tidy sum I had acquired by stealing. I of course realized that I would no longer have to return to my humble life as a craftsman, for actually I was comparatively wealthy. The thought of my new role in society seemed to overcome my disappointment in having to leave the hotel. Also, when I reflected deeply on all the pleasures which I had derived there, I was forced to admit that, although my "love affairs" had been many, they had all been with foreign women and that somehow something had always been lacking.

I then realized fully and deeply that as a Japanese I really craved a lover of my own kind. While I was turning these thoughts over in my mind, my chair—with me still in it—was sent to a furniture store to be sold at auction. Maybe this time, I told myself, the chair will be purchased by a Japanese home. With my fingers crossed, I decided to be patient and to continue with my existence in the chair a while longer.

Although I suffered for two or three days in my chair while it stood in front of the furniture store, eventually it came up for sale and was promptly purchased. This, fortunately, was because of the excellent workmanship which had gone into its making, and although it was no longer new, it still had a " dignified bearing."

The purchaser was a high-ranking official who lived in Tokyo. When I was being transferred from the furniture store to the man's palatial residence, the bouncing and vibrating of the vehicle almost killed me. I gritted my teeth and bore up bravely, however, comforted by the thought that at last I had been bought by a Japanese.

Inside his house I was placed in a spacious Western-style study. One thing about the room which gave me the greatest of satisfactions was the fact that my chair was meant more for the use of his young and attractive wife than for his own.

Within a month I had come to be with the wife constantly, united with her as one, so to speak. With the exception of the dining and sleeping hours, her soft body was always seated on my knees for the simple reason that she was engaged in a deep-thinking task.

You have no idea how much I loved this lady! She was the first Japanese woman with whom I had ever come into such close contact, and moreover she possessed a wonderfully appealing body. She seemed the answer to all my prayers! Compared with this, all my other "affairs" with the various women in the hotel seemed like childish flirtations, nothing more.

Proof of the mad love which I now cherished for this intellectual lady was found in the fact that I longed to hold her every moment of the time. When she was away, even for a fleeting moment, I waited for her return like a love-crazed Romeo yearning for his Juliet. Such feelings I had never hitherto experienced.

Gradually I came to want to convey my feelings to her ... somehow. I tried vainly to carry out my purpose, but always encountered a blank wall, for I was absolutely helpless. Oh, how I longed to have her reciprocate my love! Yes, you may consider this the confession of a madman, for I *was* mad—madly in love with her!

But how could I signal to her? If I revealed myself, the shock of the discovery would immediately prompt her to call her husband and the servants. And that, of course, would be fatal to me, for exposure would not only mean disgrace, but severe punishment for the crimes I had committed.

I therefore decided on another course of action, namely, to add in every way to her comfort and thus awaken in her a natural love for—the chair! As she was a true artist, I somehow felt confident that her natural love of beauty would guide her in the direction I desired. And as for myself, I was willing to find pure contentment in the love even for a material object, for I could find solace in the belief that her delicate feelings of love for even a mere chair were powerful enough to penetrate to the creature that dwelt inside . . . which was myself!

In every way I endeavored to make her more comfortable every time she placed her weight on my chair. Whenever she became tired from sitting long in one position on my humble person, I would slowly move my knees and embrace her more warmly, making her more snug. And when she dozed off to sleep I would move my knees, ever so softly, to rock her into a deeper slumber.

Somehow, possibly by a miracle (or was it just my imagination?), this lady now seemed to love my chair deeply, for every time she sat down she acted like a baby falling into a mother's embrace, or a girl surrendering herself into the arms of her lover. And when she moved herself about in the chair, I felt that she was feeling an almost amorous joy. In this way the fire of my love and passion rose into a leaping flame that could never be extinguished, and I finally reached a stage where I simply had to make a strange, bold plea.

Ultimately I began to feel that if she would just look at me, even for a brief passing moment, I could die with the deepest contentment.

No doubt, Madam, by this time, you must certainly have guessed who the object of my mad passion is. To

317

put it explicity, she happens to be none other than yourself, Madam! Ever since your husband brought the chair from that furniture store I have been suffering excruciating pains because of my mad love and longing for you. I am but a worm ... a loathsome creature.

I have but one request. Could you meet me once, just once? I will ask nothing further of you. I of course do not deserve your sympathy, for I have always been nothing but a villain, unworthy even to touch the soles of your feet. But if you will grant me this one request, just out of compassion, my gratitude will be eternal.

Last night I stole out of your residence to write this confession because, even leaving aside the danger, I did not possess the courage to meet you suddenly face to face, without any warning or preparation.

While you are reading this letter, I will be roaming around your house with bated breath. If you will agree to my request, please place your handerchief on the pot of flowers that stands outside your window. At this signal I will open your front door and enter as a humble visitor . . . .

Thus ended the letter.

Even before Yoshiko had read many pages, some premonition of evil had caused her to become deadly pale. Rising unconsciously, she had fled from the study, from *that chair* upon which she had been seated, and had sought sanctuary in one of the Japanese rooms of her house.

For a moment it had been her intention to stop reading and tear up the eerie message; but somehow, she had read on, with the closely-written sheets laid on a low desk.

Now that she had finished, her premonition was proved correct. That chair on which she had sat from day to day ... had it really contained a man? If true, what a horrible experience she had unknowingly undergone! A sudden chill came over her, as if ice water had been poured down her back, and the shivers that followed seemed never to stop.

Like one in a trance, she gazed into space. Should she examine the chair? But how could she possibly steel herself for such a horrible ordeal? Even though the chair might now be empty, what about the filthy remains, such as the food and other necessary items which he must have used?

"Madam, a letter for you."

With a start, she looked up and found her maid standing at the doorway with an envelope in her hand.

In a daze, Yoshiko took the envelope and stifled a scream. Horror of horrors! It was another message from the same man! Again her name was written in that same familiar scrawl.

For a long while she hesitated, wondering whether she should open it. At last she mustered up enough courage to break the seal and shakingly took out the pages. This second communication was short and curt, and it contained another breath-taking surprise:

Forgive my boldness in addressing another message to you. To begin with, I merely happen to be one of your ardent admirers. The manuscript which I submitted to you under separate cover was based on pure imagination and my knowledge that you had recently bought *that chair*. It is a sample of my own humble attempts at fictional writing. If you would kindly comment on it, I shall know no greater satisfaction.

For personal reasons I submitted my MS prior to writing this letter of explanation, and I assume you have already read it. How did you find it? If, Madam, you have found it amusing or entertaining in some degree,

THE FORTUNES OF SIR ROBERT ARDAGH

By Joseph Sheridan Le Fanu

In the south of Ireland, and on the borders of the county of Limerick, there lies a district of two or three miles in length, which is rendered interesting by the fact that it is one of the very few spots throughout this country, in which some fragments of aboriginal wood have found refuge. It has little or none of the lordly character of the American forests; for the axe has felled its oldest and its grandest trees; but in the close wood which survives, live all the wild and pleasing peculiarities of nature—its complete irregularity—its vistas, in whose perspective the quiet cattle are peacefully browsing—its refreshing glades, where the grey rocks arise from amid the nodding fern—the silvery shafts of the old birch trees—the knotted trunks of the hoary oak —the grotesque but graceful branches, which never shed their honours under the tyrant pruning hook—the soft green sward—the chequered light and shade—the wild luxuriant weeds—its lichen and its moss—all, all are beautiful alike in the green freshness of spring, or in the sadness and sear of autumn—their beauty is of that kind which makes the heart full with joy—appealing to the affections with a power which belongs to nature only. This wood runs up, from below the base, to the ridge of a long line of irregular hills, having perhaps in primitive times, formed but the skirting of some mighty forest which occupied the level below.

But now, alas, whither have we drifted?—whither has the tide of civilization borne us?—it has passed over a land unprepared for it—it has left nakedness behind it—we have lost our forests, but our marauders remain—we have destroyed all that is picturesque, while we have retained everything that is revolting in barbarism. Through the midst of this woodland, there runs a deep gully or glen; where the stillness of the scene is broken in upon by the brawling of a mountain stream, which, however, in the winter season, swells into a rapid and formidable torrent.

There is one point at which the glen becomes extremely deep and narrow, the sides descend to the depth of some hundred feet, and are so steep as to be nearly perpendicular. The wild trees which have taken root in the crannies and chasms of the rock, have so intersected and entangled, that one can with difficulty catch a glimpse of the stream, which wheels, flashes, and foams below, as if exulting in the surrounding silence and solitude.

This spot was not unwisely chosen, as a point of no ordinary strength, for the erection of a massive square tower or keep, one side of which rises as if in continuation of the precipitous cliff on which it is based. Originally, the only mode of ingress was by a narrow portal, in the very wall which overtopped the precipice; opening upon a ledge of rock which afforded a precarious pathway, cautiously intersected, however, by a deep trench cut with great labour in the living rock; so that, in its original state, and before the introduction of artillery into the art of war, this tower might have been pronounced, and that not presumptuously, almost impregnable.

The progress of improvement, and the increasing security of the times had, however, tempted its successive proprietors, if not to adorn, at least to enlarge their premises, and at about the middle of the last century, when the castle was last inhabited, the original square tower formed but a small part of the edifice.

The castle, and a wide tract of the surrounding country had from time immemorial, belonged to a family, which, for distinctness, we shall call by the name of Ardagh; and, owing to the associations which, in Ireland, almost always attach to scenes which have long witnessed alike, the exercise of stern feudal authority, and of that savage hospitality which distinguished the good old times, this building has become the subject and the scene of many wild and extraordinary traditions. One of them I have been enabled, by a personal acquaintance with an eye-witness of the events, to trace to its origin; and yet it is hard to say, whether the events which I am about to record, appear more strange or improbable, as seen through the distorting medium of tradition, or in the appalling dimness of uncertainty, which surrounds the reality.

Tradition says that, sometime in the last century, Sir Robert Ardagh, a young man, and the last heir of that family, went abroad and served in foreign armies, and that having acquired considerable honour and emolument, he settled at Castle Ardagh, the building we have just now attempted to describe. He was what the country people call a *dark* man; that is, he was considered morose, reserved, and ill-tempered; and as it was supposed from the utter solitude of his life, was upon no terms of cordiality with the other members of his family.

The only occasion upon which he broke through the solitary monotony of his life, was during the continuance of the racing season, and immediately subsequent to it; at which time he was to be seen among the busiest upon the course, betting deeply and unhesitatingly, and invariably with success. Sir Robert was, however, too well-known as a man of honour, and of too high a family to be suspected of any unfair dealing. He was, moreover, a soldier, and a man of an intrepid as well as of a haughty character, and no one cared to hazard a surmise, the consequences of which would be felt most probably by its originator only. Gossip, however, was not silent—it was remarked that Sir Robert never appeared at the race ground, which was the only place of public resort which he frequented, except in company with a certain strange looking person, who was never seen elsewhere, or under other circumstances. It was remarked, too, that this man, whose relation to Sir Robert was never distinctly ascertained, was the only person to whom he seemed to speak unnecessarily; it was observed, that while with the country gentry he exchanged no further communication than what was unavoidable in arranging his sporting transactions, with this person he would converse earnestly and frequently. Tradition asserts, that to enhance the curiosity which this unaccountable and exclusive preference excited, the stranger possessed some striking and unpleasant peculiarities of person and of garb—she does not say, however, what these were—but they, in conjunction with Sir Robert's secluded habits, and extraordinary run of luck—a success which was supposed to result from the suggestions and immediate advice of the unknown—were sufficient to warrant report in pronouncing that there was something *queer* in the wind, and in surmising that Sir Robert was playing a fearful and a hazardous game, and that in short, his strange companion was little better than the devil himself.

Years, however, rolled quietly away, and nothing novel occurred in the arrangements of Castle Ardagh, excepting that Sir Robert parted with his odd companion, but as nobody could tell whence he came, so nobody could say whither he had gone. Sir Robert's habits, however, underwent no consequent change; he continued regularly to frequent race meetings, without mixing at all in the convivialities of the gentry, and immediately afterwards to relapse into the secluded monotony of his ordinary life.

It was said that he had accumulated vast sums of money—and, as his bets were always successful, and always large, such must have been the case. He did not suffer the acquisition of wealth, however, to influence his hospitality or his housekeeping—he neither purchased land nor extended his establishment; and his mode of enjoying his money must have been altogether that of the miser—consisting, merely, in the pleasure of touching and telling his gold, and in the consciousness of wealth. Sir Robert's temper, so far from improving, became more than ever gloomy and morose. He sometimes carried the indulgence of his evil disposition to such a height, that it bordered upon insanity. During these paroxysms, he would neither eat, drink, nor sleep. On such occasions he insisted on perfect privacy, even from the intrusion of his most trained servants;—his voice was frequently heard, sometimes in earnest supplication, sometimes raised as if in loud and angry altercation, with some unknown visitant—sometimes he would, for hours together, walk to and fro, throughout the long oak-wainscotted apartment, which he generally occupied, with wild gesticulations and agitated pace, in the manner of one who has been roused to a state of unnatural excitement, by some sudden and appalling intimation.

These paroxysms of apparent lunacy were so frightful, that during their continuance, even his oldest and most faithful domestics dared not approach him; consequently, his hours of agony were never intruded upon, and the mysterious causes of his sufferings appeared likely to remain hidden for ever. On one occasion, a fit of this kind continued for an unusual time—the ordinary term of their duration, about two days, had been long past—and the servant, who generally waited upon Sir Robert, after these visitations, having in vain listened for the well-known tinkle of his master's hand-bell began to feel extremely anxious; he feared that his master might have died from sheer exhaustion, or perhaps put an end to his own existence, during his miserable depression. These fears at length became so strong, that having in vain urged some of his brother-servants to accompany him, he determined to go up alone, and himself see whether any accident had befallen Sir Robert. He traversed the several passages which conducted from the new to the more ancient parts of the mansion; and having arrived in the old hall of the castle, the utter silence of the hour, for it was very late in the night, the idea of the nature of the enterprise in which he was engaging himself, a sensation of remoteness from anything like human companionship, but more than all the vivid but undefined anticipation of something horrible, came upon him with such oppressive weight, that he hesitated as to whether he should proceed. Real uneasiness, however, respecting the fate of his master, for whom he felt that kind of attachment, which the force of habitual intercourse, not unfrequently engenders respecting objects not in themselves amiable—and also a latent unwillingness to expose his weakness to the ridicule of his fellow-servants, combined to overcome his reluctance; and he had just placed his foot upon the first step of the staircase, which conducted to his master's chamber, when his attention was arrested by a low but distinct knocking at the hall-door. Not, perhaps very sorry at finding thus an excuse even for deferring his intended expedition, he placed the candle upon a stone block which lay in the hall, and approached the door, uncertain whether his ears had not deceived him. This doubt was justified by the circumstance, that the hall entrance had been for nearly fifty years disused as a mode of ingress to the castle. The situation of this gate also, which we have endeavoured to describe, opening upon a narrow ledge of rock which overhangs a perilous cliff, rendered it at all times, but particularly at night, a dangerous entrance; this shelving platform of rock, which formed the only avenue to the door, was divided, as I have already stated, by a broad chasm, the planks across which had long disappeared by decay or otherwise, so that it seemed at least highly improbable that any man could have found his way across the passage in safety to the door—more particularly, on a night like that, of singular darkness. The old man, therefore, listened attentively, to ascertain whether the first application should be followed by another; he had not long to wait; the same low but singularly distinct knocking was repeated; so low that it seemed as if the applicant had employed no harder or heavier instrument than his hand, and yet despite the immense thickness of the door, so very distinct, that he could not mistake the sound. It was repeated a third time, without any increase of loudness; and the old man obeying an impulse for which to his dying hour, he could never account, proceeded to remove, one by one, the three great oaken bars which secured the door. Time and damp had effectually corroded the iron chambers of the lock, so that it afforded little resistance. With some effort, as he believed, assisted from without, the old servant succeeded in opening the door; and a low, square-built figure, apparently that of a man wrapped in a large black cloak, entered the hall. The servant could not see much of this visitant with any distinctness; his dress appeared foreign, the skirt of his ample cloak was thrown over one shoulder; he wore a large felt hat, with a very heavy leaf, from under which escaped what appeared to be a mass of long sooty-black hair;—his feet were cased in heavy ridingboots. Such were the few particulars which the servant had time and light to observe. The stranger desired him to let his master know instantly that a friend had come, by appointment, to settle some business with him. The servant hesitated, but a slight motion on the part of his visitor, as if to possess himself of the candle, determined him; so taking it in his hand, he ascended the castle stairs, leaving his guest in the hall.

On reaching the apartment which opened upon the oak-chamber, he was surprised to observe the door of that room partly open, and the room itself lit up. He paused, but there was no sound—he looked in, and saw Sir Robert—his head, and the upper part of his body, reclining on a table, upon which burned a lamp; his arms were stretched forward on either side, and perfectly motionless; it appeared that having been sitting at the table, he had thus sunk forward, either dead or in a swoon. There was no sound of breathing; all was silent, except the sharp ticking of a watch, which lay beside the lamp. The servant coughed twice or thrice, but with no effect—his fears now almost amounted to certainty, and he was approaching the table on which his master partly lay—to satisfy himself of his death—when Sir Robert slowly raised his head, and throwing himself back in his chair, fixed his eyes in a ghastly and uncertain gaze upon his attendant. At length he said, slowly and painfully, as if he dreaded the answer—

"In God's name, what are you?"

"Sir," said the servant, "a strange gentleman wants to see you below."

At this intimation, Sir Robert, starting on his legs, and tossing his arms wildly upwards, uttered a shriek of such appalling and despairing terror, that it was almost too fearful for human endurance; and long after the sound had ceased, it seemed to the terrified imagination of the old servant, to roll through the deserted passages in bursts of unnatural laughter. After a few moments, Sir Robert said—

"Can't you send him away? Why does he come so soon? Oh God! oh God! let him leave me for an hour —a little time. I can't see him now—try to get him away. You see I can't go down now—I have not strength. Oh God! oh God! let him come back in an

328

hour—it is not long to wait. He cannot lose anything by it—nothing, nothing, nothing. Tell him that—say anything to him."

The servant went down. In his own words, he did not feel the stairs under him, till he got to the hall. The figure stood exactly as he had left it. He delivered his master's message as coherently as he could. The stranger replied in a careless tone—

"If Sir Robert will not come down to me, I must go up to him."

The man returned, and to his surprise he found his master much more composed in manner. He listened to the message; and though the cold perspiration stood in drops upon his forehead, faster than he could wipe it away, his manner had lost the dreadful agitation which had marked it before. He rose feebly, and casting a last look of agony behind him, passed from the room to the lobby, where he signed to his attendant not to follow him. The man moved as far as the head of the stair-case, from whence he had a tolerably distinct view of the hall, which was imperfectly lighted by the candle he had left there.

He saw his master reel, rather than walk down the stairs, clinging all the way to the banisters. He walked on as if about to sink every moment from weakness. The figure advanced as if to meet him, and in passing struck down the light. The servant could see no more; but there was a sound of struggling, renewed at intervals with silent but fearful energy. It was evident, however, that the parties were approaching the door, for he heard the solid oak sound twice or thrice, as the feet of the combatants, in shuffling hither and thither over the floor, struck upon it. After a slight pause he heard the door thrown open, with such violence that the leaf struck the sidewall of the hall, and it was so dark without that this was made known in no other way than by the sound. The struggle was renewed with an agony and intenseness of energy, that betrayed itself

329

in deep-drawn gasps. One desperate effort, which terminated in the breaking of some part of the door, producing a sound as if the door-post was wrenched from its position, was followed by another wrestle, evidently upon the narrow ledge which ran outside the door, overtopping the precipice. This seemed as fruitless as the rest, for it was followed by a crashing sound as if some heavy body had fallen over, and was rushing down the precipice, through the light boughs that crossed near the top. All then became still as the grave, except the moan of the night wind that sighed up the wooded glen.

The old servant had not nerve to return through the hall, and to him that night seemed all but endless; but morning at length came, and with it the disclosure of the events of the night. Near the door, upon the ground, lay Sir Robert's sword-belt, which had given way in the scuffle. A huge splinter from the massive door-post had been wrenched off, by an almost superhuman effort—one which nothing but the gripe of a despairing man could have served—and on the rock outside were left the marks of the slipping and sliding of feet.

At the foot of the precipice, not immediately under the castle, but dragged some way up the glen, were found the remains of Sir Robert, with hardly a vestige of a limb or feature left distinguishable. The right hand, however, was uninjured, and in its fingers was clutched, with the fixedness of death, a long lock of coarse sooty hair—the only direct circumstantial evidence of the presence of a second person. So says tradition.

This story, as I have mentioned, was current among the dealers in such lore; but the original facts are so dissimilar in all but the name of the principal person mentioned, Sir Robert Ardagh, and the fact that his death was accompanied with circumstances of extraordinary mystery, that the two narratives are totally irreconcileable (even allowing the utmost for the exaggerating influence of tradition) except by supposing report to have combined and blended together the fabulous histories of several distinct heroes of the family of Ardagh. However this may be, I shall lay before the reader a distinct recital of the events from which the foregoing tradition arose. With respect to these there can be no mistake; they are authenticated as fully as any thing can be by human testimony; and I state them principally upon the evidence of a lady who herself bore a prominent part in the strange events which she related, and which I now record as being among the few well-attested tales of the marvellous, which it has been my fate to hear. I shall, as far as I am able, arrange in one combined narrative, the evidence of several distinct persons, who were eye-witnesses of what they related, and with the truth of whose testimony I am solemnly and deeply impressed.

Sir Robert Ardagh was the heir and representative of the family whose name he bore; but owing to the prodigality of his father, the estates descended to him in a very impaired condition. Urged by the restless spirit of youth, or more probably by a feeling of pride, which could not submit to witness, in the paternal mansion, what he considered a humiliating alteration in the style and hospitality which up to that time had distinguished his family, Sir Robert left Ireland and went abroad. How he occupied himself, or what countries he visited during his absence, was never known, nor did he afterwards make any allusion, or encourage any inquiries touching his foreign sojourn. He left Ireland in the year 1742, being then just of age, and was not heard of until the year 1760—about eighteen years afterwards—at which time he returned. His personal appearance was, as might have been expected, very greatly altered, more altered, indeed, than the time of his absence might have warranted one in supposing likely. But to counterbalance the unfavorable change which time had wrought in his form and features, he had acquired all the advantages of polish of manner, and refinement of taste, which foreign travel is supposed to bestow. But what was truly surprising was, that it soon became evident that Sir Robert was very wealthy—wealthy to an extraordinary and unaccountable degree; and this fact was made manifest, not only by his expensive style of living, but by his proceeding to disembarrass his property, and to purchase extensive estates in addition. Moreover, there could be nothing deceptive in these appearances, for he paid ready money for everything, from the most important purchase to the most trifling.

Sir Robert was a remarkably agreeable man, and possessing the combined advantages of birth and property, he was, as a matter of course, gladly received into the highest society which the metropolis then commanded. It was thus that he became acquainted with the two beautiful Miss F——ds, then among the brightest ornaments of the highest circles of Dublin fashion. Their family was in more than one direction allied to nobility; and Lady D——, their eldest sister by many years, and some time married to a once well-known nobleman, was now their protectress. These considerations, besides the fact that the young ladies were what is usually termed heiresses, though not a very great amount, secured to them a high position in the best society which Ireland then produced. The two young ladies differed strongly, alike in appearance and in character. The elder of the two, Emily, was generally considered the handsomer—for her beauty was of that impressive kind which never failed to strike even at the first glance, possessing all the advantages of a fine person, and of a commanding carriage. The beauty of her features strikingly assorted in character with that of her figure and deportment. Her hair was raven black and richly luxuriant, beautifully contrasting with the even, perfect whiteness of her forehead—her finely pencilled brows were black as the ringlets that clustered near them—and her eyes, full, lustrous, and animated, possessed all the power and brilliancy of the black, with more than their softness and variety of expression. She was not, however, merely the tragedy queen. When she smiled, and that was not unfrequently, the dimpling cheek and chin, the laughing display of the small and beautiful teeth—but more than all, the roguish archness of her deep, bright eye, shewed that nature had not neglected in her the lighter and the softer characteristics of woman.

Her younger sister Mary was, as I believe not unfrequently occurs in the case of sisters, quite in the opposite style of beauty. She was light-haired, had more colour, had nearly equal grace, with much more liveliness of manner. Her eyes were of that dark grey which poets so much admire—full of expression and vivacity. She was altogether a very beautiful and animated girl —though as unlike her sister as the presence of those two qualities would permit her to be. Their dissimilarity did not stop here—it was deeper than mere appearance—the character of their minds differed almost as strikingly as did their complexion. The fair-haired beauty had a large proportion of that softness and pliability of temper which physiognomists assign as the characteristics of such complexions. She was much more the creature of impulse than of feeling, and consequently more the victim of extrinsic circumstances than was her sister. Emily, on the contrary, possessed considerable firmness and decision. She was less excitable, but when excited, her feelings were more intense and enduring. She wanted much of the gaiety, but with it the volatility of her younger sister. Her opinions were adopted, and her friendships formed more reflectively, and her affections seemed to move, as it were, more slowly, but more determinedly. This firmness of character did not amount to any thing masculine, and did not at all impair the feminine grace of her manners.

Sir Robert Ardagh was for a long time apparently equally attentive to the two sisters, and many were the conjectures and the surmises as to which would be the lady of the choice. At length, however, these doubts were determined; he proposed for and was accepted by the dark beauty, Emily F——d.

The bridals were celebrated in a manner becoming the wealth and connections of the parties; and Sir Robert and Lady Ardagh left Dublin to pass the honeymoon at the family mansion, Castle Ardagh, which had lately been fitted up in a style bordering upon magnificent. Whether in compliance with the wishes of his lady, or owing to some whim of his own, his habits were henceforward strikingly altered, and from having moved among the gayest if not the most profligate of the votaries of fashion, he suddenly settled down into a quiet, domestic, country gentleman, and seldom, if ever, visited the capital, and then his sojourns were brief as the nature of his business would permit.

Lady Ardagh, however, did not suffer from this change further than in being secluded from general society; for Sir Robert's wealth, and the hospitality which he had established in the family mansion, commanded that of such of his lady's friends and relatives as had leisure or inclination to visit the castle; and as the style of living was very handsome, and its internal resources of amusement considerable, few invitations from Sir Robert or his lady were neglected.

Many years passed quietly away, during which Sir Robert's and Lady Ardagh's hopes of issue were several times disappointed. In the lapse of all this time there occurred but one event worth recording. Sir Robert had brought with him from abroad a valet, who sometimes professed himself to be a Frenchman; at others an Italian; and at others again a German. He spoke all these languages with equal fluency, and seemed to take a kind of pleasure in puzzling the sagacity and balking the curiosity of such of the visitors at the castle as at any time happened to enter into conversation with him, or who, struck by his singularities, became inquisitive respecting his country and origin. Sir Robert called him by the French name, JACQUE; and among the lower orders he was familiarly known by the title of "Jack the devil," an appellation which originated in a supposed malignity of disposition, and a real reluctance to mix in the society of those who were believed to be his equals. This morose reserve, coupled with the mystery which enveloped all about him, rendered him an object of suspicion and inquiry to his fellow-servants, amongst whom it was whispered that his man in secret governed the actions of Sir Robert with a despotic dictation, and that as if to indemnify himself for his public and apparent servitude and self-denial, he in private exacted a degree of respectful homage from his so-called master, totally inconsistent with the relation generally supposed to exist between them.

This man's personal appearance was, to say the least of it, extremely odd; he was low in stature; and this defect was enhanced by a distortion of the spine, so considerable as almost to amount to a hunch; his features, too, had all that sharpness and sickliness of hue which generally accompany deformity; he wore his hair, which was black as soot, in heavy neglected ringlets about his shoulders, and always without powder—a peculiarity in those days. There was something unpleasant, too, in the circumstance that he never raised his eyes so as to meet those of another; this fact was often cited as a proof of his being SOMETHING NOT QUITE RIGHT, and said to result not from the timidity which is supposed in most cases to induce this habit, but from a consciousness that his eye possessed a power, which, if exhibited, would betray a supernatural origin. Once, and once only, had he violated this sinister observance: it was on the occasion of Sir Robert's hopes having been most bitterly disappointed; his lady, after a severe and dangerous confinement, gave birth to a dead child. Immediately after the intelligence had been made

335

known, a servant, having upon some business, passed outside the gate of the castle yard, was met by Jacque, who, contrary to his wont, accosted him, observing, "so, after all the pother, the son and heir is still-born." This remark was accompanied by a chuckling laugh, only, the only approach to merriment which he was ever known to exhibit. The servant, who was really disappointed, having hoped for holy-day times, feasting and debauchery with impunity during the rejoicings which would have accompanied a christening, turned tartly upon the little valet, telling him that he should let Sir Robert know how he had received the tidings which should have filled any faithful servant with sorrow; and having once broken the ice, he was proceeding with increasing fluency, when his harangue was cut short and his temerity punished, by the little man's raising his head and treating him to a scowl so fearful, half demoniac, half insane, that it haunted his imagination in nightmares and nervous tremours for months after.

To this man Lady Ardagh had, at first sight, conceived an antipathy amounting to horror, a mixture of loathing and dread so very powerful that she had made it a particular and urgent request to Sir Robert, that he would dismiss him, offering herself, from that property which Sir Robert had, by the marriage settlements, left at her own disposal, to provide handsomely for him, provided only that she might be relieved from the continual anxiety and discomfort which the fear of encountering him induced.

Sir Robert, however, would not hear of it; the request seemed at first to agitate and distress him; but when still urged in defiance of his peremptory refusal, he burst into a violent fit of fury; he spoke darkly of great sacrifices which he had made, and threatened that if the request were at any time renewed he would leave both her and the country for ever. This was, however, a solitary instance of violence; his general conduct

336

towards Lady Ardagh, though at no time bordering upon the uxorious, was certainly kind and respectful, and he was more than repaid in the fervent attachment which she bore him in return.

Some short time after this strange interview between Sir Robert and Lady Ardagh, one night after the family had retired to bed, and when everything had been quiet for some time, the bell of Sir Robert's dressing-room rang suddenly and violently; the ringing was repeated again and again at still shorter intervals, and with increasing violence, as if the person who pulled the bell was agitated by the presence of some terrifying and imminent danger. A servant named Donovan was the first to answer it; he threw on his clothes, and hurried to the room with haste proportioned to the urgency of the call.

Sir Robert had selected for his private room an apartment, remote from the bed-chambers of the castle, most of which lay in the more modern parts of the mansion, and secured at its entrance by a double door; as the servant opened the first of these, Sir Robert's bell again sounded with a longer and louder peal; the inner door resisted his efforts to open it; but after a few violent struggles, not having been perfectly secured or owing to the inadequacy of the bolt itself, it gave way, and the servant rushed into the apartment, advancing several paces before he could recover himself. As he entered, he heard Sir Robert's voice exclaiming loudly "wait without, do not come in yet," but the prohibition came too late. Near a low truckle-bed, upon which Sir Robert sometimes slept, for he was a whimsical man, in a large arm chair, sate, or rather lounged, the form of the valet, Jacque; his arms folded, and his heels stretched forward on the floor so as fully to exhibit his misshapen legs, his head thrown back, and his eyes fixed upon his master with a look of indescribable defiance and derision, while, as if to add to the strange insolence of his attitude and expression, he had placed upon his head the black cloth cap which it was his habit to wear.

Sir Robert was standing before him at the distance of several yards in a posture expressive of despair, terror, and what might be called an agony of humility. He waved his hand twice or thrice, as if to dismiss the servant, who, however, remained fixed on the spot where he had first stood; and then, as if forgetting every thing but the agony within him, he pressed his clenched hands on his cold damp brow, and dashed away the heavy drops that gathered chill and thickly there. Jacque broke the silence.

"Donovan," said he, "shake up that drone and drunkard, Carlton; tell him that his master directs that the travelling carriage shall be at the door within half an hour."

The servant paused as if in doubt as to what he should do; but his scruples were resolved by Sir Robert's saying hurriedly, "Go, go, do whatever he directs; his commands are mine, tell Carlton the same."

The servant hurried to obey, and in about half an hour the carriage was at the door, and Jacque having directed the coachman to drive to B———n, a small town at about the distance of twelve miles, the nearest point, however, at which post horses could be obtained, stept into the vehicle which accordingly quitted the castle immediately.

Although it was a fine moonlight night, the carriage made its way but slowly, and after the lapse of two hours, the travellers had arrived at a point about eight miles from the castle, at which the road strikes through a desolate and heathy flat, sloping up distantly at either side into bleak undulatory hills, in whose monotonous sweep the imagination beholds the heaving of some dark sluggish sea, arrested in its first commotion by some preternatural power; it is a gloomy and divested spot; there is neither tree nor habitation near it; its monotony is unbroken, except by here and there the grey front of a rock peering above the heath, and the effect is rendered yet more dreary and spectral by the exaggerated and misty shadows which the moon casts along the sloping sides of the hills. When they had gained about the centre of this tract, Carlton, the coachman, was surprised to see a figure standing, at some distance in advance, immediately beside the road, and still more so when, on coming up, he observed that it was no other than the person whom he believed to be at that moment quietly seated in the carriage; the coachman drew up, and nodding to him, the little valet exclaimed, "Carlton, I have got the start of you, the roads are heavy, so I shall even take care of myself the rest of the way; do you make your way back as best you can; and I shall follow my own nose;" so saying he chucked a purse into the lap of the coachman, and turning off at a right angle with the road he began to move rapidly away in the direction of the dark ridge, that lowered in the distance. The servant watched him until he was lost in the shadowy haze of night; and neither he nor any of the inmates of the castle saw Jacque again. His disappearance, as might have been expected, did not cause any regret among the servants and dependants at the castle; and Lady Ardagh did not attempt to conceal her delight; but with Sir Robert matters were different; for two or three days subsequent to this event, he confined himself to his room; and when he did return to his ordinary occupations, it was with a gloomy indifference which showed that he did so more from habit than from any interest he felt in them; he appeared from that moment unaccountably and strikingly changed, and thenceforward walked through life as a thing from which he could derive neither profit nor pleasure. His temper, however, so far from growing wayward or morose, became, though gloomy, very, almost unnaturally, placid and cold; but his spirits totally failed, and he became silent and abstracted.

These sombre habits of mind, as might have been

anticipated, very materially affected the gay housekeeping of the castle; and the dark and melancholy spirit of its master, seemed to have communicated itself to the very domestics, almost to the very walls of the mansion. Several years rolled on this way, and the sounds of mirth and wassail had long been strangers to the castle, when Sir Robert requested his lady, to her great astonishment, to invite some twenty or thirty of their friends to spend the Christmas, which was fast approaching, at the castle. Lady Ardagh gladly complied, and her sister Mary, who still continued unmarried, and Lady D—— were of course included in the invitations. Lady Ardagh had requested her sisters to set forward as early as possible, in order that she might enjoy a little of their society before the arrival of the other guests; and in compliance with this request they left Dublin almost immediately upon receiving the invitation, a little more than a week before the arrival of the festival which was to be the period at which the whole party were to muster.

For expedition's sake it was arranged that they should post, while Lady D——'s groom was to follow with her horses; she taking with herself her own maid and one male servant. They left the city when the day was considerably spent, and consequently made but three stages in the first day; upon the second, at about eight in the evening, they had reached the town of K——k, distant about fifteen miles from Castle Ardagh. Here owing to Miss F——d's great fatigue, she having been for a considerable time in a very delicate state of health, it was determined to put up for the night. They, accordingly, took possession of the best sitting room which the inn commanded, and Lady D—— remained in it to direct and urge the preparations for some refreshment, which the fatigues of the day had rendered necessary, while her younger sister retired to her bed-chamber to rest there for a little time, as the parlour commanded no such luxury as a sofa.

Miss F——d was, as I have already stated, at this time, in very delicate health; and upon this occasion the exhaustion of fatigue, and the dreary badness of the weather, combined to depress her spirits. Lady D—— had not been left long to herself, when the door communicating with the passage was abruptly opened, and her sister Mary entered in a state of great agitation; she sate down pale and trembling upon one of the chairs, and it was not until a copious flood of tears had relieved her, that she became sufficiently calm to relate the cause of her excitement and distress. It was simply this. Almost immediately upon lying down upon the bed she sank into a feverish and unrefreshing slumber; images of all grotesque shapes and startling colours flitted before her sleeping fancy with all the rapidity and variety of the changes in a kaleidoscope. At length, as she described it, a mist seemed to interpose itself between her sight and the ever-shifting scenery which sported before her imagination, and out of this cloudy shadow, gradually emerged a figure whose back seemed turned towards the sleeper; it was that of a lady, who, in perfect silence, was expressing as far as pantomimic gesture could, by wringing her hands, and throwing her head from side to side, in the manner of one who is exhausted by the over indulgence, by the very sickness and impatience of grief, the extremity of misery. For a long time she sought in vain to catch a glimpse of the face of the apparition, who thus seemed to stir and live before her. But at length the figure seemed to move with an air of authority, as if about to give directions to some inferior, and in doing so, it turned its head so as to display, with a ghastly distinctness, the features of Lady Ardagh, pale as death, with her dark hair all dishevelled, and her eyes dim and sunken with weeping. The revulsion of feeling which Miss F——d experienced at this disclosure—for up to that point she had contemplated the appearance rather with a sense of curiosity and of interest, than of any thing deeper—was

341

so horrible, that the shock awoke her perfectly. She sat up in the bed, and looked fearfully around the room, which was imperfectly lighted by a single candle burning dimly, as if she almost expected to see the reality of her dreadful vision lurking in some corner of the chamber. Her fears were, however, verified, though not in the way she expected; yet in a manner sufficiently horrible—for she had hardly time to breathe and to collect her thoughts, when she heard, or thought she heard, the voice of her sister, Lady Ardagh, sometimes sobbing violently, and sometimes almost shrieking as if in terror, and calling upon her and Lady D——, with the most imploring earnestness of despair, for God's sake to lose no time in coming to her. All this was so horribly distinct, that it seemed as if the mourner was standing within a few yards of the spot where Miss F——d lay. She sprang from the bed, and leaving the candle in the room behind her, she made her way in the dark through the passage, the voice still following her, until as she arrived at the door of the sitting-room it seemed to die away in low sobbing.

As soon as Miss F——d was tolerably recovered, she declared her determination to proceed directly, and without further loss of time to Castle Ardagh. It was not without much difficulty that Lady D—— at length prevailed upon her to consent to remain where they then were, until morning should arrive, when it was to be expected that the young lady would be much refreshed by at least remaining quiet for the night, even though sleep were out of the question. Lady D—— was convinced, from the nervous and feverish symptoms which her sister exhibited, that she had already done too much, and was more than ever satisfied of the necessity of prosecuting the journey no further upon that day. After some time she persuaded her sister to return to her room, where she remained with her until she had gone to bed, and appeared comparatively composed. Lady D—— then returned to the parlour, and

342

not finding herself sleepy, she remained sitting by the fire. Her solitude was a second time broken in upon, by the entrance of her sister, who now appeared, if possible, more agitated than before. She said that Lady D—— had not long left the room, when she was roused by a repetition of the same wailing and lamentations, accompanied by the wildest and most agonized supplications that no time should be lost in coming to Castle Ardagh, and all in her sister's voice, and uttered at the same proximity as before. This time the voice had followed her to the very door of the sitting room, and until she closed it, seemed to pour forth its cries and sobs at the very threshold.

Miss F——d now most positively declared that nothing should prevent her proceeding instantly to the castle, adding that if Lady D—— would not accompany her, she would go on by herself. Superstitious feelings are at all times more or less contagious, and the last century afforded a soil much more congenial to their growth than the present. Lady D—— was so far affected by her sister's terrors, that she became, at least, uneasy; and seeing that her sister was immoveably determined upon setting forward immediately, she consented to accompany her forthwith. After a slight delay, fresh horses were procured, and the two ladies and their attendants renewed their journey, with strong injunctions to the driver to quicken their rate of travelling as much as possible, and promises of reward in case of his doing so.

Roads were then in much worse condition throughout the south, even than they now are; and the fifteen miles which modern posting would have passed in little more than an hour and a half, were not completed even with every possible exertion in twice the time. Miss F——d had been nervously restless during the journey. Her head had been out at the carriage window every minute; and as they approached the entrance to the castle demesne, which lay about a mile from the building, her anxiety began to communicate itself to her sister. The postillion had just dismounted, and was endeavouring to open the gate—at that time a necessary trouble; for in the middle of the last century, porter's lodges were not common in the south of Ireland, and locks and keys almost unknown. He had just succeeded in rolling back the heavy oaken gate, so as to admit the vehicle, when a mounted servant rode rapidly down the avenue, and drawing up at the carriage, asked of the postillion who the party were; and on hearing, he rode round to the carriage window, and handed in a note which Lady D—— received. By the assistance of one of the coach-lamps they succeeded in deciphering it. It was scrawled in great agitation, and ran thus—

My Dear Sister—my dear Sisters both,— In God's name lose no time, I am frightened and miserable; I cannot explain all till you come. I am too much terrified to write coherently; but understand me— hasten—do not waste a minute. I am afraid you will come too late. E.A.

The servant could tell nothing more than that the castle was in great confusion, and that Lady Ardagh had been crying bitterly all night. Sir Robert was perfectly well. Altogether at a loss as to the cause of Lady Ardagh's great distress, they urged their way up the steep and broken avenue which wound through the crowding trees, whose wild and grotesque branches, now stript and naked by the blasts of winter, stretched drearily across the road. As the carriage drew up in the area before the door, the anxiety of the ladies almost amounted to sickness; and scarcely waiting for the assistance of their attendant, they sprang to the ground, and in an instant stood at the castle door. From within were distinctly audible the sounds of lamentation and weeping, and the suppressed hum of voices as if of those endeavouring to soothe the mourner. The door was speedily opened, and when the ladies entered, the first object which met their view was their sister, Lady Ardagh, sitting on a form in the hall, weeping and wringing her hands in deep agony. Beside her stood two old, withered crones, who were each endeavouring in their own way to administer consolation, without even knowing or caring what the subject of her grief might be.

Immediately on Lady Ardagh's seeing her sisters, she started up, fell on their necks, and kissed them again and again without speaking, and then taking them each by a hand, still weeping bitterly, she led them into a small room adjoining the hall, in which burned a light, and having closed the door, she sat down between them. After thanking them for the haste they had made, she proceeded to tell them, in words incoherent from agitation, that Sir Robert had in private, and in the most solemn manner, told her that he should die upon that night, and that he had occupied himself during the evening in giving minute directions respecting the arrangements of his funeral. Lady D—— here suggested the possibility of his labouring under the hallucinations of a fever; but to this Lady Ardagh quickly replied,

"Oh! no, no! would to God I could think it! Oh! no, no! wait till you have seen him. There is a frightful calmness about all he says and does; and his directions are all so clear, and his mind so perfectly collected, it is impossible, quite impossible;" and she wept yet more bitterly.

At that moment Sir Robert's voice was heard in issuing some directions, as he came down stairs; and Lady Ardagh exclaimed, hurriedly—

"Go now and see him yourself; he is in the hall."

Lady D—— accordingly went out into the hall, where Sir Robert met her; and saluting her with kind politeness, he said, after a pause—

"You are come upon a melancholy mission—the

345

house is in great confusion, and some of its inmates in considerable grief." He took her hand, and looking fixedly in her face, continued—"I shall not live to see tomorrow's sun shine."

"You are ill, sir, I have no doubt," replied she; "but I am very certain we shall see you much better tomorrow, and still better the day following."

"I am *not* ill, sister," replied he: "Feel my temples, they are cool; lay your finger to my pulse, its throb is slow and temperate. I never was more perfectly in health, and yet do I know that ere three hours be past, I shall be no more."

"Sir, sir," said she, a good deal startled, but wishing to conceal the impression which the calm solemnity of his manner had, in her own despite, made upon her, "Sir, you should not jest; you should not even speak lightly upon such subjects. You trifle with what is sacred—you are sporting with the best affections of your wife—"

"Stay, my good lady," said he; "if when this clock shall strike the hour of three, I shall be anything but a helpless clod, then upbraid me. Pray return now to your sister. Lady Ardagh is, indeed, much to be pitied; but what is past cannot now be helped. I shall see you and Lady Ardagh before my death; try to compose her —her sufferings distress me much; but what is past cannot now be mended."

Thus saying he went up stairs, and Lady D—— returned to the room where her sisters were sitting.

"Well," exclaimed Lady Ardagh, as she re-entered, "is it not so?—do you still doubt?—do you think there is any hope?"

Lady D—— was silent.

"Oh, none, none, none," continued she; "I see, I see you are convinced," and she wrung her hands in bitter agony.

"My dear sister," said Lady D——, "there is, no doubt, something strange in all that has appeared in

346

this matter; but still I cannot but hope that there may be something deceptive in all the apparent calmness of Sir Robert. I still must believe that some latent fever has affected his mind, as that owing to the state of nervous depression into which he has been sinking, some trivial occurrence has been converted, in his disordered imagination, into an augury foreboding his immediate dissolution."

In such suggestions, unsatisfactory even to those who originate them, and doubly so to her whom they were intended to comfort, more than two hours passed; and Lady D—— was beginning to hope that the fated term might elapse without the occurrence of any tragical event, when Sir Robert entered the room. On coming in, he placed his finger with a warning gesture upon his lips, as if to enjoin silence; and then having successively pressed the hands of his two sisters-in-law, he stooped over the almost lifeless form of his lady, and twice pressed her cold, pale forehead with his lips, and then passed motionlessly out of the room.

Lady D—— followed to the door, saw him take a candle in the hall, and walk deliberately up the stairs. Stimulated by a feeling of horrible curiosity, she continued to follow him at a distance. She saw him enter his own private room, and heard him close and lock the door after him. Continuing to follow him as far as she could, she placed herself at the door of the chamber, as noiselessly as possible; where after a little time, she was joined by her two sisters, Lady Ardagh and Miss F——d. In breathless silence they listened to what should pass within. They distinctly heard Sir Robert pacing up and down the room for some time; and then, after a pause, a sound as if some one had thrown himself heavily upon the bed. At this moment Lady D——, forgetting that the door had been secured within, turned the handle for the purpose of entering; some one from the inside, close to the door, said, "Hush! hush!" The same lady, now much alarmed, knocked violently at the door—there was no answer. She knocked again more violently, with no further success. Lady Ardagh, now uttering a piercing shriek, sank in a swoon upon the floor. Three or four servants, alarmed by the noise, now hurried up stairs, and Lady Ardagh was carried apparently lifeless to her own chamber. They then, after having knocked long and loudly in vain, applied themselves to forcing an entrance into Sir Robert's room. After resisting some violent efforts, the door at length gave way, and all entered the room nearly together. There was a single candle burning upon a table at the far end of the apartment; and stretched upon the bed lay Sir Robert Ardagh. He was a corpse—the eyes were open—no convulsion had passed over the features, or distorted the limbs—it seemed as if the soul had sped from the body without a struggle to remain there. On touching the body it was found to be cold as clay—all lingering of the vital heat had left it. They closed the ghastly eyes of the corpse, and leaving it to the care of those who seem to consider it a privilege of their age and sex to gloat over the revolting spectacle of death in all its stages, they returned to Lady Ardagh, now a widow. The party assembled at the castle, but the atmosphere was tainted with death. Grief there was not much, but awe and panic were expressed in every face. The guests talked in whispers, and the servants walked on tiptoe, as if afraid of the very noise of their own footsteps.

The funeral was conducted almost with splendour. The body having been conveyed, in compliance with Sir Robert's last directions, to Dublin, was there laid within the ancient walls of Saint Audoen's Church—where I have read the epitaph, telling the age and titles of the departed dust. Neither painted escutcheon, nor marble slab, have served to rescue from oblivion the story of the dead, whose very name will ere long moulder from their tracery—

Et sunt sua fata sepulchris.

The events which I have recorded are not imaginary. They are FACTS; and there lives one whose authority none would venture to question, who could vindicate the accuracy of every statement which I have set down, and that, too, with all the circumstantiality of an eye witness.

RETURN TO THE SABBATH

By Robert Bloch

It's not the kind of story that the columnists like to print; it's not the yarn press-agents love to tell. When I was still in the Public Relations Department at the studio, they wouldn't let me break it. I knew better than to try, for no paper would print such a tale.

We publicity men must present Hollywood as a gay place; a world of glamor and stardust. We capture only the light, but underneath the light there must always be shadows. I've always known that—it's been my job to gloss over those shadows for years—but the events of which I speak form a disturbing pattern too strange to be withheld. The shadow of these incidents is not *human*.

It's been the cursed weight of the whole affair that has proved my own mental undoing. That's why I resigned from the studio post, I guess. I wanted to forget it, if I could. And now I know that the only way to relieve my mind is to tell the story. I must break the yarn, come what may. Then perhaps I can forget Karl Jorla's eyes. . . .

The affair dates back to one September evening almost three years ago. Les Kincaid and I were slumming down on Main Street in Los Angeles that night.

Les is an assistant producer up at the studio, and there was some purpose in his visit; he was looking for authentic types to fill minor roles in a gangster film he was doing. Les was peculiar that way; he preferred the real article, rather than the Casting Bureau's ready-made imitations.

We'd been wandering around for some time, as I recall, past the great stone Chows that guard the narrow alleys of Chinatown, over through the tourist-trap that is Olvera Street, and back along the flophouses of lower Main. We walked by the cheap burlesque houses, eyeing the insolent Filipinos that sauntered past, and jostling our way through the usual Saturday night slumming parties.

We were both rather weary of it all. That's why, I suppose, the dingy little theatre appealed to us.

"Let's go in and sit down for awhile," Les suggested. "I'm tired."

Even a Main Street burlesque show has seats in it, and I felt ready for a nap. The callipygy of the stage-attraction did not appeal to me, but I acceded to the suggestion and purchased our tickets.

We entered, sat down, suffered through two strip-tease dances, an incredibly ancient black-out sketch, and a "Grand Finale." Then, as is the custom in such places, the stage darkened and the screen flickered into life.

We got ready for our doze, then. The pictures shown in these houses are usually ancient specimens of the "quickie" variety; fillers provided to clear the house. As the first blaring notes of the sound-track heralded the title of the opus, I closed my eyes, slouched lower in my seat, and mentally beckoned to Morpheus.

I was jerked back to reality by a sharp dig in the ribs. Les was nudging me and whispering.

"Look at this," he murmured, prodding my reluctant body into wakefulness. "Ever see anything like it?"

351

I glanced up at the screen. What I expected to find I do not know, but I saw—*horror*.

There was a country graveyard, shadowed by ancient trees through which flickered rays of mildewed moonlight. It was an old graveyard, with rotting headstones set in grotesque angles as they leered up at the midnight sky.

The camera cut down on one grave, a fresh one. The music on the sound-track grew louder, in cursed climax. But I forgot camera and film as I watched. That grave was reality—hideous reality.

The grave was *moving!*

The earth beside the headstone was heaving and churning, as though it were being dug out. Not from above, but from *below*. It quaked upward ever so slowly; terribly. Little clods fell. The sod pulsed out in a steady stream and little rills of earth kept falling in the moonlight as though there were something clawing the dirt away . . . something clawing from beneath.

That something—it would soon appear. And I began to be afraid. I—I didn't want to see what it was. The clawing from below was not natural; it held a purpose not altogether *human.*

Yet I had to look. I had to see him—it—emerge. The sod cascaded in a mound, and then I was staring at the edge of the grave, looking down at the black hole that gaped like a corpse-mouth in the moonlight. Something was coming out.

Something slithered through that fissure, fumbled at the side of the opening. It clutched the ground above the grave, and in the baleful beams of that demon's moon I knew it to be a human hand. A thin, white human hand that held but half its flesh. The hand of a lich, a skeleton claw . . .

A second talon gripped the other side of the excavation top. And now, slowly, insidiously, arms emerged. Naked, fleshless arms.

They crawled across the earth-sides like leprous

white serpents. The arms of a cadaver, a rising cadaver. It was pulling itself up. And as *it* emerged, a cloud fell across the moon-path. The light faded to shadows as the bulky head and shoulders came into view. One could see nothing, and I was thankful.

But the cloud was falling away from the moon now. In a second the face would be revealed. The face of the thing from the grave, the resurrected visage of that which should be rotted in death—what would it be?

The shadows fell back. A figure rose out of the grave, and the face turned toward me. I looked and saw—

Well, you've been to "horror pictures." You know what one usually sees. The "ape-man," or the "maniac," or the "death's-head." The papier-mâché grotesquerie of the make-up artist. The "skull" of the dead.

I saw none of that. Instead, there was *horror*. It was the face of a child, I thought, at first; no, not a child, but a man with a child's soul. The face of a poet, perhaps, unwrinkled and calm. Long hair framed a high forehead; crescent eyebrows tilted over closed lids. The nose and mouth were thin and finely chiseled. Over the entire countenance was written an unearthly peace. It was as though the man were in a sleep of somnambulism or catalepsy. And then the face grew larger, the moonlight brighter, and I saw—more.

The sharper light disclosed tiny touches of evil. The thin lips were fretted, maggot-kissed. The nose had *crumbled* at the nostrils. The forehead was flaked with putrefaction, and the dark hair was dead, encrusted with slime. There were shadows in the bony ridges beneath the closed eyes. Even now, the skeletal arms were up, and bony fingers brushed at those dead pits as the rotted lids fluttered apart. The eyes opened.

They were wide, staring, flaming—and in them was the grave. They were eyes that had closed in death and opened in the coffin under earth. They were eyes that had seen the body rot and the soul depart to mingle in worm-ravened darkness below. They were eyes that held an alien life, a life so dreadful as to animate the cadaver's body and force it to claw its way back to outer earth. They were *hungry* eyes—triumphant, now. as they gazed in graveyard moonlight on a world they had never known before. They hungered for the world as only Death can hunger for Life. And they blazed out of the corpse-pallid face in icy joy.

Then the cadaver began to walk. It lurched between the graves, lumbered before ancient tombs. It shambled through the forest night until it reached a road. Then it turned up that road slowly . . . slowly.

And the hunger in those eyes flamed again as the lights of a city flared below. Death was preparing to mingle with men.

2

I sat through all this entranced. Only a few minutes had elapsed, but I felt as though uncounted ages had passed unheeded. The film went on. Les and I didn't exchange a word, but we watched.

The plot was rather routine after that. The dead man was a scientist whose wife had been stolen from him by a young doctor. The doctor had tended him in his last illness and unwittingly administered a powerful narcotic with cataleptic effects.

The dialog was foreign and I could not place it. All of the actors were unfamiliar to me, and the setting and photography were quite unusual; unorthodox treatment as in *The Cabinet of Dr. Caligari* and other psychological films.

There was one scene where the living-dead man became enthroned as arch-priest at a Black Mass ceremonial, and there was a little child. . . . His eyes as he plunged the knife. . . .

He kept—*decaying* throughout the film . . . the Black Mass worshippers knew him as an emissary of

354

Satan, and they kidnapped the wife as sacrifice for his own resurrection . . . the scene with the hysterical woman when she saw and recognized her husband for the first time, and the deep, evil whispering voice in which he revealed his secret to her . . . the final pursuit of the devil-worshippers to the great altar-stone in the mountains . . . the death of the resurrected one.

Almost a skeleton in fact now, riddled by bullets and shot from the weapons of the doctor and his neighbors, the dead one crumbled and fell from his seat on the altar-stone. And as those eyes glazed in second death the deep voice boomed out in a prayer to Sathanas. The lich crawled across the ground to the ritual fire, drew painfully erect, and tottered into the flames. And as it stood weaving for a moment in the blaze the lips moved again in infernal prayer, and the eyes implored not the skies, but the earth. The ground opened in a final flash of fire, and the charred corpse fell through. The Master claimed his own. . . .

It was grotesque, almost a fairy-tale in its triteness. When the film had flickered off and the orchestra blared the opening for the next "flesh-show" we rose in our seats, conscious once more of our surroundings. The rest of the mongrel audience seemed to be in a stupor almost equal to our own. Wide-eyed Japanese sat staring in the darkness; Filipinos muttered covertly to one another; even the drunken laborers seemed incapable of greeting the "Grand Opening" with their usual ribald hoots.

Trite and grotesque the plot of the film may have been, but the actor who played the lead had instilled it with ghastly reality. He *had* been dead; his eyes *knew*. And the voice was the voice of Lazarus awakened.

Les and I had no need to exchange words. We both felt it. I followed him silently as he went up the stairs to the manager's office.

Edward Relch was glowering over the desk. He showed no pleasure at seeing us barge in. When Les

355

asked him where he had procured the film for this evening and what its name was, he opened his mouth and emitted a cascade of curses.

We learned the *Return to the Sabbath* had been sent over by a cheap agency from out Inglewood way, that a Western had been expected, and the "damned foreign junk" substituted by mistake. A hell of a picture this was, for a girl-show! Gave the audience the lousy creeps, and it wasn't even in English! Stinking imported films!

It was some time before we managed to extract the name of the agency from the manager's profane lips. But five minutes after that, Les Kincaid was on the phone speaking to the head of the agency; an hour later we were out at the office. The next morning Kincaid went in to see the big boss, and the following day I was told to announce for publication that Karl Jorla, the Austrian horror-star, had been signed by cable to our studio; and he was leaving at once for the United States.

3

I printed these items, gave all the build-up I could. But after the initial announcements I was stopped dead. Everything had happened too swiftly; we knew nothing about this man Jorla, really. Subsequent cables to Austrian and German studios failed to disclose any information about the fellow's private life. He had evidently never played in any film prior to *Return to the Sabbath*. He was utterly unknown. The film had never been shown widely abroad, and it was only by mistake that the Inglewood agency had obtained a copy and run it here in the United States. Audience reaction could not be learned, and the film was not scheduled for general release unless English titles could be dubbed in.

I was up a stump. Here we had the "find" of the

year, and I couldn't get enough material out to make it known!

We expected Karl Jorla to arrive in two weeks however. I was told to get to work on him as soon as he got in, then flood the news agencies with stories. Three of our best writers were working on a special production for him already; the Big Boss meant to handle it himself. It would be similar to the foreign film, for that "return from the dead" sequence must be included.

Jorla arrived on October seventh. He put up at a hotel; the studio sent down its usual welcoming committee, took him out to the lot for formal testing, then turned him over to me.

I met the man for the first time in the little dressing-room they had assigned him. I'll never forget that afternoon of our first meeting, or my first sight of him as I entered the door.

What I expected to see I don't know. But what I did see amazed me. For Karl Jorla was the dead-alive man of the screen *in life*.

The features were not fretted, of course. But he was tall, and almost as cadaverously thin as in his role; his face was pallid, and his eyes blue-circled. And the eyes were the dead eyes of the movie; the deep, *knowing* eyes!

The booming voice greeted me in hesitant English. Jorla smiled with his lips at my obvious discomfiture, but the expression of the eyes never varied in their alien strangeness.

Somewhat hesitantly I explained my office and my errand. "No pub-leecity," Jorla intoned. "I do not weesh to make known what is affairs of mine own doeeng."

I gave him the usual arguments. How much he understood I cannot say, but he was adamant. I learned only a little; that he had been born in Prague, lived in wealth until the upheavals of the European depression, and entered film work only to please a director friend of his. This director had made the picture in which Jorla played, for private showings only. By mischance a print had been released and copied for general circulation. It had all been a mistake. However, the American film offer had come opportunely, since Jorla wanted to leave Austria at once.

"After the feelm app-ear, I am in bad lights weeth my—friends," he explained, slowly. "They do not weesh it to be shown, that cere-monee."

"The Black Mass?" I asked. "Your *friends?*"

"Yes. The wor-ship of Lucifer. It was real, you know."

Was he joking? No—I couldn't doubt the man's sincerity. There was no room for mirth in those alien eyes. And then I knew what he meant, what he so casually revealed. He had been a devil-worshipper himself—he and that director. They had made the film and meant it for private display in their own occult circles. No wonder he sought escape abroad!

It was incredible, save that I knew Europe, and the dark Northern mind. The worship of Evil continues today in Budapest, Prague, Berlin. And he, Karl Jorla the horror-actor, admitted to being one of them!

"What a story!" I thought. And then I realized that it could, of course, never be printed. A horror-star admitting belief in the parts he played? Absurd!

All the features about Boris Karloff played up the fact that he was a gentleman who found true peace in raising a garden. Lugosi was pictured as a sensitive neurotic, tortured by the roles he played in the films. Atwill was a socialite and a stage star. And Peter Lorre was always written up as being gentle as a lamb, a quiet student whose ambition was to play comedy parts.

No, it would never do to break the story of Jorla's private worship. And he was so damnably reticent about his private affairs!

I sought out Kincaid after the termination of our

unsatisfactory interview. I told him what I had encountered and asked for advice. He gave it.

"The old line," he counseled. "Mystery man. We say nothing about him until the picture is released. After that I have a hunch things will work out for themselves. The fellow is a marvel. So don't bother about stories until the film is canned."

Consequently I abandoned publicity efforts in Karl Jorla's direction. Now I am very glad I did so, for there is no one to remember his name, or suspect the horror that was soon to follow.

4

The script was finished. The front office approved. Stage Four was under construction; the casting director got busy. Jorla was at the studio every day; Kincaid himself was teaching him English. The part was one in which very few words were needed, and Jorla proved a brilliant pupil, according to Les.

But Les was not as pleased as he should have been about it all. He came to me one day about a week before production and unburdened himself. He strove to speak lightly about the affair, but I could tell that he felt worried.

The gist of his story was very simple. Jorla was behaving strangely. He had had trouble with the front office; he refused to give the studio his living address, and it was known that he had checked out from his hotel several days after first arriving in Hollywood.

Nor was that all. He wouldn't talk about his part, or volunteer any information about interpretation. He seemed to be quite uninterested—admitting frankly to Kincaid that his only reason for signing a contract was to leave Europe.

He told Kincaid what he had told me—about the devil-worshippers. And he hinted at more. He spoke of being followed, muttered about "avengers" and "hunters who waited." He seemed to feel that the witch-cult was angry at him for the violation of secrets, and held him responsible for the release of *Return of the Sabbath*. That, he explained, was why he would not give his address, nor speak of his past life for publication. That is why he must use very heavy make-up in his film debut here. He felt at times as though he were being watched, or followed. There were many foreigners here . . . too many.

"What the devil can I do with a man like that?" Kincaid exploded, after he had explained this to me. "He's insane, or a fool. And I confess that he's too much like his screen character to please me. The damned casual way in which he professes to have dabbled in devil-worship and sorcery! He believes all this, and—well, I'll tell you the truth, I came here to-day because of the last thing he spoke of to me this morning.

"He came down to the office, and at first when he walked in I didn't know him. The dark glasses and muffler helped, of course, but he himself had changed. He was trembling, and walked with a stoop. And when he spoke his voice was like a groan. He showed me—this."

Kincaid handed me the clipping. It was from the London *Times,* through European dispatches. A short paragraph, giving an account of the death of Fritz Ohmmen, the Austrian film director. He had been found strangled in a Paris garret, and his body had been frightfully mutilated; it mentioned an inverted cross branded on his stomach above the ripped entrails. Police were seeking the murderer . . .

I handed the clipping back in silence. "So what?" I asked. But I had already guessed his answer.

"Fritz Ohmmen," Kincaid said, slowly, "was the director of the picture in which Karl Jorla played; the director, who with Jorla, knew the devil-worshippers.

Jorla says that he fled to Paris, and that *they* sought him out."

I was silent.

"Mess," grunted Kincaid. "I've offered Jorla police protection, and he's refused. I can't coerce him under the terms of our contract. As long as he plays the part, he's secure with us. But he has the jitters. And I'm getting them."

He stormed out. I couldn't help him. I sat thinking of Karl Jorla, who believed in devil-gods; worshipped, and betrayed them. And I could have smiled at the absurdity of it all if I hadn't seen the man on the screen and watched his evil eyes. He *knew!* It was then that I began to feel thankful we had not given Jorla any publicity. I had a hunch.

During the next few days I saw Jorla but seldom. The rumors, however, began to trickle in. There had been an influx of foreign "sight-seers" at the studio gates. Someone had attempted to crash through the barriers in a racing-car. An extra in a mob scene over on Lot Six had been found carrying an automatic beneath his vest; when apprehennded he had been lurking under the executive office windows. They had taken him down to headquarters, and so far the man had refused to talk. He was a German . . .

Jorla came to the studios every day in a shuttered car. He was bundled up to the eyes. He trembled constantly. His English lessons went badly. He spoke to no one. He hired two men to ride with him in his car. They were armed.

A few days later news that the German extra had talked. He was evidently a pathological case . . . he babbled wildly of a "Black Cult of Lucifer" known to some of the foreigners around town. It was a secret society purporting to worship the Devil, with vague connections in the mother countries. He had been "chosen" to avenge a wrong. More than that he dared not say, but he did give an address where the police might find cult headquarters. The place, a dingy house in Glendale, was quite deserted, of course. It was a queer old house with a secret cellar beneath the basement, but everything seemed to have been abandoned. The man was being held for examination by an alienist.

I heard this report with deep misgivings. I knew something of Los Angeles' and Hollywood's heterogeneous foreign population; God knows, Southern California has attracted mystics and occultists from all over the world. I've even heard rumors about stars being mixed up in unsavory secret societies, things one would never dare to admit in print. And Jorla was afraid.

That afternoon I tried to trail his black car as it left the studio for his mysterious home, but I lost the track in the winding reaches of Topanga Canyon. It had disappeared into the secret twilight of the purple hills, and I knew then that there was nothing I could do. Jorla had his own defenses, and if they failed, we at the studio could not help.

That was the evening he disappeared. At least he did not show up the next morning at the studio, and production was to start in two days. We heard about it. The boss and Kincaid were frantic. The police were called in, and I did my best to hush things up. When Jorla did not appear the following morning I went up to Kincaid and told him about my following the car to Topanga Canyon. The police went to work. Next morning was production.

We spent a sleepless night of fruitless vigil. There was no word. Morning came, and there was unspoken dread in Kincaid's eyes as he faced me across the office table. Eight o'clock. We got up and walked silently across the lot to the studio cafeteria. Black coffee was badly needed; we hadn't had a police report for hours. We passed Stage Four, where the Jorla crew was at work. The noise of hammers was mockery. Jorla, we felt, would never face a camera today, if ever.

Bleskind, the director of the untitled horror opus, came out of the Stage office as we passed.

His paunchy body quivered as he grasped Kincaid's lapels and piped. "Any news?"

Kincaid shook his head slowly. Bleskind thrust a cigar into his tense mouth.

"We're shooting ahead," he snapped. "We'll shoot around Jorla. If he doesn't show up when we finish the scenes in which he won't appear, we'll get another actor. But we can't wait." The squat director bustled back to the Stage.

Moved by a sudden impulse, Kincaid grasped my arm and propelled me after Bleskind's waddling form.

"Let's see the opening shots," he suggested. " I want to see what kind of a story they've given him."

We entered Stage Four.

A Gothic Castle, the ancestral home of Baron Ulmo. A dark, gloomy stone crypt of spidery horror. Cobwebbed, dust-shrouded, deserted by men and given over to rats by day and the unearthly horrors that crept by night. An altar stood by the crypt, an altar of evil, the great black stone on which the ancient Baron Ulmo and his devil-cult had held their sacrifices. Now, in the pit beneath the altar, the Baron lay buried. Such was the legend.

According to the first shot scheduled, Sylvia Channing, the heroine, was exploring the castle. She had inherited the place and taken it over with her young husband. In this scene she was to see the altar for the first time, read the inscription on its base. This inscription was to prove an unwitting invocation, opening up the crypt beneath the altar and awakening Jorla, as Baron Ulmo, from the dead. He was to rise from the crypt then, and walk. It was at this point that the scene would terminate, due to Jorla's strange absence.

The setting was magnificently handled. Kincaid and I took our places beside Director Bleskind as the shot opened. Sylvia Channing walked out on the set; the

363

signals were given, lights flashed, and the action began.

It was pantomimic. Sylvia walked across the cob-webbed floor, noticed the altar, examined it. She stooped to read the inscription, then whispered it aloud. There was a drone, as the opening of the altar-crypt was mechanically begun. The altar swung aside, and the black gaping pit was revealed. The upper cameras swung to Sylvia's face. She was to stare at the crypt in horror, and she did it most magnificently. In the pic-ture she would be watching Jorla emerge.

Bleskind prepared to give the signal to cut action. Then—

Something emerged from the crypt!

It was dead, that thing—that horror with a mask of faceless flesh. Its lean body was clothed in rotting rags, and on its chest was a bloody crucifix, inverted—carved out dead flesh. The eyes blazed loathsomely. It was Baron Ulmo, rising from the dead. *And it was Karl Jorla!*

The make-up was perfect. His eyes were dead, just as in the other film. The lips seemed shredded again, the mouth even more ghastly in its slitted blackness. And the touch of the bloody crucifix was immense.

Bleskind nearly swallowed his cigar when Jorla ap-peared. Quickly he controlled himself, silently signalled the men to proceed with the shooting. We strained forward, watching every move, but Les Kincaid's eyes held a wonder akin to my own.

Jorla was acting as never before. He moved slowly, as a corpse must move. As he raised himself from the crypt, each tiny effort seemed to cause him utter agony. The scene was soundless; Sylvia had fainted. But Jorla's lips moved, and we heard a faint whispering murmur which heightened the horror. Now the grisly cadaver was almost half out of the crypt. It strained upward, still murmuring. The bloody crucifix of flesh gleamed redly on the chest . . . I thought of the one found on the body of the murdered foreign director, Fritz Ohm-men, and realized where Jorla had gotten the idea.

The corpse strained up . . . it was to rise now . . . up . . . and then, with a sudden rictus, the body stiffened and slid back into the crypt.

Who screamed first I do not know. But the screaming continued after the prop-boys had rushed to the crypt and looked down at what lay within.

When I reached the brink of the pit I screamed, too. *For it was utterly empty.*

5

I wish there were nothing more to tell. The papers never knew. The police hushed things up. The studio is silent, and the production was dropped immediately. But matters did not stop there. There was a sequel to that horror on Stage Four.

Kincaid and I cornered Bleskind. There was no need of any explanation; how could what we had just seen be explained in any sane way?

Jorla had disappeared; no one had let him into the studio; no make-up man had given him his attention. Nobody had seen him enter the crypt. He had appeared in the scene, then disappeared. The crypt was empty.

These were the facts. Kincaid told Bleskind what to do. The film was developed immediately, though two of the technicians fainted. We three sat in the projection booth and watched the morning's rushes flicker across the screen. The sound track was specially dubbed in.

That scene—Sylvia walking and reading the incantation—the pit opening—and God, when *nothing* emerged!

Nothing but that great red scar suspended in midair —that great inverted crucifix cut in bleeding flesh; no Jorla visible at all! That bleeding cross in the air, and then the mumbling . . .

Jorla—the thing—whatever it was—had mumbled a few syllables on emerging from the crypt. The sound-track had picked them up. And we couldn't see anything but that scar; yet we heard Jorla's voice now coming from nothingness. We heard what he kept repeating, as he fell back into the crypt.

It was an address in Topanga Canyon.

The lights flickered on, and it was good to see them. Kincaid phoned the police and directed them to the address given on the sound-track.

We waited, the three of us, in Kincaid's office, waited for the police call. We drank, but did not speak. Each of us was thinking of Karl Jorla the devil-worshipper who had betrayed his faith; of his fear of vengeance. We thought of the director's death, and the bloody crucifix on his chest; remembered Jorla's disappearance. And then that ghastly ghost-thing on the screen, the bloody thing that hung in midair as Jorla's voice groaned the address. . .

The phone rang.

I picked it up. It was the police department. They gave their report. I fainted.

It was several minutes before I came to. It was several more minutes before I opened my mouth and spoke.

"They've found Karl Jorla's body at the address given on the screen," I whispered. "He was lying dead in an old shack up in the hills. He had been—murdered. There was a bloody cross, inverted on his chest. They think it was the work of some fanatics, because the place was filled with books on sorcery and Black Magic. They say—"

I paused. Kincaid's eyes commanded. "Go on."

"They say." I murmured, "that Jorla had been dead for at least three days."

THE WILL OF LUKE CARLOWE

By Clive Pemberton

Mr. Jonas Fenwick, the lawyer, unclasped his bony, wrinkled hands as he came to the end of the short document he had perused for the third time, and carefully placing it in a convenient pigeon-hole in his bureau, peered sharply over his gold-rimmed *pince-nez* at Mr. Reuben Tunny, his confidential clerk.

"It was quite the most extraordinary document that has ever come under my notice," he said, slowly. "A little more than eccentric, eh, Reuben, eh?" and the lawyer chuckled—a dry, eminently legal chuckle in which mirth found no place. Mr. Reuben Tunny—an angular, sallow-faced man of middle age who had grown up in Mr. Fenwick's service—slowly and gravely shook his head.

"I don't understand it, sir," he said, solemnly. "I don't understand it at all."

"What don't you understand, Reuben?" returned the lawyer quizzically. "This"—laying his hand on the document under discussion—"is plain enough for a child to comprehend."

"I did not mean that I could not understand the meaning of Professor Luke Carlowe's last written words, sir," said Mr. Tunny slowly. "As you rightly

367

say, a child could comprehend the meaning of that document, for it is a perfectly plain statement. No, what I *cannot understand* is a sane man doing such an extraordinary thing. It—it is almost uncanny!"

"*Almost* uncanny!" echoed the lawyer, laying a strong emphasis on the first word. "I call it *very* uncanny, and with a hint of the devilish in it, too, Reuben! Of course, I—in common with everybody acquainted with Luke Carlowe—knew that he was very eccentric, and expected him to do something extraordinary before he died; but this matter relating to his will—Well, well! we will hear presently what the young man has to say about it."

"You appointed twelve o'clock in your letter, and I do not doubt that he will be punctual," and with a dry smile at his employer, the sedate old clerk withdrew to the outer office with a sheaf of parchments. Precisely at twelve o'clock the outer door of Mr. Fenwick's office opened, and a tall, good-looking young man of about twenty-five years of age entered quickly.

"I have an appointment with Mr. Fenwick," he said, handing Mr. Tunny a card on which was neatly engraved the name Cyril Carlowe. "I suppose—I presume he is in?"

"If you will be so good as to wait one moment, I will inform Mr. Fenwick that you are here," returned Mr. Tunny, and a moment later he ushered Mr. Cyril Carlowe into the lawyer's presence.

"Good morning, Mr. Carlowe," said Mr. Fenwick briskly, bowing his visitor to a chair. "I daresay—I expect you are wondering why I have asked you to see me this morning?"

The other shifted in his chair a little; then he gave the lawyer a frank, clear look.

"I will confess that I am most curious to learn the reason, Mr. Fenwick," he replied quickly, "for I can think of nothing to—to——"

"Well, well, Mr. Carlowe, I will set the matter before you at once. I have sent for you with regard to your uncle's will. You are aware, of course," he went on, slightly hesitating as he looked at the other, "that your uncle, Professor Carlowe, died just a month ago?"

Cyril Carlowe nodded disinterestedly, and the lawyer proceeded:

"I think I may say that I enjoyed the fullest confidence of my late client, and I never knew him take any step or do anything important without first consulting me. Of course, I need not say that I am cognizant of the strange and, now that I have seen you"—with a courtly little bow—"inexplicable dislike he bore towards his brother—your father—and you."

Cyril Carlowe nodded gloomily.

"I always told the guv'nor he was mad," he rejoined slowly. "Before he refused to see either of us again, he used to talk the wildest rot you ever heard by the hour. All about the spirits of the dead returning from the grave—supernatural agencies and intermediate states —that kind of mad foolery! I verily believe it was our scepticism and—and ridicule that turned him so violently against us, Mr. Fenwick."

The lawyer nodded quietly.

"He was eccentric—most eccentric, I agree with you; but to return to what I was saying. With regard to his will, I drew it up, but he kept it, and——"

"And of course, left all his money—a good bit it must be too—to some society for the furthering of his mad theories, eh?"

"Yes—and no," answered the lawyer, paradoxically. He took a paper from the pigeon-hole and turned it about thoughtfully in his hand. "That will he left in my care, and in it he bequeathed his fortune to a—a society. This paper,"—holding it up— "contains his last written instructions, and leads me to believe that he made a later will, leaving everything instead to—to you."

"To me?" If a thunderbolt had fallen at his feet,

Cyril Carlowe could not have looked more astounded. "Good heavens Mr. Fenwick, what do you mean? What —what is that paper? Where is the last will?"

"Ah! where, indeed?" rejoined the lawyer, handing him the paper. "Just read that, Mr. Carlowe, and you will know as much as I know."

There was a space of silence, while Cyril Carlowe, with amazed eyes, read the following few lines—the last words of the late Professor Luke Carlowe, written but a few hours before his death.

"This message, which I leave in the care of my trusted friend and lawyer, Jonas Fenwick, is to be read by him one month after my decease, and then handed to my nephew, Cyril Carlowe. I now state that I have made a later will, in which I leave everything I possess to my nephew, Cyril Carlowe, on certain conditions. The whereabouts of this will I alone know, and it is to prove my life theory—that is, that there is a means of communication between the dead and the living— that I have planned this proof. On a certain night—to be arranged by the members of the Occult Association —my nephew, Cyril Carlowe, is to descend into the vault where I am buried, and I—from the spirit world —will return and reveal where the will is. A committee of ten of my colleagues will wait outside, and a lasting proof will be given to the world of that which is now treated with ignorant scepticism. If the said Cyril Carlowe will not undertake the test, the will now existent, which Jonas Fenwick holds, will be proved."

"He must have been mad when he wrote this, Mr. Fenwick," said Cyril Carlowe, looking up from the amazing document. "I can't quite grasp it. He says here that in his last will he has left me everything. That will, nobody, save himself, knows the whereabouts of, and unless I—I— Good heavens! Am I awake or dreaming?"

"What it means is this, Mr. Carlowe," replied the

lawyer, looking keenly at him. "The will which I hold, and which I thought was the only one and the last, is evidently not so. That document distinctly states that he drew up a fresh will, leaving you his sole heir. To find that will and establish your right, he states what I candidly confess is beyond my powers of credulity—that is, that he himself will reveal to you—alone—where it is."

"But—but it is too—too monstrously fantastic!" cried the other excitedly. "A dead man reveal where his will is hidden?"

"It was his pet theory, remember," put in the lawyer, "the theory that there is a means of communicating between the dead and the living—a bridge of communication I think they call it."

There was another long silence. Professor Carlowe had ended an eccentric life by an eccentricity which almost passed belief.

Cyril Carlowe spoke at last, slowly and thoughtfully.

"What is your opinion about it, Mr. Fenwick?" he said. The lawyer coughed and deliberated carefully before replying.

"If you were rich, I would say, 'don't do it,'" he replied slowly; "but as things are—you are young; you don't seem nervous——"

"What is the law on the point?"

The lawyer chuckled.

"There is no point of law in it," he said drily. "It is purely an optional matter as far as you are concerned. You can carry out the—er—instructions, or—you need not."

"And if I don't?"

"Then the will I hold—in which everything is left to the Occult Association—will be proved, and the money will go to further more—ahem!—extraordinary theories."

"I see!"

There was another long silence—a thoughtful one on

Mr. Cyril Carlowe's part, judging from his facial expression.

He looked up suddenly, and his firm chin set in a determined manner. "I shall do it, Mr. Fenwick," he said in a decisive tone.

The lawyer looked sharply at him.

"You will——?" he began, then stopped abruptly.

"I shall carry out the instructions left in that document," said Cyril Carlowe firmly. "I am not afraid, and to show I am not afraid I will do it. You will make all the formal arrangements?"

"I will," replied the lawyer, and a strange light—a light of admiration—flickered in his dull eyes for one moment.

*   *   *

In the large, comfortably-appointed room where the Occult Association held its spiritualistic and psychological séances, a group of men were gathered round the solid mahogany table. At one end sat the chairman—Professor Michael Andover—and ranged along either side were six of the association's foremost members. At the other end, facing the chairman, sat Mr. Fenwick, the lawyer, and Cyril Carlowe. The former's face was expressive of dry cynicism; the latter looked slightly pale, but perfectly calm and self-possessed. The room was very still, for the hour was late—ten o'clock—and the quiet street was empty and deserted. Amid perfect silence, the chairman rose to speak.

"Gentlemen," he began, "the purpose for which we are gathered together here tonight is know to you all. Our valued and deeply lamented colleague, Professor Luke Carlowe, has left in our hands the proving of a much discussed and—and scepticized theory. Everything is arranged, and I have only to ask Mr. Cyril Carlowe if his wishes to—to say anything before a start is made."

"I have nothing to say—no comment to make," replied Cyril Carlowe, "save to have done with this matter as speedily as possible."

"Very good! Then a start had better be made, for the drive to the cemetery will occupy a full hour."

Four carriages were waiting without, and in a few minutes they were progressing at a fair speed towards the distant cemetery. The night was heavy and overcast—a sullen sky and a peculiar oppressiveness in the air suggesting that thunder was not far distant. Indeed, before the cemetery was reached, a few large drops of rain fell, and a distant muttering of thunder joined the rumbling of the carriage wheels.

"This is a strange project, Mr. Fenwick," said Cyril Carlowe, breaking the silence for the first time. He and the lawyer had the last carriage to themselves. "Even now, I half wish——"

The lawyer looked sharply at him.

"It is not too late to draw back if you wish," he said, quietly. "As you say, the whole thing is—er—very strange!"

"I cannot understand how they have arranged it," went on the other, thoughtfully. "The access to the vault at this time of night, I mean."

The lawyer shrugged his shoulders.

"Enthusiasts can do anything with money to help them," he said, drily. "I don't know how they have worked it—it is no concern of yours and mine. Suffice to say they have, by bribing the keeper, I suppose."

At that moment the carriages came to a stop, and the party alighted. The cemetery, dark and gloomy, was barred by heavy gates; but, as the carriages withdrew, a man came quickly out of the lodge and unlocked the side gate. The party quickly filed through, and the gate clanged behind them. Led by Professor Andover, they proceeded down a side path which led to the vault. The silence of death was over everything, and only the pattering of the hurrying rain and the

373

crunching of their footsteps broke the intense hush. Now and again, arrows of lightning darted from the black sky, lighting up the white stones and lending an added weirdness to the scene. In a few minutes they were standing opposite the vault wherein the body of Professor Luke Carlowe was interred. It was a huge stone mausoleum, square in shape, and guarded by a massive black iron-studded door. Lighting a lamp, the leader of the party unlocked the door, and all descended the short flight of stone steps. In a niche on a level with their heads was the massive coffin with its velvet pall. Flowers still withered on the ledge of the stained-glass window, and a dank atmosphere pervaded the echoing interior.

"We shall now leave you, Mr. Carlowe," said Professor Andover, in a hushed voice. "The conditions you know—that you wait here until the last stroke of twelve has sounded. It is now a quarter to twelve."

The young man inclined his head, but said nothing, and one by one they filed up the steps. Mr. Fenwick, with the lantern, was the last to go, and he hung back to say a last word.

"I feel that I advised you wrong," he said in a hurried whisper. "Have done with this mad business—no good can come of it!"

But Cyril Carlowe shook his head.

"I shall go through with it now, Mr. Fenwick," he said, firmly. "I am not afraid. I have my revolver, and I will see it through."

The lawyer said nothing further, but holding his hand for a moment, hurried up the steps. The gate shut with a dull clang, and Cyril Carlowe found himself in the dark darkness—alone!

The moments passed slowly—very slowly. Without, the storm was coming up fast. The rain rattled dully on the roof of the vault; a bright flash of lightning darted through the stained-glass window and revealed the coffin for a fleeting second. High up in the domed space of the roof, a harsh screech sounded, followed by the whirr of beating wings as a bat flew round and round, and then clung panting to the groin. Strange, wild fancies crowded on his brain. With the revolver gripped in his hand, he turned slowly round and once he was certain something touched him. Yet he was alone, save for the dead in the massive casket. Alone! was he alone? A strange shrinking sensation suddenly crept over him; a deadly nausea shook him, and he slowly sank on the stone floor. A crash of thunder split the air—a blinding flash of lightning suddenly illumined the whole vault as with the light of day, and in that moment he saw——

* * *

Above the war of thunder, the waiting group heard it—a cry that none had ever heard the like of before, and that would ring in their ears for ever.

"Great heaven!" cried the lawyer, looking into the others' white faces; "That was—that was Cyril Carlowe's voice!"

He waited for no reply, but dashed headlong into the open, and made for the vault at frantic speed. In less than ten seconds he was at the gate and tugging at the iron handle. Holding the lamp high above his head, he paused and peered into the darkness below with a horrible presage of evil.

"Carlowe!" he cried, "are you all right?"

No answer—only the dull, reverberating echo of his own voice. With the others pressing behind him, he cleared the steps in two bounds, then he fell back, half fainting with a horrible dread, for this is what he saw.

A huddled body on the stone floor—the body of Cyril Carlowe—dead! He knelt down beside him and looked into a face so distorted as to be hardly recognizable. But it was not that which sent the creeping chill

375

EYES DO MORE THAN SEE

By Isaac Asimov

After hundreds of billions of years, he suddenly thought of himself as Ames. Not the wave-length combination which, through all the universe was now the equivalent of Ames—but the sound itself. A faint memory came back of the sound waves he no longer heard and no longer could hear.

The new project was sharpening his memory for so many more of the old, old, eons-old things. He flattened the energy vortex that made up the total of his individuality and its lines of force stretched beyond the stars.

Brock's answering signal came.

Surely, Ames thought, he could tell Brock. Surely he could tell somebody.

Brock's shifting energy pattern communed, "Aren't you coming, Ames?"

"Of course."

"Will you take part in the contest?"

"Yes!" Ames's lines of force pulsed erratically. "Most certainly. I have thought of a whole new art-form. Something really unusual."

"What a waste of effort! How can you think a new variation has not been thought of in two hundred billion years. There can be nothing new."

For a moment Brock shifted out of phase and out of communication, so that Ames had to hurry to adjust his lines of force. He caught the drift of other-thoughts as he did so, the view of the powdered galaxies against the velvet of nothingness, and the lines of force pulsing in endless multitudes of energy-life, lying between the galaxies.

Ames said, "Please absorb my thoughts, Brock. Don't close out. I've thought of manipulating Matter. Imagine! A symphony of Matter. Why bother with Energy. Of course, there's nothing new in Energy; how can there be? Doesn't that show we must deal with Matter?"

"Matter!"

Ames interpreted Brock's energy-vibrations as those of disgust.

He said, "Why not? We were once Matter ourselves back—back—Oh, a trillion years ago anyway! Why not build up objects in a Matter medium, or abstract forms or—listen, Brock—why not build up an imitation of ourselves in Matter, ourselves as we used to be?"

Brock said, "I don't remember how that was. No one does."

"I do," said Ames with energy, "I've been thinking of nothing else and I am beginning to remember. Brock, let me show you. Tell me if I'm right. Tell me."

"No. This is silly. It's—repulsive."

"Let me try, Brock. We've been friends; we've pulsed energy together from the beginning—from the moment we became what we are. Brock, please!"

"Then, quickly."

Ames had not felt such a tremor along his own lines of force in—well, in how long? If he tried it now for Brock and it worked, he could dare manipulate Matter before the assembled Energy-beings who had so drearily waited over the eons for something new.

The matter was thin out there between the galaxies, but Ames gathered it, scraping it together over the cubic light-years, choosing the atoms, achieving a clayey consistency and forcing matter into an ovoid form that spread out below.

"Don't you remember, Brock?" he asked softly. "Wasn't it something like this?"

Brock's vortex trembled in phase. "Don't make me remember. I don't remember."

"That was the head. They called it the head. I remember it so clearly, I want to say it. I mean with sound." He waited, then said, "Look, do you remember that?"

On the upper front of the ovoid appeared HEAD.

"What is that?" asked Brock.

"That's the word for head. The symbols that meant the word in sound. Tell me you remember, Brock!"

"There was something," said Brock hesitantly, "something in the middle." A vertical bulge formed.

Ames said, "Yes! Nose, that's it!" And NOSE appeared upon it. "And those are eyes on either side, "LEFT EYE—RIGHT EYE.

Ames regarded what he had formed, his lines of force pulsing slowly. Was he sure he liked this?

"Mouth," he said, in small quiverings "and chin and Adam's apple, and the collarbones. How the words come back to me." They appeared on the form.

Brock said, "I haven't thought of them for hundreds of billions of years. Why have you reminded me? Why?"

Ames was momentarily lost in his thoughts, "Something else. Organs to hear with; something for the sound waves. Ears! Where do they go? I don't remember where to put them?"

Brock cried out, "Leave it alone! Ears and all else! Don't remember!"

Ames said, uncertainly, "What is wrong with remembering?"

"Because the outside wasn't rough and cold like that but smooth and warm. Because the eyes were tender and alive and the lips of the mouth trembled and were

379

soft on mine." Brock's lines of force beat and wavered, beat and wavered.

Ames said, "I'm sorry! I'm sorry!"

"You're reminding me that once I was a woman and knew love; that eyes do more than see and I have none to do it for me."

With violence, she added matter to the rough-hewn head and said, "Then let *them* do it" and turned and fled.

And Ames saw and remembered, too, that once he had been a man. The force of his vortex split the head in two and he fled back across the galaxies on the energy-track of Brock—back to the endless doom of life.

And the eyes of the shattered head of Matter still glistened with the moisture that Brock had placed there to represent tears. The head of Matter did that which the energy-beings could do no longer and it wept for all humanity, and for the fragile beauty of the bodies they had once given up, a trillion years ago.

PINNACLE BOOKS

Hornblower,
make way for Hazard!

An exciting and authentic new historical adventure series
traces the exploits of a rugged naval officer, Phillip Horatio
Hazard, as he leads his men into the bloody battles of the
Crimean War.

THE
HAZARD
SAGA
by V. A. Stuart

Order		Title	Book No.	Price
_____	#1	THE VALIANT SAILORS	PO60N	95¢
_____	#2	BRAVE CAPTAINS	PO70N	95¢
_____	#3	HAZARD'S COMMAND	PO83N	95¢
_____	#4	HAZARD OF HUNTRESS	PO99N	95¢

more to come . . .

Violence is
a man!
His name is
Edge...

The bloodiest action-series ever published, with a hero who is the meanest, most vicious killer the West has ever seen.

It's sharp —
It's hard —
It's EDGE

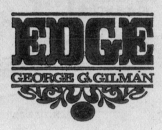

Order		Title	Book No.	Price
_____	#1	The Loner	P109N	95¢
_____	#2	Ten Grand	P115N	95¢
_____	#3	Apache Death	P133N	95¢
_____	#4	Killer's Breed	P148N	95¢

more to come...